RUSSIAN TEMPEST

Pogrom

NORKA SERIES BOOK 1

DANNY HENKEL

Tellwell Talent
www.tellwell.ca

ISBN
978-0-2288-9037-9 (Hardcover)
978-0-2288-9036-2 (Paperback)
978-0-2288-9038-6 (eBook)

This book is dedicated to my father Orville. A proud Henkel.

"FOR I HAVE LIVED, YOU SHALL LIVE ALSO."
JOHN 14:19

GLOSSARY OF TERMS

Abba – *(Yiddish) means father or dad.*

Anti-Semitic – *hostile or prejudiced against Jews.*

Bar Mitzvah – *a religious initiation ceremony of a Jewish boy who has reached the age of thirteen and is regarded as being ready to observe religious precepts, and eligible to take part in public worship.*

Bashert – *(Yiddish) means destiny. Often used to refer to one's divinely foreordained spouse or soulmate.*

Bat Mitzvah – *a religious ceremony for a Jewish girl aged twelve years and one day. It is regarded as the age of religious maturity.*

Beisitzer – *councilmen in Norka's village government.*

Bimah – *the podium or platform in a synagogue from which the Torah and Prophets are read.*

Challah – *braided bread, traditionally eaten by Jews on the Sabbath and holidays.*

Cholent – *a Jewish Sabbath dish of slowly baked meat and vegetables prepared on a Friday and cooked overnight, then eaten as lunch on Shabbat.*

Frau – *(German) title or form of address for a German-speaking woman. The English equivalent is 'Mrs'.*

Fraulein – *(German) title or form of address for a German-speaking unmarried woman. The English equivalent is 'Miss'.*

Goy (plural goyim) - *(Yiddish) the standard term for a gentile or non-Jew.*

Hanukkah (Chanukah) - *the Jewish eight-day wintertime 'Festival of Lights', celebrated with a nightly menorah lighting combined with special prayers and food.*

Herr – *(German) title or form of address for a German-speaking man. The English equivalent is 'Mr'.*

Huck – *a German village near Norka.*

Ima – *(Yiddish) means mother or mom.*

Kaddish – *Jewish prayer for the dead.*

Kiddush – *a ceremony of prayer and blessing over wine, performed by the head of a Jewish household ushering in the Sabbath.*

Kosakenwald - *(German) forest to the north of Norka. Translates as 'Cossack's Forest', a place notorious for where robbers and bandits hid out.*

Kosher – *food that is prepared or stored in accordance with Jewish dietary laws.*

Kugel – *in Jewish cooking, a kind of sweet or savory pudding made of noodles or potatoes.*

Lekach – *(Yiddish) a honey-sweetened cake made by Jews.*

May Laws - *temporary regulations concerning Jews; they were enacted on May 15th 1882, but remained in effect for 30 years.*

Mitzvah – *Jewish tradition of doing a meritorious or charitable act.*

Mutti – *(German) means mother or mom.*

Novaskaya – *fictional Jewish village located to the north of Norka.*

Onkel – *(German) uncle.*

Pale of Settlement – *areas in Imperial Russia where Jews were allowed to settle. In existence from 1791 to 1917.*

Pikuach Nefesh – *the principle in Jewish law that the preservation of human life overrides virtually any other religious laws. For example, a Jew could consume unkosher food if no kosher food was available, because without the food the person would die.*

Pogrom – *an organized massacre of a particular ethnic group, in particular that of Jews in Russia or Eastern Europe.*

Rabbi – *a spiritual leader or religious teacher in Judaism.*

Rebbetzin – *the wife of a rabbi.*

Roubles – *basic monetary unit of Russia.*

Rysincek – *the Russian village that was located to the northeast of Norka.*

Saratov – *Russian city lying on the middle course of the Volga River. Saratov was the first point of arrival for German colonists coming to settle in the Volga Region. Norka was included in the Saratov Oblast.*

Schilling – *a German settlement located on the Volga River to the east of Norka.*

Schmaltz – *(Yiddish) chicken fat.*

Shabbat (Shabbos or the Sabbath) - *the day of rest and worship in Jewish tradition. It is the seventh day of the week, commencing on Friday evening and ending on Saturday evening.*

Shiva – *the seven days of mourning in Jewish tradition for first-degree relatives.*

Shtetl – *a small Jewish town or village in Eastern Europe.*

Slavic – *relating to Slavs, the most numerous ethnic and linguistic body of people residing chiefly in Eastern and Southeastern Europe.*

Steppes – *a large area of flat unforested grassland in Southeastern Europe or Siberia.*

Synagogue – *Jewish house of worship.*

Talmud – *central text of Rabbinic Judaism and the primary source of Jewish religious laws and Jewish theology.*

Tante – *(German) aunt.*

Treif – *(Yiddish) any form of non-kosher food.*

Tsar – *an emperor of Russia before 1917.*

Unkosher – *food not prepared in accordance with Jewish dietary laws.*

Vati – *(German) means father or dad.*

Vorsteher – *head of the colony council in Norka, (roughly equivalent to being a mayor).*

Yeshiva – *a Jewish school for the study of the Talmud.*

Yiddish – *a language used by Jews in Central and Eastern Europe before the Holocaust.*

CHAPTER 1

Norka, Russia 1880

Sixteen-year-old Jacob Henkel pushed his wheelbarrow deeper into the birch forest near his home. Jacob, one of the middle children of Johann and Sigrid Henkel, was tasked with the gathering of kindling and small firewood for the family's cook stove. It had been a long and harsh Russian winter, and the family's wood supply had dwindled significantly.

Jacob could not wait until the following year. His father had promised that he would teach Jacob how to fell and chop trees for the family's winter wood supply. Until then, Jacob had to be satisfied with using his hatchet to chop up the large twigs and branches that he gathered. A couple of trips each day helped to stretch their wood supply. Now that spring had arrived, the family would need less wood for heating their farmhouse, although it was still needed for cooking, as well as for heating water for weekly baths and the washing of clothes.

Jacob enjoyed coming to the forest. He loved its earthy smell, but most of all he loved the solitude it provided. Living in a farmhouse with so many siblings, Jacob had grown up with the clamour of many voices. It was never dull, he had to admit that. There was always someone talking or doing something.

But sometimes, the thing he craved was just a little bit of peace and quiet.

The forest was not totally quiet; it had a different kind of noise. There was the wind rustling the leaves, the birds singing joyously from their perches high-up in the branches, and even the crunch of dried leaves underfoot. These things seemed quiet compared to the noise at home.

On this particular day, Jacob heard something that was not part of the regular forest sounds. Jacob was not sure at first what it was, for he could barely discern it over the chattering of the birds. He moved towards the sound. It was someone singing.

He listened intently. Although he could make out the words, he did not understand them. The song wasn't in German, that was for certain. Some of the words did sound like German though. Even though Jacob knew Russian, he knew it was not being sung in that language either.

Intrigued, Jacob continued listening to the melodies of this strange song.

He reached a small meadow that stood in a clearing of the forest. There, sitting in the middle of the meadow, was the singer. A girl. She was dressed in a pale blue dress. Her back was to him so Jacob was unable to see her face. All he could see was a head of dark curly hair that cascaded down to her shoulders. She wore a bright green kerchief that covered the top of her head.

Even though he didn't know what the girl was singing about, Jacob could feel such passion and longing in the words. He was overwhelmed with this beautiful song, and was enchanted by its singer.

Jacob hesitated. *Should he make his presence known? What should he say to this girl?* He felt a bit like an intruder. Jacob decided that he had to see who the singer was. From his current vantage point, he couldn't see much of her.

He made his way slowly through the trees, keeping himself hidden from the view of the singer until he was able to see her more clearly. From her features he could tell that she was not a Russian (she did not have the distinctive Slavic features in her face). The more he studied her, the more he became convinced that she was German. He had thought her much younger when he had observed her from behind. Now, he saw that she was close to his age.

He had never seen her in Norka. *So where did she live and why was she here in this meadow, singing this beautiful melody?*

Jacob wanted his questions answered, but he felt as though it was an intrusion on the girl's privacy. The girl, like him, had come here to be alone. He felt he must respect her privacy. He slowly backed away from the clearing, keeping his eye on the girl. He didn't see the large twig on the forest floor, and it snapped with an audible crack when he stepped on it. The girl stopped singing instantly and shouted "Who's there?"

Jacob froze. For a fleeting moment he considered turning and fleeing the way that he had come, but something stopped him. He had been taught to be respectful of others. Fleeing and giving the girl a fright was surely not what a proper young man should do.

Sheepishly, Jacob stepped into the clearing. Upon seeing him emerge into the clearing, the girl jumped to her feet and held a small knife menacingly in her right hand.

"Who are you? And what do you want?" she demanded.

Although he knew she probably couldn't hurt him with that pitiful knife - it was small like the one his mother used for peeling potatoes - Jacob knew that a frightened person, much like a frightened animal, could become quite unpredictable and dangerous. So, Jacob held his hands out in a submissive gesture and kept his voice soft and calm.

"I am Jacob Henkel. I won't hurt you."

The girl eyed him suspiciously and did not lower her knife, even though he'd made himself as unthreatening as possible. He tried to reassure her once more that he posed no danger.

"I won't hurt you; I promise. I was just listening to you sing. That's all."

"Why were you spying on me?" she demanded.

"I . . . I . . . was not," Jacob stammered.

"If you weren't spying, then what were you doing?"

"I was collecting firewood for my family," Jacob replied.

"That still doesn't answer my question."

"I was collecting firewood and then I heard someone singing. I followed the sound until I came upon you singing in this meadow. I was not spying on you, honestly. I was just listening to you sing."

"Listening and spying on me," she challenged. "Otherwise, you would have made your presence known." Her green eyes flashed in anger.

Those eyes! Jacob had never seen anyone with green eyes before. They were a deep emerald green. He was staring intently into those green pools, lost in their liquid opalescence.

"Jacob!"

Jacob was shaken out of his reverie. He realized that the girl had been asking him a question and that he had not replied to her inquiry.

Jacob dropped his gaze and focussed on what the girl was saying.

"Jacob, if you weren't spying, what were you doing hiding in the bushes listening to me?"

Jacob knew from her tone that she would accept nothing but the truth from him.

"I was just listening to you singing. It was . . . it was . . . the most magnificent thing I've ever heard. I am telling you the truth. That was all I was doing. What was that song? And what language is that?" Jacob could not contain himself. He knew he shouldn't be so forward in his questions, but he had to know more about this enchantress and her beguiling song.

The girl must have accepted his explanation because she had lowered her knife. But she still looked at him warily.

He, in turn, studied her. The girl was just a bit shorter than he was. Now that she was a bit less menacing, he saw that she had a pleasant face. Not a raving beauty like Lilith Schumacher, who all the boys his age in Norka had a crush on, but pretty enough. It was her eyes that set this girl apart. He had seen them spouting fire at him a few moments ago, now they changed yet again as her face became less suspicious of him.

Since the girl seemed more receptive to him, Jacob decided to find out more about her.

"I have introduced myself properly to you, but you have yet to do the same. May I ask, what is your name Fraulein?"

The girl seemed to be internally debating whether to tell him or not.

"Chaya . . . Chaya Blumenthal," she replied.

Jacob extended his hand. "Pleased to meet you Chaya . . . Chaya Blumenthal."

Chaya shook Jacob's proffered hand. With that gesture, both Chaya and Jacob smiled at one another and the previous tension that had been between them melted away.

"Where did you learn to sing like that?" Jacob asked.

"I'm really not that good," Chaya replied. "That's why I sing out here where no one can hear me. Well, only one can hear me, and that is God, but I guess there's now two, if I include you." Chaya smiled mischievously. "I am actually supposed to be gathering mushrooms for my family, not wasting time singing silly old folk tales."

"What language are the songs in? I haven't heard it before, although it does sound a bit like German."

"The song is an old Yiddish lullaby, and the language obviously is Yiddish."

"Yiddish? I have never heard of this language."

"That's because it is the language of my people."

"Your people? Who are your people?" Jacob asked.

"The Jews of course," replied Chaya.

"You're a Jew," was all that Jacob could think to say.

"Yes, I'm a Jew."

He was not sure what his reaction was supposed to be. Jew or not, he knew that after looking into those eyes, this girl intrigued him, and he decided he wanted to get to know her better. Emboldened by this thought, Jacob decided to forge ahead.

"So where are you from?" Jacob asked.

"I live in the shtetl of Novaskaya," replied Chaya.

"What is a shtetl?" Jacob had never heard that word before.

"A shtetl is a village."

"Why not just say you come from the village of Novaskaya, rather than saying the shtetl of Novaskaya? It's the same thing, so why the confusing name?" Jacob queried.

"It is because the word shtetl tells people, especially other Jews, that this village is a Jewish village."

"Please forgive me for not understanding, but why would it matter to other Jews what you called your village?" Jacob asked.

Chaya appreciated Jacob's candor, so she decided to patiently answer his question. Besides, she found that although Jacob's questions were a bit probing from someone she had just met, they were innocent enough. He truly seemed interested in what she was telling him. He was not scoffing at her answers, and the intent gaze he held with her eyes while she spoke made her believe that he genuinely wanted to know.

"The reason to tell other Jews that ours is a Jewish shtetl is because of a Jewish tradition called a mitzvah. A mitzvah is showing hospitality to strangers. We would offer them a meal and a place to stay as part of our mitzvah." Chaya explained. "So, for other Jews, it tells them that they will be taken care of should they be passing through our shtetl."

Jacob smiled as he now understood Chaya's explanation. "Chaya what. . ."

"Oh Jacob! So many questions. My basket has not gotten any fuller as we have been talking. I really cannot answer any more of your questions. I need to get picking before I get into more trouble for being so late returning home," Chaya declared.

"I'm sorry Chaya. I do not want you to get into trouble," Jacob said remorsefully. He was sad that she might be punished because of him, but he was also sad that the many questions he still had were to go unanswered. "I saw lots of mushrooms when I was searching for firewood," he said. "Would you like me to show you where they are? And . . . maybe I could help you pick them?" It was not that Jacob was really that interested in mushroom picking; that was more what girls and young women did, not a strapping lad like himself. But if he could learn more about this intriguing girl he'd just met, then he would pick a few mushrooms. He decided to ask her one more question as he led her to where he'd seen a profusion of mushrooms.

"Chaya, can I ask you one favour?"

"It depends on what it is."

"Would you sing while we pick?"

Chaya considered this for a moment. "If it makes you pick quicker, then yes."

"Most definitely!" Jacob replied enthusiastically.

So as Chaya sang, the two picked mushrooms until Chaya's basket was filled. As Jacob placed the last mushroom in her basket, he knew that Chaya would have to go and that he might never see her again.

"Chaya, I know that you have to go, but can I ask you one last question?" Jacob asked hopefully.

Chaya thought this over and nodded her assent. "Just one Jacob, and please make it quick. I truly must be on my way."

"Can I see you again?"

"I don't think that would be proper, Jacob. I should not be meeting a boy I hardly know in this deep dark forest. I am sorry."

"I understand," Jacob replied sadly (although he did not really understand).

Hurrying off, Chaya called back over her shoulder. "Goodbye Jacob. I really must get home. I enjoyed talking with you, but I really must get these mushrooms home for my family to enjoy. I might have to pick some more in three days' time. They really love their mushrooms. Goodbye . . . goodbye."

As Jacob watched Chaya disappear into the distance, a huge smile spread across his face. He now knew when Chaya would be back.

He retrieved his loaded wheelbarrow from where he had left it. As he headed back towards his home, there was a definite spring in his step. The wheelbarrow seemed to glide along almost weightless in his arms. Jacob could only think of one thing. In three days, he would see this intriguing green-eyed girl, Chaya, once more. Chaya - what a beautiful name!

CHAPTER 2

As he headed back home, Jacob could not decide whether he was more intrigued by Chaya or by her being a Jew. He admitted to himself that it really was a bit of both.

This was not the first time that Jacob had met a Jew. He remembered his first encounter very vividly. It was this encounter that became an important guiding force in his young life.

When he was eight years old, Jacob travelled with his father to the Jewish village of Novaskaya, or rather, as Chaya called it, the shtetl of Novaskaya. Jacob was excited that day because it was a treat that his father was taking him to the shtetl. Jacob usually only saw his father at the week's end. During the week, his father was working in their fields. Because their family's fields were spread out over a wide area in the steppes surrounding Norka, it just wasn't possible for his father to come home every night. So, Jacob only rarely saw him during the growing season. When winter arrived, Jacob was able to spend more time with his father, although it was still not a huge amount of time, since the Henkel family was so large and his brothers and sisters were also vying for his father's attention. So having his father all to himself on this day was better than any present he had ever received at Christmastime.

As they rode along in the wagon Jacob asked his father why they were going to the Jewish village.

"Their farrier is sick and they desperately need some horses shod," was his father's answer.

Besides being a farmer, Jacob's father was also trained as a farrier. Jacob thought his father was the best farrier in Norka, maybe even in all the German colonies in the Volga region. But that was just Jacob's opinion. Some of what he thought was fact; the rest was pure idolization. He hoped that when it was time for him to be apprenticed, he would be apprenticed as a farrier. And who better to be his master then his vati? Jacob knew it wasn't his decision to make. He just hoped that when his father decided, what he wished for would come true.

"Why don't they get the Russian farrier from Rysincek to do it?" Jacob asked his father. "Their village is much closer to the Jewish village compared to us coming from Norka."

"The Russians tend to mistrust the Jews and don't always treat them fairly. Their dealings aren't always pleasant for the Jews," his father replied.

All too soon for Jacob's liking, their wagon rolled into Novaskaya.

The first thing Jacob noticed was the poverty. The village, as well as the people, looked poor. The houses were very dilapidated and each showed piecemeal repairs on them everywhere. The one main street that ran through the town had also seen better days. It was heavily rutted with huge puddles of murky water lining it on both sides. The people wore threadbare clothing that had been mended numerous times. The men all wore strange hats which, Jacob noted, did not look like typical hats. They lacked brims and were worn on the backs of their skulls. The women wore kerchief scarves over their hair. Jacob was about to ask his father why the Jews dressed as they did, but before he could utter his question, his father pulled on the reins. The wagon stopped and he told Jacob to climb down.

They had pulled up in front of what seemed to be the stable in the Jewish village. This building was in the same state of disrepair as the rest of the buildings in the village. The only thing that distinguished it from the others was that a few horses were tied to a hitching post in front of it.

Jacob's father jumped down from the wagon and grabbed some tack that he had brought along from the wagon bed. Jacob followed his father into the stable. His father greeted a man who was wearing the same kind of cap as the others, and then introduced Jacob to the man.

"Jacob, this is Herr Morgenstern, owner of this stable." Jacob extended his hand and shook the man's hand. "Well Jacob, we best get to work." His father handed the tack he had brought to Herr Morgenstern. "While we shoe those horses out front, Herr Morgenstern will repair the tack I brought."

Jacob assisted his father as he shod the horses. He handed him the shoes, gave him nails when he asked for them, and handed him the rasp when he was finishing with each hoof. Within a couple of hours, they had completed the job.

While Jacob's father was loading up his farrier tools, Herr Morgenstern brought out the repaired tack. Jacob's father inspected the work, smiled, shook hands with Herr Morgenstern, and climbed onto the seat of the wagon. Jacob clambered up beside him. As his father flicked the reins to get the horses moving, Jacob lifted a hand to Herr Morgenstern in farewell. Herr Morgenstern smiled and lifted his hand in return.

On the road heading back to their farm near Norka, Jacob questioned his father about their visit.

"Vati, why did you bring tack to be repaired by Herr Morgenstern? I have seen you repair that yourself countless times," Jacob queried.

"As you probably noticed, Jacob, the Jews who live in this village are very poor. I couldn't ask for payment for my work because they don't have a rouble to spare. My payment might rob Herr Morgenstern or his family of food in their bellies. I could not do it for free either, because it would hurt his pride. So, by doing the trade, Herr Morgenstern is still able to feel he is providing for his family. These Jews may be poor, but they are a very proud people, and I respect that."

"Why are they so poor Vati?" Jacob asked. Their village was poorer than the Russian village of Rysincek. Even Norka had a poorer section of town, but the homes there were palaces compared to the hovels that the Jews lived in.

"The reason the Jews are so poor is because of the Russians and the Tsar," his father replied.

"What do the Russians and the Tsar have to do with the Jews being poor?" Jacob asked.

"The Russians constantly harass the Jews, demanding that they pay high taxes to them in the name of the Tsar. Actually, the money is not really taxes, but money they are forced to pay so that the Russians don't alert the militia of their presence here. So, the Jews are forced to sell their crops to the Russians for a fraction of what they are really worth. The Russians leave them with just barely enough to survive on – sometimes not even that."

"Why don't they just leave if it is so bad for them here?" asked Jacob.

"Where would they go?" his father asked. "Nowhere in the Russian Empire are they welcome. They are abused, harassed, and sometimes killed by their Russian tormentors. They have no choice if they want to live."

"But can't something be done by us to help them?" Jacob asked. "They are fellow Germans like us. Surely, we could help them."

"It's not that simple Jacob," his father replied. "You have to remember that we Volga Germans are also guests in this country. We have been given special provisions that give us special protection. We cannot overstep our bounds or we might face the same situation as the Jews. How Russia is run is for the Russians to decide, and there is nothing you or I or the rest of the Volga Germans can do that would change this. I'm sorry Jacob."

Jacob partially understood what his father was saying, but to his young mind, he still couldn't make the connection as to why the Jews lived in such squalor.

"Vati, my friend Werner says Jews are dirty and should not be trusted. At least that is what his father told him," Jacob stated. "Their village is so dirty and run down. Are Werner and his father right about the Jews?"

Jacob's father pulled on the reins and brought the team of horses to a halt.

"Jacob, do you believe this as well?" his father asked.

"I'm not sure," Jacob replied.

"Jacob close your eyes," his father commanded. "I want to ask you some questions. Answer them as truthfully as possible, but keep your eyes closed while you do it. Understand?"

"Yes Vati."

"I have stopped the wagon where there is a stranger standing beside the road. How tall is this stranger, Jacob?"

"I don't know Vati."

"Is he fat or skinny?"

"I don't know."

"What colour hair does he have?"

"I don't know."

"What religion does the person follow?"

"I don't know."

"Are his clothes nice or are they soiled and torn?"

"I don't know." Jacob wasn't sure why his father was asking him these questions, but he continued to keep his eyes closed, answering them as best as he could.

"Is the person a man?"

"Yes Vati."

"How do you know the stranger is a man, Jacob?"

"Because you said 'he' a few times," Jacob replied.

"Good boy Jacob. Is the man a human being?"

"Yes Vati."

"Is this man one of God's creations?"

"Yes."

"Are we not taught in the Bible to respect all of God's creatures, Jacob?"

"Yes Vati."

"Open your eyes," his father said gently. "Do you understand now, Jacob, why what your friend and his father said about Jews is not a very Christian thing to say, or for that matter, very enlightened thinking?"

"I think so," Jacob replied. "When I don't judge things with my eyes, I can see them in a totally different light. Maybe even in the true way God intended for us to see them." Jacob added.

"That is exactly what I was trying to get you to see," his father exclaimed proudly. "You have understood my lesson very well. You must look past what other people say and do, and make up your mind using more than your eyes to come to an opinion."

"Vati, Werner and his father are good Christians like us. Why would they say things like that about the Jews?" Jacob was confused about this and hoped that his father could clear up his confusion.

"Fear, Jacob. Fear, plain and simple," his father answered. "We fear what we don't know or what we don't understand. And sometimes this fear turns to hatred. And sometimes the hatred goes even further. The way to conquer fear, Jacob, is to face it head on. For when you do that, you will find that the fear was not as bad as you had thought. Do you understand what I am saying to you Jacob?"

"I think so Vati. In the case of the Jews, instead of fearing them because they are different, you decided that it didn't matter because they are people just like us," Jacob answered enthusiastically.

"Yes, Jacob. They are a poor people, but they are good people. They also are German like us, so rather than thinking of them as different and strange, I think of them as our fellow German brethren. Does it now make more sense why I helped Herr Morgenstern the way that I did?"

"Yes Vati."

"What is your favourite colour of flower, Jacob?"

Jacob was confused by his father's new question, but he answered nonetheless.

"Blue."

"Blue is a very beautiful colour, Jacob," his father said. "But what if every flower in the world was blue? Would flowers still be as beautiful and unique as they are now if all of them were blue?" his father inquired.

Jacob did not really understand why his father had switched to the colours of flowers, but he still answered his father's question.

"I guess not Vati. But I do not understand what the colour of flowers has to do with what we were talking about. I thought we were talking about Jews."

"What if all the people in the world were the same colour, the same size, had the same hair colour, the same religion? Wouldn't that sameness make people less special?"

Jacob finally made the connection his father was making with regards to flower colours and people. "So, people come in all different shapes, sizes, hair colour, religion and a lot of other things because those differences make them unique and beautiful in God's eyes," Jacob exclaimed triumphantly.

"Exactly," his father said proudly. "Now you understand that you must not fear the Jews, but celebrate them as unique and different, like us and all God's children."

This conversation with his father was a real turning point in Jacob's young life. From that day onward he learned to face his fears head on. And more importantly, he looked at others not only with his eyes, but with his heart and soul.

Jacob wondered if Chaya had noticed him when he had been in her village those many years ago. He could not recall seeing her, but he had been young and so concentrated on the sights of the shtetl that he might have missed her. Not that it would have made a difference. He would not have dared to approach her with his father present. And he had the feeling that she would have done the same. Even though his father had pointed out that they were all people, there were differences that could not be overlooked. *Would these come between himself and Chaya?*

He did not have time to ruminate too much on this. Helping Chaya pick mushrooms meant that he had only brought one load of wood home. He hurriedly dumped it by the woodpile, then turned his wheelbarrow around and headed back to the forest.

He piled wood onto the wheelbarrow lightning-quick, then headed for home. He dumped this load by the other and propped the wheelbarrow beside the woodshed. He would have to deal with the wood later. He could see his younger brother Manfred herding their milk cows towards the barn. At one time this had been Jacob's job, bringing the cows from the pasture to the barn twice a day to be milked. Now it had passed to Manfred.

Jacob was now responsible for the milking of the cows. He had taken over the job from his older brother Karl, who now worked in the fields with his father and his eldest brother Ernst. That was the way it was in the Henkel family: as you got older you took on the chores of an older sibling, and a younger sibling took on your former chores. Every child in the household pitched in. Only those in the cradle were exempt. Once a child could walk, they were given simple chores. All the family pulled together, and Jacob was proud of his contribution to his family's wellbeing.

His brother had herded their three milk cows into their stalls and given them each a generous pitchfork of hay. Jacob grabbed his milking stool, a wet rag, and his pail. He sat on his stool and gave the first cow, Margarethe, a gentle rub on her side. He felt that the cows produced more milk for him when he paid them this extra bit of attention. Margarethe looked back at him with her brown eyes and gave him a low moo. He smiled at her and gave her rump a pat before he washed her udder with the wet rag. The milk squirted noisily into the pail as he pulled expertly on her teats. When her first two teats were empty, he switched to the final two. When he was done, he had a pail of frothy milk for his efforts.

He poured a small amount of milk into a small dish near the stall. This was for the two barn cats. Their job was to keep the mice out of the barn. They were paid for their hard work with a milk treat once a day. When he poured the milk, they both came scrambling from wherever they'd been. They happily lapped up his offering.

He retrieved another pail and proceeded to milk the second cow. This one's name was Bertha. She was the biggest milk-giver of the three. She filled up her pail, as well as part of another.

The final cow's name was Katrin. It was his sisters' job to come up with the names of the cows. Whenever his sisters were within earshot, he would change the cow's names to one of theirs. That got them hopping mad at him. Sometimes they would try to tell on him to their mother, but it did not do them any good. They got a swat on the behind for being tattletales. Jacob never got a swat, but he did receive a dirty look from his mother, as well as more chores. He did not mind the extra chores too much, so the teasing was worth it. When his sisters did not tell on him, it was even better.

When the milking was done, he had three and a half pails. He grabbed the two full ones and headed for the farmhouse. He deposited them on the house's covered porch, and returned to the barn.

His brother had seen him taking the first pails to the house and met him at the barn door. Jacob retrieved the last two pails while his brother turned out the cows from their milking stalls. Once he had delivered the milk, Jacob returned to the barn. He mucked out all the stalls and spread new straw on the clean floor. He also forked hay into each stall for the morning milking. With his duties in the barn complete, he closed the creaky barn door and headed to the house.

While he was cleaning the barn, the milk sitting on the porch had had time to separate. Jacob fetched clean bottles and carefully skimmed cream off each pail. The remaining milk was poured into two metal milk cans.

Jacob then went in search of his mother to see what she wanted to do with the milk and cream. The three cows provided all the milk and cream that the family needed. What his mother intended to cook or bake in the next day determined how much was left over to trade with neighbours for things the family needed.

Of course, the milk was also used for drinking. Everyone in the family loved milk. Two milkings a day meant there was always plenty of fresh milk to be had. His mother also used the milk to make cheese every few weeks. Some of the cream was used to make butter. It was also a favourite ingredient to add to desserts. All the Henkels loved their desserts, especially when they had fresh cream poured over them.

His mother was planning to make cheese tomorrow, so he did not have to make any deliveries that day. It did not, however, mean that he now had free time. He returned to the woodpile, stacking what he had collected from the forest. Then he made several trips from the woodpile to the house, filling up the wood box beside the stove. It was also his job to make sure that his mother always had enough wood on hand for her cooking and baking.

He only just had time to wash up before his mother called everyone to the table for their evening meal.

The family gathered around their huge table. Everyone had their assigned places. Jacob's spot was in the middle. To his left was where his brother Karl usually sat, and to his right was his sister Heidi. However, his brothers Ernst and Karl were with his father in the fields that night, so there was more space on his side of the table than usual. His mother brought in a huge pot of stew. Once everyone was seated, she nodded at Jacob.

The family quieted. They all joined hands and bowed their heads. Jacob gave the blessing for the food and for those who had prepared it. If his father was home, he would say the blessing. If he was away, that task fell to his sons. Since Jacob was the oldest son there, he intoned the blessing. Everyone said 'Amen' when he was done, and the chatter of the family resumed.

His mother dished out portions of the stew onto plates. His sister-in-law Gerda (Ernst's wife) assisted in taking the plates and placing them in front of people. As the eldest, Jacob got his portion first. Next, his sister Heidi got hers. And so, it went until everyone had their food in front of them. His mother served Gerda her portion and put food on her own plate last.

It always amazed Jacob that his mother could judge correctly just how much food to prepare. No member of the household ever went hungry, nor were there any leftovers. Not one scrap of food was ever wasted.

Once everyone was served, they all began to eat. His mother had also baked bread that day, so that was passed around along with the butter. Two jars of his mother's dill pickles were also open on the table. These too were passed around and were soon empty.

Besides the chewing, there was a lot of banter among the family as they enjoyed the meal together. Jacob usually engaged in the chatter as well, but his mind was elsewhere. He was thinking about his encounter with Chaya in the forest. He was so preoccupied that he did not hear his sister Heidi's question. She must have asked him more than once because his mother asked him why he was ignoring his sister's question.

He apologized to his mother and sister, saying that he had not heard the question.

"I asked you three times," Heidi informed him.

"He was probably dreaming about Lilith Schumacher," Manfred teased.

"Lilith would never be with someone as ugly as Jacob." Heidi poked him in the ribs. "She is much too pretty for him."

Jacob was good-natured about the ribbing from his siblings. That way they wouldn't know what he was truly thinking. Or who he was thinking about.

When he did not rise to their baiting and teasing of him, they soon tired of it.

His sister asked her question for the fourth time. "Before your head went up into the clouds, I was asking you whether you had seen any mushrooms in the forest when you were gathering wood."

Jacob could not lie outright, for that was a sin. But he could not really tell the whole truth either. He chose his words carefully. "I saw some, yes, but someone had picked most of them already. I will keep my eye out and let you know if I see more before someone else finds and picks them." This satisfied his sister. He had not told a lie, so his conscious was clear.

When everyone's plates were clean, his youngest sisters, Lina and Anna, cleared the empty plates from the table. His mother brought in the dessert.

"Its the last of last year's apple crop," she declared. She had made stewed apples. Again, she ladled out portions and Gerda brought them to each family member. A pitcher of fresh cream was passed around. Jacob poured a generous amount on his apple and then attacked his dessert.

He wondered what kind of meal Chaya and her family were having that night. All he knew for certain was that they were having the mushrooms she had picked, or rather, the mushrooms they had both picked. They were German after all, so he believed it would most likely be many of the same foods that they ate here in the Henkel household. He would have to remember to ask Chaya when he next saw her in three days' time.

CHAPTER 3

Chaya hurried through the forest and back home with her basket of mushrooms. She had never meant to be this late. *What had possessed her to spend so much time with that goy?* she berated herself. *No good could come of this. Why, oh why, had she mentioned to him when she would be in the forest again? What was she doing? It was not proper for her to be meeting this boy, no matter that it all seemed so harmless. But was it really harmless?*

Chaya quietly entered the kitchen. She had to be quiet because her father was busy with the students of his yeshiva. Even though the shtetl of Novaskaya was quite poor, the villagers still spared some of their young men from their toil in various occupations so that they could attend Rabbi Blumenthal's yeshiva. In a place where every able body was needed to help the community eke out a living, it was a sacrifice, but they were willing to make it. For it was these young men who would ensure that the traditions, knowledge, and faith of the community would survive into the future. So, every day, save the Sabbath, these boys were given a few hours to study with the rabbi. Then they went back to the jobs they had been apprenticed to.

When Chaya put her basket on the table, her mother hissed at her. "Where have you been? I've already delivered the cholent and retrieved the challah from the baker." These were two of

Chaya's chores. Her mother was not happy that she had to do them for her. "We must hurry with our preparations. It is almost Shabbat."

"Sorry Ima. I lost track of time. The mushrooms were hard to find," she said by way of an excuse, hoping her mother did not sense that she was fibbing a bit.

"Just hurry up and get those mushrooms prepared. Your father is just finishing up. How will it look if the rabbi and his family aren't ready for the Sabbath?"

Chaya carefully cleaned each mushroom. She had to make sure that they were totally clean. If even the tiniest bug was missed, the mushrooms would be considered unkosher. A bug, even if ingested accidentally, was not acceptable. Her hands worked at a furious pace to make each mushroom totally clean.

Once every mushroom was cleaned, she sliced them into a pan of schmaltz she had heating on the stove. The mushrooms hit the hot pan sizzling, releasing their woodsy aroma into the kitchen. Chaya preferred to have mushrooms fried in butter, but since they were going to be eaten with the roast chicken that her mother had prepared, it was forbidden. Their dietary laws forbade them from mixing meat and dairy in the same meal.

When she had finished frying up the mushrooms, she moved the pan to the part of the stove that would keep them warm until they were ready to be served. She cleaned the area of the counter where she had been working, then left the kitchen to get ready for the Sabbath. She hurried to her room and quickly changed into her Shabbat clothes.

The sun had already set, and it would not be long until the first three stars appeared in the sky, signalling the beginning of Shabbat.

Her father and brother were already seated at the table when she arrived, as was one of her father's yeshiva students – Nicholas

Steiner. Chaya placed a veil over her hair, as did her mother. Everyone stood as her mother recited the traditional blessing and lit the Sabbath candles held in their silver candlestick holders. Her mother always ushered the Sabbath into their home with the lighting of the candles and with her prayer.

Her father then recited the Kiddush over a goblet of wine. Saying the Kiddush sanctified the Sabbath as a day of rest. After saying the prayer, her father took a small sip from the goblet. He took the embroidered cloth that was draped over it and wiped the rim where his lips had touched the goblet. He then handed the goblet to her mother, who took a sip and cleaned the rim as her husband had. Her mother handed the wine to their guest, Nicholas Steiner.

Nicholas was her father's most promising student in the yeshiva. He was becoming a common diner at their Sabbath feasts. Chaya wasn't sure if Nicholas was invited so often because he was her father's favourite, or if there was some other ulterior motive for his constant presence.

When he'd first been invited to partake in their Sabbath meals, he had sat across from Chaya at the table. But lately, her mother had seated him next to her. Chaya preferred him across from her. When Nicholas passed the wine to her, he intentionally did not clean the rim of the goblet. Chaya would have liked to clean it before she took her sip, but that wasn't allowed as part of the ritual. Chaya suspected that Nicholas did this intentionally so that her lips would have to touch where his had once been. He was a guest so she couldn't complain to her mother or father about his actions. She was sure that both knew what Nicholas was doing, but neither said a word to him.

The other thing that bothered her about Nicholas was that his hands paused longer on hers than necessary when passing her things like the goblet. She could not pull her hand away like she wanted to, because that would be considered rude behaviour towards a guest. And the feeding of guests was considered an important mitzvah.

After the wine had been passed and sipped by everyone at the table, the family and Nicholas washed their hands as part of a ritual, before her father recited the blessing over the challah. Her father broke off pieces from the loaf, dipped them into salt, and handed them to everyone. Chaya loved challah. She bit into her piece, savouring the velvety insides and the crusty exterior. After everyone had eaten their bread, Chaya helped her mother serve the rest of the meal.

Their Sabbath meal was a roasted chicken accompanied by roasted beets and Chaya's mushrooms. Chaya wondered if one of their hens had been sacrificed for the meal, or if it had been provided by a member of the community. The rabbi was not paid for his work in their shtetl. Instead, he and his family were given food from the villagers. Sometimes they did not have a lot to give. That is why Chaya's mother had a large garden. They also got food from the forest (such as Chaya's mushrooms) to supplement their diet. They never went hungry, but when times were lean her father would always say not to worry, because God would be sure to provide.

Her father was correct. The villagers did their best to ensure that the rabbi and his family were taken care of, just as her father ensured that the spiritual needs of his flock were met.

But her father was more than just the spiritual leader of their shtetl; he provided the people with much more. People constantly came to see her father seeking advice.

"Rabbi, my cow is lame again. Should I take her to the butcher Smeltz, or should I try to find someone who can cure her of this malady?"

"Rabbi, my wheat crop got attacked by insects last year. Should I try wheat again this year, or is rye a better choice?"

"Rabbi, my eldest son Ezekiel should take a bride and start a family. Do you think Yankel's daughter Eva is a good match?"

And so, it went. Her father spent just as much time giving advice as he did conducting services for his flock. Some days Chaya hardly saw her father.

As they ate, her mother made it a point to tell Nicholas that it was Chaya who had picked and cooked the mushrooms specially for him. Chaya had done no such thing. She had picked them for the family, not Nicholas. But she could not contradict what her mother had said. So, she just lowered her head.

Nicholas commented that the mushrooms were delicious and he asked for another serving. He told Chaya that she was a good cook, saying that she was almost as good a cook as her mother. Chaya noticed that her mother blushed at Nicholas' praise. Chaya thanked him for his nice words (she had to remain polite). She kept her eyes lowered, and wished her mother would quit trying to impress Nicholas.

When every one was finished eating, Chaya cleared the plates from the table. It was nice to get away from Nicholas for a short time. His thigh had brushed up against hers when they first sat down. Chaya wanted to move away from touching him, but could not without being rude. So, she endured it, trying to block out the feeling of his touch.

She sat back at her place while her mother served dessert – kugel. She had sat as far away from Nicholas as possible without appearing to be rude. Thankfully, Nicholas did not slide towards her, so she was able to enjoy her dessert in peace. Nicholas praised her mother's kugel and had a second helping. As the meal concluded, her father said a final blessing.

Chaya helped her mother clear the table. Nicholas said he had to leave (Chaya was so happy about that). He shook her father's and brother's hands and wished them a good Shabbat. He kissed her mother on the cheek and wished her a good Shabbat. Chaya was not sure if Nicholas intended to kiss her like he had her mother, or if he'd shake her hand. She was grateful when he extended his hand to her. He shook her hand, wishing her a good Shabbat. As with the Kiddush cup, his hand lingered longer than necessary.

Chaya was glad to see the back of Nicholas Steiner as he left their house.

In the kitchen, her mother washed the dishes while Chaya dried.

"Nicholas really enjoyed your mushrooms, Chaya. You could have been more gracious to him when he praised you," her mother lectured.

"You made it sound like I made them especially for him, Ima, and that wasn't true. I picked and made them for everyone."

"Oh Chaya. Can you be so blind? Nicholas has eyes for you, you silly girl. He is a catch. I was just helping you. He is your father's best student. One day, God willing, he will take over for your father as rabbi of this shtetl. I think he would make a fine son-in-law. Another rabbi in this household would truly be a blessing as well. Your abba had hoped that your brother Herschel would have taken up the calling, but he has his mind set on working with his hands and becoming a carpenter. A noble trade, but not a rabbi."

Chaya resented the fact that her mother thought that her marriage to Nicholas was the way to ensure that another generation of rabbis continued in the family. *Yes, Blumenthals had been rabbis for centuries, but why did it fall to her to continue the tradition? It should have been her brother, not her. Why did he get a choice, when she got none?* Chaya would have loved to voice all her protests but she knew it was futile. Her mother would never let her challenge what she had set her mind on. All she could do was try to avoid the inevitable.

"I'm too young to marry, Ima. Even Abba says so. I don't think it is right to encourage Nicholas when I am too young." Chaya hoped that this would get her mother to drop the subject.

"Yes, you are young," her mother conceded. "But in a few years time it won't be the same. A few more years of studying with your father and I am sure that Nicholas will want to choose a wife. Then the groundwork I have been laying will come to fruition and our families will be united. It will be my happiest day."

Your happiest day, Chaya thought. *The beginning of my life sentence with a man I have no feelings for.*

Her mother patted her arm affectionately. "You will see in time, Chaya, that I am right and that Nicholas is the one."

After that, her mother thankfully dropped the subject of Nicholas Steiner. And for that, Chaya was grateful.

Her thoughts turned to the young man she had met in the forest earlier that day. She wondered if he too had to do exactly as he was told. Maybe she would ask him when she saw him again.

CHAPTER 4

After Chaya awoke the next morning, she dressed in her best dress and joined her family who were waiting at the door. They did not eat breakfast on the Sabbath. Her father said being with God and singing his praises was all the food their souls would need. When she and her brother Herschel were younger, her mother had given them something to eat before they attended synagogue. But that had been years ago. Sometimes Chaya wished that they could eat breakfast before they went to the synagogue.

Her mother was especially impatient to leave. She reminded Chaya yet again of how it would look if the rabbi and his family were to arrive after the other worshippers.

When they arrived at the synagogue, which was the largest building in Novaskaya, they did not enter the building. Rather, her mother insisted that the family remain outside, greeting all those who came to attend the Sabbath service. Her father had once tried to convince her mother that it was not necessary to stand outside (especially when it was freezing cold), but her mother wouldn't budge on the issue. Her father just threw up his hands and did as his wife desired. Chaya knew her mother was stubborn and understood why her father gave into her demand. Chaya was grateful on this day that spring had arrived, so standing outside and greeting people was pleasant.

Only when the last person had entered the synagogue did her family finally enter this most sacred place in their shtetl. Her father proceeded to the front of the synagogue where he would conduct the service. Her brother Herschel took a seat on the men's side.

Chaya followed her mother to the women's side. In their synagogue, a rough screen separated the two sections. The women could see the service, but the screen prevented them from looking into the men's section. The focus of those assembled was to be on God, not on the opposite sex.

Chaya and her mother took their places at the front of the women's section. Chaya wished that she was not required to sit in that spot. She glanced behind her. Girls of her own age were clustered together towards the back. She knew that as the service commenced, they would spend that time whispering and gossiping. Chaya envied them. She must have looked back too long because her mother rapped her arm and told her to look forward.

She knew her mother was always worried about what other people might think. For Chaya, it meant that she had to behave in a certain manner because she was 'the rabbi's daughter'. Her mother was constantly reminding her of this. If she was slow to do something that was expected of her, or if she did something wrong (like looking to the back of the women's section), her mother was quick to point out her failing.

Chaya tried to focus her mind and concentrate on her father's service, but her mind kept wandering. She had not meant for that to happen. She was thinking again of the young man who she had met in the forest. She tried to push him out of her mind, but he kept popping back in. She finally gave up trying to focus on the service, and on putting Jacob out of her mind.

She started a private conversation with God. She told Him all about her encounter in the forest. Even though He was God and knew everything already, it felt good to unburden her soul. After she had told God everything, she posed the question of what she should do. She had foolishly told Jacob that she would be back in the forest again. *Was it wrong? Is that why she could not get him out of her head, because she felt guilty for what she had done? What should she do?*

As always, God listened patiently to her, but did not offer any advice about what she should do next. So, she had to figure out her own solution (which was probably God's plan all along). She decided that she would go to her father and tell him about her encounter with Jacob in the forest. He was always dispensing advice to others; his daughter should also have access to his counsel. If her father told her not to meet Jacob again, then she would follow his advice. It would help her to come to terms with the fact that she should never have made such an impulsive decision in telling Jacob she would be back. Meeting him again was not a good idea. She decided she would talk to her father as soon as the Sabbath ended.

Chaya had been so engrossed in her talk with God that she had not noticed that the service was over. A poke in her side from her mother told her that she had yet again done something wrong.

"Your head is in the clouds today, Chaya. People are watching. What will they think of your behaviour – especially on the Sabbath! Go and retrieve the cholent. I will make excuses for your behaviour."

Chaya left the synagogue quickly. She politely acknowledged those she met as she rushed to the door. She was sure that her mother would later lecture her on what she deemed poor behaviour.

She was the first to arrive at the baker's. The previous day, her mother had delivered their family's pot of cholent to the baker. Chaya usually delivered it, but she had been late coming home from mushroom picking (which had also added to her mother's ire). Every family in their shtetl had done the same. Since cooking on the Sabbath was forbidden, wives would place their ingredients in their cast iron pots. The pots – full of vegetables, some sort of meat, and water – simmered in the baker's oven overnight. That way, the families could have a warm meal after the Sabbath service without doing any cooking.

Chaya pointed out her family's pot to the baker's wife, although it wasn't really necessary as the baker's wife knew whose pots were whose. The pot was very heavy. It was much larger than a family of four needed. Chaya lugged it back to her house and placed the pot on their cold stove. While she waited for the rest of her family to arrive, she set the table and cut up what remained of last night's challah.

To appease her mother, she ladled generous portions of the cholent into bowls. The family arrived just as she was placing the filled bowls on the table. Her mother did not thank Chaya for doing this, nor was Chaya expecting praise – none would ever be forthcoming. There was not much conversation at the table because everyone was famished.

When the meal was over, Chaya assisted her mother with the cleaning up. Her mother did not broach the subject of her behaviour. This would come after the Sabbath. It was a small reprieve for Chaya.

After the meal, her father gathered up some of his beloved religious texts and got ready to return to the synagogue. Every Saturday, her father led sessions where he and the elders of the shtetl studied and debated the Talmud. His religious texts were there if they needed to be consulted for clarification on some matter of interpretation. Every male member of the shtetl was welcome to attend these sessions, but it was the elders who made up the majority of those who went.

Her father invited Herschel to accompany him. Herschel accepted the invitation. Her father had beamed when he had done that. Chaya wished that she would be given a choice about how she was to spend the rest of her Sabbath – but she never had a choice.

There was a reason why the Blumenthal's cholent pot was so large. It was so that Chaya and her mother could take the leftovers to those who needed help. It was a mitzvah for her and her mother to visit the sick and the poor and offer them food and comfort.

Chaya knew that her mother's role of rebbetzin within their shtetl was just as vital in the community as her father's role. That was why her mother was always being so hard on her as well. In her mind, she saw Chaya as the future rebbetzin of their shtetl (especially if she got her way and Chaya married Nicholas Steiner). So, she was grooming her daughter in the role she was one day to assume. And Chaya didn't have any choice.

Chaya carried the cholent pot as she and her mother made their way through the shtetl to their first stop. Frau Gesheim greeted them warmly when they knocked on her door. Her two small children clung to her apron. They were Marta (aged three) and Hedi (aged two). Their father, Herr Gesheim, had left his young family to seek work. He had promised to send money faithfully to his wife and children once he had settled and got a job in Odessa. But it had been months since he had left. There had been no money, or word from him. Frau Gesheim had barely enough to survive on. Had it not been for her mother, as well as the charity of others, she and her daughters would have starved to death.

Her mother doled out most of the cholent that they had brought. Chaya could see that Frau Gesheim was grateful for the food, but Chaya also noted that the woman was ashamed. *But it's not her fault,* Chaya thought. She was glad that members of the shtetl took care of one another, especially during the trying times.

Chaya and her mother did not stay long at the Gesheims, for they needed to deliver what remained of the cholent while it was still relatively warm.

They walked to the house of Herr Morgenstern and knocked to announce their presence. They did not wait for Herr Morgenstern to answer his door because he was unable to do so. Chaya and her mother walked into his house and headed to his bedroom. Herr Morgenstern was propped up in his bed, looking grayer and paler than when Chaya had seen him a few days earlier.

Her mother started to fuss over him, fluffing up his pillows and asking him how he was feeling. Herr Morgenstern's wife had died a few years ago. The couple had had no children. Now in his infirmity, he had no one to take care of him. Chaya's mother spent a lot of time ministering to Herr Morgenstern. "He hasn't got much time left," her mother had told her on their way home a few weeks earlier. "We must do all that we can to make his last days as pleasant as possible."

"Isn't there anything that can be done to help him, Ima?" Chaya had asked her mother.

"No. Herr Morgenstern's time has almost come. All we can do is pray for him and hope that his passing is peaceful."

Chaya felt guilty that she was healthy and Herr Morgenstern was not. But her mother explained it so that she felt less guilty about her health.

"Herr Morgenstern has had a long life. He was blessed with the love of a very good woman. Soon it will be time for him to join her. I am sure that he is ready and has accepted his fate. As should we."

Chaya admired her mother for her words and her wisdom. The people of Novaskaya were so fortunate to have such a caring and wise rebbetzin. She felt she would never be able to fill her mother's shoes.

Once her mother got Herr Morgenstern comfortable, she fed him the cholent they had brought. When food dribbled down his chin, she wiped it away without comment. Chaya fetched water for Herr Morgenstern when her mother had finished feeding him.

Afterwards, Chaya sat and listened while her mother relayed all the details of that morning's service. If Chaya had been asked to tell Herr Morgenstern about the service, she knew her mother would have been disappointed in her for not being able to do so. Luckily, her mother had not asked her to add anything.

Once her mother had finished telling Herr Morgenstern all about the Sabbath service, she had Chaya help her to get Herr Morgenstern into a chair. Her mother stripped his bed and put on freshly laundered sheets. Chaya noted that Herr Morgenstern had soiled himself and his bedding. Her mother said nothing. She took the soiled sheets and placed them into a basket. She would launder them later.

Before they helped Herr Morgenstern back into bed, Chaya and her mother took off his soiled clothing. Her mother lovingly cleaned him up. They got him into clean night clothes and then got him back into bed. Although he did not say anything, Chaya could see the gratitude on his face as they tended to him.

Her mother made sure that he was comfortable before she told him that she would look in on him tomorrow. Before they left the room, her mother gave Herr Morgenstern a peck on his cheek.

Chaya carried the now empty cholent pot while her mother carried the soiled bedding and night clothes. They took them home where they dropped them off. Chaya would have loved to stay at home at that point, but they were not finished yet. Her mother retrieved the lekach that she had baked on Friday. Then they headed out on their next errand.

They walked to Frau Blau's house. They knocked softly. Frau Blau answered their knock. They could both see the grief on the young widow's face. Her husband had been killed a few weeks before in a farming accident. The young couple did not have any children, and Frau Blau was taking her husband's death particularly hard.

Chaya and her mother were invited into the house. Her mother had Chaya make tea for them all as she asked Frau Blau whether she was eating and taking care of herself.

When the tea was ready, Chaya poured it into chipped cups. She cut the lekach and placed slices on plates for the three of them. Frau Blau pushed her cake away from herself, but her mother insisted that she had to eat it, declaring that they would not leave until she had eaten every crumb.

Chaya ate her lekach and sipped her tea. She loved her mother's honey cake. She would have liked to have another piece, but she knew she was not allowed. The rest of the cake would be left with Frau Blau. She could serve it to others who came to call and check up on her, as her mother had explained. Chaya doubted whether Frau Blau would eat it herself. She was only eating it now because her mother had insisted.

As Frau Blau begrudgingly ate her cake and drank her tea, Chaya's mother talked to her about what she needed to do to pick up the pieces of her shattered life. Her mother was not pushy with what she told Frau Blau; she was just trying to help her deal with her grief and continue on with her life. Although it did not seem like Frau Blau was listening to what her mother was saying, Chaya knew that all of the women in the shtetl respected her and followed her advice.

As they were leaving, Frau Blau asked her mother when she was coming back. As always, her mother's words and wisdom had helped. Chaya doubted if she ever could do what her mother did so well.

They walked home in silence. Night had fallen. The Sabbath was now over.

Once they arrived home, Chaya and her mother started preparing the evening meal. Chaya peeled the potatoes for the latkes that her mother was making for their evening repast. Since the Sabbath was over, her mother could have admonished Chaya for her poor behaviour. But if there was one thing about Sara Blumenthal that held true time and time again, it was that she was nothing but consistent. She never raised her voice, or was acrimonious while cooking. She believed that bad thoughts transferred into the food. So, while she cooked, all was peaceful.

Chaya enjoyed her latkes. The family put sour cream or apple sauce on them. No meat was served at this meal since they were eating dairy. The dishes her mother had for dairy were also used. Her mother kept a strict kosher kitchen.

Chaya tried to savor her last latke, but when her mother started clearing the table she finished quickly and helped her. Once they started washing the dishes, her mother started.

Chaya had heard this lecture many times before. She could almost recite it from memory.

Her mother reminded her yet again that she was 'the rabbi's daughter' and that she must do better to behave as she was expected to. That included conducting herself in a way that meant no one could reproach her behavior. Her mother told her how disappointed she was that Chaya had obviously not been paying attention during the service at the synagogue. She despaired over what the rest of the people thought of 'the rabbi's daughter' who was not listening to her own father's service. Her mother then went on to tell her how embarrassed she had been when she had to make excuses for her because she'd left right after the service. Her mother had sent her away, but she made it sound like it had been Chaya's idea to make the hasty retreat.

Chaya said nothing. She knew there was no point arguing with her mother or trying to defend herself and her actions. Again, her mother was predictable. She would have her tirade and nothing would stop her. Only when she had expended her frustration at Chaya's failings would she calm down and allow Chaya to say something.

But her mother did something different this time. Her tirade changed focus. She went on and on about Chaya needing to try much harder. Her mother told her that one day she would be rebbetzin, and that her conduct would be measured even more critically than it is now while she is 'the rabbi's daughter'. Her mother firmly believed that Chaya was going to marry Nicholas Steiner. Chaya despaired. This was not what she wanted for her life. But she did not dare tell her mother that.

When her mother had finally said all that, she needed to say, and when she had somewhat calmed down, Chaya knew that she could talk. But she had to tread carefully. If she brought up the fact that she did not want to be Nicholas Steiner's wife, or the future rebbetzin of Novaskaya, she knew that her mother would fly into another fit. So, all she could do was tell her mother what she wanted to hear.

"I am sorry, Ima, for my behaviour. I am sorry that I have distressed you so. I will try harder to conduct myself so that I am able to be above reproach. I will try to make you and Abba proud."

The words her mother wanted to hear softened her a bit. "I am only trying to help you and the family as best I can. I expect you to do better. I am tired. It has been a long day. Good night, Chaya."

There was never an apology for her harsh words, nor was there ever a word that she was proud of Chaya. That was just how her mother was. Chaya accepted her as she was. She just wished sometimes that her mother would accept her as she was.

Her mother's words echoed in her head. It was always about being 'the rabbi's daughter'. She loved her father, but at times she secretly wished that he was not a rabbi. Everyone treated her differently because she was 'the rabbi's daughter'. It happened all the time.

She would go to the butcher's and all the women waiting to be served would stop talking once she entered the shop. Obviously, they had been gossiping while they waited for their turn to be served. They could not let 'the rabbi's daughter' hear them. It might get back to the rabbi. Not that she would say anything to her father, but the women didn't know that.

The people of the community would greet her as 'the rabbi's daughter'. Not as Chaya, or Chaya Blumenthal. It was always 'the rabbi's daughter'. She felt sometimes that Chaya Blumenthal did not even really exist.

She always had to think about her actions and the consequences of her choices; something that none of the other girls her age had to do. She remembered a Hanukkah celebration a few years ago. On the third night of Hanukkah, Chaya had been invited to her friend Katrina's to be part of their celebrations. Her mother had allowed her to go, but not before reminding her that her behaviour was to be exemplary.

Chaya enjoyed the evening with Katrina and her family. All was going very well until dessert was served with the holiday meal. Katrina's mother had made an apple strudel. As Katrina's mother cut into the thin pastry, Chaya's mouth salivated from the aroma emanating from it. Her hostess placed a generous slice in front of her. She was about to take her first bite when she noticed that Katrina's mother had put a generous dollop of whipped cream on the plate with the strudel. The other members of the family were already murmuring signs of pleasure as they tucked into their desserts. Chaya did not know what to do.

They had just eaten meat with the Hanukkah meal and so should not be eating dairy. Chaya considered just eating the strudel and leaving the whipped cream, but could she? The dairy had touched this plate. It had tainted the strudel. Chaya thought about asking for a different piece without whipped cream, but that would be showing poor manners.

What she really wanted to do was to tuck into the strudel, whipped cream and all, and enjoy one of her favourite desserts. But she could not do that because she was 'the rabbi's daughter'. Even though Katrina's family was not following the dietary law, it would be the fact that Chaya had not that would make the rounds through the shtetl and eventually back to her parents' ears. She hated being judged with different standards than everyone else.

Her hostess noticed that she was not eating her dessert. "It is Hanukkah. We break this law only once a year. Surely you can do the same, Chaya."

Chaya would have loved to indulge herself – but she could not. All she could do was say that she was full from the excellent Hanukkah meal and beg her hostess for forgiveness for not eating dessert. Katrina's mother accepted her excuse and nothing more was said.

'The rabbi's daughter' was never invited back to Katrina's for another Hanukkah. Chaya knew it was because Katrina's family believed that she had told her parents about how they had broken a dietary law – but she never did. However, whether she did or didn't never mattered, it was what other people thought that dictated many things in Chaya's life.

She shook herself out of her reverie because she still had to speak to her father about her chance meeting with Jacob in the forest. She had promised God that she would tell him. And she was sure that he would tell her that it was wrong for her to meet a goy, and that she must not do it again.

She went to find her father. Usually, he was sitting in his favourite chair by the fireplace. This chair, however, was empty, which surprised Chaya. She found her father at the door preparing to go out.

"Abba, where are you going? It is late. I need to talk to you."

"If it's to ask me to talk to your mother, Chayaleh, you know that I cannot. Your mother has said all that needs to be said about your behaviour. I agree with her."

Chaya had hoped her father might take her side, especially when it came to the subject of Nicholas Steiner, but it looked like she could not rely on his support. She pushed aside her disappointment. "Abba, it's about an entirely different matter that I need to talk to you about."

"I'm sorry, Chayaleh, but it will have to wait. I must be on my way."

"Where are you going Abba? Is someone dying?" *Maybe it was Herr Morgenstern.*

"Some questions are best left unanswered, and let's leave it at that Chayaleh. I really must go. We can discuss what you want to talk about another time."

Her father did not give her a chance to say another word. He slipped out into the night, leaving behind a bewildered Chaya.

Chaya wondered why her father was being so secretive. Usually he told her everything, but not this time. *What did he mean by 'some questions are best left unanswered'? What she had asked had not been too prying, but her father had made her feel like she was poking her nose in where it didn't belong.*

It was a strange way for her father to react and it left her feeling more unsure of what she should do about Jacob. She had tried to talk to her father like she'd promised God, but that hadn't worked. *Should she try again? Or should she just deal with the matter herself?*

Chaya knew nothing could be resolved now. So, she decided she would wait until tomorrow and see if she could talk to her father then.

She headed to bed.

CHAPTER 5

Jacob attended church with his family on Sunday. As always, the church was full as the residents of Norka came together to worship and sing their praises to God.

Jacob and his family took their places on the two pews that the Henkel family had been sitting on ever since the church had been built decades ago.

The church was constructed entirely of wood. Huge windows let in lots of light shining on the different biblical scenes which adorned the walls and altar of the church. All of them had been hand carved and painted by expert hands. Jacob always marvelled at their beauty. He could only guess at how many hours, days, weeks or months each character and scene had taken to create. In Jacob's mind, their church in Norka rivalled all the cathedrals he'd seen in pictures.

Jacob also liked coming to church with his family because from his family's pews he could see the Schumacher clan. As the service progressed he would catch glimpses of Lilith as she prayed with her family. Jacob, like the rest of the boys his age, was besotted by the beautiful Lilith. Once during a service, she must have sensed that he was watching her, for she glanced in his direction. He had seen her smile at him before he'd quickly averted his eyes.

He knew that he was supposed to be focussing on God, but it was hard to concentrate on Him when Lilith was there. He looked over to where the Schumachers sat and there was Lilith. But today he only gave her a glance. His mind was elsewhere.

For some reason he just could not get Chaya out of his mind. Now that he was not busy having to perform his many chores, he thought about what would happen the next day. She had said she was picking mushrooms again in three days, which was tomorrow, but she had not mentioned what time she was going to be in the forest again.

Was she going to be there at the same time as the other day? She said she was going to pick mushrooms, but she did not say if she was going to pick them again in the same forest. These questions rattled around in Jacob's head.

Chaya intrigued him. He wanted to see her again. But would it be possible? He could not wait for her in the forest all day hoping she'd appear. He had too many chores to do. He could not shirk these.

He had to make two trips to gather firewood tomorrow. He decided he would try to do them near the time he had seen her on Friday. He knew where her shtetl was, but he could not just waltz into her village and find her. That was not proper. He hoped that she would be in the forest like she had said she would be.

He had a feeling she might visit the birch forest again. Otherwise, why would she have made a point of telling him when she was picking again? He looked at the altar and considered praying about it. But he believed it would be wrong to enlist God's help in this matter. All he could do was hope that she would be there tomorrow.

—⁂—

The next day, Jacob went about his daily chores as usual. His body was doing what it always did, but his mind was elsewhere. Luckily, no one in his family noticed that he was distracted.

He checked his watch. It was close to three o'clock in the afternoon: the same time he had seen Chaya the previous Friday. He grabbed the wheelbarrow and headed towards the birch forest. He headed to the meadow where he had seen her before. He stopped a few times and listened, hoping to hear her singing, but only the regular sounds of the forest greeted him.

He saw the meadow up ahead. He left his wheelbarrow and walked into the clearing. The meadow was empty. There was no sign of Chaya.

Jacob was disappointed that she was not there. *Maybe she was not coming after all.* He had felt in his heart that she would be there – but she was not. *Why? Maybe she had no intention of ever coming. Maybe she changed her mind. What should he do?*

He waited.

She did not appear after he'd waited ten minutes.

Disappointed, he returned to his wheelbarrow and pushed it away from the meadow. He couldn't delay any longer. He started gathering wood.

—⁂—

Chaya had tried to talk to her father again, but there was never a time where the two of them could be alone. She had to be extra careful because she did not want to arouse her mother's suspicion that something was amiss with her.

By Monday morning, the day she was to go mushroom picking again, she still had not resolved her dilemma. *Was God purposely making it so that she couldn't enlist the help of her father? Was he making it so that she would have to resolve this on her own?* The more Chaya thought about it, the more she believed that this was what God was doing. It was up to her to do the right thing and to tell Jacob that her words had been impulsive and that it was not proper for a Jew and a goy to meet like they had in the forest. She felt that Jacob would accept her explanation and her candour. He seemed very intelligent, and from what she could tell from their brief encounter, he seemed like a good person.

—⁂—

As Chaya stepped into the meadow, she expected to see Jacob waiting for her, but the meadow was empty. She had not told him exactly when she would be mushroom picking on that day. She was here a bit earlier than she had been the previous Friday. She decided to wait for Jacob's arrival.

After fifteen minutes he still had not appeared. *Maybe he isn't coming after all,* was her first thought. She would have liked to wait longer, but she had to start picking.

She started where Jacob had shown her where there were mushrooms during their previous encounter. There were a few mushrooms, but not enough to fill her basket. She searched deeper into the forest.

She wondered why Jacob had not come. She felt bad that she could not tell him why they couldn't meet again. *Maybe God had interceded on her behalf and made Jacob realize that it was for the best, them not meeting again. Yes, it had to be that.*

Chaya focussed on her mushroom-picking singing as she picked. She did not hear Jacob approach because she was so engrossed in her picking and singing. She jumped in fright when he suddenly appeared in front of her.

"Jacob! You gave me such a fright."

"I'm sorry Chaya. I never meant to scare you. I thought maybe you were not coming when you were not at the meadow. I am glad you are here though. How are you?"

Chaya was glad that she would be able to talk to Jacob and tell him that this was their last meeting. "I am well, Jacob. But I must clear something up with you."

Jacob could see by the serious expression on Chaya's face that something was troubling her. "You look troubled. Is there something I can help you with?"

"Jacob, forgive me, but I misspoke when I told you about coming to pick mushrooms again today."

"I don't understand."

"I should never have done that. It is not proper for me to meet you alone in this forest. You are a goy and I am a Jew. We cannot do this."

"What is a goy, Chaya?"

"A goy is the term we use for a non-Jew."

"What does it matter if a Jew and a non-Jew meet just to talk? We are not doing anything wrong?"

"It's complicated, Jacob. My rabbi has said that goyim and Jews shouldn't mix."

"With all due respect to your rabbi, Chaya, I myself have been to your shtetl. As has my father. Your rabbi says that goyim and Jews shouldn't mix, but we were invited to your shtetl."

"You were in my shtetl? When?"

"Many years ago. My father, who is a farrier, came to shoe some horses for a Herr Morgenstern. I helped him with the task."

"When was this?"

"I was eight years old at the time. I am now sixteen. So, eight years ago."

"You know Herr Morgenstern?"

"Yes. He was the only person I met there. He fixed some of my father's tack while we shod the horses. I remember him having very kind eyes. Does he still run the stable in your shtetl?"

Chaya was reeling from Jacob's announcement that he had been in her shtetl. And even more incredible was that he knew Herr Morgenstern. To Chaya, this was the strangest of coincidences.

"Herr Morgenstern is not doing well. My mutti says that he hasn't much time left." Chaya was not sure why she was telling such a personal detail to Jacob. She saw that the news of Herr Morgenstern upset Jacob.

"Is there nothing that can be done for him?"

Chaya was touched by Jacob's concern for someone he barely knew. And for a Jew at that. "No, there is nothing. It is in God's hands. My mutti and others do what they can to make his last days as comfortable as possible."

"Do you also help him like your mother?"

"Yes." Chaya had come to tell Jacob that their meeting was not appropriate, but somehow, she had gotten sidetracked. She had to tell Jacob, then leave as quickly as possible. "Jacob, I'm sorry but I cannot stay and talk with you anymore. In fact, I cannot do this ever again. It was a mistake to meet you here again and I apologize for my impulsiveness. Please forgive me. I never meant for this to happen."

Chaya's words were the last thing he had expected. He had thought they would continue talking and getting to know each other, but he could see that this wasn't going to be the case. To say that he was disappointed would be an understatement. He wished he could ask Chaya all the questions that he wanted to know the answers to, but she was telling him it wasn't possible. With regret in his voice, Jacob let Chaya know that he was disappointed that they could not speak more and meet again. He let her know that he understood her wishes and that he wouldn't bother her with any more questions.

As Chaya left, he called out after her. "I am so glad to have met you, Chaya Blumenthal. And if you see Herr Morgenstern again, please tell him that Jacob Henkel remembers him and that I will pray for him. Tell him that for me, Chaya."

Chaya never turned around or acknowledged what he had said. He felt sad that her religion was making it impossible for them to meet and learn from one another. *If only things were different.*

Chaya had to hurry away from Jacob before her resolve to leave him evaporated. She wanted to stay and talk with him, but she knew it was wrong. Better to get away from him as quickly as possible and not to think of him again. This was not that easy. Especially when he asked her to relay that he was thinking of poor Herr Morgenstern. *Why was life so complicated?*

When she arrived home, Chaya placed her basket of mushrooms on the kitchen counter next to the sink. She would clean them later. She had another chore she had to attend to first.

She headed to the chicken coop. It was now her job to clean the coop. Previously, it had been her brother's chore, but with his carpentry apprenticeship and his attendance at their father's yeshiva, he just did not have the time. So, it fell to Chaya to do this chore as well as the many others she already had.

She fetched the wheelbarrow and a shovel. She took her kerchief off her head and tied it over her face, covering her nose and mouth. She felt like a bandit from the old American West, but if she did not do this then she'd be choking and gagging as she cleaned the manure out of the coop. No matter how careful she was, a lot of dust was churned up with every shovelful. She filled the wheelbarrow then dumped it next to the garden. In the fall the manure would be worked into their garden plot.

When she had shovelled the last of the manure out of the coop, she put down a thin layer of straw on the hard-packed earth floor. She then went to the egg boxes to collect the eggs. They had twelve laying hens as well as a rooster. She was disappointed when she only found five eggs. She checked all the fencing of the chicken run, seeing if maybe a fox or a weasel had made off with some eggs. The run was secure.

She re-entered the chicken house. "You need to do better than this ladies." She waved the basket she had collected the eggs in. "Ima is making dumplings. She will not be happy with this amount." She looked at the rooster who was strutting around the coop. "Your ladies are obviously not happy about something. You need to do a better job of taking care of them, or I will tell Ima that maybe you have outgrown your usefulness and that it is time for the soup pot."

The rooster ruffled his feathers and let out a loud cock-a-doodle-doo.

"That display won't save you. Remember what I said: it's the soup pot unless things improve." She closed the coop's door and made sure it was securely latched. She hoped that her mother wouldn't make too much of a fuss over the small number of eggs.

She found her mother in the kitchen. She was cleaning the mushrooms. "I was going to do that, Ima. I just had to do the chicken coop first."

"It is fine, Chaya."

Chaya had not expected her mother to be so willing to do her chore. "I will finish them now, Ima."

"I will finish them, Chaya. I want you to do something else instead. You are to go and feed Herr Morgenstern. Also change his bedding and his night clothes. I want you to tend to him from now on."

"Alone?" Chaya had always gone to Herr Morgenstern's with her mother. It sounded like her mother wanted her to tend to him all by herself.

"Yes, alone, Chaya. It will be good practice for you. Once you become rebbetzin it will be one of your duties. Herr Morgenstern is very little trouble. He needs someone there more now that his time is almost near."

"What of my other chores?" Chaya did not want to do this mitzvah, but she could not object to doing it outright. Her mother had brought up the rebbetzin notion once again. And once again it annoyed Chaya that she had no say over what she wanted in her life.

"I will do the chores that need tending to. I have talked to your abba about this. He thinks that it is a good idea. He will excuse your brother from the yeshiva for the time being. Your brother is very happy with this arrangement, whereas I am not happy that he is so exuberant about missing his studies."

Again, her brother got his way. If only she had been born a male. Things would have been so different. Her mother had thought of everything so she could not refuse.

"Do I come home at night?" she asked her mother hopefully.

"No. Herr Morgenstern needs constant care. I will check on you once a day to bring you food. There is a pot of soup on the stove. Take that for supper for you and Herr Morgenstern. Natalie Schatzman is watching him now. She needs to get home to her family."

Chaya grabbed the soup and left her house. There were no words of gratitude from her mother for taking on this huge task. Nor would there ever be. It was what was expected of her.

Chaya knocked on Herr Morgenstern's door to announce her presence (more to Frau Schatzman than to Herr Morgenstern). Frau Schatzman was in a hurry, barely acknowledging her as she rushed out the door.

She tiptoed into Herr Morgenstern's bedroom. He was asleep. She tiptoed back out and gently closed the door.

She went to Herr Morgenstern's sitting room and sat on the settee. She was not sure what she should do next.

CHAPTER 6

The house was eerily quiet. Chaya did not want to make any noise because she didn't want to disturb Herr Morgenstern. There was nothing to do, so Chaya thought about her last encounter with Jacob. She wished she had not been so abrupt with him, but there was no other way. Jews and goyim just were not allowed to mix.

Chaya got up from the settee and went into Herr Morgenstern's kitchen. There was a bit of firewood stacked beside the stove. She got a fire going and put the pot of soup on it to reheat. The kitchen became engulfed with the fragrant smell of the soup. Chaya hoped that Herr Morgenstern would enjoy the soup as much as she did.

She peeked into his room – he was awake. She returned to the stove and ladled out a bowl of soup. She left it to cool a bit; she did not want to scald poor Herr Morgenstern's mouth with hot soup. She opened the bedroom door and entered.

"Good afternoon, Herr Morgenstern." She smiled at him and made her voice cheery. "I hope that your rest was good. I am the rabbi's daughter, Chaya. I was here the other day with my mother, the rebbetzin. Oh, I'm sorry Herr Morgenstern. You are ill, not absent-minded. I am sure that you remember me. I don't know if anyone has told you, but I will be taking care of you from now on. I will be here night and day to . . .

to . . ." – *She couldn't say to help him die* – "To help you until you get better." *Not the truth, but better than saying she's his death helper.* "I have brought you some chicken soup for your supper. Now I have made it sound as though I cooked it. I am sorry Herr Morgenstern. My mother made the soup. It is one of my favourites."

Chaya felt like she was babbling nonsense. But she did not know what else to do. Herr Morgenstern gave her a faint smile – so maybe he did not mind her ramblings.

She helped him so that he was sitting upright in the bed. She propped a couple of pillows behind his back so that he was comfortable, and went and got his soup.

Copying her mother, she patiently spooned soup into his mouth. She felt like a mother bird feeding her chick. She smiled to herself. She did not let on what she was thinking to Herr Morgenstern.

When he was done, she cleaned his chin. She gave him a big smile. Now came the hard part. It took all her strength to help Herr Morgenstern to the chair while she changed his bedding. It had been easier to move him when it was her and her mother. She noticed that he was also considerably weaker than he had been a few days before.

She stripped the bed and put on fresh bedding. Then she helped Herr Morgenstern up. She quickly changed his bed clothes and cleaned him up. He was very unsteady on his feet. Chaya had him hold the back of the chair to steady himself. As quickly as she could, she got him back into his clean bed. She propped him up again.

"After all that I'm sure that you could do with a nice cup of tea."

Herr Morgenstern did not say anything. He looked at her with gratitude and gave her hand a slight squeeze.

Chaya took the empty soup bowl to the kitchen. She ladled out another portion. Finding tea leaves in a cupboard, she put them into the kettle with some water. While she waited for the kettle to boil, she went back to the bedroom and retrieved the soiled bedding and clothes. These she deposited into a basket by the front door. She assumed her mother would pick them up and launder them the next day. The water in the kettle had not boiled so she wolfed down her soup as she waited.

When the tea had boiled and steeped long enough, she poured it into two chipped mugs. She could not find any sugar or honey, so they would have to just drink it plain. She returned to the bedroom with the tea.

"I'm sorry Herr Morgenstern, but I couldn't find any sugar or honey to sweeten the tea. I will ask my mother when she stops by to bring us some. I am sure you would prefer it sweetened. At least that's how I like it." She felt like she was rambling again. Herr Morgenstern said nothing.

Chaya waited for the tea to cool. She did not say anything. The silence in the room felt more oppressive than her ramblings. She checked the tea – still too hot. *What should she talk about?*

"I met an acquaintance of yours from many years ago. When he learned that you were feeling poorly, he asked me to send his best wishes to you for a quick recovery." She noted that Herr Morgenstern had a puzzled look on his face. "I'm sorry Herr Morgenstern, I didn't tell you who the acquaintance was. Well, he was not really an acquaintance, he only met you once. He was a young boy at the time. You might not remember him, but he remembers you. His name is Jacob Henkel and he came to our shtetl and to your stable with his father. His father came to shoe some horses and Jacob helped him. He remembers meeting you all those years ago. He was quite concerned about your health. Do you remember him Herr Morgenstern?"

Herr Morgenstern didn't say anything, but he did give her that slight squeeze again.

He remembered Jacob. And before she could stop herself, she found herself telling Herr Morgenstern all about how she had met Jacob in the forest while picking mushrooms. As she gave him sips of tea, she unburdened herself of all the guilt she felt for meeting with Jacob not once, but twice.

As always, Herr Morgenstern said nothing. Chaya wondered whether a speaking Herr Morgenstern would have told her that what she had done was wrong. The only way she could try to understand what he was thinking was through observing his reaction to her words. His eyes did not accuse her. Rather, they seemed to say that he understood.

But what did he understand? Did he understand that she felt like her life was not her own? Did he understand that she did what was expected of her, but wished that she had a choice? Did he understand just how frustrated she felt every day?

He gave her a small smile and a gentle pat.

Maybe he did understand.

Chaya told him about how everyone always judged her as 'the rabbi's daughter'. She told him how she just wished everyone would see her simply as Chaya. She poured her soul out to Herr Morgenstern. She had not realized she'd been talking for so long. Herr Morgenstern's eyes started to droop. She apologized for keeping him awake and got him settled in his bed to sleep. Before she left his bedroom, she patted his shoulder and bid him goodnight.

Chaya returned to the kitchen and washed the dishes from their meal. She rinsed and dried their mugs. She found an old blanket and stretched out on the settee.

She was asleep in minutes.

—⁂—

Early the next morning, her mother arrived. Herr Morgenstern had not woken yet. She wondered if her talking for so long had taxed him too much. She did not tell her mother that though. Her mother checked on Herr Morgenstern and seemed to be satisfied with the care Chaya was giving him. She did not praise Chaya for her care, nor did Chaya expect it from her mother.

Her mother had brought a large basket of food. She informed Chaya that it would last them for days. Chaya was now expected to cook all the meals for the both of them. Her mother informed her that the Goldstein boy would be coming in a while to bring some firewood. The Horowitz's daughter would bring water from the well later as well. She told Chaya she would be back the next day. She expected Chaya to do everything to make Herr Morgenstern's last days comfortable. "This house could do with a good cleaning," were her parting words.

Chaya noticed that her mother had forgotten to take the soiled laundry. She was about to run after her, but she saw the lye soap her mother had brought with the food. She knew she was expected to do Herr Morgenstern's laundry as well. She would have to tend to that after she fed Herr Morgenstern and got him cleaned up.

He was awake when she went to check on him. Her mother's visit must have awoken him. She began to prepare his breakfast. Her mother had brought eggs. She started the stove and scrambled two of them for his breakfast. She also put the kettle on for tea. There was honey, so this time she added it to his cup.

She got Herr Morgenstern propped up in bed and fed him his breakfast. He only ate half of the eggs. He seemed to enjoy having the tea with honey, for there was that faint smile when he sipped it. She again changed the bedding as well as him. Once she had him settled, she cleaned the crockery after she ate the rest of his eggs. Food was too precious to waste.

She put a huge galvanized tub on the stove. She would get the Horowitz girl to fill it so she could do laundry later in the day. Almost on cue, the Horowitz girl showed up. Chaya instructed her to fill the washtub. The Goldstein boy arrived with the firewood. She stoked the stove and got the water heating. She felt bad that she was neglecting Herr Morgenstern.

Chaya returned to the bedroom and apologized to Herr Morgenstern for leaving him alone. He said nothing. He did not seem sleepy. So, Chaya talked to him some more about her life. When he grew tired, she stopped and let him rest. While he was asleep, she attended to his laundry.

When he awoke, she fed him. Then she spent time talking to him until he grew tired. Then she let him rest again. She started to clean the house and prepare his evening meal.

Over the next few days, Chaya and Herr Morgenstern fell into a familiar routine.

After three days, Chaya was unable to get Herr Morgenstern out of his bed to the chair to change his bedding. He had been growing weaker and weaker. Although it was hard, she managed to get him and the bedding changed while he remained in the bed. His appetite was waning as well. He barely touched the food that she prepared. He did, however, seem to enjoy the cups of tea that she prepared for him.

Each day she noticed that he faded away a bit more. She began to worry that he might pass away all alone while she slept. She moved into his bedroom, sleeping on the floor just so that she could be near, should his time come.

Chaya had been seeing him decline for days, so she was surprised when she awoke one morning to see him smiling at her from his bed. His pallor looked better and he was not as lethargic. *Maybe he is going to get better,* Chaya thought. She had become very fond of him in the short time they had been together. *Maybe her ministrations had helped.*

"You look wonderful today, Herr Morgenstern, whereas I must look a fright," she added cheerily. "Are you hungry?"

He did not answer, but he did smile at her again.

"How about I get you some breakfast? And some tea of course." She left the bedroom, happy that Herr Morgenstern was doing so much better. Her mother would be impressed as well.

She brought his breakfast to him. As she helped to prop him up, he grabbed her arm. She was surprised at the strength of his grip. He surprised her yet again, because he spoke.

"Thank you, Chaya."

Three words that spoke volumes to her. She did not prod him to say more. There was no need. He had called her Chaya. She was Chaya to him, not 'the rabbi's daughter'. She smiled at him.

"It is I who should be thanking you, Herr Morgenstern. Thank you for listening to me. I do not mean to seem ungrateful for my life, it is just hard sometimes to be me. I think you understand that very well. I am truly grateful to you Herr Morgenstern." She gave him an affectionate peck on the cheek before she went to prepare his breakfast.

He did not eat as much as she expected, but his smile was still there so she was certain that he was on the mend. The rest of the day was spent as it usually was, tending to him and doing chores around the house.

As she bid Herr Morgenstern good night, Chaya felt so happy that he had had such a good day.

She was awoken in the middle of the night by Herr Morgenstern's laboured breathing. She quickly lit a lamp. She was alarmed by the change in Herr Morgenstern. His colour was gray and his breathing was rapid and wheezy. Chaya wanted to run and get help but she did not want to leave him alone. *What if he died while she was gone?* She did not want him to die, but she especially didn't want him to die alone. So, she stayed. She felt so helpless as she watched him struggle with each breath. All she could do was hold his hand and assure him that he was not alone, that she was there with him.

He struggled for an hour. Finally, he took a raspy breath and did not take another. She knew that he was gone. Chaya wanted to summon someone but she could not. Jewish tradition dictated that the body was not to be left alone. All Chaya could do was wait until someone arrived in the morning.

She went to the kitchen, took a knife, and made a small cut on her dress at the shoulder. Even though Herr Morgenstern was not her relative, she felt it appropriate to show that she was in mourning. He had no one left to mourn him. She wanted his soul to know he was mourned. She found a cloth and draped it over the only mirror in the house. Then she returned to the bedroom and wept for the man she barely knew, the man who had accepted her as the one person she wished to be – Chaya.

She spent the remaining hours of the night talking to Herr Morgenstern's still form.

—◦◦◦—

The Horowitz girl was the first to arrive the next morning. She summoned her father, who came with some other men to wash and prepare Herr Morgenstern's body. Chaya was able to return home.

The funeral service was held later that day. Since Herr Morgenstern had no family, many members of the shtetl volunteered to sit shiva for the deceased. Chaya did it along with the rest of her family. Chaya was happy to do this for Herr Morgenstern.

At the end of the week, Chaya's life returned to normal; the normal life of 'the rabbi's daughter'. She wished it could be different.

CHAPTER 7

Market day. Jacob had to get up earlier than usual when it was market day. He hitched up the team to the wagon and then started to load it. He made multiple trips as he loaded up the cheese that his mother would sell at Norka's market. When Jacob was younger, he had not been able to go to the market since it was held on a school day. Now that he was finished with school, one of his responsibilities was to accompany his mother to the market.

Previously, it had been Karl who had accompanied his mother to the market, but since Karl was working full time in the fields, the task now fell to Jacob.

He had most of the cheese loaded when Manfred herded the cows into the barn for their morning milking. It was earlier than usual for this, and the cows protested with an inordinate amount of mooing. Jacob got them all milked as quickly as possible. While his brother was herding the cows back to the pasture, Jacob skimmed the cream off the pails of milk. He added this to the can that had the cream from the previous evening's milking. He poured the remaining milk into a large can that also had the leftover milk from the previous evening. Jacob hefted the cream can and the milk can into the wagon bed. His brother arrived just in time to help him lift the heavy trestle table into the wagon.

Jacob was famished and would have liked to eat his breakfast, but he would not be able to until later. His mother wanted to be in Norka as early as possible so that she could get a good spot at the market to sell her dairy products. She only sold the products when she had a wagon full, so she did not have a regular spot at the market, hence her eagerness to get there early.

She too had started her day earlier than usual. She had prepared breakfast for all the family while Jacob had been loading the wagon and doing the milking. His mother had packed food for herself and Jacob that they would eat once they had set up at the market.

Jacob helped his mother up to the seat on the wagon, then he climbed up beside her. He grabbed the reins and expertly guided the team of horses out of the farmyard. Watching his mother scan the road, Jacob could tell that she was worried they had left too late. But it could not be helped – the cows had to be milked. The milk and cream from the morning's milking were sure to sell very quickly.

The Henkel farm was near the outskirts of Norka, so they did not have to travel far anyway. Jacob urged the team to move faster to appease his mother. As they entered Norka, Jacob noted that the settlement was still relatively quiet. A few dogs could be heard barking here and there.

Jacob turned down Norka's main street where several businesses were located. The stores were dark now, but in a few hours' time they would be open and would do a brisk trade. Jacob guided the team to the town square. This was where the market was held every Thursday. His mother pointed to the spot she wanted. Jacob guided the wagon to where she had indicated. Even with the early start, the Henkels were not the first to the market space. Jacob counted eight other rigs. At least his mother seemed satisfied with the spot she had chosen.

Jacob helped his mother down from the wagon. She helped him carry the cumbersome trestle table. They set it up, then they carried all the things that they were selling that day. The cream and milk cans they placed under the table to keep them cool.

They stacked the cheese in neat piles on the table. One pile was their smoked cheese, the other pile was unsmoked. Of the two varieties, the smoked kind invariably sold out first. The Russians especially enjoyed his mother's version of smoked cheese and were regular customers.

Once the wagon was unloaded, Jacob drove it to a spot where there was plenty of grass for the horses to munch on while he and his mother were engaged at the market. When Jacob returned, his mother had food laid out on the table for them to eat before the market got busy.

In the time that it had taken them to unload their wagon, others had arrived to set up as well. Even though it was still early, Jacob noted that there weren't many spots left.

Market day was important for both the buyers and the sellers. For the Henkels, the monies made from market day went to buying the things that they could not grow or make themselves. Jacob's father always joked that market day was actually cobbler's day. With such a large family, it seemed that the cobbler was always needed. Shoes were handed down between siblings as much as possible, but there were still shoes that had to be bought or repaired every year. "I should have apprenticed to be a cobbler instead of a farrier," his father would exclaim when his wife expressed the need for shoes. "Then at least I could have shod all my children. I guess I still could though. What size horseshoe do you think you would take, Jacob?" Jacob thought his father's sense of humour was funny. Some of his siblings did not appreciate it as much.

At the market, people had the opportunity to buy things that they could not make themselves. The Henkel's dairy products were in high demand because not everyone had milk cows.

The church bell rang, signalling that the market was now open. The previously empty square started to fill with people. Jacob and his mother were very busy. The milk and cream were gone within ten minutes. The cheese piles were also shrinking. As expected, the smoked cheese was the most popular. Some of the customers even bought two blocks. Some of those who came to their table were repeat customers. They praised his mother on the smoked cheese. Some even told her that they had tried to replicate her cheese, but that they had been unsuccessful. They asked her what her secret was. His mother never divulged any of her secrets to anyone. Even Jacob was not exactly sure what made his mother's cheese so special. She did tell him that whoever took over cheesemaking in the family would be told the secret, but that was all she had said.

When their customers dwindled, his mother left him alone to tend to their table while she went in search of a few things from the other sellers. Since there was no one currently at his table, Jacob scanned the crowd. He was looking for friends he knew from his school days. He noticed two Jews at a table near his. He could not see what they were trying to buy, but he was able to observe them as they tried to make their purchase.

It seemed to take them a long time to buy whatever they were getting. He noted from their animated gestures that they must be bargaining for whatever item they were trying to purchase. Jacob watched. The negotiations took over ten minutes. Finally, a deal was struck. The men shook hands with the seller and the sale was completed.

The men headed towards his table. Jacob put on a big smile and greeted the men. "The finest cheese in Norka," he announced to the men. The men did not stop. They just shook their heads and moved on. By the way they reacted, Jacob wondered if Jews ate cheese. If Chaya had not said that they couldn't meet again, this was a question he'd ask her. *Ah, Chaya.*

Then it hit him. *Chaya had said that Jews and non-Jews weren't allowed to mix, but if that was true, what were Jews doing at Norka's market?* Jacob studied the people milling about more closely. There were a few more Jews in the crowd. The men were easy to spot because of the strange cap that they wore on their heads. He studied some of the women in the crowd. Some of them wore kerchiefs on their heads like Chaya had. He felt certain that they too must be Jewish. They must also be from Chaya's shtetl. But the question still plagued him. *Why were they here if they weren't supposed to mix with non-Jews?*

"Jacob! What are you doing? You have a customer and you are ignoring them."

Jacob shook himself out of his reverie. His mother's disapproving look told him that she was not impressed that he hadn't acknowledged their customer.

"Sorry Mutti. I got distracted."

"Jacob, serve Frau Trautman."

Jacob sold Frau Trautman a brick of regular cheese. When she was gone, his mother wanted to know why he had not noticed their customer. Jacob knew better than to try to lie to his mother. She had an uncanny ability in knowing when her children were being untruthful with her. Jacob suspected her ability came from raising so many children.

"I'm sorry Mutti. I got caught up watching some Jews. They seemed to take a very long time bargaining for something at that table there." Jacob pointed out the table where the Jews had been a short time ago.

"I don't care about what the Jews are doing at other tables, nor should you, Jacob. You almost cost us a sale."

"Sorry Mutti."

Jacob accepted his mother's reprimand and focussed on the stall in front of him. When they sold out of everything, Jacob went to retrieve the wagon. He would have liked to walk around and view what was still on offer at the other tables, but he knew better than to ask his mother. Since they had sold everything, she wanted to return home as quickly as possible. There were many chores to attend to, for both of them. By the time they got home it would be almost milking time again.

His mother helped him load the table. He threw the two empty cans into the wagon bed, and they were ready to depart. Jacob let the team go at a more leisurely pace on the return journey. The main street was very busy because all the businesses were now open. He waved to people he knew as he guided the team towards their farm. His mother was smiling beside him. She was happy that everything had sold.

Jacob helped his mother from the wagon when they got to the farmyard. He then drove the wagon to its spot in the farmyard. He unhooked the team and led them to their stalls. He gave them oats and water. He had just finished that task when his brother arrived with the cows. Before he started the afternoon milking, he had his brother help him unload the trestle table from the wagon.

"How was the market?" his brother asked.

"Very busy, but I had no time to look around. We sold everything. How was school?"

"Very boring. You are so lucky that you do not have to go anymore. Lilith Schumacher told me to tell you that she misses you terribly." His brother snickered. "I told her you were very busy with your girlfriends Margarethe, Bertha and Karin. She seemed to be very disappointed that you have left her for your other girlfriends."

Jacob grabbed his brother in a headlock. "You better not have told Lilith any such thing. If you did, then the next time I see her I will be sure to tell her that you follow those three around like some lost little puppy."

Manfred squirmed out of the headlock. "Okay, I didn't tell her that. Can't you take a joke Jacob?"

Jacob knew that his brother had only been joking. He just wanted him to know that his teasing had consequences.

Chuckling to himself, he entered the barn to spend time with his three girlfriends.

CHAPTER 8

"Chaya, I want you to pick some mushrooms today. It rained recently, there should be lots," her mother informed her.

The routine of her life had returned to what it was before she had tended to Herr Morgenstern. In some ways, it felt like nothing would ever change in her life.

"I have invited Nicholas to have supper with us tonight. He especially liked your mushrooms the last time you prepared them."

"But it isn't Shabbat, Ima. Why is Nicholas having supper with us? You invite him only on the Sabbath."

"I invited him because he should feel welcome in this house to eat with us not only on special occasions. It will give us a chance to get to know him even better. And it will be a chance for him to get to know you better as well."

This again, Chaya thought. *I wish I could just tell her that I'm just not interested in Nicholas Steiner.* But what she felt or wanted did not matter. She must do what she was told. She was 'the rabbi's daughter' – she had no choice.

"Yes Ima." She grabbed her basket and small knife and left the house.

Nothing dictated that Chaya should go mushroom picking in the birch forest; there were plenty to be found in all the forests surrounding Novaskaya. But that did not matter. She was going to the birch forest. She had told Jacob that they should not meet again, but here she was, going to the spot where she might just run into him. She secretly wanted to see Jacob. She just hoped that he would be there.

She had decided that she wanted to tell Jacob about Herr Morgenstern's passing. He had shown genuine concern for the man. He deserved to know what had happened. This was the sole reason she chose to return to the birch forest.

She made her way to the meadow. She sat on the grass that was waving gently in the wind. Then she began to sing.

Jacob was just gathering his second load of wood for the day when he heard Chaya singing. He thought about just ignoring her and continuing with his chore. Chaya had made it perfectly clear during their last meeting that she could not be with him because it was forbidden for Jews and non-Jews to mix. But then he had seen Jews at the market in Norka.

He left the wheelbarrow and headed towards the singing. He wanted Chaya to clear up his confusion.

He found her much like he had on their initial meeting. She was sitting in the meadow singing. Her basket for mushroom picking lay near her feet. He stepped into the clearing.

"Hello Chaya." She did not jump like she had the first time. She stood up.

"Hello Jacob. I am glad that you came. There is something that I need to tell you."

"Is it to tell me that you lied, Chaya? You told me that Jews and non-Jews were forbidden from mixing. But just the other day I saw a few Jews in Norka. And do you know what they were doing Chaya? They were mixing with the rest of the inhabitants of my town."

Chaya could see and hear that Jacob was mad with her. *And who could blame him really?*

"I'm sorry Jacob. It was never my intention to deceive you. It's just . . . it's just complicated . . . that's all. I don't know if I can explain it so that you'd understand why we cannot meet like this."

"Chaya you are talking in riddles. We cannot meet – yet here you are." He must have sounded harsher than he had meant to because Chaya burst into tears. Jacob instantly regretted his outburst. "I'm sorry Chaya. I did not mean to be so harsh. I never meant to make you cry."

"It's not you," she sniffed. "Everything is just so complicated. Sometimes I wish things could just be simpler. I came here to tell you something I think you needed to know, but now it's a complicated mess."

"Chaya I'm sorry. I truly am. I am not sure what is so complicated, but let us not worry about that for now. Just tell me what you wanted me to know."

Jacob was so understanding that it made Chaya feel a bit better. "I wanted to let you know that Herr Morgenstern died. You showed concern for him. I just thought that you'd like to know."

"I am sorry to hear that. Did he suffer?"

"No, he didn't suffer. I was with him. It was relatively quick."

"You were there when he died?"

"I was."

"Was your family there as well?"

"No, only me."

"You had to watch a man die all by yourself. Why wasn't your family there with you?"

"I was alone because it was my job to take care of him."

"But why you? Couldn't an adult have done it?"

"No, it was my duty as the rabbi's daughter."

"Were you scared?"

"No, I just wanted to help Herr Morgenstern. I was hoping that he was going to get better . . . but he didn't."

"What did you do after? You know, after he passed?"

"I sat with him until someone came."

"Why didn't you go and get help?"

"I wasn't allowed. We are not allowed to leave the departed alone. It is our custom."

"I'm sorry that you had to go through that Chaya, but I am glad that Herr Morgenstern had you there when he passed and that he didn't die alone."

"As am I. I told him about meeting you. He seemed to remember you even though it has been many years since he had seen you and he wasn't speaking. But when I mentioned your name, his eyes lit up a bit, so I think he remembered."

"May I ask what happened after someone came?"

"Yes. His body was washed by my father and the other elders of the shtetl. He was placed in a simple shroud and then placed in a coffin. We had Herr Morgenstern's burial later that day. Afterwards, for seven days, we sat shiva for Herr Morgenstern. Shiva is where family members remember the departed for the seven days of mourning. Since Herr Morgenstern had no living family to sit shiva for him, members of the shtetl, including myself, sat shiva."

"I am sure that from his place in Heaven, Herr Morgenstern was touched by the members of the shtetl mourning his passing."

"I wish he had gotten better. I will always remember him. Even though our time together was short, I felt such a hole in my life once he was gone. He helped me."

"Helped you how?"

"It's complicated Jacob."

"So, you said Chaya. I will not press you on the matter. All I can say is thank you for telling me of his passing. And for sharing some of the details. I would like to learn more, but I think I know your views on that as well."

"I'm sorry Jacob. I wish it could be different, but it cannot. I have talked for too long. I best get my mushrooms picked."

"I am happy to help you."

"I think it would be best if you didn't."

Jacob was disappointed, but he understood. "Before you go, can I ask you one question?"

Chaya felt that Jacob had been understanding and patient, so answering one more question would be fine.

"Yes."

"Why don't Jews eat cheese?"

Chaya laughed. "Of course, Jews eat cheese. Wherever did you get the strange notion that we didn't?"

"I observed some Jews at the market. They walked right by my mother's table. I do not mean to brag, but my mutti's cheese is sought after by everyone who comes to the market. The Jews walked right on by so I assumed that they didn't eat cheese, otherwise they would have bought some."

"I can see how you might have drawn that conclusion, Jacob, but Jews do eat cheese. Your mother's cheese may be as good as you claim, but we Jews cannot eat it."

"Why?"

"It's complicated, Jacob."

"I'd like to know, Chaya."

"Fine I will tell you, but we will have to pick mushrooms while I tell you."

"I will be glad to do that, Chaya."

So, as they foraged for mushrooms, Chaya did her best to explain to Jacob why Jews such as herself couldn't eat his mother's cheese.

"Do you know what the word 'kosher' means Jacob?"

"No."

"In the simplest of terms, kosher foods are the foods which we are permitted to eat, the foods that conform to our dietary laws. God has told us what foods we are permitted to eat. Those that we can eat are called kosher, and those we are not permitted to eat are called treif. Take these mushrooms for example. When I clean them, I must remove every speck of dirt, but more importantly, I have to make sure that no insects remain on the mushrooms. The mushrooms are kosher, but if a bug remains, then it is treif. If you eat the treif food, it is considered to be unclean and you are breaking our dietary laws."

"Even if you ate it without knowing it was there?"

"Yes. As I said, it's complicated."

"Why do Jews have such strict rules about what they can and cannot eat?"

"It's a covenant that we Jews have with God. As part of our faith, we honour these dietary laws. By honouring these laws, we honour God. I hope I have explained it well enough for you to kind of understand, Jacob."

"Following your dietary laws brings you closer to God?"

"Yes Jacob, it does."

"So, Chaya, I'm still confused about why you eat cheese, but not my mother's cheese."

"It has to do with being kosher again. The dietary laws also apply to how food is prepared. In my house, we prepare and eat meat and dairy separately. We even have dishes specifically for both. Say your mother cooks meat in a pot, then she uses that same pot to heat the milk to start the cheese making process.

According to our laws, your mother's cheese, no matter how good it is, has now become treif, so we Jews cannot eat it. It also has to do with the rennet that is used, but explaining that is even more . . . complicated. Does that make sense Jacob?"

"Yes, it does, Chaya. I see now how it is, as you say, complicated. Thank you for taking the time to explain it to me and to help me understand. It must be hard remembering all of these rules."

"Not really. It is just part of our faith. Why do you have such interest in learning about us Jews and our ways?"

"Well Chaya, it all has to do with the day that I met Herr Morgenstern. I would love to share it with you sometime, if you would let me. Your basket is full and I assume that you must leave. I have enjoyed talking with you again, Chaya."

Chaya was sad to see that her basket was full. She had really enjoyed talking with Jacob.

"I cannot promise anything Jacob."

Jacob smiled at her. "I know."

"Thank you for helping me pick mushrooms."

"It was my pleasure, Chaya. And thank you again for setting me straight about Jews and cheese."

"Goodbye Jacob."

As he watched Chaya walk away, Jacob felt as though he might see her again. She seemed more receptive to meeting again than she had been previously. He would never look at his mother's cheese in the same way. *It must be hard at times to be a Jew with so many rules,* he thought. He retrieved the wheelbarrow and continued collecting firewood.

As Chaya headed for the shtetl she thought of how eager Jacob was to learn about what it was like being a Jew. She had enjoyed talking with him. She did not feel the same guilt she had experienced previously. Their meeting was harmless and nothing untoward had happened. She was also curious about Jacob's story about Herr Morgenstern. It would be nice to know more about the way that they had met. Maybe she would go mushroom picking in a few days' time.

CHAPTER 9

Chaya's mushrooms were once again a hit with Nicholas Steiner when he dined with them. So, when Chaya suggested that she pick some more two days later, her mother thought it an excellent idea.

As she headed for the birch forest, Chaya was looking forward to hearing Jacob's story about Herr Morgenstern. She sat in the meadow and started to sing. Jacob appeared soon after with a huge grin on his face.

"Hello Chaya. You came."

Chaya smiled back at him. "I wanted to hear the story about Herr Morgenstern."

He sat down beside her. "I remember that day so well. I remember meeting Herr Morgenstern, but it was what happened after that changed me."

"What happened after, Jacob?"

"All in good time Chaya. All in good time. I must tell you the story in the order that it happened. I can't tell you the end then go back to the beginning; it would be too complicated."

Chaya noted the big grin on Jacob's face. "You are teasing me Jacob, using my own words." She laughed at the way he was poking fun of her use of the word 'complicated'.

"I am, Chaya, but it would make the most sense if it I told it in order. Before I begin though, I have very important question for you."

"What is it?"

"Do we need to pick mushrooms while I tell the story?"

Chaya felt content sitting in the meadow. It was such a beautiful day. He could tell his story, then they could pick mushrooms after.

"Let's enjoy the sunshine. We can pick after you have told your story."

Jacob was happy to enjoy the sun with Chaya while he told his story.

"I was eight years old when I visited your shtetl."

First, Jacob told Chaya about his impressions of her shtetl. He described all that he had seen and observed that day. He explained why he and his father were there that day, and he told her his impression of Herr Morgenstern.

Chaya listened as he described her shtetl, seeing it as he saw it as a visitor and as a non-Jew. The things he described, she took for granted because they were familiar. She also knew the reasons why her shtetl looked poor and rundown, but she did not tell Jacob. Those reasons were secret. He talked about his encounter with Herr Morgenstern.

Then he got to the part of his story where he and his father were returning home.

"It was my first experience visiting your shtetl. It was also my first time meeting a Jew. Not to be disrespectful, Chaya, but I had many questions. The visit had confused me. I had a friend whose father made it sound like Jews were dirty and not to be trusted. But when I met Herr Morgenstern, I did not get that impression of Jews at all. So, I asked my father about this."

"And what did your father say?"

"It is better, if I show you."

"Why can't you just tell me?"

"Because I want you to experience what my father had to tell me the same way that I did. Trust me Chaya, it will be better this way."

Chaya was curious, so she agreed to do what he asked.

"Close your eyes, Chaya."

"What? Why do I have to close my eyes?"

"Because that is what my father had me do. Go on, close your eyes. You cannot fully understand unless you do."

Chaya hesitated. She did not understand what closing her eyes would do. But obviously Jacob would not tell her more unless she did. So, with a bit of reluctance, Chaya closed her eyes and waited for what came next.

Once Chaya closed her eyes, Jacob proceeded to pose questions much like his father had those many years ago.

"Chaya, a stranger has just joined us in the forest," he began.

"A stranger, Jacob." A note of panic rose in Chaya's voice.

"Calm down, Chaya. You are safe. The stranger is not here to harm you, he just happened upon us in the forest. He is no threat to you or I, I promise. Keep your eyes closed and trust me. Just answer the questions as truthfully as you can. Can you do that for me, Chaya?"

"I . . . I . . . guess I can," Chaya replied nervously.

"Good," Jacob replied. "Now for the questions. How tall is the stranger, Chaya?"

"I don't know, Jacob."

"Is the stranger a male or a female?"

"Male."

"How do you know the stranger is male?"

"You have referred to the stranger as a 'he' a couple of times."

"Good, Chaya. Is the stranger tall and skinny, or short and plump?"

"I don't know, Jacob."

"What colour eyes does the stranger have?"

"I don't know."

"What religion does the stranger follow?"

"I don't know."

"Is the stranger a human being?"

"Yes."

"Is the stranger one of God's creations?"

"Yes Jacob. We are all God's creations."

"Exactly," said Jacob. "And aren't we all taught, Christians and Jews alike, to respect all of God's creatures, no matter who they are, where they come from, and how they worship?"

"Yes. But I still don't understand."

"Open your eyes Chaya and you will."

Chaya opened her eyes and looked around. There was no one there in the forest with her and Jacob.

"What do you truly see in front of you, Chaya?"

Chaya understood. "A human being. One of God's creations."

"When we judge with our eyes only, we make many mistakes about what and who that person truly is. It all boils down to the most basic of things, which is, although we may be different, we are all human beings lovingly created by God."

Maybe she had been too hasty to dismiss Jacob as just a goy. Maybe he could teach her more about himself and his people. For were they not also German, just like herself and her fellow Jews? But more importantly, was not everyone a human being, like he said?

Chaya knew that she had totally misjudged Jacob. She also knew that she had to apologize to him and make him understand that she had not set out to judge him, despite having done so. To make things right, she wanted to extend an olive branch to Jacob. She reached out her hand to him.

"Hi, my name is Chaya Blumenthal and I am very pleased to meet a fellow human being."

Jacob took her proffered hand and shook it. "Pleased to meet you Chaya Blumenthal, human being. I am Jacob Henkel, human being."

As they shook hands they looked into each other's eyes. They held each other's gaze for a moment, then they both burst out laughing.

The tension that had previously existed between them melted away with this small gesture. Now they could start anew, learning about each other. They were no longer Jew and goy, but rather two human beings who, with open minds, hearts and souls, could learn so much from one another.

"Chaya, I know that we come from different religious backgrounds. But I think we have much more in common with each other than you think. I would like to get to know you better."

"I would like that," Chaya replied. "I would like to get to know you better as well. If today is any indication, I am in for quite an education on who Jacob Henkel is."

"I think we better do it while we work," Jacob stated. "You have a basket of mushrooms to pick."

"Yes, we'd better start picking. Thank you for sharing your experience and for opening my eyes. I am sorry that I misjudged you. I hope that you can forgive me?"

"I cannot forgive you."

Chaya had not expected him to reject her apology. "Why not?"

"I will only forgive you if you agree to come back to the forest and talk with me more. I think that this human being would like to know so much more about my fellow human being."

Chaya noted that Jacob had a twinkle in his eye as he said this last thing.

"I will come, but I cannot be sure when I will be able to."

"As long as you come."

Chaya for once did not consider that 'the rabbi's daughter' should not consent to continue seeing Jacob. She wanted to do something that made her happy for once in her life, without worrying about what other people thought or expected.

Damn the consequences, she decided. *It was time she did something for herself.*

Chaya felt more like herself with this small act of defiance.

CHAPTER 10

As spring changed into summer, Chaya and Jacob continued to meet in the birch forest.

For Chaya, it was the happiest she had been in a long time. She enjoyed getting to know Jacob, but the thing that made her the happiest was that she was finally just Chaya. When she was with Jacob, she no longer felt that she was being judged as 'the rabbi's daughter'. Nor did he make her feel like she was different because she was a Jew. Yes, he asked her a lot of questions about what it was like being a Jew, but he never judged. He just wanted to know so that he understood things better. And by understanding those things, he understood her better. Others were not so understanding. She felt so fortunate to have found such a good friend. Jacob had truly become her best friend. She had never had a best friend before. It was not that she had not wanted one. It was just that she was always 'the rabbi's daughter' to her peers. Now with Jacob, she could truly just be herself.

She told him about the expectations she had to live with every day just from being 'the rabbi's daughter'. She told him about how frustrated she felt when, even in her own family, she was treated differently from her brother; how the expectations for her were always so much higher and more inflexible. She told him how her life had already been mapped out for her, including a possible marriage to Nicholas Steiner in the future.

Chaya bared her soul to Jacob. He listened, sympathized, and gave her support. The last time she had felt this much like herself was when she had been tending to Herr Morgenstern.

The thing that she appreciated the most about Jacob was that he never judged her. She had spent her entire lifetime being judged, and it was such a relief not to have to live up to someone else's perceptions and standards. Jacob accepted her for who she was and nothing more. Chaya knew that she could tell Jacob anything and that he would never judge her or hold anything against her. Chaya was glad that she had decided to continue meeting with Jacob. It was selfishness on her part, but when had she ever done anything just for herself?

The guilt she had had during their first meetings was gone. She no longer felt the need to confess to her father or to seek his guidance on the matter. Fate had brought her and Jacob together. They were doing nothing inappropriate, so she stopped stewing over the matter. All that was happening was two people learning about each other. Maybe if others did the same then there wouldn't be so much hatred in the world. Jacob had said it best when he told her something his father had told him. His father had said we fear and hate what we do not understand. How true those words were. He had also said that fear and hate can be removed with understanding and love; two things that seemed to be in short supply in Russia.

—⚶—

Jacob was not sure why Chaya had had a change of heart about their meeting in the forest. Maybe it had come about because of the story he told about his visit to her shtetl all those years ago. Maybe it was because she finally realized that he was right, that there was no harm in them getting to know each other. They were both just people after all. Maybe she just enjoyed his company. He never knew the reason, and in many ways, it was not important. She came and they spent time together. He enjoyed getting to know her and to learn more about what it was like to be a Jew.

However, they did not only talk about her Jewishness. They talked of many things. They talked about their families, they talked about their chores, and they talked about their favourite things. They talked about their hopes and their dreams.

Jacob felt so sad for Chaya when she talked about what her life was going to be in a few years' time. She believed she was destined to become the wife of Nicholas Steiner. Jacob listened as she lamented the fact that she had no say in the matter. He could not solve her dilemma. All he could do was provide her with was a sympathetic ear and let her know that he felt it was wrong – but that was all he could do. He felt so bad for her. She did seem less sad once she had unburdened herself. At least he felt like he had helped her in a small way.

Most of the time, their talks were light-hearted and lively. The time they spent together flew by in the wink of an eye. They worked as they talked. There was the mushroom picking of course. Sometimes, Chaya would also be in the forest looking for certain plants that her mother needed for different medicinal concoctions for her family or for others in the shtetl. When the berries came into season, they also picked those while they talked. They also gathered wood for Jacob's wheelbarrow. Initially, Jacob had refused Chaya's help, but she had persisted.

"Four hands can do more than two. Just look how fast we pick mushrooms or gather berries," she added to further her point.

Jacob had finally agreed to let her help, not so much because of her argument, but because it meant that he could spend more time with her.

—⚹—

The halcyon days of summer were quickly coming to an end. So was the time that the two friends were spending together. Harvest was just a few weeks away. Both would be too busy to meet in the forest, as the harvesting of the grains from the fields needed every available body, whether it be in Norka or in Novaskaya.

After the harvest, Jacob would accompany his father and brothers to the Kosakenwald to gather the family's firewood supply for the coming winter. Many of their fellow farmers from Norka would do the same. Bandits roamed the Kosakenwald, so the farmers worked together to gather their winter wood supplies. Those who toiled felling trees and cutting up the wood were protected by their fellow farmers who were armed. The bandits knew better than to attack the wood gatherers.

There would be no chance for the friends to meet once the steppes became frozen. They would have to just wait until spring arrived once again in this part of Russia.

It was a bittersweet parting on their final day in the forest. The levity of their meetings was not there. Both would miss the companionship of the other. They only thing that they had to look forward to was the promise that they would meet up again the following spring.

As a final request before they said goodbye, Jacob asked Chaya to sing one of her songs as they went their separate ways. Jacob listened as Chaya's song got fainter and fainter. Then it was gone. He grabbed his wheelbarrow and headed for home.

CHAPTER 11

Jacob did not have a lot of time to think about Chaya after they parted. He was just too busy. At the end of the work day, he was exhausted. He toiled with his father and brothers in the fields. The rush was on to get their crops off the fields and into the granaries before the weather turned.

He cut swathes through the crop using his scythe almost as well as his father and brothers. He had also learned how to make the sheafs so that the grains could dry in the autumn sun. Sometimes he even drove a loaded wagon from the fields to the threshing floors in Norka. It was exhausting, backbreaking work, but Jacob enjoyed every minute of it.

Jacob's younger siblings also enjoyed harvest time as well. They were given time off school to help. It was not a holiday though. Every pair of hands were kept very busy.

It had been a good crop year. In fact, it looked like it was going to be a bumper crop. The granaries in Norka filled up very quickly. There was enough grain this year that many wagons were sent directly to Schilling. There it would be sold and shipped on the Volga to feed other places in Russia.

As the final field was cleared, the people of Norka knew that there would be plenty of food to get them through the winter.

Some years it had not been so easy. They thanked the Lord for their bountiful harvest.

—m—

In the shtetl of Novaskaya, they too were engaged in getting their crops off. Their crops had done well, but not as well as those in Norka's farms.

Chaya toiled along with several women and young girls in their shtetl's threshing floor. She swung her flail, hitting the grain spread on the threshing room floor. Eventually, the grain would separate from the stalk. The straw was gathered for bedding for the animals of the shtetl. Young girls gathered up the grain and placed it on tarps. With one girl on each corner, they would take the tarp outside. They would toss the grain into the air, letting the wind blow away the chaff from the grain. When all that was left was clean grain, the girls dumped it into a wagon bed. Chaya had done the job the girls were doing for many years. For the last two years, she had been given the harder task of using the flail.

The work was hard, but no one complained. There would not be food in their bellies unless they all worked hard to get the grain harvested as quickly as possible.

Even though it had been a good crop year, there was still some doubt as to whether there was enough to see the shtetl through the winter. There would be enough if they did not have others who took their grain from them.

Towards the end of each day, everyone worked at a frenetic pace. Wagons that stood outside the threshing room floor had to be loaded before night fell. The filled wagons were tarped and everyone retired to their homes exhausted and in need of a meal.

In the morning those filled wagons would be empty. Under the cover of darkness their precious cargo was stored safely away in a secret granary. If it was not for this secret granary, the inhabitants of Novaskaya would have starved to death many times over.

It was one of the secrets of her shtetl. She did not learn about it until she had had her bat mitzvah. It was when others also found out about it as well, either at their bat mitzvah if they were a girl, or bar mitzvah if they were a boy. These rites of passage in Judaism, signalling the transition from girl to woman and boy to man, were also the occasions for learning some very important secrets about their shtetl. As newly-introduced adults to their shtetl, they were told the secrets and tasked with keeping them.

The secret granary was located under the synagogue. Access to it was through a trapdoor under the bimah. The secret granary was constructed of wood to keep their grain safe from pilferers as well as from rodents. Chaya had only seen it once when she was shown it by her father. During the harvest, young men from the shtetl transferred grain from the wagons to the secret granary during the wee hours of the night. She never knew who was tasked with the job because everyone in the shtetl looked exhausted during harvest, but she was grateful to them for their mitzvah to the shtetl.

For the elders, the challenging part of the harvest was deciding just how much grain could be hidden. A good year such as this one should mean that the shtetl's granary would be relatively full. If there was not enough grain in the granary, it might arouse suspicion. And the one thing that the Jews of Novaskaya did not want was to have people not taking things at face value.

Day after day, Chaya toiled in the threshing room. It was dusty work, but she soldiered on. She would have liked to take more breaks to rest, but she was 'the rabbi's daughter' and was expected to lead by example. When she did take a break, it was only when it was urged by an older lady. Chaya would go outside to get some fresh air and to stretch her tired limbs. She would lean against the wagons they were filling to give herself a short reprieve from her physical exertions. Then she would go back inside and resume her flailing.

As she rested one day, she sensed that something was different. It took her a minute of puzzling over what it was before she figured it out. It was the wagons. More specifically, one wagon. There were the same number of wagons that had been there the previous day when they loaded them up, so she had not really taken any notice of the change right away. The number was the same, but one of the wagons was different. Chaya pondered this. She did not have time to ask questions or to investigate this further because she had to get back to work.

She thought nothing more of it until the next day, when the wagon that was there two days ago reappeared in line. A different wagon was now gone. Now Chaya's interest was piqued. *What was going on?*

She continued to observe the wagons over the next week. A wagon disappeared and was replaced with another. Then it would reappear a day or two later. Something was going on. She wanted to go to her father and ask him about it, but he was so busy and the right time to ask him just never presented itself. She decided to ask him once the harvest was complete.

But as soon as the harvest was over, the Jews of Novaskaya had to quickly prepare for the arrival of the Governor from Saratov. Chaya, like her fellow Jews, were kept busy as they prepared for his arrival. The preparations were not to welcome the Governor, but to hide and protect all those things that they did not want the Governor to confiscate. 'Confiscate' was just a nicer way of saying what he was really doing: stealing from the Jews of Novaskaya. The Governor purported to be doing his duty for the Tsar, but the Jews knew better. He was doing it to line his own pockets at their expense. Anything they did not want 'confiscated' they had to hide so that the Governor and his men did not discover them.

Like the harvest and the hiding of grain, not everything of value could be saved. Some things had to be given up to keep the Governor and his men satisfied that the Jews had lost things of value.

Chaya carefully wrapped up her mother's silver Sabbath candlesticks. She would bury them in their garden until the threat of the Governor passed. In their place, she put out two brass ones that had seen better days. She went around the house collecting items that had to be hidden. She also had to decide on a few items that would be left. A beautiful goose down quilt would be one of the sacrificed items. *Damn the Russians for taking such things from them.*

She remembered when she was little and had lost something dear to her heart. Her mother had made her a beautiful doll who she had named Sonja. She took Sonja everywhere. She told Sonja all her secrets as she lay in bed at night. Sonja was her best friend. Then the Governor and his men had come and taken Sonja. Chaya was devastated. She cried for days afterwards, but Sonja was not coming back. She had lost her best friend and confidant. She hated the Governor and his men.

On the day of the Governor's arrival, Chaya stood in front of her house with her family. She wondered how the people of Novaskaya always knew what day he was to arrive. Every year, she and her family waited in front of their house for the Governor to come and take what he wanted in the name of the Tsar. They were ready. Some of their prize laying hens had been whisked away to the forest to be hidden in a makeshift pen until it was safe to bring them home. Others in the shtetl had done the same with some of their animals.

They had dressed that morning with the Governor's visit in mind. They were not in their best clothes (which were the clothes they wore to synagogue). Rather, they were in their most worn-out clothes. It was all part of what they and the rest of the shtetl were conveying to the Governor: that they were so poor and they were barely surviving. Their shtetl looked run-down and derelict, its inhabitants looked much the same. If the Governor and his men believed what their eyes saw, then they would not take more than the Jews could afford to replace. It was what they had to do to survive.

When the Governor arrived, he took in the pitiful sight of the residents of Novaskaya. Mothers had deliberately neglected feeding their children so that the wails of hungry babies and small children filled the air. The Governor ignored this. He did not care about these Jews and their plight. He had a job to do.

The Governor's entourage included his own personal militia as well as several wagons. Four wagons made their way to the granary. The Governor inspected the contents and then instructed his men to load the wagons. The grain he took was tax on behalf of the Tsar. At least that was what he told the Jews. The grain did make its way to the Tsar's granaries, eventually. The Governor used a middleman to sell the grain to the Tsar's stores. All involved in the illegal transaction were compensated handsomely for their efforts. The Governor made a very tidy sum off the transaction for his own coffers.

A fifth wagon was left in the centre of the village. Militiamen went into the houses of the Jews searching for anything of value. No one could protest this invasion of their homes; it had been going on for decades. A Jew had once tried to resist the militia entering his home. The militia shot him and executed the rest of his family. After that incident, there was no more resistance.

Chaya watched as the quilt was thrown onto the wagon. Four hens were also thrown on, their necks broken. One of her mother's pots was thrown on as was her father's pipe. The militia must have been satisfied because they moved onto the next house. They continued throwing items in until the wagon was close to overflowing.

The Governor did not say anything to the assembled Jews, he just ordered his men to move out. The Jews of Novaskaya watched as their wagonloads of grain disappeared down the track. The last wagon with all their stolen goods trundled along behind the procession. Two cows were tethered to the back of it, followed by two calves that were bawling for their mothers. The Jews shook their heads for their losses, but they returned to their homes knowing that most of their things were still safe.

It could have been much worse. But their troubles were not over yet. Another set of visitors were expected.

CHAPTER 12

Chaya went to her father after the harvest was over. She was sure that he had the answers as to why a couple of the wagons kept on appearing and disappearing. Her father listened as she explained what she had noticed. When she was finished, she looked at her father expectantly, waiting for him to explain.

"Who else have you told this to?"

"No one, Abba."

"Not even your ima? Or Herschel?"

"No Abba. Only you."

"It is best that you forget what you saw and not mention this to anyone ever again. Do I make myself clear, Chaya. No one."

"But Abba I don't understand. What is going on? I am only telling you what I saw. I told no one else, I swear, although I am not sure why I am made to feel like I have done something wrong. If I have done something inadvertently then please tell me what it is, Abba, so that I don't do it again."

"Chayaleh, just drop the matter. Some things are best left alone."

"I'm sorry, Abba," although she was not sure what she was apologizing for. She had obviously observed something she was not supposed to, but that was all that it was - an observation. *Why was her father so reluctant to explain what she had observed? And why had he told her to drop the matter? She would be the* dutiful daughter and do as he had asked. But it still incensed her that she had not been told what was going on.

—⁂—

The second visitors to the shtetl arrived a couple of weeks after the Governor's visit. These visitors were Russians as well. They were peasants from the nearby village of Rysincek. Every year like clockwork, they appeared in Novaskaya just after the harvest and the appearance of the Governor. It was not a social call they were making though. Like the Governor, they came to Novaskaya to take what did not belong to them.

As soon as the Russians appeared, people scurried to their homes. Chaya had strict orders from her father to stay out of sight every time the Russians came. This time she disobeyed her father and hid herself in the loft of the shtetl's storehouse. She usually did as her father told her, but since she had not been given an explanation about the wagons, she decided it must have something to do with the Russians. They always brought a wagon with them when them came to the shtetl. Maybe it was one that kept appearing and disappearing during the harvest.

She heard the doors to the storehouse open. Voices drifted up to her hiding spot. She carefully peeked down into the storehouse. She could see the peasants' wagon parked just outside of the open door. She was disappointed to see that it was not one of the ones that had appeared and disappeared. Her theory had been wrong.

She listened to those who were assembled below. Her father was there as well as all the elders of the shtetl. She was shocked when she saw them embrace the Russians and slap them on the back like they were long-lost friends. A bottle of vodka was produced and glasses were filled. Her father toasted the Russians and all drank. Glasses were filled once again. This time, Chaya noticed that her father and the elders did not drink but poured their glasses on the ground when the Russians were not looking. Glasses were filled again and again. The Russians got louder and the Jews kept refilling their glasses.

Finally, one of them bellowed that it was time for the Jews to pay up. Her father and the other elders started carrying food from the storehouse to the wagon. The Russians might have helped, but most were staggering around. When the wagon was half full, her father showed the Russians two wooden crates with bottles in them. Judging by the response of the Russians, Chaya surmised that the bottles were full of vodka. Her father put the crates on the wagon and the Russians eagerly jumped into the wagon bed. One fellow tried to get onto the driver's seat but was so drunk that he fell while climbing up and landed flat on his bottom. He roared in laughter, finding falling funny. Her father and another elder helped him up into the seat. Chaya did not see any more because someone closed the storeroom's door.

She did hear the receding sounds of the drunk Russians as they left the shtetl. She thought about what she had just witnessed. Every year, the Russians came and took from them. Food that they had all worked so hard to grow and gather was taken away by these people who had no right to it. That really made Chaya angry, but what made her even angrier was how her father and the elders had treated these thieves like they were old friends. *It was appalling. How could they do this?* She wanted to go and confront her father but knew she could not. For if she told him what she had witnessed, he would know that she had defied his order to stay hidden. Well, she had hidden, just not where he had expected her to.

"Where were you?" her mother asked as Chaya entered the house after the Russians had left. "You were supposed to be here."

"The arrival of the Russians surprised me. I couldn't get home without being seen by them, so I hid until they left."

"Where did you hide?"

She wished her mother had not asked that question. She could not lie. Now her father would know she had witnessed what had happened in the storehouse.

"I had to hide in the storehouse – in the loft." She looked at her father.

"Stupid girl. That is where the Russians go to steal from us." Her mother's voice was angry. "What if they had seen you?"

"Sara, she is safe. The Russians didn't see her and that is all that matters."

Chaya could see that her father was trying to diffuse the situation, but her mother was not going to have it.

"What were you thinking Chaya?"

"Enough Sara." Her father tried to intercede again.

"She knows better."

"I said enough Sara! The girl is safe, and there is no use making her feel worse than she already does. Now I am hungry. Let us eat before the food you prepared goes cold."

Her mother stopped. Not because she wanted to, but rather because her husband rarely put his foot down. When he did, like in this case, she knew better than to pursue the matter any further.

As the family ate, there was not the usual atmosphere in the house. Everyone was tense and the meal passed mostly in silence.

Chaya knew that her mother had been forced to drop the matter, but she sensed that her father had not.

After her mother and brother had retired to bed, Chaya busied herself in the kitchen making tea. Even though her father had not mentioned the need to talk about what she had witnessed, Chaya knew he would want to have words with her.

She poured them each a cup of tea, then carried the cups into the sitting room.

Her father was sitting by the fire. A book rested on his lap. Usually, he would smoke a pipe while he read by the fire, but his pipe was gone. Chaya remembered it being thrown into the Governor's wagon. She wondered if her father would replace it. She handed her father a cup of tea, then took a seat opposite him.

He took a sip, then looked at her. "Tell me everything that you saw and heard in the storeroom."

Chaya told him everything that she had seen and heard. She only left out one detail: why she was there in the first place. Her father listened to her account, not saying anything. He just nodded. When she was done, she expected him to lecture her just like her mother had done. But he did not. Instead, he asked her what she thought it all meant.

"I don't understand what you mean, Abba."

"You are a very clever and observant girl, Chaya, I want you to tell me why you think the things you saw and heard were done."

Chaya thought about everything, trying to understand what her father wanted her to conclude from her observations.

"Some things I understand. Others I don't," she answered honestly.

"So, start with what you understand."

"I understand why you give the Russians vodka. It is so that they get drunk and forget what they really came for. I noticed you and the elders only had one drink so that you did not lose your heads. Because the Russians got drunk, they did not really notice that their wagon was not even full. Especially after you brought out the two crates of vodka."

"What else did you understand?"

"That you brought the Russians to the storerooms purposely. Not all the shtetl's food is stored there, only some that each family has contributed. Most of the food from our gardens are stored in our own homes. You want the Russians to go only to the storeroom so that they ignore the food we have stored in our homes."

"Good, Chaya. What else?"

"I think that you also want the Russians to stay in the storeroom so that they also stay away from the granary. I'm not totally sure about this, it is just a feeling I have, that's all."

"Is there anything else, Chaya?"

"I don't think so, except for the one thing I don't understand."

"And what is that?"

Although it felt like she was judging her father and the elders' actions, she felt her father expected her to tell the truth.

"I don't understand why you treat the Russians the way that you do. They are coming here to steal from us, yet you and the elders treat them as if they are our friends and as if we are happy to give them what they want."

Her father nodded. "I am glad that even someone as smart as you cannot see the gesture for what it really is."

"I don't understand Abba."

"Exactly."

Why was her father talking in circles? It was so exasperating sometimes.

"You aren't telling me what I'm not seeing. Just like you wouldn't tell me about the wagons," Chaya blurted out before she had time to consider her words. She had let her frustration get the better of her.

Her father stared at her.

"I'm sorry, Abba. I should not have brought up the wagons again. I didn't mean any disrespect."

Her father continued to stare at her. She squirmed under his gaze. His face softened.

"Chayaleh, you are sometimes too smart for your own good. I love you with all my heart, but sometimes you can be so obstinate. Why can't you let the matter drop?"

Chaya hated disappointing her father, but what she was asking was not all that difficult. Her father obviously knew the answer, but he obviously did not trust her enough to tell her. She should have let the matter drop, but her obstinate side wanted to know.

"I have answered your questions, Abba. Why can't you answer mine? Don't you trust me?"

Chaya could see by the hurt look in her father's eyes that she had really touched a nerve.

"It's not about trust, Chaya. It is about survival. Not just about our family's survival, but the whole shtetl's."

"I would never place either of those in jeopardy. Why won't you trust me, Abba?" Chaya got up. She was mad and frustrated. She was going to storm out of the room.

"Sit down Chaya." The tone of her father's voice made her comply immediately. "I wanted to know your impressions because it is important that we are not discovered. We must do many things, Chayaleh, to ensure that our shtetl and its people survive and are protected. It is not easy, some of the things that we must do, but it is necessary. You want to know all, Chaya, but it is for your own protection and for the protection of others that you are not told everything. Only myself, the elders, your mother, and those whose help we enlist know the entire truth.

That is all there is to it. Once you become rebbetzin, then you will be given the answers that you seek."

Chaya wanted to be privy to the secrets her father alluded to, but they would be gained at a high cost. To learn them, she would have to consent to marrying Nicholas Steiner.

"Thank you, Abba, for putting up with your impetuous daughter. I will respect your wishes and drop the matter."

She hugged him and then made her way to her bedroom. *What could she do to convince her father that she didn't want to marry Nicholas?* She sensed that he was considering such a match. Her mother must be doing her best to convince him of the merits of the match. *How long would it be before her father pursued the matter more vigorously?* Luckily, her father still thought of her as his 'little girl'. But she was not a little girl anymore. She was a young woman. A young woman who was quickly nearing marrying age.

—◊◊◊—

Yuri Gregorvich (who many called 'Pockface' because of the lesions on his face from a bout of small pox when he was small) and his pal Pavel were riding in the back of the wagon, enjoying the vodka the Jews had provided. He looked at the wagonload that the Jews had loaded, only half full of vegetables. He scoffed at how easily his fellow villagers had been duped by the Jews, but since he was one of the younger ones in attendance, he held his tongue. *Not even a full wagonload. How stupid these oafs were.* If he were in charge, the Jews would not have been able to get away with this farce. He felt that the Jews needed to be put in their place, and he was just the man to do it. However, he would have to wait for a more opportune occasion.

The vegetables and vodka were not as valuable as something he had glimpsed only briefly. Tomorrow, he and Pavel would pay the Jewish village another visit. He wanted to see if there were more treasures the Jews were trying to keep hidden.

—⁓—

The next day when he was supposed to be splitting wood, Pockface slipped away from his father's farm. He collected Pavel and they made their way to the Jewish village.

They did not enter the village, but rather observed it from the cover of the forest that surrounded it. They did not have to wait long before he saw what he was hoping to see. There she was, the beauty he had briefly glimpsed as they had arrived in the village. He took note of which house she came out of. He was about to tell Pavel that it was time to leave when another beauty emerged from the same house. *This must be the sister.* Pockface could not believe his luck, for there were two beauties.

He and Pavel watched the house for a while longer, then they left to return to their village.

When the time was right, they would return to the Jews' village. His manhood stirred just thinking of those two beauties and what he had in store for them.

CHAPTER 13

It had been a successful harvest. Bumper crops abounded in the fields and in the gardens. The wood supply for the winter had been harvested and the butchered animals had been hung in the smokehouses. It was time to celebrate. It was time for Kerbfest.

For three days, the residents all over Norka celebrated the successful harvest. The Henkel family jubilantly joined the celebrations.

Jacob was happy that on the first night of the Kerbfest celebrations, the Henkels had been invited to celebrate at the Schumacher's.

Jacob noticed Lilith as soon as he entered her house. She was wearing an emerald green dress that took Jacob's breath away. Jacob did not go over to her; he was too shy. Instead, he glanced in her direction as discreetly as possible. On one of his quick glances, he noticed that Lilith was talking with Liesel Hauser. He knew Liesel from school. She had been in the same grade as him.

Jacob had to stop peering at Lilith when his sister Heidi insisted, he dance with her. After taking a turn with Heidi, his sisters Lina and Anna also requested a dance. Jacob obliged, but he would have preferred to dance with Lilith. He was trying to work up the nerve to ask her when his mother came along and told him that a proper young man should ask for a dance, not the other way around (like it had been with his sisters). Jacob asked his mother to dance, which she accepted, but she insisted that they wait for a slower dance due to her condition. She was pregnant with Jacob's next brother or sister.

After dancing with his mother, Jacob watched other couples dancing, again working up the courage to ask Lilith for a dance. His father came over and sat beside him. His father gave him an affectionate hug. His father was not usually so demonstrative, but that was because he had been enjoying some alcoholic libations. Jacob could smell it on his father's breath. He wished that he could imbibe as well. Maybe a little liquid courage would help him to take the plunge and ask Lilith to dance with him.

"Don't Karl and Magda look happy? I do not think they have danced with anyone else since their engagement was announced. That Magda sure is a pretty one. Although I am not sure that she really comes from Huck. They are not quite as easy on the eye in that village." His father laughed at his own attempt at humour.

Jacob laughed along with his father. He was a happy drunk. Jacob did not begrudge his father for his drunkenness. He worked very hard providing for his family. He deserved to let off a little steam.

"Soon it will be your turn, Jacob."

Not if I can't work up my nerve with Lilith, Jacob thought. "Yes Vati, when I find the right girl." *Find her – she's right across the room.*

"Jacob my boy, I have decided that your apprenticeship starts after Kerb."

This was news Jacob had been waiting to hear.

"Who am I to be apprenticed to, Vati?"

"Why me of course. You silly goose. I will make you the best farrier in Norka. Correction, I will make you the second-best farrier. The best farrier needs another drink."

Jacob watched his father stagger away. He rose. He strode purposely towards Lilith. He did not know where his newfound courage came from. Maybe it was his father's announcement.

When he was halfway across the room, his bravado started to abandon him. He was about to change his course, but Lilith had spotted him and was watching him. He would really look foolish if he turned away now. He willed his legs to keep walking.

Then he was standing in front of her. She smiled at him when their eyes met. Jacob panicked. For the life of him he could not figure out what he wanted to say. He continued to stare at Lilith. Jacob felt like such a fool. He tried to salvage what little dignity he still had.

"I'm sorry Lilith," he stammered. "But I wondered if you would mind if I asked Liesel to dance. I know you are talking and all. I didn't mean to interrupt and be rude." Jacob felt that his nervousness was making him ramble.

Lilith smiled at him again. "You will have to ask Liesel, not me."

Jacob looked at Liesel, "would you like to dance?"

Thankfully, she accepted. Jacob was able to recover a small shred of his dignity. As he led Liesel to the dance floor, he whispered thank you to her.

Jacob felt bad that he had used Liesel to cover his own inadequacies. He asked her what she had been doing since he last saw her. Since he was no longer in school, he had not seen Liesel for almost a year.

"I am helping out in my parent's store. Why didn't you ask Lilith to dance? It was clearly who you intended to ask when you came over. Although, I don't mind being your second choice."

"I'm sorry Liesel. That was rude of me."

"I'm not complaining, Jacob. You are a really good dancer."

"Thank you."

Jacob felt so bad that he asked Liesel to dance with him again for the next song. It was a lively polka. They were both smiling and laughing as they sailed around the dance floor.

Jacob thanked Liesel for the dances and went to find something to drink. After he was refreshed, he thought again about his missed opportunity with Lilith. He considered trying to work up his courage again, but every time he looked for Lilith, she was on the dance floor dancing with different partners. He watched her wistfully, knowing that her partners did not realize just how lucky they were.

The second night of Kerbfest, the Henkels attended the celebrations at the Miller residence. The Schumachers were not there, so Jacob didn't have a chance to dance with Lilith that night. Liesel was there with her parents. Jacob danced with her a few times.

The last day of Kerbfest, the Henkels went to the Bucher's. Jacob saw that Lilith and her family were there. He now had a chance to make up for his lost opportunity. Jacob did not wait to work up his courage. He strode up to Lilith and asked her to dance before his courage deserted him. To his surprise and delight, Lilith accepted his invitation.

"Why haven't you asked me to dance before?" Lilith asked him as they made their way around the dance floor.

"I wasn't sure if you would say yes," Jacob replied truthfully.

"Well, I am dancing with you now. So that should be answer enough." She smiled at him.

Jacob felt like he was floating on air. All too soon the dance ended. He would have liked to ask Lilith for another, but another dancer swept her away before he had a chance. He decided that he would ask her later.

Every time he went to ask Lilith, she was already being escorted onto the dance floor by someone else. Jacob did not bemoan the fact, and he still enjoyed himself. Liesel was also at the dance and he danced with her several times over the evening.

Finally, he saw his chance. Lilith was sitting down sipping a drink. She was having a rest and some refreshment after being on the dance floor for so long. Jacob approached her.

"Might I have the next dance, Lilith?"

She smiled at him. "That would be nice, Jacob. I just need a bit of rest. Dancing so much makes me so thirsty." She drank from her cup.

Jacob could see that her cup was now empty. "Would you like me to get you more punch?"

"That would be lovely, Jacob."

He took her cup and made his way to the table where the punch was. He filled the cup and returned to where Lilith had been sitting – the seat was now vacant. Another dancer had coaxed Lilith back onto the dance floor. Jacob watched them. As the music ended another dancer swooped in and became Lilith's new partner. He kept waiting for her to return but she was constantly being asked to dance by new partners. He placed the cup on her seat and went to find Liesel. But before he could find her, his mother intercepted him.

"Your vati has had too much to drink. I need your help to get him home."

Jacob was disappointed that he would not have the opportunity to dance with Lilith again, but he could not refuse his mother's request. As he left, he looked enviously at Lilith's current dance partner. Jacob wished that he could trade places with him.

CHAPTER 14

Christmas came and went in Norka. The Henkel household had been busy since the end of Kerbfest. First were all the preparations for Christmas, and now the household was in a frenzy as the family prepared for the upcoming nuptials between Jacob's brother Karl and his soon-to-be-bride Magda.

The wedding was to take place just after the new year. As the day grew closer, the atmosphere in the farmhouse was one of anticipation and excitement. Jacob's younger siblings, especially his sisters Lina and Anna, were beside themselves with excitement. Every day they got louder and louder, squealing over everything wedding related. The way that they were carrying on, Jacob thought it could have been them getting married, not Karl. They had not even been this excited at Christmastime. Sometimes Jacob stayed in the barn longer than he needed to, just to have a bit of time to himself away from the wedding preparations. The cows did not complain about his presence in the barn.

Starting three weeks before the big day, an announcement was made in their church of the upcoming nuptials between Karl and Magda. It was all part of their wedding traditions. It was a chance for anyone who opposed the match to come forth and air their reason for opposing the union. Most marriages were not challenged. No one opposed Karl and Magda's upcoming marriage.

Jacob helped his father as they hand carved canes for the wedding invitations for the invited guests. Once the canes were finished, Karl and Magda used them to fulfill another tradition. The prospective bride and groom went to the houses of the guests they wanted at their wedding. If the guests were able to attend, they tied a ribbon onto the cane.

Jacob only cared about one ribbon. He pestered Karl until he admitted that the Schumachers had accepted their invitation. Jacob was so happy because it meant that Lilith would be at the wedding, as well as at the celebrations that happened before and after the actual wedding.

The day before the wedding, the Henkels would host a dance for the young people. It was meant to be a last fling for Karl before he took on married life. Jacob saw it as an opportunity to dance with Lilith again. This time he resolved that he would dance with her as many times as he could. He was not going to stand aside and let others enjoy what he desired most.

On the evening before the wedding, Jacob waited expectantly for Lilith to arrive. An hour into the dancing, neither she nor her family had appeared. *Why was she late?* Jacob wondered. He kept watching for her, but she did not appear. He saw Liesel. *Maybe she knew something.* He asked her to dance.

"I noticed Lilith isn't here. Her family accepted our invitation to the wedding. You are her friend. Do you know why she is not here?"

"I thought you knew, Jacob. Lilith is very sick. Her family are tending to her. She won't be attending the wedding or the festivities, neither will the rest of her family."

Jacob was crestfallen. He tried to hide his disappointment, but Liesel could probably see it written all over his face.

"I'm sorry, Jacob. She was looking forward to seeing you."

Liesel's words were meant to comfort him he knew, but they had the opposite effect, making him feel miserable instead. He stopped dancing.

"I'm sorry Liesel. I am not being very good company. I need to be alone."

"Jacob, Lilith told me to tell you that she is sorry and that she will make it up to you when she feels better. She was worried that you would take her absence this way, so she asked me to take her place, just for the evening. I do not think being alone is a good idea, Jacob. Let's just dance and have some fun – for Lilith's sake."

Jacob knew he was being unfair to Liesel.

"Okay, if it's what Lilith wanted then I will do as she asks. May I have the pleasure of the next dance, Liesel?"

Liesel consented and they danced the next dance, and a lot more after that. Even though he wished Lilith was there, he still had a good time thanks to Liesel.

—✤—

The wedding day arrived. His brother and father hitched up the sleigh to the team and journeyed to Huck to collect Magda from her childhood home. Upon their return to Norka, they joined the procession of the other brides and grooms who were also getting married at the same time.

Magda looked beautiful and radiant in her white gown, as did the other brides. His brother was absolutely beaming, dressed in his Sunday best. The couples paraded down the aisle and then sat on the front pews in the church. The pastor gave a sermon, then each couple was called up for the ceremony to be wed. His brother placed a ring on Magda's finger. The pastor blessed the union and they were married. When all the marriages were complete, the new couples walked down the church aisle.

Once outside, the couples led a procession to their respective homes where their wedding receptions would be held. Jacob walked with Heidi as they followed Karl and Magda to the Henkel farmhouse. When the couple arrived at the farmhouse, Jacob's mother welcomed Magda to her new home. The bride and groom, as well as the other members of the family, formed a receiving line outside of the farmhouse. They all greeted the guests who came to celebrate the wedding. Some guests could not attend because they were at the reception of another couple, but that did not matter because the reception would last for three days.

Lilith and her family were absent from the wedding ceremony, so Jacob did not expect them to be at the first day's reception. The first day went by in a flurry of eating, dancing, drinking, and visiting. Jacob could see that his mother was run off her feet. With Magda, she would have another pair of hands to help her in the house. Ernst's wife Gerda and his sisters did their best to help his mother out.

On the second day, Jacob was disappointed when the Schumachers had not appeared. All he could do was hope that Lilith would recover so that she and her family could attend the final night of revelry.

Early the next morning, the church bell in Norka tolled. Jacob knew from how it was tolling that someone had died. His brother Ernst was sent into Norka to find out who had passed away. When he returned, he informed the family that Lilith had died in the night. The festive air in the house instantly turned somber. Jacob could not believe that it was true. *Lilith was so young and vibrant. It just did not make any sense.*

It became real for Jacob when he and his family went to pay their respects to the Schumachers once Lilith's body had been prepared by a local midwife.

Lilith was lying in a coffin in the green dress that Jacob remembered her wearing to the Kerbfest party. Paper flowers had been placed in the coffin so that they covered a lot of her body, but not her face. When Jacob looked at her, he was still struck by her beauty. She looked like she was sleeping. *How could this have happened to someone so beautiful?* He conveyed his condolences to her parents and to her younger siblings. She was the oldest in the family. She was only a year younger than himself - much too young to die.

After paying their respects, the Henkels returned home. The wedding celebrations were cancelled, and the food that had been prepared for the wedding reception was taken to the Schumachers.

Lilith would remain in her house for three days before her funeral and burial. Jacob's father had volunteered to spend one night with her body. It was their tradition that the body never be left alone between death and burial. He thought of Chaya and Herr Morgenstern. The Jewish tradition of siting shiva was almost the same as what they were doing for Lilith.

Jacob wished that he could volunteer to sit with Lilith, but he knew he was considered too young (which he felt he was not). He wanted to be alone with Lilith to tell her all the things that he hadn't had the courage to tell her when she was alive. But much like his timing with asking her to dance, he was too late.

On the day of Lilith's funeral, the sky was a slate gray. It signalled that somewhere on the steppes a storm was starting to brew.

All of Jacob's family attended Lilith's funeral, except for his mother who was feeling poorly. It was not a sickness like the one that had taken Lilith, but rather her pregnancy. The wedding had worn her out. She sent her regrets to the Schumachers, hoping that they would understand.

Jacob joined the procession with his family as Lilith's coffin was carried from the Schumacher's home to the church. Their pastor led them as they sang hymns. He talked of Lilith and what she had meant to her parents and siblings. After the eulogy, Lilith's coffin was carried to the cemetery. As he watched her coffin being lowered into her grave, Jacob and the others gathered at her graveside to sing a final hymn.

Members of her family each threw a shovelful of dirt onto the coffin. Then the mourning party left the cemetery. Her grave would be filled in by the village gravedigger and his assistant once the mourners left.

They all returned to the Schumacher's for a meal with the deceased's family.

Jacob stared out the window and picked at the food on his plate. Fat snowflakes were drifting lazily to earth. He hardly noticed them. He was thinking of Lilith lying dead in the cold frozen ground. He did not notice that someone had sat beside him until he felt them gently shaking his arm. He looked over to see Liesel looking at him. Jacob had not seen Liesel since the wedding.

"Did you know that Lilith was so sick?" he asked.

"I knew that she was quite sick, but I never thought she would die." There was a catch in Liesel's voice.

"She was just so young and full of life. It's hard to think of her as dead."

"I know, Jacob. It is hard for me too. I know that you liked her."

Jacob did not want to talk about his feelings for Lilith with Liesel. "It is just sad. I feel so sorry for her parents and for her brothers and sisters."

"Yes. It has been very hard on them, as it has been on you."

It seemed like Liesel was not going to let Jacob keep his feelings to himself. Luckily, his father appeared and told him that they had to leave because it looked like a storm was coming. Jacob looked outside. The snow was not falling gently anymore. The wind had picked up and was whipping it at the window.

It looked like they might be in for a blizzard.

He said his goodbyes to Liesel and the Schumachers, and followed his family into the beginnings of the storm.

CHAPTER 15

Pockface was happy to see the gentle snowfall transform into the makings of a good storm. It was what he had been waiting for. The storm would provide the necessary cover for him to do what he had been planning ever since he had been in the Jews' village.

He collected his friend Pavel and they headed towards the Jewish village. Pockface wasn't afraid of getting lost in the snowstorm, he'd been through worse. Besides, what awaited them in the Jews' village was all that mattered.

No one was about as they approached the village. The storm had sent everyone inside, just as he hoped it would. He led the way to the bakery. Even with the wind blowing, a yeasty smell emanated from it. The storefront was dark, but Pockface could see a light in the rear. He threw his weight against the door. The lock splintered under his assault. He walked into the dark interior of the bakery. A bearded man appeared in a doorway at the rear of the shop.

"What is the meaning of this?"

Pockface grabbed the man by the scruff of his neck and pushed him against the wall.

"Where are they?"

"What are you doing? Get your hands off my husband." The baker's wife had appeared in the doorway. Pavel grabbed her and she shrieked. Pockface and Pavel pushed the two into the room they had come from. The room was their living quarters. The aroma of stew filled the air. It was on the stove bubbling away. Their table was set for the evening meal.

"Where are they?" Pockface repeated.

"Who?" the baker asked.

"Your lovely daughters, of course. They have two gentleman visitors and they need to come and entertain them."

"Our daughters are dead."

"Oh, I'm sorry to hear that." He feigned sympathy. "When did they die?"

"This past summer," the baker replied.

"LIAR!"

"My daughters are dead," the baker repeated. "They died in the summer of the fever."

"Liar!" roared Pockface. "I saw them just a few months ago when Pavel and I were watching this little Jewish paradise."

"You are mistaken."

Pockface smashed his fist into the baker's face. "You are mistaken," he mimicked. "Now, you are going to start telling me what I want to hear, or we will deal with you in a less pleasant manner. So, I will ask you one more time old man. Where are your daughters?"

"Dead."

"Dead," he replied mockingly. "Since when do the dead eat with their parents?" He pointed to the four place settings at the table. "You insult my intelligence, Jew. I have tried to be reasonable with you and all you have done is repay my reasonableness with lies and deceit. So now, Jew, you will reap what you sew."

"Okay Pavel, the old Jew wants to do this the hard way. Every time I ask him a question that he doesn't answer correctly, I want you to cut off one of his wife's fingers."

Pavel nodded his head enthusiastically. He was obviously going to enjoy doing this.

"Okay, first question Jew. Where are your daughters?"

"Dead," the baker replied, desperation creeping into his voice.

"Wrong answer," Pockface declared. "Off with her finger, Pavel."

"With pleasure," Pavel said.

"Please . . . please," the baker implored. "I beg of you, show mercy. Cut off my finger instead."

"I don't negotiate with Jewish scum. Off with her finger Pavel."

"No please – don't hurt our mutti!" Mia and Petra, the baker's daughters, ran into the room, tears streaming down both of their faces. "We are here. We are here. Please don't hurt our mutti," they both wailed.

"Well, look at what we have here," Pockface declared.

"Please," the baker implored his tormentors. "Please just beat me, spare my daughters. They have done nothing wrong."

"I think that they deserve everything they get. As do you. You lying sack of Jewish shit."

Pockface unleashed his fury on the baker, pummeling his face over and over with his fists. When the baker sank to the ground, lying in the fetal position, Pockface continued to kick him and curse him.

Seeing her father being beaten so severely was too much to bear for the youngest daughter Petra. She launched herself at Pockface, trying desperately to claw his eyes out. Pockface laughed at her futile attempt and punched her in the side of the head. Petra fell in a heap by her father's feet.

He then looked at Pavel, who was still holding a knife to the baker's wife's finger.

"This old Jew is making me waste my energy on teaching him a lesson. This is not what we came for."

He tossed a rope to Pavel. He relieved Pavel of his knife while Pavel tied the baker's wife to a chair. The baker was still unconscious, so they dragged him to another chair and tied him up as well. They stuffed gags into the mouths of the baker and his wife.

The youngest daughter, Petra, was just regaining consciousness (considering what happened next, it would have been better if she had not recovered her senses). Her older sister, Mia, was cowering in the corner whimpering.

Pockface lunged at Mia and pinned her against the wall. Mia started kicking and thrashing, screaming at the top of her lungs for help.

"There isn't anyone who is going to help you, so shut up," he commanded.

Mia was hysterical and did not stop her screaming. Pockface had had enough. He stuffed a rag into Mia's mouth and started to rip off her clothes. He took her in full view of her mother.

Pavel had grabbed the semi-conscious Petra and started to rip her clothes off. When he entered her, Petra let out a long high-pitched wail. As soon as she let out the wail, Pavel knocked her unconscious again with a well-aimed punch.

Tears streamed down the mother's face as she bore witness to her daughters being raped.

After their lust was slaked, Pavel bound the two girls just in case they tried to escape.

Each grabbed a plate and helped themselves to the Jews' supper. Pockface found the stew very tasty, but he was not going to tell the Jews that. The bread on the table was also fresh. Both tore off hunks of it as they devoured their meal. The bread was made with white flour, not the coarse rye flour they had to use in his village. *These Jews have more than they deserve*, he thought.

Once they had eaten their fill, Pockface rose and approached the baker's wife.

"Your stew, though good, was actually missing an important ingredient." He walked over to the pot and spat into it. "There, that's what it was missing."

With his stomach full, Pockface could feel his lust returning. He grabbed a pitcher of water and threw it onto the baker. The water had the effect he desired. The baker was now conscious. Pockface smiled at him.

"You slept through the first round of your daughters entertaining us. It would be a pity if you missed the second act."

The baker strained at his restraints, causing Pockface to laugh. This time, Pockface took the younger one, while Pavel had his fun with the older one.

Had the two young men left after debasing this family and defiling the daughters, maybe the deaths that followed might not have happened. But their lust was not fully slaked.

"Now that we've had a bit of fun, Pavel, it is time to teach this Jewish dog and all these other filthy Jews that when we ask for something, they give it to us. For if they don't, then this is what happens."

The baker had to watch as the two men took turns raping his wife.

The two perpetrators ransacked the bakery and house, stuffing food and anything of value into empty flour bags. Before they stole away in the pre-dawn light, they left the baker with a message he was to tell all the Jews of the village. Their message was simple: We will be back. And we will take what we want when we return.

It was still snowing when they left, so their tracks were covered very quickly (not that the Jews would pursue them). They had also made it very clear to the Jews that if the authorities were alerted, then the baker's life, as well as the lives of his family, were forfeit.

—⚏—

No one in the shtetl knew of the horrors that had occurred at the baker's until early the next day, when a woman came to purchase bread. After discovering the broken door, she went to fetch her husband. He discovered the family in their kitchen, all bound and gagged. It did not take long for the news of what had happened to make its way through the close-knit community. Mia and her mother had given detailed descriptions of their assailants. Petra had not spoken a word since the attack.

The men ministered to the baker's many bruises, but they were not able to erase what his eyes had seen and what had been done to his family.

The women of the shtetl, Chaya and her mother included, tended to the battered and bruised bodies of the baker's wife and his daughters. When Chaya returned home to prepare a meal for her family (her mother was staying at the bakery longer), she found her father sitting by the fire just staring into the flames.

Chaya approached her father.

"Abba, why haven't the authorities been summoned to find those responsible for what happened at the baker's house?"

Her father looked at her with sad eyes which showed remorse and regret.

"They will not be summoned, Chaya."

"But why, Abba? Both Mia and the baker's wife described their attackers. They need to be found and arrested for their crimes."

"It is over and done with Chaya. They are gone and we must all carry on."

Chaya had a hard time hearing her father's words. *Carry on as if nothing had happened. But something had happened. Why wasn't her father going to the constable in Saratov and demanding justice? It just did not make any sense.*

"Abba, why aren't you doing anything? What if it had been our family? What if it had been me or Ima who were violated? What if they attacked you? Or Herschel?"

"Chaya, you don't understand."

"Then make me understand, Abba. I want to know why we cannot do anything to bring them to justice."

"Chaya, we are living amongst people who hate us. They hate us because we are Germans, and they hate us even more because we are Jews. How could they help us? They would only blame us, claiming that we somehow encouraged the attack."

"But that is not true, Abba."

"Who is the constable going to believe? A Jew or a Russian? Since the constable is Russian, there is no question of whose side he will be on."

"Then we should go to the Governor."

"Another Russian. A man who exploits us whenever the opportunity arises. No one can help us, nor will we ask for help either."

"Abba there has to be a way."

"Chaya, there is no other way. I was hoping to spare you the bitter facts until you became the rebbetzin, but for you to truly understand, I will tell you now. However, what I tell you must never be shared with anyone. I am only telling you this so you will see that everything we do or do not do in this shtetl has consequences. Do you understand?"

"I will try my best to understand, Abba."

"I will start at the beginning. When our ancestors came to this country, they were heading to the Black Sea to settle. Their guide abandoned them here after robbing many of their valuables. He had left them here to die on these steppes. And they would have if it hadn't been for the people of Norka. They took these poor unfortunates into their homes and sheltered and fed them. Their intercession helped our ancestors to survive that first harsh Russian winter. The next spring, they helped them to establish this shtetl. Our ancestors abandoned the idea of continuing to the Black Sea because of the support they received from their German brethren. It wasn't easy during those early years, but they survived and the shtetl grew. Some Jews who were passing through also decided to call Novaskaya their home."

"The Governor eventually caught wind of our settlement. He came to investigate. He could have evicted our ancestors and sent them on their way, but he didn't. He was greedy and he saw an opportunity. Since our settlement was not permitted because it was not in the Pale of Settlement, he decided he could take advantage of them."

"Why didn't they just leave then?" Chaya had not meant to interrupt her father, but the question seemed important enough to ask it.

"By this time, all of the good land which they might have claimed before was long gone. Times were tough all over. It was likely that they would have ended up starving to death had they moved on. The risk seemed too great – so they stayed. They put up with the Governor and his bribes, as well as the incursions by the local Russians, because even with these, there was still food in their bellies and roofs over their heads. And when times got tough, they knew that the people of Norka would come to their aid."

"One thing that our ancestors did, and that we still uphold, is to not flaunt what we have. We purposely make the Governor and the other Russians think that we are just a poor shtetl. We hide our valuables when they come and we hide some of our grain under the synagogue. If they knew about these things, they would not hesitate to take them from us. We are always keeping up the pretense that we are barely surviving. The truth is that we are not, but it requires a lot of effort to maintain this illusion to the Russians."

"You were partially correct when you guessed why we treat the Russian peasants so cordially. Getting them drunk and diverting their attention prevents them from seeing our shtetl for what it really is. It is part of the pretense that we are just poor Jews who do not have much that they can take. They had been content taking what little we gave them, but those animals who attacked the baker's family did not act like the rest of the peasants. Although I would like to see justice served, just like you would, I cannot let my personal feelings change the decision to do nothing. If we were to go to the authorities, the story would circulate amongst the Russians that we are vulnerable and easy pickings for the dregs of society. We would have more of those lowlifes invading our shtetl and abusing our people. It is hard, but we must keep quiet."

"We also must protect those who help us. You were very observant, Chaya, when you noticed the different wagons during the harvest. Every night during harvest, we send a wagonload of grain to a farmer in Norka. It is unloaded in secret. As you have seen, the Governor taxes our harvest heavily. The farmers of Norka help us to keep our grain out of the Governor's clutches.

They are taxed much more reasonably than we are. When the farmer sells his grain with ours included, no one is the wiser. We pay the farmer the tax, plus a little extra. Some farmers do not accept the extra payment. With the money from those grain sales, we buy things that the people of this shtetl need to survive and prosper. We use different farmers every year so as not to arouse suspicion with the authorities. Our farmer friends from Norka risk a lot by helping us."

It all now made sense to Chaya. She remembered her father's mysterious errand when she wanted to tell him about meeting Jacob in the forest. He would have most likely been going to meet in secret with the German farmers to plan for the upcoming harvest.

"I now understand, Abba, why we must keep quiet about everything. I will do my part and keep the secret. Thank you, Abba, for confiding in me."

"Chayaleh, we all must do what we can to ensure that our shtetl and its people remain safe. For the baker and his family, it will not be easy, but we will all pitch in to help them through this terrible time. I am sure that in time they will all recover from their ordeal."

—⁂—

Her learned father, who usually had sound advice and wisdom, was wrong in his assessment of the baker's family. The shame of watching his wife and daughters being brutally raped was too much for the baker. He was found hanging from a rafter in the stable two days after the attack.

With the baker dead, people of the shtetl banded together to try to help the women of his family rebuild their broken lives. But some things could not be rebuilt.

Prior to the attacks, both girls had had very promising matches arranged by the matchmaker. After the attack, the parents of both young men rescinded the promise of marriage. Who could blame them? Their prospective brides had been sullied.

Five months later, just as winter was reluctantly loosening its grip on Russia, a roundness of Mia's belly became a reminder of that fateful night.

Now pregnant with Pockface's bastard, Mia had no chance for a reputable husband of any kind. Like her father, she gave into the despair of her situation. Her bloated corpse was found floating in the Norka River. Two lives lost.

Petra was never the same after the attack. Before, she had been a carefree girl, always laughing and smiling. Now she jumped at the slightest noise. Worse yet, she stopped talking altogether. She went through her days with a haunted look in her eyes. Some believed that she might never be the same again.

As for the baker's wife, she tried her best to make her family whole again, but failed in her attempt. After the death of Mia, she announced that she was taking Petra and moving to the Pale of Settlement. At least there she would be with other Jews who were under better protection from the Tsar. Or so she thought.

People tried to convince her that it was safer for them to stay in the shtetl.

"Don't talk to me about safety," she spoke vehemently. "How safe was it here while my husband was beaten and my daughters and I were raped?"

So, the baker's wife and her daughter left the shtetl for the Pale of Settlement. Two women travelling alone in a land filled with many cruelties.

No one ever heard from them again. Most likely, tragedy followed them out of the shtetl to their fates. Another two fatalities.

As the tragedy of the baker's family unfolded over those months, Chaya came to realize how lucky she and her family had been to escape that fate. She also understood even more what a precarious situation the Jews of Novaskaya were in.

But it seemed that the Jews were always in difficult situations. Hopefully, like her ancestors who came to this place long ago, they would be able to persevere and live through this crisis.

CHAPTER 16

Jacob could not dwell on Lilith's death and the what-ifs for long. Life went on in Norka. Death was part of their everyday lives. The next death was even closer to him: his mother's miscarriage. This pregnancy had been a difficult one for his mother. She lost the baby in the middle of winter. Jacob was sad for his parents, especially his mother. He wondered why his mother did not grieve. She was back in the kitchen working barely a day after the miscarriage. He did not understand any of it.

There was not a lot of time to dwell on such things. Jacob's apprenticeship kept him very busy. He had been helping his father since he was young, so he already knew a lot about the jobs and tasks of a farrier. Now he did a lot more of the work under his father's guidance. The thing he enjoyed the most about his apprenticeship was spending so much time alone with his father. He marvelled at his father's knowledge and tried his best to learn everything he could from him. His father was very happy with his progress, and praised Jacob on numerous occasions. The winter months passed by very quickly. With the arrival of spring, his apprenticeship would have to be paused for awhile so that his father could return to the fields. Before he did that, he fulfilled a previous promise he had made to Jacob.

That spring, Jacob's father came with him to the birch forest to teach him how to fell trees for the family's wood supply.

Jacob's foraging had supplemented the family's wood supply. Now, Jacob would be responsible for providing all of it. Jacob was proud that he could do this for his family. Plus, he was releasing his father and older brothers from doing this task in the fall.

Every year, his father and two brothers would go to the Kosakenwald to harvest wood for the winter. Most of the people of Norka did not venture into the Kosakenwald alone because it was known that bandits roamed there. Since there were many families gathering wood at that same time, the bandits left them alone. All were armed with axes, so the bandits knew that attacking the German farmers was a suicide mission.

It took Jacob's father and brothers about two weeks to gather enough wood for the winter. It was a huge operation that involved most of the family. Jacob's father and brothers felled the trees. Then they cut them into lengths that would fit into the stove. When they had enough wood cut, they then loaded up the wagon. One of his brothers would drive the loaded wagon home while his father and other brother remained behind and continued to log.

Once the wagon reached the farm, Jacob and his younger siblings unloaded the wood.

While the empty wagon went for another load, Jacob would split the wood. Sometimes, when Jacob needed a break, Manfred would split for a while. But for the most part, Jacob split the lion's share of the wood. The younger girls and his younger brother stacked the wood Jacob split. Sometimes the toddler would even carry a small piece or two to help. Splitting all that wood developed muscles quickly on Jacob's body.

Jacob had proven his worth with the splitting of the wood. Now he would be given the opportunity to do even more for his family.

Since Jacob was going to be working alone, his father said that they were not going to get their wood from the Kosakenwald – it was just too dangerous. Jacob had suggested the birch forest instead, and his father agreed that it was as good a place as any. He of course did not tell his father that his choice included an ulterior motive: continuing to see Chaya.

—⁓—

When they arrived at the forest, Jacob's father first showed him which sizes of trees to select. He also advised Jacob that he should not cut down all the trees in one area, but should only take a few in each spot so that the forest could recover.

His father showed him how to safely fell a tree. He stressed to Jacob that he was never to turn his back on a falling tree. He pointed out snags and how they could pose potential dangers.

After felling a few trees, his father then let Jacob try his own hand at it. The muscles which Jacob had developed splitting wood were very helpful as he swung the broad axe. Before long, a dozen trees had been chopped down.

Next, they chopped and stripped the branches off the trunks. Jacob was sweating profusely by then – even though it was a cool spring day – but he was also enjoying himself thoroughly.

After stripping all the branches off, they then started chopping the trunks into lengths that the two of them could carry. Jacob asked why they did not use one of their horses to pull the trees out of the forest. His father told him that it would be easier using the horses, but that the ground in the forest was uneven, and if the horse tripped and came up lame, the family would not have them for their regular work around the farm. Jacob joked that it was fine for him to come up lame instead. His father laughed at his little joke.

When Jacob and his father had chopped the trunks to a manageable length, they hefted each onto their shoulders and carried them to the forest's edge.

When they had packed them all to the spot, Jacob's father selected six logs that were approximately the same length and diameter. He chopped notches into the middle of all six, chopping halfway into each. He then fitted two logs together at the notches that he had made. Put together, the logs resembled the letter 'X'. He made sure they stayed together by driving nails into them at their shared joint.

With Jacob's help he constructed two more X's. These he lined up in a row a few feet apart from each other. He and Jacob hefted one of the logs onto the X frames. They each got on one side of the crosscut saw and proceeded to cut the logs into lengths that would fit in the woodstove.

It was quite easy sawing with two people. Jacob's father also showed him how to saw solo. It was a bit slower and harder, but Jacob soon mastered it. After they had sawed all the logs they had brought, they made perfect stacks of the cut logs. In the stacks, the wood would cure and dry over the spring and summer. After the harvest was complete, the wagon would be brought and the wood Jacob had cut and stacked would be taken home.

Finished with the first logs, Jacob and his father returned to the forest to continue harvesting more wood.

At the end of the day, Jacob's father told him that he was proud of how hard Jacob had worked, mentioning that he was going to be a good provider for the family. The words from his father were a balm for his sore, aching muscles.

He knew that his family could count on him. If he worked hard, he might even be able to get more wood than his family needed. This they could use to barter with other farmers for things that the family could use.

Jacob was so happy about his new role in the family. He was also very happy because he could still see Chaya while he logged in their forest.

But Chaya did not appear.

While his father was in the forest with him, he had not expected her to appear, but he had expected her to come after that when he was alone. A week went by and she had not returned. Then another week passed and still she was absent. Jacob started to worry. *Had something happened to her?* He had an urge to go to her shtetl, to see if she was okay, but he knew he could not. All he could do was continue to log and hope that she was okay and that she was only delayed. There was one other possibility that he also considered. *Maybe she had decided that it just was not proper for her to meet and talk with him anymore.*

—⁂—

Chaya wanted to return to the birch forest, but it was not possible. Everyone was still on edge from the attacks on the baker's family. For Chaya, it meant no more trips into the forest alone – it was just too dangerous. Not that her family could stop her foraging altogether; they needed the extra food. Her mother insisted that she was to be accompanied by another person. Most of the time it was her brother Herschel, but sometimes it was another girl from the shtetl.

Chaya exchanged her small knife for a much larger one. She wanted to go to the birch forest, but her having an escort prevented this. She did not want to run into Jacob accidentally. She took her escorts to a different forest to the north of the shtetl. There were hardly any mushrooms there, but she could not risk going where she knew they grew in abundance. Her mother complained about the lack of mushrooms.

In time, the tension in the shtetl ebbed. Soon it became more important for her brother to study at the yeshiva or work in his apprenticeship. The girl who accompanied her also went off on her own because her mother was complaining about the poor results of their foraging. Chaya was secretly happy that finally she could return at last to the birch forest. She wondered if Jacob would be there as well.

—❦—

Jacob was busy sawing a log on the day that Chaya reappeared. He was so engrossed in his work that he had not noticed that she had arrived and was watching him work. He looked up and she was there.

"Chaya. I didn't hear you approach."

"How could you? You are making such a racket here in my tranquil forest."

"Your forest!" he laughed. "When did it become your forest?"

Chaya smiled at him. She had missed him and his cheerful banter. After the awful winter, it was so nice to see a friendly face.

"Where have you been? I was worried when you never came after the snows melted."

Chaya was touched by his concern. "It was a hard winter, Jacob. A very bad thing happened." She then told him all about the attack on the baker and his family. When she was finished, he was visibly upset.

"Why didn't anyone alert the authorities? They shouldn't get away with what they've done to that poor family."

"It's complicated, Jacob. I wish that we could do something, but we cannot."

"Why not?"

"I told you – it's complicated."

"I am a pretty intelligent fellow if I do say so myself. I'm sure that if you told me I'd understand, no matter how complicated it is."

Chaya would have liked to tell him, but she had promised her father.

"I can't. I've been sworn to secrecy. If I could tell you I would. You have to believe me."

"I understand Chaya, you have made a solemn oath. I will respect that, but if you ever need to unburden yourself, I too would keep your secret."

Too many lives depended on her keeping the secret, no matter how sincere she knew Jacob was.

"Thank you, Jacob." She decided to change the subject. Chaya surveyed Jacob's worksite. "I see you have been hard at work."

"Yes, I have," he replied excitedly. "I am now responsible for getting all of the wood for my family. I might even be able to cut some extra which we can trade to other farmers for things that we need." Jacob proudly showed her all the wood that he'd cut since he had commenced logging a few weeks back. Chaya looked like she was impressed.

"That is great, Jacob. But since you have so much to do, I better leave you to your work."

"Nonsense Chaya. I can take a break to help you with your gathering. In fact, I insist upon it. Plus, it will give us time to catch up, and I still haven't shared my best news."

"What news is that?"

"Even though I am now the chief procurer of wood for my family, I am still so valuable to my family that I have retained my milking duties. The Henkel family would be in dire straits if not for the hardworking and ever-so-humble Jacob Henkel." Jacob put a silly grin on his face as he said this.

"Jacob, I think you are being a lot more than humble," Chaya said with a gleam in her eye. "I think maybe the whole world works better because of The Great Jacob Henkel."

Jacob burst out laughing. "You really understand my sense of humour, Chaya. Most people wouldn't have caught on that I was joking."

"That's because they don't know you as well as I do," Chaya replied. "I'm still trying to decide if that's a good thing or a bad thing." She smiled at Jacob as she said this.

Jacob laughed at Chaya's comment.

"All joking aside, I better tell you what the really big news is."

"You mean it's not that you are the humblest man in the world?" Chaya mocked.

"I guess I deserved that. The news is that my father has finally arranged my apprenticeship. I started to apprentice as a farrier with my vati this past winter."

"That is great news. I am so happy for you."

"Thank you, Chaya, I'm so happy that my wish came true."

"You deserve it. I am sure your father is going to enjoy teaching you all about his trade."

"I'm grateful that I get to spend time with my vati as I learn from him as well."

"I think we better get to the mushrooms."

They chatted animatedly as they picked. Both choosing light-hearted topics to converse about. Jacob didn't tell Chaya about Lilith's death or of his mother's miscarriage. These he would bring up another day. Chaya's distressing news about what happened in her shtetl was enough sadness for this day.

When Chaya's basket was only just over half full, she insisted that she had to go immediately. Jacob was sad to see her go, but he understood that she had other obligations. She did promise to return in a few days' time. He waved goodbye to her as she left him at his worksite. He picked up his saw and continued to work on the log he had been sawing on before Chaya appeared.

—⁂—

Chaya had not told Jacob the entire truth. She was needed at home, but she could have stayed a bit longer to fill up her basket. She did not want her basket to be full – that was her deceit. She did not want to appear in the shtetl with a full basket after weeks of poor pickings. It would be sure to arouse her mother's suspicions. If she was going to keep her meetings with Jacob secret, she had to make sure that no one in her household or in the shtetl were any the wiser as to what she was actually doing.

She hated being deceitful, but being with Jacob again reawakened the Chaya she'd been missing since she last saw him. The Chaya who was just herself, not someone's daughter, or sister, or a Jewess of her shtetl who was expected to act, think, and behave as others wanted instead of how she really felt. Her meetings with Jacob were so liberating for her soul.

CHAPTER 17

Chaya and Jacob continued meeting in the forest. Jacob eventually told her about Lilith and his mother. Regarding Lilith, she was sympathetic. She never pressed him for information on any feelings he might have had for Lilith, and for this, Jacob appreciated Chaya even more.

As for his mother's miscarriage, she was very consoling. He found out that her mother had had three miscarriages since her younger brother Herschel was born. She told Jacob how hard those miscarriages had been on her mother. When he got home at the end of his work day in the forest, he hugged his mother fiercely before he went to do the afternoon's milking. His mother was very surprised by Jacob's overt display of affection. When she asked him what brought this on, Jacob just told her that he knew she was having a hard time. He did not mention the miscarriage, but he did notice her wiping away a tear before she shooed him outside. Jacob was grateful to Chaya that she had helped him make his mother feel a little better.

Every day that they met, they learned more about each other, their families, and their lives. Sometimes Jacob would have more questions about Judaism, which Chaya patiently explained. But more and more the questions were less about religion and more about the wants, dreams, and desires of two young people. Their friendship grew stronger and stronger.

Jacob continued to help Chaya with her foraging. Chaya insisted that she help him as well since he was not logging when he was helping her. Jacob tried to dissuade her by telling her that the logs were too heavy, and that it was not like filling a wheelbarrow with kindling. But Chaya finally convinced Jacob that she could at least stack the wood. Jacob, with some reluctance, at last agreed that she could do this. He showed her how to make the stacks into neat piles, then he went back to his sawing while she stacked.

Eventually, Chaya convinced him that she could help him a lot more. He let her help him saw the lengths of wood. He had to admit that with two people on the saw, the logs got cut up even more quickly. Then she insisted that she could help him carry the logs back to the worksite. Again, he marvelled at her strength. The wood piled up quicker and quicker with all of Chaya's help.

—⟨⟨⟩⟩—

One hot muggy July day, he and Chaya had met again in the forest. After doing just two logs, they were both drenched in sweat. Even with the forest providing shade from the blazing sun, the air in the forest was stifling. If only there was a slight breeze, then there would at least be a little relief. They switched jobs to gathering mushrooms, but that was not much better. It was just so terribly hot!

"We should go swimming, Chaya. It is just too hot to do anything. I need to cool off."

Chaya would have liked nothing more than to go for a swim. She was sweating profusely even just picking the mushrooms. But no matter how good Jacob's suggestion sounded, or the thought of the cool water refreshing her, she knew that she could not.

"Although a swim would be so nice – I cannot."

"Why not Chaya? We are both so hot. We can swim in our clothes."

"Jacob we cannot. We Jews bathe separately – that is our law. I cannot bathe with you even with our clothes on. It isn't allowed."

Another of those Jewish rules, Jacob thought, but he did not say anything to Chaya. Sometimes he wished she was not bound by so many rules. Sometimes he sensed that Chaya felt the same way.

"Okay let's not go swimming, but it will be cooler by the river. There is always a breeze blowing there. At least that might help to cool us off a bit."

Chaya liked the idea of a cool breeze and agreed that they could go to the river.

They sat on the riverbank and enjoyed the slight breeze that was blowing.

"The breeze is stronger on the sandbar. Is it okay for you to wade out to it?"

Chaya could not think of any objection her faith might have to wading. It was quite different from swimming.

"Yes Jacob, that would be fine."

They both shucked off their shoes and socks. Jacob had to roll up his pant legs. Rather than waiting for him, Chaya hitched up her skirt and started to wade to the sand bar.

"Careful Chaya. There are holes."

Chaya was just about to acknowledge Jacob's warning when she stepped into one of the holes. She lost her balance and toppled into the water. She swallowed some water and came up sputtering.

Jacob ran to aid Chaya who was floundering in the water. He could not help himself from laughing though. She looked like a drowned rat. Her wet hair was plastered across her face. He offered her his hand, intending to help her back to her feet.

Chaya was not impressed that Jacob was laughing at her. She ignored his proffered hand. Instead, she grabbed a handful of mud from the bottom and flung it at him. The mud clog hit him on the chin.

Jacob had not expected Chaya's surprise attack. Some of the mud that hit his chin spattered into his mouth, causing him to stop laughing. He spat out the slimy sludge and reached down and grabbed a handful of the gross stuff himself. Then he flung it at Chaya. It splattered into her hair. She reached up, felt the mud on her hair, and then ran at him, tackling him. They both fell into the water. When they came up, they had fistfuls of mud which they flung at the other. They pelted each other over and over with their gooey concoctions, each laughing uproariously if they scored a direct hit on the other.

Finally, both held up their hands begging the other for a truce. Mud covered them from head to toe. Neither could stop laughing because the other looked so hilarious. When their giggles had finally subsided, they both seemed to grow serious at the same time. Or rather, they tried to be.

"What have you been doing, Jacob Henkel? Grubbing around in the mud with the hogs again?" Chaya tried to make her voice stern, trying to emulate a disappointed parent, but she burst into giggles halfway through her lecture, and in the end her lecture was more giggles than words.

"Chaya! How many times have I told you to wash behind you ears? I think you missed a spot." Jacob also had a hard time trying to get his words out without laughing.

They had another bout of laughter. They laughed until their sides hurt and tears were streaming from their eyes. It took them awhile before they could finally control themselves.

"We better wash this mud off. I think the fun is over."

Jacob was sad that their fun was over, but Chaya was right. He dove into the water then surfaced. He looked back. Muddy water was in his wake. He dove under again, relishing the cool water.

Chaya followed Jacob and dived into the water. She dived a few more times until she felt sure that she had removed every trace of the mud. Instead of getting out of the water immediately, she stayed. Soon she and Jacob were frolicking around. The rules were forgotten. They splashed each other and tried to dunk one another. Chaya had so much fun. They were swimming together and nothing bad happened.

They swam to the sandbar and lay there while their clothes dried on them. Then they waded back to shore. Chaya was careful this time to avoid the hidden holes. They retrieved their socks and shoes and went back to the forest. They filled her basket before she had to quickly leave, as she had spent more time than she had intended to with Jacob that day.

As she walked back to the shtetl, she smiled at the thought of their mud fight. It had been so fun having the mud fight and swimming with Jacob, but at the same time, she felt guilty that she had done something that she should not have. It would be nice to do things without worrying about how they might look to others. All they had done that day was have a little bit of innocent fun. If only life were not so complicated.

CHAPTER 18

Pockface hadn't forgotten that he'd threatened to return to the Jewish village; he'd just been unavoidably detained.

Not long after the rapes, he and Pavel had journeyed to Saratov. They had been caught red-handed stealing from the Tsar's granaries. It was an impetuous mistake that had cost him and Pavel six months of their lives doing hard labour. After being released, Pockface was even more surly than he'd been before his incarceration.

They returned to their village. Pockface tried to get some physical company from the girls of his village, but they rebuked him like they always had. His face was what had the girls scurrying away whenever they saw him. He had urges and needs that went unfulfilled, and so he took what he wanted from those with no choice.

The stirring in his loins told him it was time to visit the Jewish village once more. There had to be more tasty tidbits in that village. The last two had been so very tasty.

Had he and Pavel waited until winter, they might have gotten away with their crime, just like last time. But Pockface's desire pushed him to be more reckless. He was reckless, but not stupid.

As they had done before, Pockface and Pavel hid at the forest's edge and observed the inhabitants going about their daily activities. He kept an eye on the bakery hoping that one of the sisters might appear, but they did not. He noticed a girl come out of a house near to where they were hiding. She had a basket draped over one arm. Pockface expected her to collect something from the few shops which lined the dirt track running through the settlement. But she surprised him when she headed into the forest, not far from where they were. He signalled to Pavel that they should follow her.

She wasn't as beautiful as the sisters, but for what he had in mind, she would do just fine. As they followed her, she seemed to be unaware of their presence. She wasn't quite far enough away from the village yet – he didn't want to chance her screaming and alerting the villagers. So, they followed her deeper and deeper into the forest.

—···—

Chaya was just about to enter the small meadow where she had first met Jacob when she heard a twig snap behind her. She peered back into the forest, but saw nothing. *Probably just a deer,* she told herself.

As she stepped into the clearing two men materialized out of the forest. Chaya stopped dead in her tracks, partially because they had startled her, but more so because of who they were.

One was skinny with a thick, bushy mustache. The other was shorter, his face covered with scars. There was no mistaking who these men were. The baker's wife and daughter had described them when they'd told of their attack.

Chaya froze in fear.

Pockface spoke. "Well, what do we have here? I do believe, Pavel, that we have found ourselves another of those tasty Jewish bitches."

Chaya, in desperation, groped inside her basket for the one thing that might save her. She grasped the knife, dropped her basket, and prepared to defend herself.

Pockface and his companion did not try to attack her. Rather, they started to circle her like a pack of wolves. She kept trying to keep both in her sight line, but one was always slipping behind her with practiced precision. So, she kept shifting around, trying without avail to keep both in front of her.

"It seems the little bitch thinks she can stop us from getting what we want using that little pig sticker." Pockface let out a loud guffaw following his declaration. "You better drop that, you little bitch, if you know what's good for you. Or we aren't going to be very nice to you," he snarled.

Defiantly, Chaya stood her ground, holding the knife menacingly in front of her. Her focus was on the taunting Pockface, and for a split second she lost sight of Pavel.

Pavel darted in and slammed his fist down on Chaya's arm. Chaya yowled in pain from the attack. The knife fell into the grass and out of her reach. Totally defenseless, Chaya tried to keep both in sight, but they continued to circle her.

"Now bitch, you are going to give us what we want, like a good little Jew."

While Pockface was saying this, Pavel darted in and snatched the kerchief off her head.

Chaya felt like they were like cats tormenting and playing with a mouse they had caught. She just did not know how she was going to escape from them – or if she could.

"Okay bitch, time to get what's coming to you."

With that statement, Pockface darted in and grabbed Chaya's breast.

That is when she started to scream.

—◊◊◊—

Jacob had been sawing a log when he heard the scream. It only took him a second to realize that it was Chaya doing the screaming.

He dropped his saw and pelted through the forest towards the sound.

When he burst into the meadow, he saw Chaya thrashing and kicking on the ground while a man was pawing at her clothes. The man's friend was laughing and swinging Chaya's headscarf around in glee.

Jacob processed this all in a split second. With a roar like an angry bull, Jacob set upon the kerchief waver, landing a powerful blow on his chin that dropped him like a sack of potatoes. Jacob then turned his aggression to the man on top of Chaya. He wretched him so hard off Chaya that the man went sprawling into the grass. Before he had time to recover, Jacob was upon him pummelling him. Jacob was in a blind rage. He rained blow upon blow upon the man's face. Even when the man's face was a bloody mess and he no longer cried out in pain, Jacob continued to hit him. Only one thought pulsed through Jacob's mind: *How dare this animal touch Chaya.* Every blow Jacob landed only fueled his anger even more. He got up and repeatedly kicked the man over and over.

And then he saw it. A glint of metal lying in the grass – Chaya's knife.

Jacob grabbed the knife and raised it to kill the animal once and for all.

"NO JACOB!" Chaya shouted. "NO JACOB!"

Chaya's words brought him out of his murderous rage. He looked at the knife in his hand poised to kill. *He had almost killed a man.*

The one he had knocked out was just coming to. The other one was not moving.

"Get your friend and yourself out of here – NOW!" Jacob yelled. "And if I ever catch either of you in this forest again, I swear to God, I will kill you both."

The mustached one helped the beaten one to his feet and half-dragged half-carried him out of the clearing and back into the forest.

Jacob hoped he would never cross paths with either of them again, because he knew that if he did, he would be responsible for their deaths.

With Chaya's attackers dealt with, Jacob could now focus on Chaya herself.

"Chaya, are you okay?"

No response.

"Chaya, are you hurt?"

She still did not respond.

"Chaya?"

When Jacob looked into her eyes, the fire he had come to know was not there. Her eyes just stared blankly back at him, the life in them gone.

Jacob started to panic. *What should he do?* Chaya was not responding to his questions, or to him shouting her name. *What if he couldn't get her to snap out of it?* He could only think of one thing to do. He grabbed Chaya and shook her vigorously. His shaking worked because she collapsed onto the ground and started sobbing uncontrollably.

Jacob enveloped her into his arms and reassured her over and over that she was safe. Even with his assurances, Chaya continued to cry.

Finally, Chaya's sobs subsided to a few sniffles and hiccups. She quieted, seeming to be more in control of herself. Jacob peered at her tear-stained face.

"Chaya, are you hurt?"

She shook her head 'no', and then started to sob again.

"Please Chaya, don't cry, it makes me sad."

"I . . . I'm . . . I'm sorry," Chaya hiccupped. "I . . . I didn't mean to make you sad."

"Hush Chaya, its okay." Jacob looked deep into her eyes and could see a bit of the fire returning. "I'm just glad that you are okay."

"Jacob, you saved me."

"I wish I could have gotten here sooner."

"But you came and you saved me and you stopped them from what they were going to do to me."

"Chaya, you know . . ." But before Jacob could finish his sentence, Chaya was pressing her lips to his.

Jacob was completely taken aback by the kiss – at first.

Things had been building between the two of them for quite some time. The friendly banter and teasing were indications that the friendship was blossoming into something more. Neither had admitted to themselves that the feelings they had for the other was more than just friendship. This traumatic event had propelled their friendship over the precipice and into love; into something new and wonderful and so full of hope, as young love is.

So, rather than breaking off the kiss, Jacob returned it with the same passion and ardour as Chaya.

CHAPTER 19

Chaya had not meant to kiss Jacob. She did not know what had come over her to make her do that. But she had kissed him . . . and he had kissed her back. She did not regret her actions. Jacob had saved her from the scum who had attacked her. But it was not just her gratitude which had made her act upon her growing feelings for Jacob. There was more to it than that. Jacob made her feel something that she had been trying to bury within herself for years: the feeling that she could be loved for who she truly was and not for who other people expected her to be. Jacob had feelings for her, Chaya, not 'the rabbi's daughter'. And she had feelings for him as well. She had never felt so alive and free as when she was with Jacob. When she kissed him, her heart was all aflutter, but her head was telling her that it was a bad idea.

Chaya had listened repeatedly to her head. She did what was expected of her and never voiced what she truly felt or wanted. For once, she wanted something for herself. It was selfish she knew. But where had listening to her head gotten her? Her heart was going to lead the way for once. She knew it was wrong, but she just wanted this one small thing.

When she and Jacob finally broke apart from their kiss, she looked deep into his sky-blue eyes. What she saw in them confirmed what her heart was telling her: Jacob was in love

with her too! She was elated. She moved to kiss him again, but
he stopped her.

—⁓—

Jacob had not expected Chaya's kiss, but his mouth had
responded to her kiss before he could think to stop it. Not
that he really wanted it to stop. For weeks he had been looking
at Chaya differently. Sometimes when he knew she was not
looking, he'd steal secret glances at her. But he felt guilty when
he did this because she was his friend after all, and friends did
not look at friends the way that he was looking at her. He loved
Chaya as a friend. They had many things in common and he
was happiest in her presence. But he longed for more than
friendship. However, Jacob had never let on that he thought of
Chaya as more than a friend; he did not want to scare her off or
lose her. So, he kept his thoughts and desires hidden, although
at times this was very hard.

When they had had the mud fight it had been a wonderful,
playful romp with his friend. When they had ended up
swimming he had enjoyed splashing and dunking her. It all
would have been fine had they not gone to the sandbar to
dry off. Even though they had both been fully clothed, Jacob
had experienced stirrings when he'd looked at Chaya. Her wet
clothing clung to her body. Jacob had seen just how beautiful
her body was. His friend had somehow transformed into a
beautiful young woman. A woman he desired, but felt he should
not. So, he did his best to supress his feelings.

However, when Chaya kissed him, those feelings came
flooding out. When they broke apart and he looked into her
eyes, he was ecstatic when he saw that she had deep feelings for
him as well. She tried to kiss him again, but he stopped her.

"Chaya, as much as I'd love to continue what we are doing, we must stop. It is getting late. You haven't gathered anything and your prolonged absence might arouse suspicion."

Chaya knew that Jacob was right, although she wished that she did not have to leave him and what they'd discovered.

"I wish it were different, Jacob. But I know you are right."

"Chaya, I too wish it could be different. I will escort you back to your shtetl. We can gather mushrooms along the way. I also want to make sure that those thugs are truly gone."

Chaya could not have loved Jacob more in that moment. She was dreading going back to the shtetl through the forest. Although Jacob had nearly beaten one of the attackers to death, she was worried that the other one would be looking for more trouble.

They gathered enough mushrooms on their journey to make it look like Chaya had been moderately successful in her foraging. They quickly embraced at the forest's edge, and Chaya walked towards her house. When her mother saw her soiled clothes, she asked Chaya what happened. Chaya had no choice. She had to lie again to her mother. She told her that she had tripped and taken quite a bad fall near a stream. Some of the mushrooms she had gathered had fallen into the stream and floated away. She hated lying, but the truth had to be kept hidden. Her mother accepted her story and sent her to the chicken coop to collect the eggs. Chaya was relieved that her secret remained safe.

She could not warn anyone in the shtetl that another attack had occurred by the same scum who had attacked the baker's family. Questions might be asked. Questions that might lead someone to discover what she was really doing in the birch forest. She was in love with Jacob, and no one must find out. 'The rabbi's daughter' was involved in something she shouldn't be.

The attackers were long gone. Jacob had threatened their lives. If they were smart, they would never return.

—⚬⚬—

Pavel helped his battered and bruised companion through the forest. His friend groaned constantly. Pavel had a splitting headache from the lucky punch his assailant had landed, but his friend had borne the brunt of the attack.

When they reached Rysincek, Pavel carried the now unconscious Pockface to the nearest hovel. Although there were peasants in the village who professed to be healers, Pavel knew that his friend needed a lot more medical attention than they could provide.

He demanded that a peasant give him his wagon. The peasant begged him not to take his wagon, but he knew better than to cross a man such as Pavel. So, as they drove off, all the peasant could do was hurtle curses at them.

It took them many hours to cover the forty miles from Rysincek to Saratov. They arrived late in the evening. A passerby on the street directed them to a small hospital. He carried his friend into the building and demanded to see a doctor. It took longer than he thought it should for a doctor to appear.

"Who did this?" the doctor asked as he was examining Pockface.

"That is none of your concern."

"Have the authorities been notified?"

Pavel had had enough of the doctor's questions. He grabbed the doctor and held his blade to the doctor's throat. "You are here to fix my friend, not to ask questions." To further make his point, Pavel nicked the doctor's throat with his blade.

"I need to call for a nurse."

"You will tend to him yourself. Now get on with it."

The doctor removed his jacket since he did not want to get blood on it. He rolled up his sleeves, washed his hands thoroughly, then tended to the wounded man.

The man's face was a bloody pulp. The doctor cleaned it up the best that he could. The nose had been broken in at least two places. If Pockface survived, his nose would be permanently disfigured, and his face would be forever covered in scars. The doctor then moved on to the man's torso which was a mass of ugly purple bruises. He discovered that several of his ribs had been broken. All he could do was wrap the man's chest in linen cloth to keep the ribs as immobilized as possible.

The part that scared the doctor the most was what he could not see. How much damage the beating had done to the man's insides was unknown. If too much damage was done, he would inevitably die.

When he looked up, he saw that the man who had threatened him with the knife was holding a picture of his daughter, a picture that he kept in his jacket pocket. The man must have searched his coat while he'd been tending to his friend. Fear coursed through his veins again.

"You have a very beautiful daughter, Doctor. It would be a shame if you went to the authorities after this and something happened to her. I know people, bad people, who could do bad things to her. So, I suggest, Doctor, that you do everything in your power to make sure that my friend recovers, and then you need not worry about anything. Do I make myself clear?"

The doctor could only nod his head.

He had done all that he could do for the man – the rest was in God's hands. He prayed that God would help the man recover. Maybe then the nightmare he was living in would be over.

CHAPTER 20

Chaya lived in two worlds. In the world where Jacob resided, she was ruled by her heart. In her home and in the shtetl, she was the dutiful 'rabbi's daughter' who was ruled by her head. Although Chaya was one person living in two worlds, she wished that both of her worlds could somehow become one. However, she knew that could never be. It just was not possible.

After kissing Jacob, Chaya examined her feelings for him, thinking about how she had been meeting with this young man for over a year. Recognizing her true feelings, she was both elated and scared. She was madly and hopelessly in love with this young man whom she had no right falling in love with. And every time she looked into his eyes, Chaya knew that he felt the same way about her.

She loved her family. She loved her home. She loved her community of Novaskaya and the people who lived there. But this love between her and Jacob was so different. When she was with him, her heart sang a new melody, a melody it had never sung before. Chaya had never felt so loved in all of her life, and she in turn shared her love with Jacob.

Every minute they shared together was bliss. It was not all just kissing and being physically closer to each other (although there was some of that, of course). It was just that their relationship was evolving into something deeper and more meaningful because love had entered it. Working side by side felt different somehow now that they were in love. A look, a touch, a smile, passed electricity between both of them. They treasured every minute when they were together, and looked forward to their next reunion each time they had to part.

Although they kissed and touched, they did not pursue their love any further, not that they did not want to. Their bodies responded to one another in ways they did not know existed. Often, they felt their ardour building up to a crescendo, but both pulled back before it was too late. They were young. They were in love. But they could not make love because of the one big, insurmountable hurdle that still lay in their way.

—⁂—

Jacob and Chaya had gone swimming on another occasion. For modesty's sake and for other obvious reasons, they had swum fully clothed again. While they were letting the sun dry them off on the sandbar, they discussed the subject that neither of them had spoken about until then.

Jacob lay flat on his back. Chaya was lying beside him with her head on his chest. She could hear Jacob's heart beating strongly under her ear, the heart that she knew belonged to her. She was so happy, but at the same time a wave of melancholy passed through her.

"What are we going to do, Jacob?"

"About what, Chaya?"

"About this . . . about us . . . I love you with all my heart. But what are we going to do? I want to be with you always. But how can we? What are we going to do?"

Jacob knew that they would have to discuss what Chaya was addressing, but he was hoping that it would be later, that it wouldn't be so soon after they'd discovered their love for each other. He stroked her hair as he tried to think of a solution.

"Is there no way in which we could marry without our religions standing in our way?"

"No Jacob. There is no way for me to marry someone outside of my faith."

"Surely if two people love each other as we do, there has to be a way."

"Jacob, it's complicated. There is more to it than just love."

"I know that it is complicated, Chaya, but maybe there is a way that we just haven't discovered yet."

"There isn't a way. I wish there were." Chaya loved Jacob with all her heart. She felt as though she had finally found the piece of herself that had been missing all her life. With Jacob, she felt like she was finally whole. Every day he made her heart sing. She had never been happier in her life. And she had never been so sad at the same time.

"I can't bring you home to meet my family. Nor can you declare your intentions to my father."

"Your father is a rabbi. From what you have told me, he is also a wise man. Surely, he could find a way for us to be together. Especially once he sees how right for each other we are. He will see how in love we are and how much I love his daughter."

"The only way we could be together, Jacob, is if I turn my back on my faith. But I cannot do that – not even for you. I have been born a Jew, Jacob. It is who I am and it will never change. It is a part of me, just like my hand or my heart or my head. I cannot give it up for it would be like cutting off a part of me that would never be there again, and the loss of it would mean that all that I am would be lost as well. Do you understand?"

"I never asked you to give up your faith, Chaya. I understand it is what makes you who you are. It is one of the many things about you that I admire and love. I just want to be with you always. My heart doesn't want to accept the fact that our love cannot overcome something that makes you truly happy. It just doesn't make any sense."

Chaya's heart melted some more at Jacob's words. Her heart screamed that he was right and that they should be together and damn the consequences. But her brain told her it just was not possible. Even though she was in Jacob's world, her head dominated her thoughts and her thinking. Her heart wept at her decision.

"If I turn my back on my faith, I will be considered dead by my family. My parents and my brother will mourn me even though I still live. But unlike a regular mourning, my name will never again be spoken in my home. It will be like I never existed. As for the rest of the shtetl, they will do the same. If I walked among them, they would ignore me and treat me as if I was a specter and nothing more. I would be turned out by my own people. As for my family, the shame of having their daughter renounce her faith would be something that they would have to endure every day. I am the daughter of the rabbi. Would my father's flock forgive the transgression of his daughter? How could they have faith in a man who couldn't stop his daughter from abandoning the faith that he was entrusted to administer to his fellow Jews? They would turn their back on my father and my family, just like they would do with me. My family would have to leave Novaskaya. Where could they go? News travels in Jewish communities. Even if they relocated, my family's shame would follow them. I am sorry Jacob, but I cannot put my family through such misery just because of my own selfish desires. I just cannot."

"What if I converted?"

She touched Jacob's cheek tenderly. His gesture, though sweet, wasn't possible.

"You aren't of the faith, Jacob. Even if you converted, people would still treat you as an outsider. In a small community like our Novaskaya you would never be accepted. Outsiders are always treated with suspicion. It is just our way. No matter what you did, it would never make a difference. What if we had children, Jacob?" She paused, feeling an overwhelming sadness. She would like nothing more than to have children with Jacob . . . but it could never be. "Could you live with the fact that they too would be treated as outsiders, even amongst their own? They are innocents in the matter, and our decisions, though based on love, could do them irreparable harm. And what of your family, Jacob? Would they welcome the fact that their son wants to marry a Jew? What of the people of Norka? Would they shun you and your family because you chose a Jew for a wife? I love you Jacob, but could our love survive all of this?"

"I think my parents just want me to be happy. And if my happiness came from marrying you, I am sure that they would support me in my decision and welcome you into our family and community."

"They might Jacob, but don't be so sure about the others. Anti-Semitism is not a new thing, here, or many other places where Jews have lived. We live with it in our history and we deal with it in our every day lives. The Russians think nothing of taking advantage of us, raping our women, stealing from us . . . killing us." Chaya knew her words were harsh, but they were the truth of the situation.

Both knew deep down that their relationship was doomed. They should have stopped seeing each other and gone their separate ways. But after finding their love, they were not willing to abandon it. They both knew there was no future together possible for them. But they refused to let something so wonderful go. Love is special when it comes along. Even when it is doomed.

So, they stopped talking about the subject altogether. Instead, they revelled in the time they were able to spend together. Neither knew how long they could go on like this, but the alternative was worse – never seeing each other again. That was just too heart wrenching.

The one thing that they did discuss was whether they had seen the last of those two Russians. Chaya still feared that they might reappear. Chaya always ran as though the devil was chasing her when she left her shtetl to meet Jacob at his worksite. And in many ways, Chaya was indeed running from the devil. Just the memory of those two thugs urged her to run even faster. Only when she saw Jacob's familiar shape did she slow and finally relax a little.

It would be easier if Jacob could meet her at the edge of the forest and escort her like he did when she returned to the shtetl, but it just was not possible. Chaya never knew exactly when she would be able to slip away from the shtetl. Jacob couldn't just wait in hiding until she was free – he had to tend to his wood cutting. He could not afford to lose time waiting. So, she endured the fear and the trepidation of going through the forest alone because of what awaited her once she'd found Jacob.

—⁂—

What Chaya and Jacob didn't know was that the two Russians posed no threat to them. Both were currently in Saratov, where they'd been ever since Jacob beat Pockface so badly. Pockface continued to hover between life and death months after the beating.

CHAPTER 21

The summer soon came to an end. Even though Jacob and Chaya wanted to be together, they both knew that they would have to part. The harvest was nearing, and again it would take precedent in both of their lives.

The last day that they met went by much too quickly for the both of them.

Chaya had been dreading the day she would have to say goodbye to Jacob yet again. She knew it would be many months before she would see him. Anything could happen in that time. The one thing she was sure of, though, was that she did not want to give up on their love. She would endure the separation and count the days until they were reunited in the spring. She hoped that Jacob felt the same.

He did. Jacob was also not looking forward to their separation. He was worried that those two Russians might reappear again that winter. He feared for Chaya's safety because he could not be there to protect her. Although he kept his worry hidden from Chaya, he knew that she sensed it. So, on their final day together, he tried to keep the atmosphere between them light and carefree, but his effort was only half-hearted, and Chaya tuned in to his real feelings.

"It will be hard not being able to see you," he confessed.

Chaya tried to keep herself from bursting into tears, but a tear escaped from her eye. Jacob wiped it lovingly as it coursed its way down her cheek. This intimate gesture caused her dam to burst and her tears flowed freely. Jacob held her close, softly stroking her hair as she let her heart pour out her grief. *Why was life so hard?* When she felt more in control of herself, she looked into his eyes. She smiled.

"You are my bashert, Jacob."

"What does bashert mean, Chaya?"

"Bashert means that you are my soulmate."

"Bashert. I like that. You, Chaya Blumenthal, are also my bashert. You hold my heart. And you are a part of my soul. Even though we have to be apart for a while, know that in here and here we are always together." Jacob touched his heart and his head as he told Chaya this.

"I will think of you every day."

"As will I. Spring cannot come soon enough for me."

"Soon enough for us," Chaya corrected.

They clung to each other, neither one wanting to let go of the other. Finally, Jacob pulled away slightly.

"As much as I'd love to stay this way forever, Chaya, we need to fill your basket and I have to get back to my wood."

"You are right, Jacob. Maybe we can pick slowly – to make it last a bit longer."

"And maybe you will sing one of your songs as we pick, so I can relive the first time I found you in this forest."

Even picking slowly, the basket filled faster than either of them liked. When it was full, they could delay no longer. Jacob escorted Chaya back to her shtetl. In the cover of the trees, they kissed long and passionately. As they parted, each whispered their undying love, repeating that the other was their bashert.

—⁓—

The routines of the harvest quickly took over both of their lives.

Chaya once again toiled on the threshing room floor. As usual, grain was squirreled away in the secret granary under the synagogue. And once again, Chaya noted the wagons that she now knew took some of their grain secretly to different farmers in Norka. She wondered if Jacob's father was one of the ones chosen this year to assist the Jews. She knew she could not ask her father, nor would he tell her if she asked. But in her mind, she believed that Jacob's father was one of their helpers. Jacob was such a kind and loving person. She felt sure that he got these traits from his parents.

The Governor arrived as usual after the harvest was complete. It had not been as bountiful of a harvest as the previous year. The Governor was not pleased with the amount of grain in the shtetl's granary. That did not stop him from taking a generous portion though. To further show his displeasure, he took an extra wagonload of goods from the Jews. He had only brought one wagon with him for his pillaging of their homes and businesses. He commandeered one of their wagons as well as the shtetl's best team of horses. These they also lost to his greed. The Jews were glad when he and his militia soldiers left the shtetl.

But their worries were not over. The Russians from Rysincek would still make an appearance. Every person in the shtetl was on edge because they feared that the two who had attacked the baker's family would be amongst them. Everyone breathed a collective sigh of relief when the Russians arrived and the two were absent. Even after plying the Russians with copious amounts of vodka, the Russians still demanded more than they usually did. The shtetl's food supplies that were left would not have sustained the community through the winter. Even with the hoarded grain under the synagogue, as well as the money from the grain sold by the German farmers, life in the shtetl was going to be challenging. They would not starve, but they had to make what food stores they had stretch as far as they could. It would be hard, but the Jews were used to hardship – their history was full of it.

—ᴍ—

For Jacob, the harvest was so busy that he didn't have a lot of time to moon over missing Chaya. He missed her, but he just didn't have the luxury of time to miss her every second. At the end of each work day, he fell into bed exhausted. Just before he fell asleep, he did say a quick prayer, entreating God to watch over her and to keep her safe through the winter.

After the harvest, Jacob, his father, and his two brothers hauled all the wood that Jacob had cut to their farm. After their supply was replenished, there was still enough wood left over that they could trade it for things the family needed. Jacob could not have felt prouder.

His apprentice duties resumed with his father after the harvest was complete. His father continued to be impressed with his progress.

Before he knew it, Kerbfest had arrived once more. Jacob accompanied his family to the different nightly celebrations. The Schumachers hosted one of the nights. For Jacob, it seemed strange being there when Lilith was not. It was not like he was still besotted with Lilith; his heart now truly belonged to another. Lilith was just a crush. He did not dance much though. Lilith was gone. *Would he have even asked her to dance if she was still alive?* And Liesel, who he'd danced with a lot at the last Kerbfest, was also absent. Liesel's mother had recently passed away and he knew that she and her father were in mourning. So rather than dancing, he brooded. He knew who he really wanted to dance with, and that was Chaya. But that was not possible – it would never be. So, he missed her presence even more, and became more and more sullen as the festivities dragged on. When his father made a comment one night about Jacob spoiling the fun, he knew that he had to put on a cheerful front, lest someone find out why he was so down. Luckily for Jacob, his father had imbibed a lot so he did not remember pointing out Jacob's melancholy.

He was grateful when Kerbfest finally ended. He knew he could not be truly happy until he could be with the one who held his heart.

His bashert.

CHAPTER 22

Pockface remembered very little of his first few months in the hospital. He had vague recollections of a doctor hovering over him many times. The doctor had an extremely worried expression on his face.

A weaker man might have succumbed to his injuries. Pockface had one thing that kept him fighting for life: revenge. He clung to his tenuous thread of life because he had unfinished business. *Those Jewish dogs are going to pay for everything they did.* Pockface had incorrectly assumed that Jacob was also a Jew. *I will make them rue the day they crossed me.*

His recovery was very slow. It seemed that every cell in his body was screaming out in pain. A weaker man would have wished for death to come and relieve him from the pain, but Pockface was no ordinary man. Instead of succumbing to the pain, he relished it. It gave him purpose and fired up his will to live even more. It reminded him every day that he would have his revenge and that it would be oh-so-sweet when it came. Everything he was feeling was nothing compared to the pain he was going to unleash on those Jews. When he was done with them, they would be begging him to end their pitiful lives. But that would require giving them mercy. Mercy was not something he would ever give those two.

It took months before Pockface showed any improvement. His doctor seemed the most surprised that he had improved at all.

Ever-dutiful Pavel was there at his bedside watching over him and making the doctor tend to him far more than the doctor would have wanted. Pockface knew his friend well enough to know that the doctor's life was forfeit if he died. Every day that he lived, the doctor survived as well.

It was many more weeks before Pockface could finally sit up in his bed. He was still as weak as a kitten though, and even small movements taxed his little strength.

Another month passed before he was able to move around, albeit very gingerly. He could now get out of bed, sitting on a chair near his bedside. His slow progress started to get on his nerves. Boredom set in. Pavel, faithful friend that he was, got him some newspapers for him to read to pass the time. Many of them were months old, but that did not matter to Pockface. The newspapers were full of stories of Tsar Alexander II's assassination. As he read, he found out that Jews had been implicated in the plot. And most interesting of all were the stories of the pogroms that had occurred as a form of retaliation for the Jews' role in the murder. *Serves the dirty Jewish pigs right,* he thought.

A plan began to formulate in his mind about how he could exact his revenge. A plan where he could do what he wanted against those Jews and not fear the consequences of his actions.

He was excited to carry out his ingenious plan. He just wished his recovery would hurry up. *Revenge was going to be oh-so-sweet.*

CHAPTER 23

Liesel Hauser woke in her bed and wished that she could remain there forever. But she knew she could not do that. She forced herself to get up. Her body was sore, her heart was broken, and her soul despised the turns her life had taken.

What was she to do?

She had had such a good life. After finishing her schooling, she worked with her parents in their family store. She loved working alongside her parents and serving their many loyal customers. She always gave every customer a big smile when they entered the store. Her father had even commented that business was up after Liesel started working there. This made Liesel burst with pride because her father wasn't one to give praise easily.

She loved her father, although sometimes he could be quite brusque with her. Liesel did not hold it against him though. She respected him and accepted that it was just his manner. He had a hard time showing any emotions to do with love. She knew that he loved her, he just was not demonstrative. Her mother, on the other hand, was the exact opposite of her father.

Where her father was cold and aloof, her mother was warm and loving. Daily she showered Liesel with praise and with love. She doted on Liesel and Liesel thrived under her mother's love. The love she did not receive from her father was made up ten-fold by her mother. Anything that would make Liesel happy, her mother did for her. Liesel was not spoiled. She was just loved. Her world was perfect – until it all started to all fall apart.

It had started out innocently enough. Her mother had made a comment one day about not feeling like herself. Liesel was not alarmed because her mother had made it sound trivial. A few days later, however, Liesel became worried.

Her mother didn't get up like she usually did to prepare breakfast for the family before the store opened. Liesel's father told her that her mother just needed a day of rest. Liesel prepared breakfast for herself and her father. Before she went into the store to help her father, she also took a tray in to her mother. She was fast asleep, so Liesel left the food on her bedside table.

It was very busy in the store that day with a steady stream of customers. Liesel was able to slip away only for a short period to prepare a quick lunch. When she brought some more food to her mother, she noticed that her mother hadn't touched the food she'd left her for breakfast. Her mother was still sleeping. *Had she even woken?* she wondered. As much as she hated to disturb her mother, she gently shook her shoulder. Her mother barely opened her eyes. Liesel told her that she needed to eat to get better. Her mother promised to eat. Liesel wanted to stay and tend to her, but she knew her father wanted her back in the store as soon as possible. She gave her mother a quick kiss on her forehead, then rushed back to the store, taking her father's lunch with her. Liesel did not eat lunch. She was worried about her mother and it was causing her stomach to be upset.

When the last customer was served at the end of the day, Liesel wanted nothing more than to rush to tend to her mother, but she couldn't. She had to help her father count the money from that day's sales. Then the amount had to be recorded in the ledger where they kept their accounts. Stock had to be replaced on the shelves, and finally, the store had to be swept. Liesel wanted to rush through these chores, but she knew that if she did her father would chastise her. So, she did the jobs at her usual pace and with her usual care.

When she got to their living quarters, which were at the back of the store, she made to go to her mother's room to check on her, but her father stopped her. He was hungry and he wanted her to cook his supper. Liesel did as she was told. She made enough so that she could take a plate to her mother once she and her father had eaten.

As Liesel picked at her food, she noticed how quiet it was. Usually her mother was there and conversation between all three of them was present as they ate. Now with just the two of them, all that reigned at the supper table was silence. Liesel asked her father if he liked the food she'd prepared, but all he said was that, considering how good of a cook her mother was, he'd expected Liesel to have made something more edible. Liesel usually accepted her father's brusqueness, but this comment really hurt her feelings. So, she said nothing to him after that.

Liesel had to clean up after the meal was done because that was what was expected of her. She cleaned everything just as her mother did. It was her mother's kitchen after all, and she wanted it to be perfect for when her mother returned. She took her mother's plate to her bedroom. Her father had gone there after eating, so she knocked gently to let them know she was coming in. She was denied entry. Her father opened the door and stepped out of the bedroom before she could enter it. She looked at her father.

"I have Mutti's supper."

"She's asleep. She will not be eating it. Put it away and go to bed, Liesel."

"But she has hardly eaten, Vati. When I checked on her at lunch, she hadn't even touched her breakfast. It isn't much, but she needs to eat Vati."

"I said go to bed Liesel." Her father's tone told her that her protests about her mother not eating were not going to be discussed.

"But Vati"

"Enough of this nonsense. Your mother needs rest. Do as I say. You are not too old that I cannot take the belt to you. Your mother will be better tomorrow."

But she was not. She did not come out of her room the next day. Her father insisted that she just needed to rest a bit more.

Liesel wanted to see her mother, but her father forbade her, saying he could tend to her needs. Liesel knew it was pointless arguing with him. All she could do was prepare the food that her father took to her mother.

Even though Liesel could not see her mother, she could see that most of the food which she prepared for her remained untouched.

Every day that Liesel was separated from her mother was hell. Every day when she awoke, she expected to see her mother emerge from her bedroom healthy and happy. Every day she was disappointed.

She thought about defying her father and sneaking in to see her mother when he was occupied in the store, but the opportunity did not present itself. Lunchtime would have provided a perfect opportunity. Liesel could have slipped in to see her mother while she prepared the midday meal. But in a strange turn of events, her father had closed the store for half an hour at lunchtime. It gave him time to eat what Liesel had prepared, as well as to take the food into her mother. Liesel was exasperated with the actions of her father.

Every day that passed she resented her father more and more. Whenever she would ask to see her mother, he'd flatly refuse her request. If she challenged him on anything to do with her care, he'd fly into a rage and tell her that he knew what was best for his wife. He did not consider her feelings, nor did he mince words about what he would do to her if she disobeyed him.

Her living hell continued for months, until one day things finally changed.

When she saw her father the morning of that fateful day, Liesel sensed that something had changed. Something that caused her to feel like her world, which had been plummeting for quite some time, was about to crash. Her father's eyes were full of pain when he uttered the words – "She wants to see you".

It had been months. Liesel should have run to her mother's bedroom. Finally, she was going to see her mother whom she had missed so much, but something, some invisible force, caused her not to run, but to shuffle slowly towards that closed door, unsure if she should proceed. Her hand was on the door handle. It seemed frozen. She willed her hand to turn the handle, but it would not respond to what her brain was instructing it to do. She might have stood there for all of eternity had her father not come and opened the door, pushing her inside. At that moment, she could have used his support, but he had shut the door behind her after shoving her into the bedroom.

She surveyed her parents' bedroom. All was familiar to her except for one thing: the woman lying in their bed was nothing like her mother.

"Come here Liesel." The specter lying on the bed motioned weakly for her to come to the bed. The voice was that of her mother's, but it was very weak and raspy. Liesel hesitantly went towards the bed. She tripped and was only able to stop herself from falling by clutching the bedpost, a movement which jarred the bed. The specter let out a moan of pain. Liesel looked to see what had tripped her. A tangled mess of blankets were strewn on the floor. Liesel realized that her father had been sleeping on the floor. He did not even sleep in the same bed as her mother while he tended to her. Liesel grew angry with her father for this. However, her anger towards him would have to wait. Taking care of her mother was more important now.

Her mother lifted her hand weakly. Liesel took it into her own hands, cradling it gently. The hand was devoid of flesh, the skin was taunt against the bones. Liesel could make out all the veins and arteries. Liesel swallowed hard as she looked at the rest of the body attached to the hand that she held. So much had changed since she had seen her mother last. Her eyes were sunken in her face and the colour of her skin was alarmingly gray. Her once vibrant and strong mother had become an emaciated person whom she did not recognize. Her beautiful tresses, once so full and luxurious, now hung limp, clinging to her skull. Tears started to flow from Liesel's eyes.

"Mutti?"

"Yes, Liesel dear." Her mother's voice was barely a whisper. "I just wanted to see you one last time before . . . before . . ."

Her mother did not finish her sentence, but Liesel sensed what she was going to say. Liesel did not want to hear the words, so she said what she wished, even though she knew what she wanted was impossible.

"Before you get better."

"Liesel, there is something you need to know," her mother rasped. Liesel could see that talking was draining her mother's energy. Her mother lay still for a few moments. Then she took a deep breath and continued. Liesel could see that her mother was struggling. She wished she could help her, but there was nothing she could do except be patient and wait until her mother was able to say what she needed to say.

"You are my darling girl. You are the best thing I ever did in my life." Again, her mother stopped and rested. "I only wish I could be there for your wedding. To hold my first grandchild. I'm sorry, Liesel."

Her mother's words were breaking her heart.

"No Mutti. Do not give up. You are just weak from not eating. You need to eat more, then you will get your strength back. You will get better, Mutti, if you do that. You will dance at my wedding. You will spoil all your grandchildren. You have to get better Mutti."

"Enough, Liesel. You are tiring out your mother. Leave her alone to rest."

Liesel had not heard her father enter the bedroom. He stood at the door with his arms crossed and a stern expression on his face.

"Vati, Mutti needs me. I need to tend to her. I need to help her. She needs to eat to get stronger."

"I said leave."

"But Vati!"

"Leave before I take my belt to you."

Liesel could see that her father was not going to let her stay, no matter how much she begged or pleaded. She still held her mother's hand. As she reluctantly let it go, her mother whispered, "Be happy Liesel."

She walked past her father and then ran to her room. She slammed the door (she did not care if her father punished her for that), threw herself onto her bed, and sobbed and sobbed uncontrollably for the next hour.

She knew she should go and work in the store, but she just could not bring herself to do it. She could not put a smile on her face for the customers when all she felt was misery. So, she just lay on her bed and stared at the wall, not caring if her father was mad about her absence or not. She expected that he'd be very mad at her and would come looking for her, but he never came. She was grateful that he was at least letting her have some time to herself.

She would have remained in her room had her stomach not grumbled in protest to the fact that she hadn't eaten anything that day. She hadn't expected to see her father, but he sat at the table staring at nothing. She assumed that he was waiting for her to prepare him something to eat. Even though Liesel did not want to talk to her father, she knew that her mother would want her to make sure that her father was fed. For her mother's sake, she addressed her father.

"Would you like some lunch, Vati?"

Her father looked at her as if he had just noticed that she was there.

"She's dead," was all that he said in response to her question.

Mutti dead. It just was not possible. She just needed to eat some more and she would be fine. No, she wasn't dead.

"Vati you are mistaken. I am going to her. She needs me." She headed to her parents' bedroom door, but before she could open it her father grabbed her.

"No Liesel, she's dead. She's been dead for hours."

Hours? Her mother had been dead for hours. Why had she not known? Why hadn't her father summoned her? She let out a long wail, then started to scream. She pummelled her father's chest with her fists.

"Why didn't you let me take care of her? You let her die. Oh Mutti . . . oh Mutti. I COULD HAVE SAVED HER! YOU SELFISHLY KEPT ME FROM HER!" The slap on her face shocked her. Her father's eyes showed not sadness and grief, but fury. She had not meant to call him selfish. It was grief speaking, but she couldn't take the word back. She tried to apologize but her father just slapped her again. He stomped off after hitting her the second time. Liesel burst into tears yet again.

—⁂—

The days that followed her mother's death were a blur for Liesel. Her mind was drowned in grief for most of it, and she could comprehend little of what occurred. She remembered snippets of those days. Some things she remembered with distinct clarity, others were muddled and her mind could make little sense of them.

One distinct memory she had was standing at her mother's graveside. She stared at the pine box containing her beloved mother's earthly body, but could not remember how she had gotten to her mother's graveside, nor anything after the box was lowered into the ground. She remembered a few faces of those who came to pay their respects to her and her father. They seemed to float in front of her as ghostly memories. She had no idea what they said to her. She only remembered their lips moving and that their eyes were sad.

For Liesel, time lost all meaning. The days flowed into one another. She would have liked to wallow in her grief and mourn for her mother, but her father had different ideas.

She was not entirely sure how many days had passed when her father demanded that she get out of bed and attend to her duties. Liesel wanted to yell at him to leave her alone, but she thought of her mother and she knew her mother would be disappointed by this behaviour, so she dragged herself out of bed and went to make breakfast for her and her father.

They did not talk as they ate. Only when her father was finished did he tell her that he expected her to work in the store all day. The store had been closed since her mother's death. Her father informed her that it could no longer remain closed, because they could not afford to lose any more money by not being open. Liesel knew this was not true. They had plenty of money. After all, she helped count it at the end of each day. She could not understand why her father was so adamant that they reopen, but he left before she could ask him.

It was very hard for Liesel to work in the store. Every customer that came in extended their deepest condolences. Liesel tried her best to put on a brave face, but she was soon overwhelmed and burst into tears when yet another customer extended their condolences. She ran into the storeroom and started to cry. Her father followed her there after the customer left the store (she heard the tinkling of the bell that hung over the door as they left). Liesel, seeing her father standing at the storeroom door, thought that he had to come to comfort her. His words, however, were far from comforting.

"Liesel, stop this blubbering. You are upsetting the customers. Now get back to work."

Her father's harsh words made her even more upset and she started to sob. Her father advanced towards her with his hand raised. With a great effort, Liesel stopped crying. Her father very slowly lowered his hand.

"Go wash your face. Then get back to work." As he turned to leave, he shot back – "And put a smile on your face. The customers expect it."

Liesel wanted to cry once more, but held herself together. She knew that her father would strike her like he had after her mother's death. She was only grieving for her mother, just like him. *Why was he acting this way towards her? They should be supporting one another through this difficult time – not drifting apart. Maybe this was all her fault.*

She did as she was told for the rest of the day. She stayed out of her father's way and did as he'd instructed her, pasting a smile on her face. It was hard, but she did not want to upset him anymore.

As they ate their supper in silence, she decided she would make things right between them by apologizing.

"I'm sorry, Vati, if I've upset you. We are both grieving over the loss of Mutti. Together we will get through this. Mutti would have wanted us to be strong together." She had laid out the olive branch. She expected her father to accept it.

"You are not to speak of your mother ever again, Liesel. She is dead and gone. Speaking of her will not bring her back. Get out of my sight and leave me alone."

Liesel was shocked by her father's rebuke. She knew he was hurting just like she was, but his lashing out at her cut her to the quick. She ran from the table to her room. She flung herself on her bed and sobbed and sobbed into her pillow. What hurt the most about her father's words was that she could never speak her mother's name again in his presence. Her resentment for her father was transforming into something she had never thought possible – it was turning into hatred. *What would her mother think, her hating her father?* She had never felt so ashamed of herself.

In the weeks that followed, Liesel never let on to her father that she despised him. She became a master of pretending. Pretending that everything was fine, pretending that she was a dutiful daughter, pretending that she cared about the store and the customers. It was all one big lie and she was living it. To Liesel, it felt like she was living in hell. But she was about to find out what hell truly was.

CHAPTER 24

The embodiment of Liesel's new hell was the Widow Fromm. She flounced into the store barely two weeks after her mother had been laid to rest. Liesel went to wait on her, but the Widow waved her off. The Widow focussed her attention on her father.

The Widow inquired about how he was coping. She spent a lot of time speaking about the fragility of life and telling her father that he shouldn't grieve too long, for he was still a young man. Liesel was disgusted with the Widow's behaviour. *My mother is barely cold in her grave and this woman is making advances towards my father. The gall of the woman.*

The Widow left without purchasing anything. Liesel breathed a sigh of relief when she finally departed.

She was back the next day, fawning over her father yet again. Liesel wished he would tell her to just go away. Liesel wanted to do it, but she knew it was not her place. Besides, if she said anything, she feared that her father might fly off the handle at her once more. Her one and only hope was that Widow Fromm might finally realize that what she was doing was disrespectful towards her mother, and cease her advances. But Widow Fromm, it seemed, did not have a conscience.

She appeared every day in the store, and sometimes she was there more than once a day. Each time she came, she fussed over her father. She ignored Liesel, which was just fine for her. She was an irritant in Liesel's day, but she tolerated her because eventually she would leave. Then Liesel could do her job without having to listen to the constant nattering of the woman. But Liesel's reprieves from the Widow were not to last.

One evening, while she and her father were eating their supper in silence, her father made an announcement that shocked her.

"Widow Fromm is going to work in the store. I expect you to train her properly."

That was all he said. From his tone, Liesel could tell that his announcement was final and he would brook no discussion from her on the matter at all. Liesel felt hurt that he had not even asked her about this beforehand – it was partially her store as well. Or was it? Considering her father's callous disregard for her feelings, maybe she was mistaken. She could only nod at her father. She was fuming inside, and was sure that if she said anything she would regret it. Only when she was alone in her room later did she take out her frustration on her pillow, pummeling it furiously. Then she burst into tears and eventually cried herself to sleep.

Widow Fromm appeared an hour after the store opened in the morning. Liesel wondered why she had not appeared when they'd opened. In passing, she mentioned that they opened at eight o'clock. She could tell that her comment was not well received from the Widow, because the expression that passed across her face was very unpleasant.

As much as she hated the job she had been tasked with, Liesel did as her father instructed and showed Widow Fromm the things she needed to know. Rather, she showed her the things that an employee needed to know. Some things she omitted because they were private, especially the financial side of the business.

Widow Fromm did not do the tasks Liesel assigned her very well. Liesel would show her the correct way and she would still do it incorrectly. By the end of the first day, Liesel was mentally exhausted. No matter how hard Liesel tried to be patient, Widow Fromm would go out of her way to challenge her at every turn. She declared over and over that Liesel's way of doing things was stupid and that a wise woman, such as herself, knew how to do these things the proper way. It was an insult to Liesel, but there was more to it. Her mother had taught her how to do the things she was now expecting Widow Fromm to perform. Her refusal to respect Liesel's instruction, and her belittling of the way things were done, was a direct insult to her mother. Liesel was not sure who she hated more now: Widow Fromm or her father, who had brought her to work in the store in the first place.

The days that followed were no better. Widow Fromm continued to do things her way, and Liesel grew more and more fed up with her attitude and behaviour. It came to a boiling point very quickly.

At closing one day, Widow Fromm complained to Liesel that she hadn't been shown how to record sales in the ledgers, or been allowed to count the money of the day's sales. Liesel had had another trying day of putting up with the Widow, and had snapped at her, saying that an employee did not need to know how to do those things. Widow Fromm only said "We will see about that." Then she stormed out of the store in a huff. Liesel was glad to see her go. She did not take her threat seriously; she was just an employee after all, and not a good one at that. But Liesel had underestimated just how much Widow Fromm had her father's ear.

Liesel had made a stew for their supper that night. Her father had taken just a few bites when he stopped eating and glared at her.

"I told you to show Enid how to do everything in the store. Can you not do anything right? This stew tastes disgusting."

Enid. Now her father was calling her Enid instead of Widow Fromm. It made Liesel sick inside. She had prepared the same stew a few weeks ago and her father had not complained about it. He had even finished two bowls of it. Her father was displeased with her and he was trying to find fault with her. She tried to defend herself.

"I taught her everything that an employee needs to know."

"She is to be shown how to do everything – how to order, write receipts in the ledger, count the day's tallies. EVERYTHING! DO I MAKE MYSELF CLEAR?"

Liesel should have agreed meekly and shut up then, but she did not think that what her father wanted her to do was right.

"I show her how to do things, but she does them incorrectly or poorly. Mutti would never have put up with her working in the store."

Her father's hand slapped her cheek hard. Liesel was shocked by how quickly he had struck her. But she didn't have time to react because her father swept his arm over the table, sending food, plates, and cutlery crashing to the floor. He then stomped out of the kitchen.

Liesel placed her hand on her stinging cheek. Her father had never treated her like this before. He was so volatile now, and it seemed that everything she did set him off. She wanted to cry, but that had solved nothing lately. So she got the broom and started sweeping up the mess scattered on the floor.

What was she going to do?

She had no choice but to do as her father demanded and show Widow Fromm how to do everything. Of course, Widow Fromm did the new tasks poorly and to her own liking. Liesel said nothing. She continued on hoping that things might change if her father saw that she was obeying his orders.

Things did change.

Liesel had to put up with Widow Fromm all day in the store. And soon she had to put up with her after the store closed as well. The Widow decided to invite herself and her brood to their table for suppers. She was cooking in her mother's kitchen, which made Liesel furious. Her father permitted it, though, and Liesel knew it was futile to protest. More and more she felt like an intruder in her own home.

While it was just the two of them, her father had virtually forbidden conversation while they ate. Now with Widow Fromm and her brood, their supper table was lively and noisy. Her father talked with the Widow as well with her snot-nosed brats. Liesel ate in silence. No one talked to her, which was just fine with her. When the youngest threw food at her that stuck in her hair, she just lowered her head more and said nothing, although she felt like strangling the little brat.

Liesel endured those meals as best as she could. She had no choice but to put up with this new arrangement. Her father seemed oblivious to her plight.

Now that the Widow had wormed her way into their personal lives, she started to focus her attention on Liesel. Widow Fromm always called her by the name she detested – Liselotte. She had tried to correct her once, but it had ended badly for her with another rebuke from her father. So, it was just another humiliating thing that she had to endure thanks to Widow Fromm.

Widow Fromm had taken to criticizing her at every opportunity. To Liesel, it seemed that the Widow revelled in making others miserable, especially herself. Her father never interceded on her behalf. Sometimes he joined the Widow in her condemnation of Liesel.

What cut Liesel to the quick was how the Widow delivered her blows. She used a sickeningly sweet voice designed to cover the acerbic comments which were not kind in their gesture or intent. Every word that came out of the woman's mouth just made Liesel feel even more miserable than she already was. The Widow loved to pick at Liesel constantly.

During one supper, the Widow, in her sickly-sweet voice, made the comment that Liesel's dress was a disgrace. She pointed out that it was worn out and that Liesel shouldn't be wearing rags to the dinner table, for she was supposed to be setting an example for the younger children. Liesel would have liked to laugh in the woman's face, retorting that her children were uncouth and behaved abominably at the table. In many ways, her comment was laughable, but Liesel held her tongue. As for the dress, it was worn, yes, but it was not a rag as the Widow was implying. She had chosen it simply because it was blue – her mother's favourite colour.

"Honestly, you are such a heathen, Liselotte. When I am your mother, things are definitely going to change around here!"

Liesel saw red. "You are not, nor will you ever be my mother," she yelled at the bully Fromm.

The room went silent. Liesel knew that her outburst would bring her father's ire, but she didn't care. She did not lower her eyes in shame, but stared defiantly at Widow Fromm.

"Liesel, you will apologize to your moth . . . to Enid at once for your rudeness," her father roared.

Liesel knew that her father would not hesitate to strike her there in front of everyone. She did not fear him striking her, but she also did not want to give that bitch Fromm the satisfaction of winning. Nor did she want to be further humiliated in front of the Widow's brats. So, she apologized.

"I'm sorry." Liesel's lips said the words, although her mind said *I'm really not sorry in the least.* She continued to stare at the Widow, not showing any weakness.

Widow Fromm pasted a smile onto her face and out came her syrupy words.

"That's alright, Liselotte. All is forgiven. I know that you are still grieving and I have been insensitive. I will try harder to be more tolerant of your feelings from now on. Just know that all I want is the best for you."

Her words sounded very nice, but Liesel knew that she did not mean them in the least. She was just saying them for her father's benefit. Later, Liesel would find out that the Widow's words were indeed false.

After the meal, Liesel had to help with the cleanup. She would have liked to retreat to the sanctuary of her room, but she knew her father would not allow that. Widow Fromm washed the dishes and Liesel was forced to endure her company as she dried them.

"Mark my words, you little hussy. I intend to marry your father and I will indeed be your mother." She hissed these words at Liesel, keeping her voice down so that her father and the children could not hear. "I will not put up with your insolence. Things are going to change once we marry."

Liesel had suspected that this was the Widow's intention all along. Now she had confirmed what Liesel had been suspecting . . . and what she feared.

"My mother is barely cold in the grave. My father is still grieving her loss. You should leave both of us alone. You will never be my mother." Liesel was fed up with this woman and everything she had done. She wanted her to take the hint and to just leave her and her father alone.

"If you get in my way you will rue the day that you were born." Widow Fromm was not backing down. Then, in her usual sickly-sweet voice, she spoke loudly enough for everyone to hear. "Of course, I forgive you, Liselotte. I accept your apology once again. I think we have an understanding now, dear, and I'm glad for that." In a whisper she continued. "It is time that you learned your place, Liselotte, and the consequences of crossing me."

Liesel could do nothing but extricate herself from the kitchen as soon as the clean up was complete.

Alone in her room later, she fretted once again over her current situation. She did not take the Widow's threats lightly. *What was she going to do?*

CHAPTER 25

"Jacob, I need you to go into Norka and get me some cheesecloth."

Jacob had just finished his morning milking and was about to join his father to shoe some horses, when his mother ordered him to go get her the cheesecloth. His father nodded that he should do as his mother said.

Jacob hurried towards town. The sooner he completed his mother's errand, the quicker he could be back at the farm helping his father.

The fields he passed on his way into town, he noted, were almost devoid of snow now. Spring was not that far off. Soon, his apprenticeship would be put on hold again as his father returned to his work in the fields. Jacob too would resume his other job: getting the family's wood supply. Jacob was so happy that it was going to be happening very soon because it meant that he would be reunited with his love once more. He wondered how Chaya and the rest of her shtetl had fared over the winter. He worried that those ruffians had made a reappearance. In a few weeks, he could put his fears to rest and see the love of his life well and happy once more.

Jacob decided to get the cheesecloth from Hauser's store. He felt bad that he had not expressed his condolences to Liesel on the passing of her mother. He also wanted to do the same for Herr Hauser.

—⟩⟩⟩—

Liesel was alone in the store when the bell jangled announcing a customer had entered. She looked up from the ledger she was writing in to see Jacob Henkel standing in front of her. She had not seen him for over a year. He looked like the Jacob she knew, but she sensed that something was different about him as well.

"Hello Jacob. How are you? It's been a long time since I last saw you." Liesel was so happy to see Jacob that she did something that she rarely did anymore – she smiled.

"Hello Liesel." Jacob shifted around in front of her as if he was uncomfortable.

"Is there something wrong, Jacob?"

"It's just, I wanted to say . . . I wanted to say I am sorry, Liesel, about your mother . . . and for not coming sooner to extend my condolences to you and your father. My father and I were away when your mother passed and we couldn't attend her funeral either. I am sorry. I am now apprenticing with my father to be a farrier. There is not much time for social calls."

Liesel was touched by Jacob's words, as well as how contrite he was about missing her mother's funeral.

"It's okay Jacob, I understand. And thank you for your condolences." She could see Jacob relax a little.

"So how are you, Liesel?"

Finally, someone who genuinely cared about how she was. Liesel was touched by Jacob's caring, but she couldn't tell him what was really going on with her life. It was just not worth dredging up the things that made her life the misery it was. Telling Jacob how things really were couldn't help her in any way.

"All is as expected in such a time," is what she offered him by way of explanation. She gave him another smile to reassure him that she was fine, when she really wasn't.

Jacob seemed to accept that she was coping and that things were relatively fine with her. Soon, they were reminiscing about old times. It helped Liesel to forget her current woes. Another customer came in and Jacob waited patiently while Liesel served her. Once the woman left, they resumed talking. For the first time in a very long time, Liesel felt something other than despair.

The spell was broken when Jacob told her that he had to get going. He was at the door when he remembered something and returned to the counter.

"I almost forgot why I came in the first place. My mother needs some cheesecloth."

Liesel retrieved it from under the counter.

"I'm afraid that we are almost out of it, but we are expecting more later today if our deliveries are not held up. Otherwise, it will be here sometime tomorrow."

"I will take what you have and come back for more tomorrow."

"Nonsense, I will deliver it. I do not want you to have to make a special trip for it. And if you come at the wrong time, it might not have been delivered yet. This way, you won't have to waste your precious time."

"Are you sure its no trouble Liesel?"

"No trouble at all, Jacob. I will deliver it myself." She wanted to do it so that she could get out of the store and away from the Widow as well. More and more she was doing the deliveries. It helped her to get through the days with 'the witch' (a nickname for Fromm that Liesel had coined, and kept to herself).

"I will tell my mother that more cheesecloth is coming. It was great to see you, Liesel, and I'm glad that you are doing okay." He gave her a big smile before he left the store with the cheesecloth bundle in his hand.

As the bell quieted after his exit, Liesel thought of how nice it was to see Jacob again. She was still smiling when the door jangled again and the Widow flounced in. Her smile quickly faded.

The shipment that included the cheesecloth arrived later that day. By the time Liesel had entered all the new merchandise into the store's ledgers, it was too late to deliver the cheesecloth to Jacob's mother. She decided she would do it first thing the next morning.

—⚬—

When the Widow arrived at the store, Liesel grabbed the cheesecloth and headed out the door. She called out "delivery" as she hurriedly exited. She did not want to speak more to the Widow than she had to.

Once she was away from that woman, she was able to relax a bit. Since threatening Liesel that evening, the Widow had not relented. Her newest torment was hinting that it was time for Liesel to get married. Liesel was not opposed to the idea of marriage, but she cringed at the thought of who the Widow was suggesting. She told Liesel that Elias Frank, the gravedigger, would be a perfect match for her. Frank's first wife had supposedly died in childbirth, but rumours which floated around Norka suggested that she had died quite differently. They said that he had liked to hit his wife, and that one time he went a bit too far. Liesel knew that many rumours were just that – rumours – but in the case of Herr Frank, she believed them. The Widow obviously sensed her fear towards the man because she brought him up quite often. Liesel knew she was purposely doing it to torment her, but she feared that the Widow might manipulate her father and get him to approve the match, just to get rid of Liesel. Liesel did not know what she was going to do.

She arrived at the Henkel's farmhouse and knocked on the door. Jacob's mother answered it. She was cradling a howling baby. Liesel remembered that the last time she had seen Frau Henkel she was pregnant during the Kerbfest. Liesel had heard that she had lost that baby. Liesel realized that she was really out of touch because she didn't know that Frau Henkel had gotten pregnant again and had another baby. Her grief over her mother's death had made her miss much of what had been going on in Norka. Liesel wondered why Jacob never mentioned that there was a new baby in the house.

She smiled at Jacob's mother.

"Good morning, Frau Henkel. Jacob said you needed cheesecloth. I'm sorry that we didn't have enough yesterday." She held up the bundle for Jacob's mother to see. "I hope that this is enough."

Even though Jacob's mother looked a bit harried because of the screaming baby, she greeted Liesel warmly.

"Good morning, Liesel. How are you? I was so sorry to hear about your mother. I am sure it is a very difficult time for you. Thank you for bringing this." She pointed at the cheesecloth. "I would like to talk with you more, but I need to tend to this one." She indicated the howling baby. "He's got colic and there is no one to tend to him – all the others have gone to the market."

The mention of her mother caused a huge lump in Liesel's throat. She fought off the urge to burst into tears, so she focussed on the fussing baby.

"Maybe I can help, Frau Henkel?"

Frau Henkel looked grateful for Liesel's offer. "Are you sure you don't have to get back to the store right away?"

"My father hired a helper. I can help you."

Frau Henkel took the cheesecloth from her and handed her a small saucer.

"Could you scrape a bit of the bird droppings from the fence on this?" Frau Henkel asked.

Liesel knew why Frau Henkel wanted the bird droppings. It was a proven remedy for babies suffering colic. A small amount was added to the baby's milk. Liesel was not sure how it worked, but many a housewife swore of its effectiveness. The colicky baby would stop fussing and fall asleep.

After Liesel had gathered the bird poop, she returned to the house. Frau Henkel was heating up some milk. She took some of the poop and stirred it into the warming milk. When she was happy with the temperature, she tried spoon feeding the milk to the baby. At first, he fussed, refusing to take the milk, but Frau Henkel persisted. Eventually she got him to take several spoons. Liesel noticed the baby was getting drowsy. Frau Henkel burped him before he dropped off totally. Then she put him down in a crib that was near the stove.

"Poor little mite. I hope that he gets over this soon. The rest of my children never suffered as much as this one."

"What is his name?"

"Hans."

"Hans Henkel, it has a nice ring to it. He looks a bit like Jacob."

"You think so? I think he looks more like Manfred, but I'm sure that once he is older, he will look like Hans." She smiled at her thought.

Liesel was not sure if she should bring it up, but she felt she should convey her condolences to Frau Henkel.

"I'm sorry, Frau Henkel, about the baby you lost. I would have come sooner and conveyed my condolences, but it was a bad time because . . . because . . ." She could not finish her sentence. The tears she'd been trying to contain just started flowing.

Frau Henkel came and embraced her, and let her cry herself out. Frau Henkel used soothing words like "there, there" as she cried.

When Liesel was drained of her tears, she felt embarrassed that she had let her emotions get the better of her. She made to leave, but Frau Henkel stopped her, saying she should stay and have a cup of tea. Liesel wanted to go, but what was she going back to? Here in the Henkel farmhouse, she felt that someone cared about her welfare. Jacob's mother, just like her son, had extended a kindness to Liesel that touched her heart. Jacob's mother made tea and they talked of things that were more lighthearted. Liesel appreciated the support she got from Jacob's mother. If things were different, she might have completely unburdened herself to this caring woman, telling her all about the tragedy of her life. But she could not bring herself to do it, for she felt that telling Jacob's mother would change nothing about her circumstances.

Liesel felt that she had taken up enough of Frau Henkel's precious time. The baby was still asleep and Liesel knew that she would want to get things done without tending to a fussing baby. Jacob's mother confirmed that she was just about to make a batch of cheese. Liesel offered to help her, but she insisted that Liesel probably had other things to tend to. Liesel told Frau Henkel that her mother had promised to teach her how to make cheese, but never had. Frau Henkel changed her mind and told Liesel that she would be honoured to show her how to make cheese.

Liesel enjoyed learning all about how to make cheese. Frau Henkel complimented her often, as she tried her best to do it well. The praise did wonders for Liesel. No one had praised her since . . . since her mother. In Frau Henkel's kitchen, Liesel started to feel like her old self.

When they were done, Frau Henkel gave her a wheel of her smoked cheese to thank her for her assistance. Liesel gratefully accepted her gift – it was the most sought-after cheese in Norka. Liesel also accepted one other thing from Frau Henkel: an invitation to join her and her family for a meal after Sunday's church service. It was going to be Easter, and Liesel was grateful that this invitation meant she would not have to spend it with her father and Widow Fromm and her brood.

When she left, she hugged Frau Henkel. Only when she was halfway back to Norka did she realize that she'd forgotten to get payment for the cheesecloth. She wasn't worried though. She knew that the Henkels always settled their accounts.

—⚬⚬⚬—

When she walked into the store, both her father and the Widow were behind the counter.

"Where have you been?" Her father did not seem pleased.

"I was making a delivery."

"Where is the money?" The Widow didn't care about the time she was away. She just wanted the money.

"I forgot to collect it. I will put it on their account." Liesel went to retrieve the accounts ledger.

"What do you have there?"

Liesel forgot that she was still carrying the smoked cheese Jacob's mother had given her. She would have liked to tell the old biddy that what she had was none of her business, but her father was standing there, so she had no choice but to answer 'the witch'.

"It is a wheel of smoked cheese. The customer gave it to me."

"Let me see it."

Liesel handed the cheese to the Widow. She sniffed it and made a face. Then she retrieved a knife and cut off a piece which she shoved into her mouth.

"Disgusting," she announced. "It's too salty and tastes like a campfire." She grabbed the wheel of cheese and tossed it into the rubbish bin.

Liesel could not believe the gall of the woman, making it sound like she was a cheese expert. She was nothing but a fraud. Frau Henkel's cheese was the best in Norka. Liesel had been looking forward to enjoying it, but now it was in the rubbish. *How dare that witch. Throwing away something that clearly wasn't hers to throw away.* Liesel seethed inside. She thought she could not hate the Widow any more than she already did, but she was wrong. Before she said or did something that would provoke her father's ire, she skulked off to the storeroom. It took her a long time before she was able to calm down. Every fiber of her being wanted to strangle the Widow.

―⚮―

As Liesel suffered through the rest of the week, the one thing that kept her going when she just wanted to scream was the invitation to the Henkel's for the Easter meal. She did not tell her father nor the Widow of the invitation. She should have told her father for propriety's sake, but she feared he would tell the Widow. And if the Widow knew, Liesel felt that she would meddle in some way. So, she remained firm in her stance that neither should know.

Keeping it a secret was easier when Liesel found out that the Widow had plans for Easter as well; plans that included her children and Liesel's father, but not Liesel. The Widow probably did this on purpose to slight Liesel. But Liesel was not slighted in the least. She was grateful that the Widow's plan had backfired, for she had inadvertently done Liesel a favour.

After attending the Easter church service, Liesel accompanied the Henkel family back to their farmhouse. Jacob's mother had not attended the church service. She had stayed at home to tend to the baby and to cook the Easter meal. When everyone arrived, she was still in the midst of cooking. Her daughters-in-law jumped in and started helping her. Liesel did too, even though Jacob's mother insisted that she was a guest and did not need to help. But Liesel insisted that she wanted to help. So, Jacob's mother finally relented.

The meal was the traditional Easter Sunday meal of roast chicken. The meal started with a noodle soup. Liesel marvelled at how tender the noodles were and how flavourful the broth was. Liesel asked Jacob's mother for the recipe. Jacob's mother told her it was a dash of this and a dash of that. But Liesel was not disappointed because Jacob's mother said that if she wanted the recipe, she'd gladly show her how to make the soup one day.

The entire meal was wonderful, and not just because of the food. Liesel was squeezed between Jacob and his sister Heidi. Both kept her entertained throughout the meal. In fact, the entire family went out of their way to make her feel welcome and like a part of the family. Liesel had never experienced such a lively repast. When her mother was alive, their meals were pleasant, if not a bit subdued. Now she saw what it was like for a large family to gather and eat. Eating with the Widow and her brats and her father was something she detested, especially due to the dastardly table manners of the Widow's children. The fact that the Widow never admonished or disciplined them, even when they were being disgusting at the table, irritated Liesel to no end. But if Liesel slouched at the table, she would instantly criticize her. Her father was no better, finding fault with her and ignoring the behaviour of the snot-nosed brats.

Eating with the Henkels had given Liesel something that she was missing in her life: a warm, loving environment. With all the bodies, it tended to be loud in the kitchen, but it was a good kind of loud. Everyone was respectful and the loudness came from the happiness everyone felt for the good meal and the gathering of loved ones. Liesel felt it, and was so thankful that they had included her.

Many topics of conversation passed as the meal progressed. Heidi asked Liesel if she was going to the Spring Dance. Liesel had been so removed from everything that she had forgotten about the dance that occurred every spring, two weeks after Easter. She explained to Heidi that she had forgotten and that she shouldn't go because she was still in mourning. Heidi had ignored her statement that she was in mourning, and said that Jacob could take her. Liesel was just going to tell Heidi that it was a bad idea when Jacob's mother entered their conversation, saying that Heidi's suggestion was a wonderful idea. She told Liesel that the dance would do her good and that her mother would want her to be happy. Mirroring her mother's last words, Liesel suddenly thought that maybe she should go to the dance; that she should make an effort to be happy.

She looked at Jacob. "Would you want to go with me?"

Jacob had been caught a bit off guard by his sister's suggestion. Liesel had had a rough time of things of late. She looked like she could use some fun. He remembered how she'd danced with him the last time at the Kerbfest, even though she knew he was pining for Lilith. The least he could do was return the favour and take Liesel to the dance to help her have some fun during her time of grief.

"Yes, Liesel, I would like to go with you, if you will do me the honour of accompanying me?"

Liesel was so touched. Jacob was such a gentleman.

"It would be my pleasure, Jacob."

"Can I go too Mutti?" Heidi piped up.

"I can't see why not," Jacob's mother answered. "Just mind your brother and behave yourself."

"What are you going to wear?" Heidi asked Liesel, excitement spilling into her words.

For the next while, she and Heidi discussed what they were going to wear, but Liesel was also thinking of how it would feel to be in Jacob's arms once again, dancing to the music. For the first time in a long time, Liesel was looking forward to something.

After the meal, Liesel helped to clean up. When it was time for her to go, Jacob's mother insisted that Jacob escort her back into Norka. Heidi also tagged along. All the way into town, she gushed about how lucky Liesel was to have a store. Heidi assumed that Liesel could help herself to whatever she wanted, like the sweets on the counter. She didn't want to curb Heidi's enthusiasm, so she just smiled, keeping the truth hidden in her mind. Sometimes Jacob would give her a sympathetic look. He knew that Heidi was a bit much, but Liesel didn't really mind. She had never had a sister. Heidi made her feel like one of the family. Liesel would've loved to have a sister like Heidi. Jacob was so lucky.

As they neared the store, Liesel started to panic. *What if her father saw her with Jacob and his sister? Or worse yet – what if Widow Fromm saw them?*

"I just remembered – I promised to stop at Elsie's and wish her a Happy Easter," she lied. "I better do that before I go home." She stopped on the boardwalk. "Thank you, Jacob and Heidi, for seeing me home."

"What time should I call on you to bring you to the dance?" Jacob asked.

"What time should WE call on you?" Heidi corrected her brother.

"I'm not sure when I will be able to leave the store." Another convenient lie. "Maybe I can just meet you both there."

"Are you sure?"

"Yes, Jacob, it's fine. I do not want you having to wait around for me. It is best if I just meet you there."

"Alright Liesel, but I – I mean WE – will escort you home at the end of the evening."

Liesel did not want them escorting her home for the same reasons she was avoiding it now, but she would have to think of some excuse then. She hated lying, especially to Jacob, but she had to. There was no other choice.

"Until the dance." She waved at the pair as she crossed the street, supposedly heading to Elsie's house. She hid behind a building and watched them until they were out of sight. Then she recrossed the street and headed for the store. She let herself in the back entrance. The house was empty – she had lied for nothing. But it was necessary. She could not have that busybody Fromm knowing her business. For if she even caught a whiff of the fact that Liesel had found a sliver of happiness, she'd do everything in her power to destroy it. Of that Liesel was certain.

CHAPTER 26

Jacob's wait was finally over. He was returning to the birch forest once more – to his job of gathering his family's wood supply, but more importantly, to a reunion with his love.

Jacob's fears that something might have happened to Chaya were put to rest when she appeared a few days after he returned to the forest. She looked breathtaking.

Both hardly spoke to the other. They fell into each other's arms and kissed passionately, the longs months of separation fuelling their ardour. Both could feel themselves being pulled to where they had not gone before. They simultaneously pulled apart before things went too far, but it was hard for both.

Jacob stared at Chaya. His heart seemed to melt even more now that he was finally back with his beloved. He wished that time could stand still and that they could live in this moment forever.

Chaya's heart was singing once more as she gazed into her beloved's eyes. She wished that they could be together forever. Their love just felt so right.

But nothing had changed. Their circumstances remained the same. Their separation had deepened their longing for one another, but that did nothing to change the cold hard truth that they could never be together.

However, rather than ruining their joyous reunion, each chose not to speak of the hopelessness of their situation. Rather, it was better to cherish being together, alone and sheltered from the rest of the world in their little birch forest.

After their passion had been requited, but before they crossed any lines, they talked of all that had happened in their lives since they last saw the other. As always, they picked mushrooms while they talked, and then Chaya helped Jacob stack the wood he'd recently cut. All too soon for both, they had to part.

However, parting was not so bad this time because they would now be seeing each other more often. Both of their hearts sang at this prospect.

Both carried on with their every day lives as best as they could. Their biggest struggle was keeping the secret. They both wanted to shout from the rooftops how much they were in love with the other person. But they could not share their happiness with anyone, and that made it very hard for both of them. The secret had to be kept, no matter their feelings.

—◊—

The evening of the Spring Dance arrived. Jacob was happy to be escorting Liesel because he felt so sorry for her. She had once been so happy, but with the death of her mother, she now seemed perpetually sad. He hoped that this evening might help her with her melancholy.

In his heart, he secretly wished that he was taking Chaya to the dance instead. *Did Jews go to dances?* He would have to ask Chaya about that the next time they met in the forest. *Did she even know how to dance?* He decided it would not really matter – if she hadn't danced before, he'd teach her. He felt certain that Chaya would be a perfect dance partner, whether she could dance or not. Just the thought of holding her in his arms made him excited. He stored that memory to enjoy by himself later.

When he arrived with Heidi, Liesel was already waiting by the barn where the dance was being held. He thought about the fact that he could have escorted her from the store after all. She was wearing a pale-blue dress that looked nice on her.

Liesel had snuck out of her bedroom window, because she did not want her father, nor the Widow, to know that she was attending this dance. She had chosen the blue dress in honour of her mother, and she was glad because Jacob complimented her on its colour.

Jacob offered his arm. Liesel hooked hers through his. His sister Heidi did the same on his other side, and then the three of them strolled into the barn.

For Liesel, what followed was a magical night. For the entire evening, Jacob never left her side. He was so attentive. He danced only with her – except for a few dances when he danced with his sister. Liesel used those dances to have a small rest and to partake in some of the refreshments.

The best part was dancing with Jacob. It was just like dancing with him at the Kerbfest, but better. He smiled at her all the time, and in his arms, she felt something that she thought she'd lost forever – happiness. For the hours that they danced, Liesel was able to forget about her problems with the Widow, and most importantly, about how much she missed her mother.

Much too soon for Liesel, the band announced that it was playing its last song. The melody they played was slow and felt mournful. It was as though the band was sad to see the night end and they were playing a sad song to relay their lament. Dancers danced closer as they bid the night a final adieu. Liesel noted that Jacob was also holding her very closely, a sensation she savoured. She kept swaying to the music even after the last chord played, so enthralled with how Jacob was holding her. He shook her shoulder gently which brought her out of her reverie.

As people made their way out of the barn, Jacob guided Liesel to the door. Outside, they waited for Heidi, whom they'd seen very little of that evening – she'd had a full dance card. Once Heidi appeared, Liesel tried to say her goodnights to Jacob and Heidi, but they insisted on escorting her home, no matter how much that she protested that she could make her way home by herself.

"My mother would skin me alive if she found out we didn't escort you home at this late hour," Jacob had stated.

In any other circumstance, Liesel would have been touched by Jacob's chivalrous gesture, but her worry about her father or the Widow seeing them caused her to be on edge. The three of them made their way through the darkened streets of Norka with Heidi gushing about all of the fun she'd had. Both of them had to shush her because they didn't want her boisterous voice to be responsible for waking up any of the slumbering residents of Norka.

They turned into Liesel's street. She could see the dark outline of the store. Everything was dark inside, and for that she was grateful. Heidi waited in front of the store while Jacob escorted Liesel to the back entrance.

"Thank you, Jacob. I had a wonderful time," she whispered.

"It was my pleasure, Liesel. You are a beautiful dancer and I had a wonderful time as well. Good night then." He gently grabbed her hand and kissed the back of it. "Maybe we can do it again sometime." He turned and walked back the way that they had come, leaving a breathless Liesel on the rear doorstep of the store.

She waited until Jacob was out of sight before she left the doorway and circled to her bedroom window. Only when she was back in her bedroom did she let out a loud sigh. Jacob's kiss had left butterflies in her stomach. She lay down on her bed and stared up at the ceiling. This time, however, she was not staring in despair, rather she was reliving every wonderful moment of the evening. She could still feel Jacob's lips from when they'd brushed across her hand.

When she finally fell asleep, it was with a smile on her face. That night she dreamed of her mother, who smiled at her joyously in her dream. Before her mother faded away in her dream, she said "be happy my girl".

—〰—

Jacob did not know what had come over him. He knew he was dancing with Liesel, but throughout the night he kept thinking he was dancing with Chaya. It was not too hard for his mind to make the substitution. Both Chaya and Liesel were similar in size and stature. They even shared the same hair colour, although Chaya's was a bit of a darker shade. Their faces were both oval shaped, with the one big difference being their eyes: Chaya's were green, Liesel's were blue.

All night long, Jacob had smiled at Liesel when he'd been thinking of Chaya instead. Luckily, Liesel could not read his mind or know that his smile was for another. She had returned his smiles.

At the end of the evening, Liesel told him that she had had a wonderful time. Jacob was glad that he had been able to help her to have some fun when her life was full of sadness. To thank Liesel for the evening, he had kissed Liesel's hand. He thought of the gesture as being nothing more than an act of chivalry – nothing more.

But this gesture was not received as he had intended.

CHAPTER 27

Months! It had been months and months of sitting in this bloody hospital, and still he was not feeling like his old self yet. His impatience was growing every day. The waiting was becoming unbearable. Waiting for his body to heal was hard, but the waiting for his revenge was harder still.

Pockface had everything planned about how he was going to make those Jews pay. At one time he had even considered the notion of sending Pavel to exact his revenge, but letting someone else do the dastardly deed would defeat the purpose of having to endure so much. Pavel was like a brother to him, but he had not endured the pain and humiliation he had. *No, the revenge would be his to mete out.*

In May, two things changed: the plan, and his recovery.

He was reading a newspaper Pavel had brought him when he saw something that made him smile (which, with his ruined face, looked more like a ghoulish grimace). There it was – the thing that gave him a new idea of how to carry out his revenge.

Tsar Alexander III had just passed new laws concerning Jews. As Pockface read them, he knew they would be the catalyst he needed to convince others to embark on his revenge with him.

He was well enough to leave the hospital, but he still was not strong enough to make the trip back to Rysincek. He figured that in a month's time he would be strong enough to travel. He was not just going to idle around Saratov, though. He and Pavel had many arrangements to make. Arrangements that he felt would make his plan a success.

If those Jews knew what was coming, they would pack up and flee. But they did not know what was about to descend upon them. Pockface grinned his evil grin once more.

—⁂—

While Pockface was musing to himself, Liesel, on the other hand, was walking on air. Even the barbs that the Widow threw at her bounced off her. She was just so . . . just so . . . happy! Happy that someone loved her. Jacob occupied her mind, and her heart. She was finally going to be happy.

The Widow must have sensed something was different with her, because Liesel saw her studying her when she thought Liesel was unaware. Liesel tried to act normal when she was around the Widow, although it was hard to contain her excitement at times. The Widow didn't say anything, which Liesel didn't mind at all. But if she had looked more closely at the Widow, she'd have seen that her face had a menacing expression painted on it.

From their night of dancing, Liesel knew that Jacob felt the same way about her as she did about him. She saw him as her saviour. If they married, he would take her away from all of the pain, sorrow and sadness. They would have a family, and she vowed that she'd honour her mother by naming their first-born girl after her. She was sure Jacob would agree to this, because he loved her.

The problem with all her planning and romantic notions was that nothing could start happening until she and Jacob became betrothed. Couples just could not profess their love and get married – that was not the way that it was done. Liesel knew that someone would have to petition the Henkels on her behalf. Liesel was grateful that these negotiations were usually done by the bride's godparents, for if it had been her father negotiating on her behalf, she wasn't sure if he'd agree to do so.

Liesel's godparents were Greta and Gunther Seebaldt. Tante Greta and her mother had been friends from their school days. When she was alive, her mother used to take her to visit her tante and onkel once a month. They lived on a small farm south of Norka. Liesel loved going there because her godparents had no children of their own, and they doted on her when she came to visit. Liesel spent many happy days on their farm. Unfortunately, her Tante Greta had died two years ago. After that, she and her mother stopped visiting the farm. She missed her Onkel Gunther. When she had asked her mother why they didn't visit anymore, her mother had replied that Onkel Gunther had taken Tante Greta's death really hard, and that he wasn't right in the head anymore. Liesel would have liked to ask more questions to find out why Onkel Gunther was not right in the head, but her mother's expression told her the subject was closed. Whether her onkel was right in the head or not did not matter to Liesel. She needed his help, and she felt sure that her onkel would oblige.

Liesel tried to think of a way she could go and see Onkel Gunther without her father or the Widow finding out. A fortuitous thing happened when the person she was trying to keep in the dark, the Widow, was the one who made Liesel's trip to her onkel's farm possible.

"Your father has a delivery he wants you to make," the Widow announced to her, just as she was coming out of the stockroom after retrieving an item for a customer. "You are to go right now. It is for Herr Seebaldt. I will finish up here." She waved Liesel away from the customer she was serving.

Liesel gathered up her onkel's order from the counter where the Widow had placed it. Luckily it was not too heavy. It was a long walk to her onkel's farm. Her father usually delivered his orders on horseback. Liesel suspected that the Widow, not her father, had decided to send her on foot, just to be spiteful. As she headed out the door, she smiled to herself. The old witch was doing her a favour.

"Don't doddle, Liselotte. You still have to stock the shelves," the old witch shot at her as she left the store.

"You can stock the shelves yourself, you lazy bitch," Liesel muttered under her breath.

It was a beautiful spring day. Liesel took her time as she walked to the farm. She loved this time of year.

She walked by a small orchard. All the trees were in full bloom. Their delicate petals were alive as bees went from one to another, gathering their sweet nectar. Liesel could hear the low buzzing of the bees as they gorged themselves on the blossoms. Liesel sniffed the air. There was a faint trace of the scent of the blossoms, but the more distinct smells of lilac and honeysuckle permeated the air. Liesel loved the smell of spring.

She crossed the bridge over the Ella Born River and headed out onto the steppes south of Norka. She passed one of the windmills that was located in Norka. Wind blew constantly across the steppes, turning their sails. Today, however, there was only a slight breeze, so the sails of the windmill were barely moving. Liesel didn't mind that the wind wasn't blowing like it usually did. The slight breeze made the walk that much more enjoyable.

As she walked, she listened to the songbirds as they too announced what a beautiful day it was. She passed a herd of cows grazing contently in a small pasture. They too seemed to be enjoying the sunshine and the placid day.

She saw farmers working in their fields. She waved at them – they returned her wave.

She heard a horse and wagon approaching her from behind. The clip-clop of the hooves of the horses, and the jangling of the harnesses, gave Liesel ample time to get to the side of the road so that it could pass her. The driver pulled the wagon alongside her and stopped. It was one of their customers. He offered to give Liesel a ride. She declined. It was just too beautiful a day. She wanted to relish it for as long as she could. The driver accepted her refusal and carried on.

The spring day had done wonders to improve Liesel's thoughts about her life. Once she talked to Onkel Gunther, she knew that everything would be all right.

The familiar farmhouse came into view. The farmyard of her tante and onkel looked more run down then the last time she had been there. A few scrawny chickens scratched around in the dirt of the yard. She expected a welcome from their dog Fritzie, but he did not come running when she entered the yard.

She went up to the farmhouse door and knocked. No one answered. She had not thought about the fact that her onkel might not be home. He was probably out working his fields like the other farmers she had seen. She really needed to talk to him, but she had no idea where his fields were. Every census year, the fields were redistributed in Norka. The last census had taken place two years ago. Liesel doubted that her onkel would have been allotted the same plot of land he had farmed previously. She banged her hand on the door in frustration.

She heard movement within the house – maybe Onkel Gunther was home. She knocked again. This time she called out Onkel Gunther's name as she hit the door more forcefully.

The door swung open and there stood her onkel. Or rather, there stood her onkel like she had never seen him before. His hair was long and disheveled. It looked like it had not been washed or combed for weeks. While her tante was alive, her onkel had always been clean shaven. Now he sported a heavy beard that was matted and grayer than his natural hair colour of black. The clothes he wore looked like they had not been washed in quite some time. Even though Liesel was in the open air she could smell his rank odour. It made her want to gag.

Onkel Gunther looked at her with rheumy eyes. It seemed to take him awhile before he figured out who she was.

"Ah, Liesel," he slurred. "Come to finally visit your dear sweet onkel. Come in."

Liesel did not want to go into the house. When her onkel spoke, she was assaulted with another repugnant smell. His breath reeked of alcohol. Liesel decided that, in his current state, her onkel could not negotiate with the Henkels on her behalf. She would have to come back another time when her onkel was sober.

"I came to deliver your order. I'm sorry that I cannot stay and visit, Onkel, but I am needed at the store." She thrust the package at him, hoping he did not detect that she was lying about needing to return to the store. He did not take the package from her.

"Nonsense. I deserve a visit. To hell with the store." He turned and retreated inside the house.

Liesel wanted to leave the package on the doorstep and go. But she knew that if she did, word would get back to her father that she had been rude to her onkel. She needed his help so she could not have him being upset with her. Liesel reluctantly entered the house, hoping that the visit would be a short one.

The house, like her onkel, had an unpleasant odour. The air smelled stale. The house needed a good airing out. Her onkel's body odour was present as well as the smell of something rotting. She saw that her onkel had sat himself on a chair in the sitting room. She approached him.

"Where do you want this?" She raised the package she was holding.

"Kitchen." He waved one hand towards it. The other hand, Liesel noted, was holding a bottle of liquor.

Liesel went into the kitchen where she found the source of the rotting smell. Half-eaten food lay rotting on the kitchen table. Some was even on the floor. Liesel surveyed the kitchen which had been the pride and joy of her Tante Greta. She had kept it spotlessly clean and tidy. Her tante's kitchen was no longer either of these things. Liesel wondered how her onkel could live like this. It was such an affront to his late wife, to desecrate her domain in this disgusting fashion. Liesel remembered her mother saying that her onkel had gone strange. Strange was an understatement. Living like a pig was more accurate. Liesel put the package on the table and left the kitchen.

She returned to the sitting room. Her onkel watching her as she entered.

"Sit down, Liesel," her onkel commanded.

Liesel looked for a place to sit. Every piece of furniture had a thick layer of dust on it. She perched on a chair, barely letting its dirty surface touch her dress.

"I cannot stay long," she reminded her onkel. She should have exchanged pleasantries with him, asking how he was, but Liesel could see exactly how he was – and he was not well at all. She was having a hard time believing this was the same Onkel Gunther who had doted on her for all those years. She could tell that he was lonely, and for that she felt bad. Maybe if she told him her wonderful news, he might become the onkel she knew and loved once more.

"Onkel, I have news. In fact, I have wonderful news. News that will make you happy, I'm sure."

"What news?" he grunted.

"I have fallen in love, Onkel. I want to marry, and I need you to negotiate with his family for my betrothal." She smiled at her onkel. "I know that you want me to be happy."

Her onkel didn't say anything. He just stared at her with his rheumy eyes. It started to make her uncomfortable.

"Love!" he roared. "Happy!" he bellowed. "What do you know of love and happiness? They do nothing for anyone. What has love given anyone except for heartache and unhappiness and loneliness?"

"Onkel, please . . ."

"Please, what?"

"Please, Onkel, can you talk to his family?"

"Who is he?"

Liesel could not mistake the distain in her onkel's question.

"Jacob . . . Jacob Henkel."

"Why, he's just a boy. Still wet behind the ears," her onkel scoffed.

"He is a man." Liesel felt the need to defend Jacob. "And he is in love with me."

"Love! Bah! What does a boy know of love?"

"He isn't a boy, Onkel. And he knows of love. As do I. I just need you to speak with his family . . . and . . . not tell my vati."

Her onkel didn't respond. All he did was stare at her once more. His staring continued to make her uncomfortable.

"I will do as you ask, Liesel. All that I ask in return is that you pay me for my efforts."

"I don't have any money, Onkel, in which to pay you."

"There are other ways that you can pay."

The way that her onkel said that last thing, along with the way he was staring at her, sent a shiver down her spine.

"I don't understand, Onkel."

"The price is a fair one, considering what you are asking me to do."

"All I'm asking is for you to speak to his parents to negotiate my betrothal."

"And you want me to do this secretly, without telling your father. You want me to keep your secret. Secrets come at a price."

She felt like she did not have a choice. "I will pay your price – as long as you negotiate and keep my secret."

"Now that wasn't too hard, was it?" he crowed. "The price is very reasonable indeed. All I ask is that you give your poor old onkel a kiss. That is all. Very reasonable indeed."

It was reasonable when she was younger, when she willingly gave him a kiss on the cheek while greeting and farewelling him with her mother. He also had kissed her on those exchanges – it was all fine back then. But now . . . now he was not the same man he'd once been. He was, as her mother had said, strange. She wanted to bolt to the door and leave this repugnant man behind, but she willed herself to stay. She had only him to help her.

"Alright," she conceded. *I can give him a quick peck on the cheek. It will be over in a split second.* She urged her feet forward. She breathed through her mouth, but she could still smell the stench emanating from him. She moved quickly towards his cheek to pay with her kiss.

Her lips never contacted her onkel's cheek. Her grabbed her wrists, and before she could react, his mouth was all over hers. She tried to cry out but his mouth covered her own. She tried to break away from him but his strong grip kept her firmly in his grasp. She tried to twist her head away from him but he pressed even harder on her lips. Then she felt her lips being forced apart by his tongue. She gagged as his foul breath entered her mouth. Her gagging turned to retching. Only then did he loosen his hold on her as she heaved over and over. Only when the heaving stopped did she do what she had not been able to do before – she screamed.

His fist slammed into her cheek, sending her sprawling across the floor. She was lying there dazed when he grabbed her by the hair and pulled her up. She screamed again. This time, her scream was not of terror, but of pain. It felt like he was tearing her hair out by its roots.

"Shut up. No one can hear you out here. It is time to pay your price. You will see what a real man knows of love." With that he yanked on her hair once more, dragging her across the room.

Liesel was in agony, but she was still able to desperately grab the doorframe of the bedroom he was dragging her into.

"Please Onkel. Please no, Onkel," she begged.

He yanked her so hard that she lost her grip on the doorframe. He dragged her to the bed and tossed her on it. Liesel was grateful that he finally let go of her hair, although her scalp was still on fire. Liesel tried to scramble off the bed, but her onkel pinned her down so that she lay helpless beneath him.

"Please Onkel. Please no more. I am sorry. Please let me go."

"Let you go," he laughed. "I haven't even showed you what love is yet. You will love it, Liesel."

Liesel tried to squirm away from the vile creature that had her trapped, but it was useless. His pelvis was pressed against her leg and she could feel him getting aroused. He shifted his weight to free one of his hands. Liesel was too slow to take advantage of this moment. By the time she realized it, the opportunity had passed. He pinned both of her arms above her head, held fast by his one hand. His free hand was the one that she feared more. It was groping near her private area. It pushed up her dress and ripped off her underwear. She felt her onkel's hand move away from her. He was fumbling with his pants. She hoped that he would never get them open. But then there was no hope left. He violated her.

It was painful. Liesel wished that she were dead. When he finished, he rolled off her – and that was when she escaped. She ran from the bedroom and out through the farmhouse door. She left the door wide open. She ran as if the devil himself were chasing her. Her onkel did not pursue her, but he yelled that she now knew what it was like to be with a real man, and that she'd be back for more. She ran even faster. Her sides started to ache, but she kept on running. Then her legs gave out and she fell into a heap at the side of the road. She lay there gasping, not being able to draw enough air into her lungs. She was eventually able to breathe a bit easier. She drew in a huge lungful of air and screamed at the top of her lungs. The scream was more animal than human. A flock of songbirds frightened by her scream took flight. She screamed until her throat was on fire. Then she broke down and cried tears of humiliation. She wept and wept and wept.

She didn't know how long she lay at the side of the road, but at some point, she dragged herself to her feet and started to walk back to Norka. She met no one on the road which she was grateful for; she burned with humiliation and did not want anyone to see her shame. The day she had marvelled at for all its beauty had now turned so ugly. She passed by the things that had delighted her a few hours earlier, not seeing, hearing, or smelling them at all. She plodded on, her head down, her shoulders slumped, and her soul shattered.

When she arrived at Norka, she slunk through the less travelled streets, making her way home as quickly as possible. She did not go into the store, but snuck in the back door of her house. She went to her bedroom and curled herself into a ball on her bed. She cried until she fell into an exhausted sleep.

She did not know how long she had been sleeping, because the next thing she knew her father was yelling at her.

"What the hell are you doing?" he yelled at her from the doorway of her bedroom.

"I'm sick, Vati. Leave me alone."

"Get your ass out of bed. I do not care. Enid tells me you have been gone for hours. Where have you been?"

You know exactly where I've been. You sent me there. Liesel wanted to scream this at the man who was supposed to protect her, but who had instead sent her to be violated by . . . She could not bear to think his name, much less to say it to her father.

"I'm sick . . . leave me alone."

"I said get out of bed NOW! Enid says you were fine a while ago. She says you have not stocked the shelves like you were supposed to. Now get up and get to work, or I swear, Liesel, I will take the horsewhip to you."

Liesel knew her father would do just as he threatened. She could not stand another humiliation on this darkest of days. She got up, passed her father while giving him a look of pure hatred, and stomped into the store. She noted a look of triumph on the bitch Fromm's smug face. Liesel so wanted to wipe that smug look off it forever, but she knew it was fruitless. She stocked the shelves, not saying anything to anyone. If a customer greeted her, she ignored them and walked away. Many sensed her mood and steered clear of her, which was just fine with her.

She tried to get out of having supper, but her father was again insistent that she be present. Neither her father nor the

Widow asked her about the huge bruise on her cheek. They obviously did not care enough about her to concern themselves. She expected this from the Widow, but her father's behaviour wounded her deeply.

After the meal, Liesel was alone in her room at last, and she could finally vent her anger and frustration by taking it out on her pillow. Her father did not love her. Her onkel had abused her love. Only one tiny tendril of love remained: the love she had for Jacob.

She vowed that she would do anything necessary to protect the only love she had left.

However, she was worried about the biggest thing that could destroy their love – she was now a soiled woman. Jacob must never find out what had happened to her at her onkel's farmhouse. If he found out the truth, he might never forgive her, even though it wasn't her fault. He must never find out. She would take this secret to her grave.

Jacob was her knight in shining armour. He was the solution to all her woes. He was her love.

—ᵐ—

The only bright spot amongst the hellish days that now made up her life, was the one day that she saw him – Sundays. The Henkels had taken it upon themselves to invite Liesel to their Sunday afternoon lunches. After attending the church service, she accompanied the family back to their farm. Here, Liesel was her happiest self. In fact, she acted happier than she was. She feared that they might guess that something unspeakable had happened to her, so she overcompensated, acting like her life was happy and carefree. As far as she could tell, no one seemed to pick up on her deception.

When she felt certain that no one was looking, she would steal quick glances at her beloved. It was not that easy with such a large family. One time, Jacob's eyes met hers and he smiled at her. His expression conveyed everything that she wanted – he definitely loved her too.

Everything was easier to bear knowing this.

But another new hell was brewing on the horizon. One that would sweep her up in a maelstrom of death and destruction.

CHAPTER 28

Chaya was helping her mother clean up after the evening meal.

"Your abba wants to speak with you, Chaya. Leave this. I will do the cleaning up." Her mother gave her a look that she could not interpret.

What could her father want to talk to her about that couldn't wait until she had finished helping her mother clean up? Her mother believed in duty first, and it was Chaya's duty to help her to clean up. It was so unlike her to let Chaya out of her chores.

"Are you sure, Ima?"

"Yes dear, just go. Your abba is waiting."

Chaya did as she was told, although her mother's behaviour towards her was baffling. She hadn't spoken to Chaya with such endearment in a long time, and as she waved her away, she was smiling – at what, Chaya had no idea. Chaya went to the sitting room where she knew her father would be. He was sitting in his favourite chair, a tome open on his lap, a pipe clamped in his lips.

"Abba, you wanted to see me?"

Her father looked up with a huge smile on his face.

"Sit, Chayaleh. I have some good news to discuss with you."

Chaya sat opposite her father. Her interest was piqued.

"What good news, Abba?"

"You are to be married, Chayaleh. Nicholas has formally asked for your hand in marriage."

His words hit her like a punch to her stomach. *Married . . . to Nicholas.* She was so stunned that she did not say anything for many minutes. She just stared at her father, feeling her world coming apart. *What should she do?*

"Abba, I am too young to marry." She had used this argument with her father before. Maybe it would work yet again. If it did, it might buy her some time so that she could figure out what to do about her and Jacob.

"You are no longer too young, Chayaleh. Other girls your age have married and have children already."

"But Abba, I'm not ready. I'm not ready to be a wife and a mother."

"It is your duty, Chaya. Your ima says that I have indulged you too much, and in this matter, I think she is right. Ready or not, it is time for you to marry and, God willing, to bless our family with many grandchildren."

Chaya could see that her father was not going to be swayed as easily this time.

"But I don't love Nicholas, Abba." What she really wanted to say, but could not, was – *My heart belongs to another, and I shall never love Nicholas.*

"Love will come in time, Chaya. Nicholas is a good man. You will grow to love him as your ima grew to love me. Our marriage was arranged and look what came from it: love and two beautiful, obedient children."

Chaya could not believe that her father had chosen the word 'obedient' to describe herself and her brother. Her brother, who should have been the next rabbi but had been able to choose to become a carpenter instead. How was that being obedient? As for herself, she knew her own shortcomings when it came to being obedient. Her greatest disobedience was her relationship with Jacob. If her father knew about what she had been doing, it might just kill him.

"Abba, I don't want to marry Nicholas. Please don't make me do this."

"Chaya, it is already decided. Stop acting like a spoiled little girl and start acting like a woman."

Her father's rebuke startled her. Her father had never spoken as harshly as he just had to her. His words hurt, but it was the expression on his face that was even harder to bear – it was one of disappointment. Chaya's heart broke seeing that expression on his face, but what hurt more was that she had caused it. Chaya could not stand seeing him look at her that way. There was only one way to fix things.

"Alright, Abba. I will marry Nicholas. I am sorry that I disappointed you."

The dutiful and obedient 'rabbi's daughter' did as she was told, accepting her fate with sad resignation. The free and happy Chaya shook her head in disgust at her capitulation, knowing that the love she should have fought harder for was now going to be sacrificed in an attempt to please others.

As soon as she agreed to marry Nicholas, her old father returned. Disappointment left his eyes. It was replaced with pride. It should have been enough to help Chaya feel better about her sacrifice – but it was not.

"Nicholas loves you, Chaya. He will make a wonderful husband and father. You, my Chayaleh, will also be a rebbetzin worthy of our humble shtetl. Your ima has told me all that you did for Herr Morgenstern and how you ministered to the baker's wife and her poor unfortunate daughters. You are such a caring and loving soul, my Chayaleh."

Any other time, her father's words would have made her feel elated that he was singing her praises. But now they were just words. Words that meant nothing to her because her heart was screaming *NO!*

All she could do was nod at her father politely as he went on and on. She only interrupted him once to ask a question that she needed to know, but feared the most.

"When are we to be married, Abba?"

"In a month's time. Nicholas wanted it to be sooner, but your ima insisted that she needed more time to complete all of the necessary preparations."

One month. Chaya could not believe how little time she had left, how little time she and Jacob had. *She had to tell him. But how? And when?*

She was glad when her father finally finished and she could retreat to her room. She hugged her father as she left the room. It did not matter that he and her mother had shattered her heart. She still loved him, even though inside she wished that he could know about the man who held her heart. She felt that if the circumstances were different, her father would like Jacob once he got to see what a great man he was. And he would surely bless their union. *If only things were different . . .*

Chaya did not sleep that night. She tossed and turned in her bed. Her body was in as much turmoil as her mind. She knew that her relationship with Jacob must now end. Chaya struggled within herself, trying to determine exactly when and how the break must occur.

The selfish side of her wanted to spare her heart for as long as possible, prolonging the inevitable. She could tell Jacob just before she was to wed. That would spare her heart, but not her conscience.

"How could she go on with Jacob acting as if nothing had changed, even if it was just for a month? It was deceitful. She had deceived her parents about her meeting with Jacob in the forest,

and it was eating her up inside. Doing the same to Jacob would be her undoing. So, as the hours ticked by in the night, she came to the sad truth. She must end it with Jacob. He needed to be told. Her heart begged for more time, but she held firm in her resolve that it had to be this way. If another day passed, she might convince herself to delay telling him. The heartache that was coming for both could not be deferred. She had to fulfill her duty. There was nothing else she could do. She hoped that Jacob would understand.

Long before the rest of her household awoke for the day, Chaya rose and made her way quietly through her slumbering house. In the kitchen, she left a note telling her parents that she needed to be alone, that she had gone mushroom picking and was sorry that she had neglected her morning chores. She knew that her mother would be very mad at her, but she was counting on her father to calm her down so that she could have time to think.

She did not break her fast, because her stomach was in knots with the knowledge of what she had to do. She grabbed her basket, gently latched the door, and slipped away from the shtetl in the pre-dawn light.

She made her way through the forest to the meadow. She was not sure what time Jacob was going to arrive to start his day of chopping wood. It was still so early. He had to milk the cows before he came to the forest as well. Chaya sat on the soft, dew-kissed grass and waited for him. She sang Yiddish folk songs to pass the time. Her melancholy meant the words were sung with such sadness and longing. At times, tears streamed down her face as she sang.

—⁓—

Jacob arrived at his worksite and was about to start sawing a log he had set up the previous day, but something stopped him. He had a very uneasy feeling. He was not sure what was causing it – but it was so strong within himself that he couldn't ignore or dismiss it. *Chaya.* Her name echoed in his head. He dropped the saw and headed for her shtetl. The foreboding feeling grew stronger. He walked faster. Then he began to run.

He heard it before he reached their meadow. It was Chaya singing. He stopped and listened. He had heard the song many times before. He had come to recognise some of the words even though they were in Yiddish. But what had made him stop, and what was sending chills up and down his spine, was not the song itself, but how Chaya was singing it.

Every note that emerged from her mouth was filled with such pain. Jacob knew instantly that something had happened. Something bad . . . something very bad.

CHAPTER 29

Pockface had been back in Rysincek for a few days; days in which he'd observed the Jew's village. He had even seen the Jewish bitch on whom he wanted to enact his revenge. He saw her walking the street on the second day he and Pavel were observing the village. They had not seen the other Jewish scum who had beaten him, but he was sure that he was there as well. Satisfied that they were there, Pockface observed the other Jews in the village. For his plan to work perfectly, he had to know where they'd be when he, Pavel, and the others struck.

The Jews would rue the day that they had crossed paths with the likes of him.

—᭟᭟—

The peasants of Rysincek were just starting their day. Pockface knew that the Jews would be doing the same. He had Pavel drive the wagon they had stolen from Saratov to the village square. Most of the villagers ignored them until Pavel passed around a few bottles of vodka. Almost immediately, men flocked to their wagon. Pavel retrieved a few more bottles and they were passed around. The peasants did not care that it was early in the day and that they should have been working, not imbibing. The vodka was of a good quality and they liked the fact that it was free. Some women had even joined the assembly. More came out of curiosity than for the free vodka. However, it was not exactly free, for they would help him in his plan against the Jews.

He stopped Pavel handing out any more vodka. He wanted the peasants to be happy, but not stinking drunk. The time was ripe for what he wanted them to do.

Pockface stood in the wagon bed so that he towered over those assembled.

"Good people of Rysincek," he began. "I know that all here have endured tough times." Many heads nodded in agreement when he said this.

"I can tell you, brothers and sisters, that our beloved Tsar knows of your pain and suffering, and he knows who is causing this for you, and he is doing everything in his power to help you." Pockface saw a few confused faces in the crowd. *These backward peasants don't understand a great speech,* he thought. *Better get to the point before these clueless clods go back to shovelling pig shit.*

With a dramatic flourish, Pockface produced a paper from his pocket.

"I have words from your Tsar, called the May Laws. The Tsar drafted this because his dear father was assassinated at the hands of the vilest creatures who live amongst us – the dirty filthy Jews. I will read his words to you now. These words are law, so we must follow them to honour our glorious Tsar."

"The Tsar has said that any Jewish settlement outside of the Pale of Settlement is forbidden." The actual decree had 'new village' in its wording. *These clods don't need to know that,* he mused.

"Why do we have a village of those Jewish pigs just down the road from us when we are not part of the Pale of Settlement?" he thundered. "What gives them the right to live where they are not supposed to be?" he roared. Some in the crowd cheered at this.

"Have we not put up with their filth for too long?" More cheers. "They have taken the best land for themselves." Shouts from the crowd, agreeing to what he was saying. "They do not belong here. They are not Russians." More cheering, along with catcalls of "how dare they!" and "dirty scheming Jews!"

Pockface just about had them where he wanted them. Now for the coup de grâce.

"Your Tsar has granted Russians the right to demand the expulsion of the Jews from their towns." Their Jewish village was not technically part of Rysincek. Pockface was sure that they would not pick up on this – and they didn't. The alcohol was doing its job, as he knew it would.

"As the sons and daughters of Russia, let's take back what is ours from these Jewish vermin. Let us drive them out of our part of Russia, never to be seen again. For the Tsar. For Russia," he yelled, the crowd echoing him. "For the Tsar!", "For Russia!" they all cried.

"When we have finished with them, we will celebrate." He waved a bottle of vodka in front of the frenzied crowd. Pavel pulled back the tarp from the wagon, showing the peasants that it contained many cases of the vodka they had been drinking. The crowd cheered and then dispersed as each person ran to their homes to collect axes, scythes, and a few ancient firearms. They followed the wagon as Pavel drove it towards the Jewish settlement, chanting "For the Tsar!" and "For Russia!" as they marched.

Like a seasoned General, Pockface directed the mob with military precision. He had them surround the entire village so that no Jews could escape. If any had left to work in the fields, he'd know where they'd be from observing the village the last few days. He sent a small contingent to the Jews' potato fields.

Some of the Jews tried to escape from their village once they discovered that they were under attack. But none slipped though the net he had cast around it. The peasants had the upper hand, and most of the Jews cowered in fear. The few that were foolhardy enough to try and break free were set upon by the mob and beaten.

Pockface had the peasants herd the defenceless Jews into the largest building in their village. He enlisted two of the peasants to board up the windows. The lucky two would be given two bottles of vodka each for doing the job. He also selected an old man who was toting an ancient firearm. He was also to be given two bottles of vodka for his job, which was ensuring that no Jew escaped from the building. With the windows nailed shut, he only had to guard the one entryway into the building. Maybe rewarding him with two bottles was a bit excessive considering how easy the task was, but Pockface wanted every Jew that was brought there to remain there.

As the peasants brought the Jews to the building, he kept looking for the two Jews he desired the most. After every house had been cleared, they had not been found.

The scum must be hiding, he thought. He sent Pavel off to look for them. The peasants had fulfilled their duty of bringing the Jews to the building. Now they turned their attention to looting the homes of the Jews. Pockface could see that his guard wanted to leave his post and join in before all the booty was gone. Only the promise of two more bottles kept him from leaving.

Pavel returned, pushing two Jews towards him – a man and a woman. Pockface was disappointed; they were not the right ones.

"I found these two hiding in the stable," Pavel informed him. "I set it alight. There were two old nags in there. Maybe the smell of roasting horseflesh will make them reconsider their decision to hide from us."

Pockface could smell smoke. The panicked squeals of the horses could also be heard.

"I will keep looking for them." Pavel seemed confident that he would find them.

Pockface looked around. With the peasants now focused on their looting, it would be easy for the two to sneak away undetected.

"No, I have a better idea. They are hiding, and someone knows where they are. Go grab a Jew, Pavel. And make sure that it is someone with a family. They will tell us everything we want to know."

Pavel entered the building and came out dragging a Jew wearing a dirty, bloodstained apron. He was the Jewish butcher. Pavel dragged him over to where Pockface stood.

"Now, you Jewish piece of shit, if you want your family to survive this little dust up, you will tell me everything that I need to know. Otherwise, Pavel here is going to carve up your family members one by one, right in front of you."

Pockface turned to Pavel. "I thought he would appreciate the carving and all, being the butcher. The butcher gets to watch you butcher his family – how poetic, don't you think?" Pockface laughed at his own joke.

"Now, butcher. Two Jewish rats are hiding somewhere in your little Jew Heaven. The woman looks like the rest of your Jewish whores, except she has green eyes. I saw her two days ago, so I know that she is here somewhere, hiding. Hiding most likely with the Jew who is bedding her. He has one feature that makes him distinct as well – he doesn't have the long hook nose you Jews tend to have. Maybe some of you Jewish swine have been defiling some poor Russian women. If that is the case, then those responsible will have to pay for their indiscretions. Now, before I send Pavel in to get your oldest child, tell me where they are."

The butcher knew exactly who he was dealing with. Although the face of one of his tormentors was massively scarred, there was no mistaking the pock marks. He was under no illusion that this man and his companion would spare the lives of his family and himself. No matter what he told him, his fate would be the same as that of his friend, the baker. He would be forced to watch as his family was defiled by these brutes.

He reached his hand into the pocket of his apron and grasped the handle of the small boning knife that he carried there. Before the scarred one knew what he was doing, the butcher plunged the knife into Pockface's chest. He was aiming for his heart, but the small knife grazed a rib and he missed the mark.

Had Pockface not still been recovering from his previous beating, he might have been able to parry the thrust or move away from the deadly blade in time. Instead, he saw the flash of the blade too late, feeling a searing pain in his chest.

Pavel, seeing Pockface stabbed by the butcher's knife, grabbed his own and stabbed the butcher repeatedly until the Jewish bastard collapsed to the ground. Pavel continued to stab him until he finally lay inert, a pool of blood seeping into the ground around him. Pavel then went to help Pockface.

Pockface wanted to pull the Jew's pigsticker out, but he found that he did not have the strength.

"Take it out," he instructed his friend.

Pavel gently helped him to sit down. Even that small movement was excruciating. He grasped the knife and yanked it out quickly. Pockface could hear a sucking sound as he did that. He screamed in pain, but it came out more like a gurgle. His chest felt very heavy. He could not get enough air into his lungs. He gasped for air. Each time he breathed in it felt like he was drowning. When he breathed out, bloody bubbles came out of his mouth.

Pockface did not know that the butcher had missed his heart and nicked his lung. He was drowning in his own blood. His breath was rasping horribly as he struggled to say the words he needed to say to Pavel.

"You . . . kn . . . ow . . . wh . . . what . . . you . . . ha . . . v . . . e . . . to . . . do."

Pavel left him to carry out the rest of their plan.

As the life drained out of him, Pockface smiled one last lopsided smile, for what he saw was the revenge that he sought. He knew that Pavel would find the missing two and complete his revenge for him.

His hearing was the last sense to go before he succumbed to death. He crossed to the other side, listening to the desperate screams of the Jews.

CHAPTER 30

Jacob stepped into the clearing. Chaya saw him and stopped her mournful song. Jacob ran to her and gave her a loving embrace.

"What's wrong, Chaya? What has happened?"

When she saw Jacob, all her resolve about breaking it off melted away. Instead of telling him, she sought his lips. She kissed him with such passion. But in her passion, there was also desperation.

Jacob had not expected such passion in the way Chaya was kissing him. And before he knew what was happening, Chaya was unbuttoning her blouse. Jacob wanted Chaya, and from her ardour, he could tell that she wanted him as well. His body was responding to her passion, but his mind told him that something was not right. He pulled away from her, even though his body screamed at him, questioning what he was doing.

"Chaya, what are we doing?"

"Make love to me, Jacob." She started to remove her skirt.

Jacob almost ignored his mind. Chaya, being half undressed, was making it hard for him to concentrate. He wanted her so badly. But not this way. He pulled away from her.

"No Chaya, not like this."

Chaya had not expected Jacob to pull away. His rejection stung, so much so that it opened up the floodgates to the emotions she'd been desperately trying to keep in check. She could not hold back her tears any longer. She buried her face into Jacob's chest and sobbed and sobbed.

First, Chaya had thrown herself at him, and now she was crying uncontrollably. Jacob knew she was not crying because he had rejected her. Her wails were not wails of rejection; they were something more than that. Chaya's crying sounded like she was being torn apart inside. Jacob felt so helpless as he stood there holding her and letting her cry until his shirt was soaked with all her tears.

It was a very long time before her crying subsided and she was a bit calmer. He sensed that it was too soon to ask her what was upsetting her, so all he could do was hold her and whisper to her that he loved her.

Chaya felt ashamed. Ashamed that she had not been strong like she had planned. Now she was a blubbering mess, and she still had not told Jacob the news that was ripping her apart inside.

Chaya was now just sniffling. The tears were over. Jacob felt that the time was right to ask Chaya what was upsetting her, what had caused her to act the way that she had.

"Chaya, my love. You have to tell me what's wrong, but before you do that, maybe you should put on your clothes."

Chaya had been so caught up in her inner turmoil that she had forgotten she was in a state of undress in front of Jacob. She did as he said, putting her skirt back on and re-buttoning her blouse. All the time that she was dressing, she kept her eyes on the ground.

Jacob averted his eyes as Chaya got dressed. When she was dressed, he repeated the questions he'd asked her when he first entered the meadow.

"What's wrong, Chaya? What has happened?" As he asked his questions, he noticed that Chaya kept her eyes averted from him. She stared down at the ground. He gently took her chin in his hand and tilted her head so that she was looking at him, gently repeating his questions a third time.

Although Chaya wanted to keep her eyes downcast, she knew that it was cowardly to do so considering the devastating news she had to deliver. She mustered up what remained of her courage. She looked deeply into her beloved's eyes and said the words that she wished she'd never have to say: "I'm sorry, Jacob, but I am to be married."

Chaya's words hit him like a punch to the stomach. *Chaya to be married.* A pain spread in his chest as his heart took in the news. Now he understood why Chaya's singing had been so sad and morose, and why, when she had burst into tears, her wails had sounded so heart-wrenching. He was now feeling similarly. He wished he could cry like Chaya had. His heart was telling him to cry its anguish for the whole world to hear. Even though he wanted to cry and vent his lament, he could not because he was a man. And a man just did not do such a thing. Crying was seen as weakness in his family – even the girls in his family rarely cried. He envied that Chaya could cry without seeming to be less than what she was.

Chaya could see that Jacob was struggling with his emotions. She appreciated that he had not pressed her when she was at her most vulnerable. She would give Jacob the same consideration, giving him time to come to terms with his emotions. All she could do was send him loving thoughts as he struggled to get his emotions in check. When she felt he was in control, she reached out her hand and squeezed his.

Chaya's gesture tugged at his heart, but that small touch conveyed to him just how much she loved him. He drew strength from her. And he, in turn, would provide strength for her.

"Let's sit, Chaya – and talk."

"Jacob . . . I'm sorry–" Jacob placed his fingers on her lips, stopping her from saying more.

"No more apologizing, Chaya. It will not change things. It will only make you feel worse. We must talk and be honest with each other, but we cannot take blame or apologize for things that are beyond our control. We both have known for quite some time that what we have could not last forever."

"Oh Jacob, I wish that it could."

"Chaya, wishing won't change things. The day we have dreaded has come, and we must be strong for each other."

"I will never love him, Jacob."

Although Chaya's words warmed his heart, he knew that she must not close her heart off to Nicholas. As much as it hurt him, he had to convince her that she mustn't deny Nicholas her heart.

"Chaya, from what you have told me, Nicholas is a good man and he clearly has deep feelings for you. You must give him a chance to know the beauty of your heart."

Chaya could not believe that Jacob was championing Nicholas.

"My heart belongs to you, Jacob, and to you only."

"Mine belongs to you as well, Chaya, but we have no choice. You will be married to Nicholas no matter what your heart wants. You will share a bed with him and bear his children. How will your children thrive if they sense that you do not have love for their father? You are not being fair to them, Chaya. One day, I too will have to marry someone else. I don't want my children sensing that I don't love their mother."

"Do you have someone you wish to marry . . . besides me?" Chaya felt a pang of jealousy as she asked Jacob this question.

"No, Chaya. There is only you, but one day there might be another. I must give my heart to that person. Even though one special part will always belong solely to you. You are a part of me now, Chaya, and I will always carry you with me wherever I go until the day that I die. And, if God is willing, into Heaven as well."

Jacob's words gave her a small bit of comfort.

"I too will take you with me every day, until we can meet again one day in Heaven. You are my bashert, Jacob. No other shall take your place – ever."

"You, Chaya Blumenthal, are and will always be my bashert. I love you."

"Our love will burn inside of me forever. No matter that we are apart."

"As will it for me."

They sealed their declarations with passionate kisses. As their ardour increased, a breathless Chaya uttered the words she had said earlier.

"Make love to me, my bashert. Let our two souls become one."

Jacob's body wanted nothing more than to comply with Chaya's suggestion, but his mind protested yet again. He gently pulled away from Chaya so that she would not think he was outright rejecting her. He looked deeply into her eyes.

"I would like nothing more than to make love to you, Chaya, but I cannot. For if I do, I know that I will never be able to let you go. As much as it pains me, we cannot do this Chaya. It will be hard to let you go as it is. Having you will make it impossible. Even though I said no more apologies – I'm sorry, Chaya."

Chaya knew that what Jacob said was the truth. She too would find it impossible to leave him if they consummated their love. She gave him a weak smile and nodded that she agreed with what he said. She wanted to say so many things to him, but feared that if she spoke, she might lose control of her emotions yet again, and she didn't want their parting to be any more sorrowful than it already was.

Jacob could see that Chaya was fighting her emotions.

"Chaya, my love, I should escort you back to your shtetl before someone comes looking for you."

Chaya wanted to stay longer, but she knew that Jacob was right. She nodded to his suggestion.

Hand in hand, they walked away from the meadow for the last time. At the edge of the clearing, they both stopped and looked back. Each of them looked sadly into their bashert's eyes, before walking slowly down the path towards Chaya's shtetl.

CHAPTER 31

Neither Chaya nor Jacob spoke. Both were in their own purgatories. The hand of their beloved gave each of them strength to put one foot in front of the other. A breeze blowing from the direction of the shtetl brought the scent of smoke. Chaya dropped Jacob's hand and she ran towards home.

Jacob ran after Chaya. As they got closer to the shtetl, he saw a huge pall of black smoke in the sky. He wondered what had caught fire.

Chaya could not get her legs to move as fast as she wanted. She feared that it might be her home on fire. She had only a few hundred yards to go when she heard the screams. It was such a heart-wrenching sound. They were the screams of horses trapped in a burning building. She knew what was on fire before she saw it with her own eyes - the stables. She hoped that someone was working to free the trapped horses, although the pitch of their screams had become even louder.

She was at the edge of the forest and was about to run into the shtetl when she stopped and stood frozen in fear. The two men who had attacked her were there in her shtetl. She feared for the safety of her parents and her brother. She needed to find them and get them away from these men, but her legs would not respond, no matter how much her brain screamed at them to move. She sensed Jacob's presence beside her, but she could not even turn her head. All she could do was look at her attackers, her heart pounding in her chest.

The one called Pavel disappeared into the synagogue. He came out a minute later, dragging the butcher towards his accomplice. The one who had a disfigured face was threatening the butcher, but she was too far away to hear his words. Then the scene in front of her seemed to slow down. She saw the butcher draw a knife out of his apron and she watched as his arm arched and embedded the knife into the disfigured one's chest. She watched the expression on his scared face as it first registered surprise, then shock, and finally pain. Still in slow motion, she saw the one called Pavel repeatedly stab the butcher over and over until he lay on the ground with a pool of blood around his prone body.

She watched as Pavel went to his friend. The disfigured one had a hand on the hilt of the butcher's knife, which still protruded from his chest. She saw the disfigured one nod to Pavel, and she saw Pavel grab the knife and pull it out of his friend's chest. She saw blood spurt out of the wound.

Her gaze was broken when she felt herself being shaken.

Jacob had caught up to Chaya. He had almost bowled into her because she had stopped so suddenly and without warning. He could see that she was entirely rigid. When he looked at the shtetl, he knew why. He saw the two who had attacked her. The one he had beaten senseless still bore the scars of their last encounter – his face was a disfigured mess. He saw the one called Pavel drag one of the villagers to his disfigured friend. He saw the flash of a knife blade and the villager plunging a knife into the disfigured one's chest. Then he watched in horror as Pavel repeatedly stabbed the villager. These men he had fought in the forest had obviously come to exact their revenge for their beating. Jacob feared most for Chaya's safety. After witnessing their savage attack, he wanted to get her as far away from these beasts as possible. When he tugged on Chaya's arm, she did not respond. He remembered how she'd been paralysed with fear in the forest. There was only one way he knew that would snap her out of it. As much as he hated to do it again, he shook her violently, trying to get her to come out of her paralysis.

Chaya became less rigid.

"Chaya, we have to go. I have to get you far away from these beasts."

"No Jacob! My parents and brother are there. I have to help them."

"They are not alone this time." He pointed out the other Russians in the shtetl. "We must get away from here. We need to get help from Norka. We have to hurry, Chaya, before there is any more bloodshed."

Her heart broke as she let Jacob lead her away from the shtetl. Jacob was right. There were too many of them. She saw the peasants bringing out things from their homes. *Where were her parents? Her brother? The rest of the members of the shtetl?* As she ran with Jacob, she said a prayer to God, entreating Him to keep them all safe until help could arrive.

As Jacob fled away from the shtetl with Chaya, he tried to think of a place he could take her where she would be safe while he raised the alarm and got help for her fellow Jews. He felt that the safest spot was his farm, but he couldn't just take her to the farmhouse. He would have a lot of explaining to do, and it would require a lot of time. Considering who was behind the attack, he feared that Chaya's people could not afford this delay. The place that seemed the best for now was the hayloft in the barn. Chaya could hide there until the immediate crisis was over. He urged her to run faster. Now that he had a plan, he felt that Chaya would be safe, and that made him feel better.

No one was in the farmyard when they arrived there, breathless. They snuck over to the barn. The barn door creaked loudly when they opened it, but luckily no one came to investigate. He led Chaya to the ladder leading up to the hayloft. He scrambled up the ladder with Chaya following him. He told her she was safe in the loft, but that she had to be quiet. He told her he loved her. Then he assured her he would find her family and bring them to her. He kissed her and went to the ladder. He glanced back at her. The expression on her face broke his heart. It was a look of such sadness and desperation. He wanted to go to her to comfort and console her, but there was no time. He had to find her family. He gave her an encouraging smile, then he hurried down the ladder.

He didn't worry as much about the squeaking barn door as he emerged from the barn. He needed to find his father. With his father's standing in the community, he was sure that he could help him to convince others to come to the aid of the Jews. Jacob was heading towards the fields to find his father, but when he heard the bells of Norka pealing, he knew his father would be heading to Norka. The bells of Norka pealed to warn of blizzards, of deaths, and of danger. They rang in distinctive patterns to inform the villagers of what was occurring. Jacob wondered how the people of Norka knew about the attack on the shtetl, but when he looked to the northern horizon, he understood. The entire horizon was a huge dense mass of black smoke. When he had stood at the forest's edge with Chaya, it was only the stable that was burning. Now, judging from the amount of smoke, Jacob assumed that more of the shtetl had caught fire.

He raced towards Norka. Others alerted by the bells were also hurrying towards town. He followed the throng of people, but he already knew where everyone was going: the village square. It was quickly filling when he arrived. He scanned the gathering crowd, hoping to find his father. He spied him standing with his two elder brothers. Jacob ran up to him.

"Vati, the Russians attacked the Jewish village. You must get some men together and help them. I saw them kill a Jewish man in the village. We have to hurry Vati."

"Jacob, are you okay?" His father gave him a big hug.

Jacob broke from his father's embrace. "Yes, Vati, I'm fine. But we must hurry. Please, Vati." Jacob was getting agitated with his father. *Why wasn't he taking his urge to hurry and do something more seriously?* "Vati, there is no time to lose."

"You need to tell me everything, Jacob."

Everything would take too long. So he told his father only the things that he needed to know, hoping that he would act quickly to help save the Jews. He elaborated more on what he had seen at the shtetl: the looting of the Jewish homes by the peasants, the burning of the stable, and the attack on that poor butcher. He left out everything that had to do with Chaya. When he was done, his father did spring into action, but not in the way Jacob had anticipated.

His father told his brothers to get to the farm as quickly as possible. He told them to get all the family safely into the farmhouse. His brothers were to arm themselves and be prepared to take on the Russians, should they attack their farm. As his brothers ran off to do his father's bidding, Jacob followed him as he sought out the Vorsteher. Herr Seidler was the current head of Norka's colony council.

The Vorsteher was with a group of men whom Jacob knew were the Beisitzer of Norka. They served as councilman in

Norka. They were all engaged in animated conversations, discussing what the smoke signified. Jacob's father approached the Vorsteher.

"The Jewish village has been attacked by the Russians. My son saw it with his own eyes. They are looting the Jews' homes. My son saw them murder one of the Jews. They set the Jews' stable on fire, but from the look of the smoke on the horizon, they have set more buildings on fire."

"Is this true?" The Vorsteher directed his question to Jacob. Jacob nodded.

"We must inform the people of Norka that they must defend their families, their homes, and their businesses from the Russians," declared the Vorsteher decisively.

"What of the Jews? They need our help. You must do something, Vorsteher, to help them," Jacob blurted out.

"Jacob!"

From his father's tone, he knew that he had spoken out of turn. He had challenged the Vorsteher and disrespected his elders. He knew he had to make amends, even though he was boiling inside from frustration.

He lowered his head. "Sorry for my insolence, Vorsteher. Sorry, Vati."

The Vorsteher did not acknowledge his apology. He started talking with the Beisitzer once again. His father did not acknowledge it either. He led Jacob away from the Vorsteher and Beisitzer. Jacob surmised that he was heading for home. They did not need to stay around for the Vorsteher's announcement, for they already knew what he was going to say to the gathered crowd.

Jacob wanted to beg his father again to help the Jews, but he knew it was futile. He was miserable because he had promised Chaya that he'd get help for her family and he had failed.

"Why were you near the Jews' village, Jacob? It is quite far from where you are working?"

His father's question caught him totally off guard. He knew he could not fabricate a story that would explain why he'd been there. Plus, he had never lied to his father before. The only thing that might save Chaya's family and her people was if he told the truth. So, the secret he'd kept for so long from his family, came pouring out of his lips as he unburdened his soul. He left out no detail. He wanted his father to understand that he was in love with Chaya and that he needed to help her to get her family to safety.

When he was done with his confession, he looked up into his father's eyes. He had expected to see disappointment in them, but he did not. Instead, they showed deep sorrow. Jacob was not sure if his father's sorrow was because Jacob was in love with a woman who could never be his wife, or if his father's sadness came from being unable to come to the aid of the Jews. Jacob did not ask him, because he had something else that he had to tell his father.

"There is something else, Vati. After seeing the attack on Chaya's village, I had to get her away from there to someplace safe."

"Where did you take her, Jacob?"

"I didn't know where else to take her, Vati. She is hiding in the hayloft. I promised her that I would help rescue her family. Now I've failed her."

"You haven't failed her, Jacob. It is just not prudent or safe to do anything now. The Russians have been stirred up like a hornet's nest. If we intervene, they might turn their attention on Norka. You said you only saw one Jew killed. Maybe the rest have escaped and are hiding in the surrounding forest. Once it is dark, Jacob, we will seek them out. We will bring them here and provide refuge for them – you can tell Chaya that. I know it is not much, but it is something. For now, her presence on our farm must remain a secret. Do not tell your brothers or sisters. I will only tell your mother because we might need her help, and she deserves to know. When we get to the farm, you can go to Chaya and tell her that we cannot help until dark. Make her understand that we will do what we can when it is safe. She must remain as quiet as possible. Once you have told her this, then you must come to the house. If you are absent when we are supposed to be together, it will arouse suspicions. I know that you would like to be with her to comfort and assure her, but our family's safety comes first, Jacob."

When they arrived at the farmyard, Jacob did as his father had instructed. He went to the hayloft and told Chaya that he could not stay with her, and that his father had assured him that they would seek out the Jews hiding in the forest after dark. He told her that her family and her people would be given shelter and refuge. He wished that he could promise her that everything would be alright, but he knew he could not provide her with false hope. She took his news with a stoic face, but he knew that underneath her brave face, she was in turmoil. With a heavy heart, he kissed her goodbye and made his way to the farmhouse.

The atmosphere inside the house was tense. Both of his older brothers were armed and pacing around the house. The rest of the family was sitting at the table. Jacob noted it was quieter than it had ever been. Very few words were spoken. Everyone sat quietly, fear was etched on every face. His mother, to keep herself busy, started cooking. When the meal was ready, she dished it up for the family. Everyone picked at their food. Eventually, his mother cleared the table. The leftover food would not be wasted. It would be eaten at another meal.

The afternoon wore on. Discussion started about the afternoon's milking. It was already an hour past the time the cows were usually milked. Manfred always brought the cows in from the pasture, but everyone agreed that it was not safe for him to do this. It was finally decided that Jacob would bring the cows home, and that Ernst would go with him, armed with one of their rifles. Karl, with their other rifle, would guard the farmhouse.

Jacob was glad that he had been chosen to bring the cows in. His father had made that decision so Jacob could be nearer to Chaya. Jacob and Ernst encountered no one when they went for the cows. The cows were easy to herd home as their full udders made them very compliant. As Jacob milked, his brother stood guard outside the barn. He worked as quickly as he could so that he could steal a few moments with Chaya. The few moments passed by very quickly. All he could really do was assure Chaya that night was coming soon and that he would ask his father if he could go with him to her shtetl.

He was not sure if his father would grant his request to go to the shtetl. It turned out that he did not need to ask.

As darkness fell, his father announced to the family that he was going to the Jewish village. He told everyone that Jacob was going to accompany him. His two older brothers were to stay and continue to protect the family, so Jacob was the logical choice (not that anyone would challenge his father's decision). His father ruled the roost – not even his mother would have dared to challenge her husband's decisions.

Jacob followed his father out of the farmhouse, glad to be finally doing something. But his father had other plans about Jacob going with him, and revealed this to Jacob once they were away from the farmhouse.

"You need to stay with Chaya, Jacob. She has been alone all day and is surely going out of her mind with worry. You need to comfort her and keep her calm. I will gather some others and we will search the forest by the Jews' village."

Jacob's father opened the barn door, which made its usual creaking noise. In the gloom, they made their way to where the lanterns were stored. His father struck a match and applied it to one of the lantern's wick. The flame caught and the barn was bathed in light. His father lit another lamp. He trimmed the flames on both, then lowered the glass on them.

"Before I go, I want to meet Chaya. Go and bring her down, Son."

Jacob scrambled up the ladder. With the glow from the lamps partially illuminating the loft, he could see Chaya crouching in the furthest and darkest corner.

"It's okay, Chaya. It is just me and my vati. He wants you to come down. Don't worry. He just wants to meet you, that's all." He extended his hand to her to assure her that everything was all right. She walked tentatively towards him. He smiled at her. Then he helped her down the ladder.

When they were in front of his father, Jacob introduced Chaya.

"Vati, this is Chaya Blumenthal. She is the girl I told you about. Chaya, this is my vati."

"Good evening, Herr Henkel."

"Good evening, Chaya. I am pleased to meet you. I only wish that it were under more pleasant circumstances. I am sure that Jacob has told you that it was too dangerous to go to your village until now. I am sorry that we have had to wait until dark. I am sure that you are going out of your mind with worry, but Jacob will stay with you now until I return. I am sorry, but I will have to take both lanterns so that it appears as though Jacob is with me. Jacob was able to bring you some food. You must eat something. Is there anything else that you need?"

"I really need to urinate."

"I'm sorry, but using the outhouse is too risky. You will have to go in one of the stalls – it is the best we can do. Jacob, go to the well and get some water for Chaya to drink later. She will be fine with me for a few moments."

Jacob grabbed a pail and tried to open the barn door slowly so that it did not squeak. Even doing it slowly caused a small noise. He went to the well and filled the pail half full, then returned to the barn. His father waited until they both ascended the ladder before he left with the lanterns. The hayloft was plunged into darkness.

Jacob and Chaya lay beside each other.

"Chaya, you need to eat something. I'm sorry it's not kosher, but I'm sure that God would forgive you."

"I'm not hungry, Jacob."

"You have to eat, Chaya. If not for me, then do it for your family. You need to keep up your strength. They will need you to be strong."

"Okay Jacob, I will eat. Thank you for caring for me so much. Even now you worry about things being kosher – you would have made a good Jew, Jacob. God has made provisions for times like this with a principle called Pikuach Nefesh. It states that the preservation of human life takes precedence over other Jewish laws. Having no kosher food would qualify."

"You are so knowledgeable about your faith, Chaya. It's one of the things that I really admire about you."

Jacob's words were supposed to make her feel proud, but they did not. Her father had taught her about Pikuach Nefesh. *Where was he? Where was her mother? Her brother?* She was safe and they were not. Her guilt was overwhelming. When they were reunited, she would never be parted from them again. She would be the dutiful daughter, the future rebbetzin, the mother of their grandchildren. She would be the Chaya, they always expected her to be. The Chaya who felt so alive when she was with Jacob would have to go and be lost forever. And so would Jacob.

Even in the darkness, Jacob could sense Chaya's sadness. He felt he had to try and do as his father had suggested, comforting her the best that he could.

"Chaya, can I tell you something funny that happened to me the other day?" He wanted to lighten the tense atmosphere in the hayloft.

Chaya knew that Jacob was trying to distract her from her worries. She loved him more for doing this. She welcomed the distraction. Anything was better than the despair she had been feeling since she saw the fire in the shtetl and the attack on the butcher.

"Yes, Jacob, I'd like to hear what happened to you."

Jacob told her the story, then another. Then she told him one. They kept their conversation light and talked about nonsensical things. It passed the time for both. As it got later and later, both became more anxious because Jacob's father had not returned. But they kept their fears to themselves, keeping up the pretense that all would be fine.

CHAPTER 32

The creaking of the barn door alerted them that Jacob's father had finally returned. The loft was bathed in a soft light from the lanterns that his father brought back into the barn.

Jacob went to the ladder and peered down. He saw his father standing near one of the stalls.

"Come down, Jacob. But only you," his father directed.

Jacob was confused as to why his father only wanted him to come down.

"Vati just wants me to come down. I will be right back, Chaya."

As Chaya watched Jacob go down the ladder, she wondered why Jacob's father had only requested that he go down. She heard the barn door creak. She peered down into the barn. Jacob's father had left the lanterns burning. The barn was empty. *Why had Jacob and his father left?*

At first, she was panicked because she thought that something bad might have happened. Then she calmed down and thought that maybe Jacob had to go with his father to help those they had found hiding in the woods around the shtetl. She held on to her belief that Jacob was bringing her family to her. But as the minutes continued to pass, doubts started to creep into her thinking once more.

When Jacob got off the ladder, his father signalled that he should follow him. He wanted to ask his father what was going on, but he also signalled for Jacob to be quiet. He followed his father out of the barn, not knowing why his father was being so mysterious. They walked towards the cow pasture. Only when they were some distance from the barn and the farmhouse did his father stop.

"What is it, Vati?" Jacob tried to remain calm., but his voice betrayed his anxiousness.

"I have news, Jacob, but I'm afraid that it is not good. I wanted to tell you by yourself, because some of what I tell you, you might not want Chaya to hear."

"Is it her family . . . are they dead?" He hated asking the question, but he had a sinking feeling in his stomach that his father was going to confirm the thing that would devastate Chaya the most.

"Yes, her family is dead . . . as well as all of the other Jews."

Jacob had braced himself to hear of the deaths of Chaya's family, but he was unprepared for the news of the others.

"Dead . . . all of them? But how, Vati?"

"Twenty of us searched the woods around where the village once was. We were armed just in case, but we encountered no one in our search – no Jews, nor any Russians. At first, we thought the Jews might have been too scared to reveal themselves to us, so we kept shouting over and over that we were from Norka and we were there to help them, but it was to no avail."

"We entered the village – not one building remained. The Russians had burned everything. Smoke still hung heavy in the air, but there was another smell that . . . that—" His father stopped, his voice was choked with emotion. He seemed to gather himself. "The smell, Jacob, was like when we singe chickens – that sickly sweet smell of burning flesh. It was the smell of the Jews. The Russians have burned them." He stopped again. Jacob could not believe what he was hearing.

"Are you sure, Vati? Maybe some escaped?"

"None escaped, Jacob. We found a peasant passed out drunk by a small stream in the village. None too gently, we brought him around. We asked him what had happened to the Jews. He cried and said he did not know that they were going to do that to the Jews. We asked him who 'they' were, and he described the two assailants you said attacked Chaya in the forest. He kept pleading his innocence, stating that it was those men and not him who were responsible for what happened. At that time, we did not know that all of the Jews had perished. We made him tell us all that he knew. And that's when we learned that they had all been killed."

"The peasant had been tasked with guarding the door of the building where the Jews had been brought by the villagers. He was given extra bottles of vodka from the two for doing this. Once all the Jews were brought there, the rest of the villagers looted their homes and businesses. The peasant wanted to do the same, but he feared defying the two ringleaders. Plus, they promised him more vodka to continue doing his job. He swore over and over that he did not think they would ever hurt the Jews. He thought they would only steal some stuff from the Jews and scare them a bit. He did not see anything wrong with stealing from the Jews, he claimed they were hiding lots of riches. It was when they dragged one of the Jews out that he knew their intentions were much more sinister. He saw the Jew stab one of the men, and then the other stepped in and killed the Jew."

"The peasant told us that Pockface died shortly after that, but not before Pavel had him barricade the door. Then Pavel set the building alight with the Jews inside it. The peasant covered his ears when he described the screams of the Jews as they were burned alive."

Jacob found his father's account hard to hear, but he knew that he had to know everything because it would be his job to tell Chaya the devastating news.

"Vati, how am I going to tell Chaya?"

"There is more, Jacob."

More! Wasn't what he'd heard bad enough? What more could there be?

"The peasant said that the one called Pavel went crazy after his friend Pockface died. He ran into every building, shouting for the cowards to come out. When they did not appear, he set that building alight. Soon the whole village was in flames."

Jacob did not have to ask his father who Pavel was looking for; it was himself and Chaya.

"Once the entire village was engulfed in flames, Pavel was still in a rage. He tripped over the body of the Jew who he'd killed. The peasant saw him pick up the body and drag it to the remains of the building where the Jews had been burned to death. He yelled that he should roast in Hell with the rest of them. The building had collapsed into a hole underneath it. As he tried to throw the body into the fire, he stumbled and fell into that fire, still clutching the dead Jew's body. The peasant heard him screaming in agony as he died."

Both of the animals who'd attacked Chaya were dead, but it was little consolation. They'd succeeded in killing Chaya's family, as well as all of the Jews in her shtetl. She too would have died if she had been in the shtetl when they attacked. Jacob shuddered as he realized just how close he'd been to losing Chaya forever.

His father had stopped talking, so Jacob knew that he had told him everything. But one question remained in his mind.

"What happened with the peasant?"

"He was an accomplice, although according to him he was an unwilling one. He was dealt with. It is best if you don't know who disposed of this man. We must protect his identity just in case the authorities investigate. No matter the circumstances, a Russian killed by a German never bodes well for us."

"Vati, Chaya will be devastated. How am I going to tell her . . . about her family . . . and about all the other Jews of her village?"

"She deserves to know, Jacob, and I know that you will do it with compassion and love. But I think it best if she does not know all of the details of what occurred in her village. It will not change the facts, nor will it bring her family back. What it will do, however, is make her feel in some way that she was responsible for this. That guilt will eat her up inside, and who knows how she will get through it, or if she is even able to. This is why I wanted you to hear the details of the attack first, so that you can see how knowing everything might be detrimental to Chaya."

Jacob was grateful that his father was so wise. He was right. Chaya knowing that Pavel and Pockface had been looking for them would make her think that the attack was all her fault. And his father was right – this knowledge would not change things or bring her family back. Jacob had an overwhelming urge to protect Chaya. He resolved that he would never tell her that those thugs attacked the shtetl because of them. This he would take to his grave. *Would those who listened to the peasant's story do the same?* Jacob voiced his concern to his father.

"We swore an oath, Jacob. None will speak of what the peasant told us about the attack. We must protect the one who killed the peasant. We all agreed I could tell you, because they know that one Jew survived and is under our protection."

His father, his mother, and now this group of men all knew of Chaya's presence. Jacob was alarmed that so many knew. One slip of the tongue and Chaya could be in even more danger.

"Vati, what if one of them accidentally lets something slip about Chaya's presence?"

"These men, Jacob, know how to keep a secret. I would trust every one of them with my life. No one will find out about Chaya. We might have to enlist the help of some of them when we figure out a plan for getting Chaya away safely."

"Where will Chaya be taken?"

"I'm not sure just yet, Jacob. I need to think on it some more. We will talk more about it another time. You had best return to the barn and tell Chaya the sad news. She is probably going out of her mind wondering where you have gone and why she hasn't been told any news about her family."

Jacob knew his father was right – Chaya needed to be told. He followed his father in silence back to the barn. The door creaked as they re-entered the barn. As Jacob climbed the ladder to the hayloft, his father went about extinguishing the lamps. He waited for his eyes to adjust to the dark. The door creaked as his father left.

He swallowed hard.

"Chaya."

CHAPTER 33

Business was slow in the store the day after the attack on the Jewish village. Many Norkans were not venturing far from their homes. A few braved the deserted streets of the village to get some necessities. Most who came were not looking for food or supplies. What most sought was information.

It did not take long for news to circulate through the town that all the Jews had perished, burned to death at the hands of the Russians from Rysincek.

When Liesel heard about this the first time, she was shocked. Her shock then transformed into sadness. She did not know any of the Jews personally, but hearing of how they'd died so savagely made her feel absolutely devastated.

Her sadness quickly turned to anger, then to fury. She was not furious at the perpetrators, but rather at Widow Fromm. Every person who came into the store got an earful from the Widow about how the Jews deserved everything they got. *How did the Jews deserve being burned alive? How could she talk about these people with such distain? What had they ever done to her?* Liesel doubted that Widow Fromm even knew any Jews. *How could this witch talk with such disregard for those poor unfortunate souls?*

Liesel would have liked to escape from the store and away from the ignorant prattling of Fromm, but with the attack, there were no deliveries to make. She hid in the storeroom as much as possible.

Usually, this was the day that she would go to the Henkel's for an evening meal. She could sneak out and still go, but she felt that it was not an appropriate time to make a social call. In addition, she was afraid to make the trek to the Henkel's farm alone. Rumours were circulating that the Russians might still attack Norka; rumours that were fueled in no small part by Widow Fromm, who put this fear into anyone who'd listen.

So, she endured the interminably long day. She tried to beg off supper by saying that she wanted to go to bed early, but her father refused to let her do that. Consequently, she had to suffer through more time with the Widow and her brood, picking at her food and waiting for the meal to end. She rushed to her room when the cleanup for the meal was done. The day had been mentally exhausting. It took her a long time before she finally fell asleep.

When she awoke the next morning, she was nauseous. She barely made it to the outhouse before she vomited. There was nothing in her stomach, so she just retched, bringing up some vile tasting bile. *Had the Widow poisoned her?* was her first thought. She wanted to crawl back into bed, but knew that her father would not permit it. So, she went to the breakfast table, even though the mere thought of food made her feel queasy.

Usually, she only had to put up with the Widow at suppertimes, but lately she and her brood had also intruded on all their meals. She sat at her usual spot at the table, feeling miserable.

"I don't feel well. I only want some weak tea." She directed her request to the Widow.

"You will have what I give you. I have gone to a lot of trouble to prepare this meal and you will not be rude by refusing to eat it." The Widow glared at her from the stove.

She dished food onto a plate and placed the plate none too gently in front of Liesel.

Liesel saw that her father was also glaring at her. She picked up her fork and gingerly took a few bites. Her stomach rebelled. She rushed out of the kitchen and straight to the outhouse where she vomited up what she had just ate. *The bitch was truly trying to poison her.* She retched again. Even after she had stopped vomiting, she remained in the outhouse. She did not want to return to the house until she was sure that breakfast was over. She did not want to give the Widow another chance to poison her.

Thankfully, the kitchen was empty when she returned. Although she knew that being caught (especially by her father) would mean receiving a slap, or his belt, she risked the punishment. She put on the kettle and made the weak tea that she had wanted before. As she sipped it, she felt a little better. Knowing that she could not prolong the inevitable, she went into the store.

That day, those who came in brought news that a memorial service was being organized for the Jews who had perished. The Widow, of course, had plenty to say about this. She carried on and on about how the Jews had gotten what they'd deserved, and that the people of Norka were wasting their time organizing a memorial. Liesel didn't listen too much to her diatribe, her stomach was again making her feel ill. She escaped to the outhouse once again.

In her misery, she missed her mother even more. She cried tears of frustration that she had no one whom she could lean on for help. Well, there was someone – Jacob – but she didn't know where he was. He might still be at home because of the attack, or he might be back in the forest cutting wood for his family. Liesel decided that she'd go to the Henkel farm the next day. Maybe she would be lucky enough to see Jacob, but if not, she could call on Frau Henkel. She hoped that she would be able to get another invitation to dine with them.

She was dismayed the next morning when she was sick again. Her plans to slip away to the Henkel's were thwarted by the Widow and her father, who had her making deliveries the entire day. She decided to go the next day.

That too was derailed when the Widow announced that she and her father were attending the memorial. Considering all her belligerent talk about the Jews, Liesel could not believe that the Widow wanted to attend. The Widow claimed that even though she did not like the Jews, it was 'the Christian' thing to do. Liesel suspected that the Widow had some ulterior motive for going, but she did not care to find out what it was. She was expected to take care of the store in their absence. Normally, Liesel would have welcomed the opportunity to be in the store without the Widow being present. But her presence would still be there, for Liesel was tasked with looking after her snot-nosed brats.

It was hours and hours of hell.

When her father and the Widow returned, Liesel made a discreet inquiry as to who had attended the memorial. The Widow only listed those she deemed worthy of her attention in Norka. Liesel was not sure if the Henkels had attended the service or not. The Widow, of course, felt she was far superior to the Henkels.

—◊—

The next day, Liesel had only a few deliveries. As she returned to the store, she hoped that she'd be able to slip away to the Henkel's for a few hours after lunch.

As Liesel entered the store, the bell rang. She froze in her tracks. Gunther was at the counter discussing something with Widow Fromm. Their heads were so close that they were almost touching. They stopped talking the instant they saw her standing and staring at the two of them.

Gunther smiled at her. Not a pleasant smile, but a smile like a ravenous wolf would give to a poor, unsuspecting sheep. He was still as disgusting as the last time – maybe even worse. She was some distance from him, but she could smell him. Her stomach churned in disgust.

Widow Fromm also smiled at her. Her smile was triumphant.

"Liselotte, don't stand there like a dolt. Come and greet your dear onkel Gunther." She said this in that sickly tone Liesel so detested.

Liesel forced herself to come closer to the repugnant creature.

"Hello Onkel Gunther. How are you?" She hated calling him 'Onkel'. After what he'd done to her, he didn't deserve to be called this. She resisted the urge to spit in his face. She would have to get closer to him to do that, and she wasn't getting anywhere near him if she could help it.

"You are looking as lovely as ever, Liesel. In fact, I'd say you have a special glow about you."

Liesel hated every word that came out of his mouth. She had to remain polite, even though she wanted to scratch his eyes out.

"Thank you, Onkel."

"We were discussing important business. Leave us Liselotte."

For once, Liesel was grateful to Widow Fromm for her dismissive nature. She fled to the storeroom. She could not get away from Gunther fast enough. She wondered what important business the two of them had to discuss. She busied herself in the storeroom, trying her best to erase the image of Gunther devouring her with his eyes. She did not notice that the Widow was at the doorway watching her until she spoke, startling her.

"Come into the store, Liselotte – NOW." The Widow used her imperious tone, making it clear to Liesel that she must obey at once. Liesel had a bad feeling.

The Widow did not beat around the bush, getting right to the heart of the matter.

"Your Onkel Gunther has taken quite a shine to you. He has said that he wants to marry you."

The Widow's words hit her like a punch to the stomach. But before she could recover from this shocking announcement, the Widow delivered more blows.

"He has told me how you threw yourself at him. You shameless hussy. And now you have gotten yourself in a family way. No man in Norka will have you if word gets out about what you have done. You are damn lucky that I was able to convince Gunther that marrying you was for the best. You owe that man and ME everything. Your father will be heartbroken, but I will be able to convince him it is for the best."

Liesel's head was reeling. *She had not thrown herself at Gunther – he was the one who'd raped her. And the family way . . . oh God.* Liesel thought about her sickness in the mornings, realizing with devastation that she had not got her monthlies. *Not since . . . not since. Oh my God, she was pregnant and carrying the monster's child.* The Widow continued to rail at her, but the buzzing in her ears drowned out the bitch's voice. *What was she going to do?*

She noticed that the Widow's mouth had stopped moving. From her expression, Liesel could tell that she expected Liesel to say something. But there was nothing to say. She fled from the store, running through the streets of Norka. She did not know where she was going, nor did she care.

She had nowhere to go to escape what had befallen her.

CHAPTER 34

Chaya could not remember much from the night that Jacob had come to her with the news of her family's death. She remembered shrieking. But nothing after that.

Not that she wanted to remember everything. She wished she could just crawl into a hole and die. Then she would be with the rest of them. The main reason she could not do this was because of her duty. There was only herself to sit shiva for her loved ones. She had to do that for them, no matter how painful every second she continued to live was.

She fingered the cut on her blouse. She did not remember doing that. It was just another thing of which she had a vague recollection.

Jacob was doing his best to comfort her, but she needed him constantly and he was not able to be there with her – it was just too dangerous. She had to remain hidden in the hayloft while Jacob and his family had to appear to carry on as normal. She knew that Jacob's father was formulating a plan to get her away from Norka, but neither he nor Jacob had shared it with her. When Jacob had mentioned that she would be safe where she was for the time being, she had pressed him about what was going to happen to her. He shared what he knew (which was not much), but it was clear that she'd eventually be taken somewhere else. Chaya made it known to Jacob that she was not going anywhere until she had finished sitting shiva. It was not negotiable. She assumed Jacob relayed this to his father.

She spent most of her time alone in the hayloft. Jacob's mother brought her food and water secretly every day. She saw Jacob only late at night. However, it was always dark, as lighting a lantern would arouse suspicion. He would empty the bucket she used for her bodily functions. Then he would talk to her quietly as she paced the barn in the dark. She wished she could go outside and walk around, but even in the dead of the night it was deemed unsafe.

She was grateful for Jacob's visits. Even with her world in shambles, she felt his love and his strength. He helped her get through each moment, even when he wasn't with her. It was hard, but she endured as best as she could.

Sometimes it was too much, and she'd break down and cry until she felt her heart would explode from the sorrow. Jacob would just hold her and whisper over and over that he loved her. She would eventually fall into an exhausted sleep in his arms. She would wake in the early dawn light, feeling his arms still around her. She wished they could stay that way forever – but he would stir and she would know that he'd have to leave. Once awake, he would kiss her, then they'd go down to the barn once more so that Chaya could relieve herself and pace about before it was milking time. She would climb the ladder alone, and then she'd listen as Jacob brought the cows into the barn to milk them.

He would leave after milking, calling up softly from below that he loved her. The creak of the door signalled that he had left for the day.

She would spend her day doing as she was required, sitting shiva and remembering those who'd passed. It was hard doing it alone. No one was there to support her in her time of grief, so the remembering was hard, so hard. She saw her abba's smiling face. She remembered the twinkle in his eye when he said her name. Her mother rarely smiled. But when she did smile, she had a smile that lit up a room. Her mother had been stern, yes, but that was her way to show you just how much she loved you. Chaya was ashamed, for she really missed her mother more than her father. She had never truly appreciated her mother until she was gone. Now it was too late to tell her how much she meant to her. And that she loved her. Her memories of her brother Herschel were mixed; some made her laugh; others made her cry. Sometimes, she'd remember some of the antics they got up to when they were younger. They had so much fun. Then she would remember that her dear sweet brother would miss out on so many things in life, and that brought on the tears again. He'd never have his first kiss, a girlfriend, a wife, children. So many things. Her poor brother.

Chaya not only sat shiva for her family, but she also did it for every member of her shtetl. She was the only one that survived, and this weighed heavily on her. She could not understand why God had spared her while condemning the rest to the flames. She rallied against God on this point. Her faith was shaken to the core. How could God have allowed this? She considered turning against her religion. She stood on the precipice, but she could not jump. It was who she was, and more importantly, turning her back on her faith would not help her loved ones. They were born Jews and they died Jews. It was up to her to remember them – there was nobody else.

Something else weighed very heavily on her heart. Something that she did not share with Jacob. Something that she knew was going to happen. There was no stopping the inevitable – she would have to leave here and never return. Where she would go, she didn't know. She would have to leave her family and the people of the shtetl behind. And worst of all, she would have to leave Jacob. She was no longer betrothed to Nicholas Steiner, but nothing else had changed. She still could not be with Jacob. A marriage between a Jew and a gentile just was not possible. The same desperate situation still existed, except now she no longer had her family for love and support. Soon she would be losing the only one she still had left who could give her that. *Why was life so cruel?*

Jacob told her that his church had organized a memorial service for the Jews of her shtetl. She could not attend it of course, but she did feel grateful that there were people aside from herself remembering those who were lost.

When Jacob described the memorial to her, he told her that there were many in attendance who were visibly upset. He was surprised that the majority were farmers like his father. Chaya suspected that these men were the ones tasked with secretly selling the shtetl's grain. They would have dealt with the men from her shtetl. Maybe some had even dealt with her father. Thinking of her father brought another wave of sadness.

She felt like crying again, but she forced herself to be strong. She wanted to talk to Jacob about what was on her mind without being an emotional wreck.

"Jacob, where will I go?"

Jacob knew that soon Chaya would have to go away, for there was no other option. His father had not yet indicated when she'd have to leave, and where she would be going. His father was respecting Chaya's need to mourn her loved ones, but Jacob sensed that his father had already worked out a plan. A plan that he wasn't yet privy to.

"I don't know," he answered her truthfully. "I understand that it is worrying you, Chaya, but we will have to trust that God will guide us to help you to be safe."

"I only feel truly safe when I am in your arms, Jacob."

Jacob pulled her closer, trying to comfort her and to let her know that he would keep her safe. He sought her lips in the dark and he kissed her, conveying his love to her.

Jacob's kiss sent tingles down her spine. She kissed him back passionately.

Their kissing became more passionate and intense. Soon they were tearing off their clothes. This time, neither tried to stop what they had stopped before. They gave themselves to each other. As they consummated their love, two bodies, two hearts, and two souls, became one.

CHAPTER 35

Liesel decided to slip away from the store while the Widow and her father were distracted with customers. She hurried towards the Henkel farm. The night that she usually had supper with the family was in two days, but she had yet to receive an invitation. Liesel was also hoping to see Jacob. She hadn't seen him in some time, and she needed to see him to assure herself that he was missing her as well.

She knocked on the Henkel's farmhouse door, but no one came to answer her knock. No one seemed to be around. She thought that maybe Frau Henkel was in the garden. She was making her way there when Frau Henkel emerged from the barn. When she saw Liesel, she jumped as if someone had frightened her.

"Good day, Frau Henkel. I did not mean to scare you. I knocked on the farmhouse door, but no one answered. How are you, Frau Henkel?"

"Liesel, you did give me a fright. I am sorry but I am very busy today. I'm sorry but I cannot stop for a visit."

"Maybe I can help you, Frau Henkel."

"No Liesel, that is quite all right. I'm sure that they need you at the store."

Liesel found Frau Henkel's behaviour very strange. She had never refused Liesel's help before. She seemed very agitated and not her usual pleasant self. Liesel also felt that Frau Henkel wanted to get rid of her, which was unusual. She was being rather standoffish, which Liesel thought was also very out of character for her.

"Are you sure everything is alright, Frau Henkel?"

"Yes Liesel." *Again with that tone.* "Is there anything else? As I said, I am very busy."

Liesel thought of an excuse for why she had come.

"I was hoping you had some milk to spare. I wanted to try to make cheese like you taught me."

"I have no milk to spare, Liesel. I will have some tomorrow morning after Jacob does the milking."

"I will come by and get some then. It would be good to see Jacob again."

"No Liesel. That will not be necessary. I will have someone bring it to you at the store." Liesel noted that Frau Henkel's response almost had a note of panic to it. *What was going on? Was she trying deliberately to keep her and Jacob apart? She had been her staunchest ally, now it seemed like she wanted nothing to do with her.* Liesel felt hurt. *Maybe Jacob could clear up why his mother's attitude towards her had changed.*

"Is Jacob here?"

"Jacob is busy in the forest cutting wood for the family. Now Liesel, I really must say goodbye." She hurried to the farmhouse and slammed the door before Liesel could say anything else.

Liesel stared at the door, wondering what she had done. She could do as Frau Henkel had suggested and return to the store, but she had to see Jacob. She was just not sure where she would find him.

His mother had said he was cutting wood in the forest. She ruled out that he would be in the Kosakenwald. It was too dangerous to be there alone due to the bandits. That left the woods either to the north or to the south of town. The northern woods were closer to Rysincek and the destroyed Jewish village. She decided that the southern one was the safer one, and it was where she would find Jacob.

However, she searched the southern woods and could not find Jacob. That left only the northern woods.

She had only been in those woods for fifteen minutes when she heard the unmistakeable sound of an axe hitting wood. She followed the sound. She was still in the cover of the forest when she saw Jacob swinging an axe. She did not let him know that she was there. She just watched him work. His shirt was off and sweat glistened on his body as he attacked the tree. Liesel admired his body. His muscles rippled as he swung the axe. Liesel felt a stirring within her as she watched him work.

He loved her and she loved him. A plan began to form in her mind. A plan that could save her.

She stepped out from the forest. Jacob did not see her yet. She continued to admire his body.

"Jacob." He continued to swing the axe. He must not have heard her. "Jacob." She said his name louder this time. He stopped.

—m—

Jacob was enjoying watching the chips fly off the tree trunk he was attacking. The tree was taking the brunt of his frustrations. Even though he and Chaya had made love, it still did not change anything. They still could not be together. In fact, making love made things more complicated. How could he let her go now? He swung his axe again and again in frustration.

He had just landed a heavy blow when he heard his name. He looked around and was surprised to see Liesel.

"Liesel, what are you doing here?"

"I needed to talk to you, Jacob. I stopped at the farm and your mother said you were here."

"My mother said I was here?" Jacob was doubtful that his mother had said such a thing, but maybe she had, for here was Liesel standing in front of him. "Why do you need to talk to me?"

"Jacob, I need your help."

"What kind of help do you need, Liesel? I am very busy right now. Maybe we can meet at a later time and you can tell me all about your troubles."

Jacob was trying to brush her off just as his mother had. What was going on? She abandoned the plan she had made. There was only one thing that she was sure would get Jacob to stop and listen to her: tears. She let out a cry of anguish and started crying. It worked. Jacob rushed to her, took her in his arms and tried to console her. She could smell his sweat. She became aroused by his touch. As he held her, she caressed his shoulder. He did not pull away.

Liesel's tears had taken him by surprise. He could tell that something was upsetting her, but she was sobbing so much that he wasn't sure what was causing her distress. All he could do was hold her and soothe her until she could get control of her emotions. Her sobs eventually subsided until she was just hiccupping. She looked at him with tear-stained eyes. He felt so bad for her. A stray tear coursed down her face. He wiped the tear with his thumb and gave her a smile, conveying to her that everything would be okay.

When Jacob smiled at her and wiped her tear away with such tenderness, Liesel knew that he loved her. She sought his lips and kissed him.

Jacob had not expected the kiss. Liesel was so vulnerable. He did not return her kiss. He pulled away from her gently. He did not want to make her feel worse. She was lonely and obviously in distress. She had kissed him on impulse. He failed to see that the kiss meant something more to her.

"Liesel, what are you doing?"

Jacob pulling away did not deter her. He was just surprised by her advances, that was all. The love in his voice told her he wanted her as much as she wanted him. She started to unbutton her blouse.

When Liesel started to unbutton her blouse, Jacob knew she had misinterpreted his concern and compassion for something else. He had to stop this before it went any further. He should have been brusque and forthright with her, but he held back, worrying yet again about her fragile state and her feelings.

"Liesel, stop. Not here and not now. You are in a vulnerable state and it is best to stop this right now. It would be best if you go."

Liesel was confused that Jacob wanted to stop. But from his look, she could see he did not want this to go any further. Liesel fumbled with her buttons and fled from the forest. At first, she was humiliated. Then, as she thought more about what Jacob had said, she saw a glimmer of hope. He had said they could not make love there because of her vulnerable state. He had not said that they could never make love. He was being a gentleman and did not want to take advantage of her if she was distraught. That was one of the many things that she loved about Jacob. He was so chivalrous, which worked perfectly with her plan. Once Jacob slept with her, his chivalrous nature would compel him to do the right thing and marry her. Gunther and the Widow's plans could go to hell when she became Jacob's wife.

Jacob had refused to sleep with her this time, but next time he would surely not refuse her. She already knew when she would see him next. Soon she would be free of the miserable turn her life had taken.

—⚇—

As soon as she stepped foot in the store, the Widow questioned her.

"Where have you been?" she demanded.

She would have loved to tell the old witch off, but knew that if she did then her father would hear of it.

"I was out."

"Out where?"

Why did the old witch have to be so nosy? "I was out on some errands."

"Don't lie to me, you hussy. If you are going to whore around, at least have the decency to make yourself presentable before you come where people can see your wanton ways." The Widow pointed at her blouse.

Liesel looked down and saw that she had buttoned her blouse incorrectly. The Widow assumed she had misbuttoned it hurriedly after an illicit assignation. Liesel would not admit to anything the Widow claimed, true or contrived.

"Might I remind you, you little hussy, that Gunther has agreed to make an honest woman of you. You cannot be running around opening up your legs to half the town."

The Widow was goading her. She did not say anything in response to her accusations. This obviously aggravated the Widow, which gave her a small bit of satisfaction.

"Maybe I should talk to Gunther." Liesel flashed her a defiant look.

A look of surprise crossed the Widow's face. "So, you were with Gunther just now. Well, you have fancied him all along. I guess I didn't have to arrange your meeting."

Liesel swallowed in disgust when the Widow intimated that she fancied Gunther – that disgusting pig. However, what shocked her the most was that final thing the Widow said.

"What do you mean you arranged our meeting?"

The Widow instantly went red. "Shut up. I meant nothing. Now quit wasting time. You have shelves to stock. Get to it right now before I tell your father that you left for so long to engage in your dalliance."

Liesel wanted to pursue the matter further, but knew it was pointless. The Widow had obviously let something slip that she had not intended. The witch would never admit she had done anything wrong. Liesel stocked the shelves and railed at the old bitch inside her head.

Only when she was alone in her room that night did she have time to think about what the Widow had meant. She had revealed that she had engineered the meeting between Gunther and her on that fateful day. *Had she sent her to Gunther knowing that he would rape her? Had Gunther also been in on her plan?* When she saw them together in the store, she remembered that they had looked as thick as thieves. She was now sure that both were working together. The Widow was using Gunther to get rid of her. Once she was gone, the Widow could marry her father and move into her mother's home with her snot-nosed brood.

As for Gunther, he would have a young wife that he could rape to his heart's content. Liesel knew that it was a death sentence. The more she thought about it, she started to wonder about her godmother Tante Greta's death. *How had she died exactly?* If her mother were still alive, she would have asked her. Her father might know, but she feared his reaction if she brought it up. She pushed aside her suspicions. Tomorrow, she would be intimate with Jacob. Then everyone – the Widow, Gunther, even her father – could all go to hell. She fell asleep thinking of Jacob smiling at her.

CHAPTER 36

Jacob felt conflicted. He still was not sure why Liesel had kissed him. She obviously felt something more for him than friendship. He wasn't sure where she'd gotten the idea that he also felt the same way. His heart belonged solely to Chaya. He struggled with whether he should tell Chaya about what had occurred with Liesel in the forest.

He was glad that when he joined her in the hayloft, she couldn't see his face in the dark. *Would she see his guilt?* He wasn't the one who'd instigated what happened in the forest; it was Liesel who'd sought him out and made advances towards him. Still, he felt guilty . . .

Chaya sensed that something was wrong with Jacob. They made love again, but she felt like he was holding back this time. She was not sure exactly what had changed. Maybe it was something she was doing, or not doing. Afterwards, neither of them said much. They fell asleep shortly after, but Jacob's sleep was restless. He kept tossing and turning, causing her to wake each time. She finally fell into a deep sleep.

She awoke with a start. She reached out to where Jacob had been only to find an empty space. She felt the hay – it was cold. He had been gone for a while. Chaya peered around. The small window in the loft showed that the dark sky was gradually lightening. *Why had Jacob left? And why hadn't he woken her so she could relieve herself and walk around in the barn before the morning's milking?*

"Jacob?" she whispered, hoping he was nearby. She waited for him to reply, but he did not. She crawled to the ladder – maybe he was in the barn. She made her way carefully down the ladder. "Jacob?" she whispered again once she reached the bottom.

"Over here," came his whispered reply.

She walked over to where Jacob was. He was lying on a bed of straw with a horse blanket thrown over it.

"Why are you here, Jacob?"

"I was disturbing your sleep. I decided to sleep down here."

"What's wrong, Jacob? You haven't been yourself. All you did was toss and turn all night."

"I'm sorry Chaya, it's just . . . it's just . . ."

"It's just what? Tell me Jacob. It is just what?"

"I feel guilty, that's all."

"Guilty about what?"

"Chaya, just know that I love you and only you. You own my heart and my soul. You are my bashert. Never doubt that."

Jacob's words were starting to scare her.

"I love you too, Jacob. You can tell me anything." She tried to keep the fear out of her voice, but could not. Her voice quivered.

Jacob told Chaya all that occurred in the forest with Liesel.

Liesel, that was the girl who had come to the farm yesterday. Chaya had heard her talking to Jacob's mother. She had also heard her ask Jacob's mother about Jacob himself. She had not thought much about their conversation – until now. It was obvious the girl had her eye on Jacob. The ugly head of jealousy reared up inside of her.

"She obviously has feelings for you, Jacob. Maybe you feel the same way?" Chaya had unintentionally raised her voice. "Well Jacob, do you?"

"I have never encouraged her in any way. I have only treated her as a friend. I felt sorry for her because she seemed so alone after her mother died. All I was doing was showing her kindness."

Chaya should have accepted Jacob's explanation, but she felt threatened by this Liesel, even though she had never met her, and had only heard her talking once. "Maybe somewhere deep down you want to be with her, Jacob, because you know . . . you know that she can give you what we can never have. You can love her and marry her and have children with her because she is not a Jew. All those things are possible with her, but will never be with me."

"Chaya, you are the one I love, not her. It is you whom I want as my wife and the mother of my children. It is you, Chaya, and only you. Liesel means nothing to me. Nothing, I promise."

A sound came from outside the barn. Both froze. In the heat of their arguing, they had forgotten to keep their voices lowered. Now someone had heard them.

"Up into the loft quickly." Jacob ushered Chaya towards the ladder. They hurried up to the hayloft and then lay down on the hay, slightly panting. They both listened intently, waiting to see if they heard any more sounds, but they heard nothing.

"I'm going to see if I can figure out what made the noise. I will be right back." Jacob crawled over to the ladder and made his way cautiously down it. He crept across the barn. He tried to open the door as quietly as possible, but it still let out a soft creak. He looked around the farmyard – it was empty. Or so he thought it was, until he saw the pail lying on its side. *Why was the pail there?* He looked beyond the farmyard, and that was when he saw a figure in the distance, hurrying away from the farm. The pre-dawn light made it impossible to see who it was. Jacob rushed back into the barn.

"Chaya!" he whispered from the bottom of the ladder. "Chaya!" Her head appeared above him. "Someone was in the yard. I am going after them to see who they are. Stay there and be completely quiet. I will be back as soon as I can."

Jacob ran out of the barn, closing the door quickly and not caring about the noise it made. The figure was now a great distance away. He ran after them.

—⁕—

Liesel had decided that she would meet Jacob in his barn before the morning's milking. It would be early in the morning so there would not be anyone else around, she'd concluded. Plus, the hayloft in the barn would be the perfect place to do what they had not done in the forest. Jacob the gentleman had not wanted to take her on the forest floor. She was sure that he would not object to making love on the soft hay.

It was still dark when Liesel snuck out of her bedroom window. She had snuck a pail into her bedroom the night before without anyone seeing. She was sure that she was not going to need it, but it was good to have it with her just in case she ran into Jacob's mother.

She pulled a shawl over her head. All of Norka was asleep, but she still had to be careful. Someone might be using the outhouse and recognize her. Liesel did not want the Widow to have any knowledge of what she was doing.

Liesel kept to the shadows. She heard someone closing a door, but she could not see anyone. She assumed it was the door of an outhouse. The first streaks of dawn were appearing as she entered the Henkel's farmyard. The farmhouse was still dark, so she knew she could slip into the barn and surprise Jacob.

She was about to open the barn door when she heard voices coming from inside. She froze and listened; one of the voices was Jacob's, the other voice was that of a woman. It was not one of his sisters, for she knew all of their voices. *So, who was he talking to?*

As Liesel listened, she realized that Jacob and the woman were not talking – they were arguing. It was not what they were arguing about that caused her to hitch her breath, but who.

They were arguing about her.

The woman was obviously jealous, for she was questioning Jacob's affection for her, Liesel. *Who was this woman?*

Liesel was shocked when she heard Jacob say that he was only nice to her because of her mother's death. *Why was Jacob saying this? He loved her!* Liesel couldn't understand why Jacob was saying these hurtful words.

Liesel could have forgiven Jacob for those words, for she loved him. But what he said next changed everything. He told the woman that he loved her and only her, which shattered Liesel's heart. He told the woman that Liesel was nothing to him. *NOTHING!*

Liesel's world crumbled around her. She threw the pail onto the ground and ran from the farmyard.

Liesel was furious. The hope that she had been clinging to, the hope that her life was about to change for the better, had evaporated. Jacob, the only one who loved her . . . didn't really love her. It was all that woman's fault.

The woman had obviously poisoned Jacob's mind and his heart. She hated the woman with every fiber of her being. If she couldn't have Jacob, then neither could the woman.

While they were arguing, she had heard the woman say that she was a Jew. *She must be a survivor from the village,* Liesel concluded. *Jacob was protecting her, and she must have bewitched him.*

She hurried her pace. She knew what she had to do to set things right.

CHAPTER 37

The mysterious figure had too much of a head start for Jacob to catch up to them. He was only able to keep the figure in sight by sprinting. It was a woman. He could tell that because he could make out that the figure was wearing a dress. He could not see much else because the woman had something draped over her head and shoulders.

Jacob had thought at first that the woman might be heading to Norka, but she was heading north instead of east. The only thing to the north was Rysincek. *The woman was heading to the Russian village – but why?*

When he arrived at the Russian village, the woman had disappeared. She could not have vanished into thin air, so he deduced that she had obviously entered one of their dwellings. But Jacob had no idea which one.

He walked down the village's main street. A few of the houses had light spilling out of their windows as the occupants got up and started their day.

Jacob was about to knock on the door of one such dwelling when he saw the figure emerge from another house further up the street. The figure headed back the way they had come.

This time, Jacob knew he could catch up to the mystery woman.

He caught up to her at the edge of the village. He grabbed her arm and spun her around. He was shocked to see it was Liesel.

"Liesel, what are you doing here?"

"I thought you loved me, Jacob. I heard you. You said I was nothing." Liesel's voice quivered. "Why couldn't you have just loved me? I came to set things right, Jacob."

"What do you mean set things right, Liesel?"

"If I can't have you . . . then neither can she. I came here, Jacob, to tell the Russians that you are hiding a Jew."

Jacob was stunned for a moment. Liesel, who he thought of as a friend, had done the unspeakable, because she believed that he loved her. And her confused feelings had put Chaya in harm's way.

Jacob no longer felt sorry for Liesel. There was no excuse for what she had done.

"You make me sick, Liesel. I rue the day that I showed you any kindness. I wish you'd never been born. Do you even understand what you have done? All of Norka is in danger because of you," Jacob yelled at her. "The Russians will do your dirty work – BUT YOU WILL HAVE KILLED HER!"

Jacob ran off.

Jacob's words hurt her deeply, but it was his look that hurt the most. His look was one of utter contempt and disgust. It finally sank in, what she had done. And worse than that, the person she had become. Jacob's words were true.

Tears streamed down her face. *She was despicable. She was so many vile things. Her life was pitiful. She had no one and nothing. How could she make things right?* She decided to seek solace with the only person she knew who would not judge her for her actions, and who would love her no matter what.

—⁂—

Jacob headed to the fields. His father and brothers had returned to them after the threat of the Russian attack had subsided.

He arrived breathless just as his father and brothers were emerging from the hut they slept in while tending the fields. His father took one look at him and knew instantly that something was wrong.

"What's happened, Jacob?"

"It's Chaya . . ." he gasped for air.

"Who's Chaya?" his brother Karl asked.

In his agitated state, Jacob forgot that only himself, his father, and his mother knew about Chaya hiding in their barn. As he continued to gasp for air, his father briefly told his brothers about who Chaya was and where she was hiding. When his breathing became more even, Jacob told his father and brothers that Liesel had learned about Chaya hiding in the barn, and that she had told someone in Rysincek about it.

"What are we going to do Vati?"

"We must get Chaya to safety. But we have to plan it carefully."

"Do you think the Russians will come looking for her at our farm?"

"It is possible. Karl, go to Rysincek and observe what is going on. Stay out of sight. If they look like they are organizing something, then I want you to get home as quickly as possible and warn Jacob."

"Yes Vati." His brother ran off towards Rysincek.

"Jacob, I want you to go and stay with Chaya. If Karl comes or something else happens, I want you to get Chaya away from the farm. Take her to the Gruen's and hide out in their barn. I know that their farm isn't too far from our own, but it will buy us some time. Once it gets dark, we will have to get Chaya out of Norka. Ernst, go with Jacob. Gather all of the family into the house and stand guard until I get home."

"Where are you going, Vati?"

"I need to make arrangements with others who can help us get Chaya away. I will be home as soon as possible."

Jacob and his brother ran towards their farm. Jacob was exhausted from all the running that he had already done, and he started to lag. He urged his brother to press on to get home quickly. Jacob wished he could keep up with his brother's pace, but all he could muster was a brisk walk.

When he finally arrived at the farmyard, he went directly to the barn. He ignored the lowing cows as he opened the door. Manfred must have brought the cows in while he was gone. The milking would just have to wait. He had to tell Chaya what had happened.

He climbed the ladder and found her sitting on the hay with her arms wrapped around her knees.

"I'm sorry, Chaya, for being away for so long . . . but it was necessary."

Chaya could tell from Jacob's body language that something was very wrong.

"What is it, Jacob? What is happening? You were gone so long? What was that noise?"

"I'm sorry, Chaya, but someone has discovered that you are here."

"Who, Jacob? Who knows that I am here?"

"Liesel. She heard us arguing. She knows you are here and that you are a Jew."

Chaya felt very vulnerable. "Did you tell her why you are hiding me?"

"It's more complicated than that, Chaya." Jacob felt guilty for the thing he had to tell her next, but she deserved the truth.

"She believes that she is in love with me. I set her straight on the fact that I have no such feelings for her. However, . . . I did not reach her in time before . . . before . . ."

"Before what?"

"Before she had time to tell the Russians that you are here."

Chaya gasped. Now that the Russians knew she was here, she was as good as dead. Jacob's family would also be in danger because they had harboured her.

"I have to leave, Jacob."

"I know." Jacob couldn't keep his voice from breaking as he confirmed what Chaya had said.

"Where will I go, Jacob?"

"I don't know, Chaya. My father is making the arrangements right now. My brother Karl is watching the Russian village to see what they are going to do. We will have to wait here until dark, then you will be taken out of Norka. If we have to flee before dark, I will take you to a neighbour's barn."

"Jacob, I'm scared."

"I know Chaya, I know."

"I'm not scared for myself, Jacob, I'm scared for your family. What will the Russians do to your family because you harboured a Jew?"

"My brother Ernst is keeping watch. The Russians would be pretty stupid to come here looking for trouble." He tried to sound confident to comfort Chaya. The truth was, if the Russians attacked, Ernst and his single rifle would be quickly overwhelmed. "I will protect you Chaya . . . with my life."

Jacob's presence comforted her, but her mind was in a turmoil worrying about what was to come. Even if they successfully got her away from here, her life without Jacob was not a life. *Maybe it would have been better if she'd died with the rest of her family.*

True to his word, Jacob stayed and comforted her. He only left her for a short time to attend to the protesting cows.

The time seemed to drag on. Both jumped at the slightest noise. Jacob was especially agitated when his father had not yet returned to the farm – and neither had Karl.

His mother appeared at lunchtime with food for them. She was accompanied by Ernst who kept a watchful eye, his rifle at the ready. Neither had eaten all day, but both of their stomachs were upset, so they only picked at the food.

It was mid-afternoon before they heard the door creak again. Jacob peered down from the loft and was relieved to see his father. Karl was also there.

"Come Jacob," his father instructed. "And bring Chaya too."

When they were all standing in the barn, Jacob introduced Chaya to Karl. Karl told him and Chaya about everything he'd observed in Rysincek.

The Russians had gathered in their village square and spent hours debating what to do about the Jew discovered in Norka. None of them had the stomach to come to the farm and do what they had done at the Jews' village. The debate centered around what they were going to do instead. After much arguing, they finally agreed that they would inform the Governor in Saratov. Then the debate began all over again as they tried to elect someone to do this task. One poor fellow was chosen, but flatly refused to go alone because of his fear about being attacked by bandits in the Kosakenwald. More discussions and arguments occurred until they finally convinced three other farmers to accompany the chosen one. It took them another hour to hitch up their horses to the four wagons that were making the trip. The wagons had left just over half an hour ago.

Jacob was grateful that the Russians were so disorganized. Travelling at a snail's pace, they would be lucky to make Saratov by dark. *Would the Governor even receive them at such a late hour?* Jacob hoped not. That would give them even more time before someone came looking for Chaya. The more time they had to get Chaya away, the better.

Jacob's father then outlined the plan for Chaya's escape. When it turned dark, four wagons would arrive at the farm. Each wagon would travel in a different direction, journeying to four different settlements. Chaya would be taken to one of the villages and be hidden there for the day. The next night, she'd be spirited away to another village. She would be moved like that until they could get her to one of the villages on the Volga. Then she would be smuggled onto a boat and taken to the Black Sea. From there she would be taken overland to a village of her people within the Pale of Settlement.

"Why not just take her to the Volga tonight, Vati?" Jacob asked.

"That is the first place the Russians will search. We must be at least three steps ahead of them. Our route, though more circuitous, is the safest for Chaya."

Jacob could see that his father's plan had merit. Although he was worried about Chaya on this journey, he didn't say anything to his father. He wanted to speak with Chaya first – alone.

There were still many hours before it would be dark enough for Chaya to be spirited away. His father told Chaya that she should rest as much as possible in the next few hours, because her trip was going to be long and arduous. When his father and brother had left the barn, Jacob suggested to Chaya that they should return to the hayloft.

"Chaya, I'm going with you. The journey will not be an easy one. There will be many dangers. I cannot let you go alone."

Chaya was touched by Jacob's love and concern for her well-being, but she couldn't ask him to do such a thing, even though she wanted him to accompany her as well. Her presence in their barn had already put him and his family in danger. She would never forgive herself if something happened to him or his family because of her.

"No Jacob. You cannot come with me. I have already put both you and your family in so much danger. I must go alone, although it will break my heart to say goodbye to you forever."

"There will be no goodbyes until I deliver you to safety."

"Jacob, no."

"I am not going to change my mind. I am going with you and that is final. Now we should do as my father suggested and rest. It will be a long night for both of us."

Jacob kissed her and then settled down in the hay. Chaya knew it was pointless to try and convince Jacob to change his mind. He was stubborn like her abba. Her abba – the thought of him did not bring a tear, nor a smile. She wondered what he would think of Jacob accompanying her on this journey. Would he be grateful that Jacob was there to help protect her, or would he disapprove because Jacob was not of the faith? Chaya wasn't sure how he'd feel – so much had happened in the last few days and her head was spinning.

Before she settled down to lie beside Jacob and get some rest, she recited the Kaddish for her family as well as for the members of her shtetl one last time. She had not completed her shiva. Would God understand why she had to break shiva? She resolved that each day, no matter where she was, she would say Kaddish for the dead. She hoped that God would understand.

She did not think she would sleep, but once she closed her eyes, sleep came quickly.

—∿—

"Chaya, wake up."

Chaya opened her eyes. She could see that the light of the day was fading. It would not be long now before she and Jacob had to leave. She gazed at the man she loved and kissed him as a way of telling him that she was ready.

Not long after, they heard the barn door creak.

"Does that mean that the cows are being brought in to be milked, Jacob?"

Jacob laughed. "The cows have already been milked. I did it over an hour ago. You were obviously exhausted if you didn't hear that."

"I hadn't realized."

"We should go down. It's almost time."

As they descended the ladder, they saw Jacob's father in the barn.

"The wagons should be arriving in an hour. Did you get some rest, Chaya?"

"Yes, Herr Henkel, I slept so soundly that I didn't hear Jacob doing the afternoon milking."

"That is good, Chaya, it will be a long night for you."

"Vati, I am going with Chaya."

"Jacob, that isn't possible. If the Governor discovers you missing, he might guess correctly that you were with Chaya. No Jacob, you cannot go."

"The journey will be dangerous. I need to go to protect Chaya and to make sure that she gets to safety."

"NO!"

"Vati, if Heidi were to go on such a perilous journey, would you want her to go alone, unprotected and at the mercy of others? As a father, would you want your daughter to be exposed to dangers that could threaten her life or her virtue? If things were reversed and Chaya's family was hiding Heidi, would you want her father to send her on such a journey without protection?"

Jacob could see that his father was reconsidering his firm no. Jacob felt him wavering. Jacob continued.

"Once I see Chaya to safety, I will return home – that I promise you. Please Vati, let me do this."

"What of the Governor? He is shrewd. How will we explain your absence?"

The barn door creaked open. The three of them jumped as they hadn't been expecting anyone to come for another hour. What was even more shocking was who had entered the barn – Liesel.

"Liesel, what the hell are you doing here?" Jacob was angry as soon as he saw Liesel. "Have you come to gloat over your treachery?"

Jacob's words stung. Liesel ignored the hurt his words had caused within her. "No Jacob, I have not come to gloat. I have come to tell you all that there is another way."

"Nothing you say can change what you have done. Look at the woman whom you have condemned to death. Her blood is on your hands."

"Jacob! These are not the words a son of mine speaks. Liesel has done wrong, but she needs our forgiveness, not our condemnation."

Liesel looked at Herr Henkel.

"I do not deserve forgiveness. Nor do I ask for it. I can only do one thing, one thing that will set everything right. You just have to listen to what I have to say."

CHAPTER 38

After Jacob broke her heart and told her how disgusted he was at her behaviour, Liesel fled to the only person who truly loved her. She ran to the cemetery and poured out her heart and soul to her mother.

As she told her mother of her unrequited love, she cried and cried. She felt as if her heart would explode at any moment. In fact, she wished it just would. Then she would be dead and her poor miserable life would be over. Maybe she could join her mother in Heaven, although she doubted whether she would be reunited with her, considering her recent actions.

Where had it all gone wrong? Could she blame everything on Widow Fromm? That was the easy solution, but it was not the truth. The woman she despised had indeed had a large hand in her life's downward turn, but Liesel had made decisions and done things herself that were not unlike what the Widow had done.

She had schemed to try and get Jacob to make love to her so that he would be forced to marry her. And if that was not bad enough, she had planned to deceive him into believing that the bastard she was carrying in her womb was his when it was not. She had deluded herself into thinking that all of that manipulating and lying was justifiable because of what had happened to her. Her plan was disgusting, and it made her disgusted with herself. This was not who she truly was. She was sweet and kind and considerate, and people loved her – well, they had loved her. *Who could love this monster that she'd become?*

A monster who, in a fit of rage and jealousy, denounced a person she did not know and who had never done anything to her. Just because the person was a Jew. Liesel had committed the same kind of narrow-minded thinking that she despised the Widow for. A monster indeed.

What a mess.

She cried until she had no more tears. She lay across her mother's grave, willing herself to die.

But she did not die. She fell into an exhausted sleep.

—⁓—

Her mother appeared in her dream. Liesel ran towards her, but no matter how much Liesel ran, she never reached her mother. She even yelled for her mother to come to her, but her mother just shook her head sadly.

"Mutti, talk to me." But her mother just shook her head again. "Mutti, tell me what to do?" When Liesel said these words, her mother turned and moved even further away. "Mutti, please don't go." She screamed. Her mother stopped and looked back at her. Then she turned and walked away, quickly fading into nothing. "No Mutti," she cried. "Don't leave me. Come back."

Her crying in her dream caused her to awaken. She broke into sobs once more. Her mother had left her, but the thing that hurt her the most was her mother's last look. Where there was once love in her eyes, Liesel saw only sadness and disappointment. This was harder to take than Jacob's rebuffing of her love. She had lost her mother's love as well.

She swiped her hand across her eyes, wiping the tears away. She sat up straight and took many deep breaths to calm herself. When she was composed, she got up and brushed the grass from her dress.

"I know what to do, Mutti." She directed this comment to her mother's grave. "I know how to get your love back, Mutti. I am sorry that I disappointed you, Mutti, but I will make it up to you. I promise. I must go now. I will make you proud, Mutti. I love you."

She touched her fingers to her lips and then touched them to her mother's headstone. Then she turned and left the cemetery. She had to make her mother proud. She just hoped that it was not already too late.

She kept to the back streets of Norka as she made her way back to the store. She did not want anyone to see her, for she had her reasons. She should have stolen back into her room through the window, but she was so hungry that she decided to risk using the side door. She had not eaten all day and she needed food to help give her strength for what she needed to do.

She opened the door slowly and furtively looked around her residence. Thankfully, it was empty. Her father and the Widow would be in the store. The door to the store was open, though, so she still had to be as quiet as possible. She went to the larder to see what she could take to her room to eat. She chose a heel of bread and some cheese. She threw the bread on a plate and cut off a generous slice of cheese from the wheel that was there. As she was putting the knife down, it slipped from her grasp and fell to the floor with a clatter. She grabbed the cheese, threw it onto the plate, grabbed the knife from the floor, and hurried towards her bedroom.

The Widow was standing in the doorway to the store with a smug look on her face.

"Your father wants you in the store, now! You are in for it now, you little hussy."

Liesel hated the Widow even more for the smug expression on her face. She was enjoying being the one to order Liesel to go to her father. She did not have time for the Widow's sadistic pleasure, nor her father's desire to see her so that he could mete out a punishment.

"Go to hell." She glared at the Widow as she brushed past her and headed to the sanctuary of her room. She slammed the door, then retrieved a chair and propped it under the knob so that if someone tried to get in, they wouldn't be able to.

She had just sat on her bed when she heard her father's heavy footsteps approaching. He pounded on her door.

"Liesel, get out here this minute."

"Go away. Leave me alone."

"The hell I will."

Liesel watched as the door knob turned. The door shook as her father tried to open it but couldn't because of the wedged chair.

"Open this door, Liesel, now!"

"Go away."

"I am going to thrash you within an inch of your life, Liesel. Where have you been? OPEN THIS DOOR!"

Liesel was not sure how long the chair would keep her father at bay, especially with his temper of late. She had to make him go away. She did not have time for this.

"If you want to know where I was so badly, then I will tell you. I was somewhere you have not been. I was at Mutti's grave, a place that you have not returned to since you put her in the cold hard ground. I have not forgotten my mother as quickly as you have forgotten your wife. At least one of us loved her." Liesel did not mince words with her father, nor did she care if they hurt him. In fact, she wanted her words to hurt him. Maybe then he would feel something.

Her words did what she had intended them to do. Her father left her door. She listened to his footsteps as he retreated – they were heavy as usual, but they plodded away, making each step sound like a chore.

I'm sorry Vati. She had no right to talk to her father that way, no matter how horribly he had treated her of late. It was another thing to regret. All she could do was try and right some of the bad things that she'd done.

She quickly ate the bread and cheese, then went to her small writing desk. The desk had been a gift on her twelfth birthday from her mother. She searched for some paper and got out her favourite fountain pen, also from her mother.

For the longest time she just stared at the pieces of paper. She agonized over how to start the letter. Finally, she started with a single word: 'Vati'.

The light of the day was fading when she finally finished her letter. She folded up the sheets of paper and inserted them into an envelope. She sealed the envelope and placed it into the pocket of her skirt. She slipped the knife in there as well. She tiptoed over to the door and carefully removed the chair. Eventually, her father would come back. He would find the door unbarred and the room empty.

Before she climbed out the window, Liesel surveyed her room one last time. She knew she was never coming back. She swiped at a stray tear and turned her back to what she had once loved. There was no turning back now.

She hurried through the quiet backstreets of Norka, hoping that she was not too late. It was almost dark when she reached the Henkel's farm. She crept in the twilight towards the barn. She heard voices coming from within – she recognized Jacob's and his father's. She breathed a sigh of relief. She had arrived in time.

She listened for a short time. Then she opened the barn door and made her presence known.

When Jacob saw her, he shot daggers at her with his eyes. He hurled words at her that hurt, but she had to ignore the pain in her heart. She had to make them see that she was there to set things right.

Jacob started to argue with his father about her presence in their barn. It gave her time to study the woman Jacob was in love with. Liesel was surprised at how similar in appearance she was to herself. *So, this was the woman who had stolen Jacob's heart.* She felt envious and jealous of this woman, but she pushed down these emotions. She had to keep a level head.

She had to convince the others that her plan was their salvation. And hers.

CHAPTER 39

The Governor of Saratov was not a happy man. Days before, he had received a report informing him that the Jewish village near Norka had been burned to the ground and that all its inhabitants had perished. News of dead Jews should not have bothered him, but it did. The Jews had been indispensable to his family. Now they were gone. He debated whether he should swoop down on the village of Rysincek and exact his revenge on the stupid peasants who had perpetrated the attack. He paced in his office, wondering what his grandfather or father would have done.

It had been his grandfather who had allowed the Jews to settle on the land near Norka so long ago. The Jews had been passing through Saratov on their way to the Black Sea. They had the misfortune of being abandoned and robbed by their guides (a ruse that his grandfather had orchestrated). The Jews were destitute and vulnerable. His grandfather swooped in. He offered the Jews land and allowed them to establish their own little village. The Jews eagerly accepted. The generosity of his grandfather came at a price though. They were taxed heavily on their grain harvests. In addition, they also had to provide a wagonload of goods to the Governor.

His grandfather had been shrewd when it came to lining the coffers of his family's fortunes. His grandfather did not report the existence of the Jewish settlement. Since it de facto did not exist, he could exploit the Jews for his own gains. The grain he purportedly took on behalf of the Tsar for the taxes, was not really tax. He took their grain and sold it to the Tsar's granaries in Saratov. His grandfather had been smart, for he did not sell the grain directly to the Tsar. Rather, he used the services of a middleman, who was compensated handsomely for their part in the transaction. This system worked perfectly in his grandfather's time, as well as in his father's and into his. Only once did a middleman get greedy. It was during his father's time as Governor. When his father got wind of the fact that the man was skimming off more profit for himself, he sent someone to make the man and his family disappear. No one had tried to skim from them again.

His grandfather had schooled his son well on the ways to make money from the Jews. He was firm on his stance that the Jews must never be left totally destitute. He decreed that no matter the harvest – good or bad – their granaries should always be left half full after they paid their supposed taxes to the Tsar.

His father had done as his grandfather had instructed. That was until his grandfather had died. After that, his father had only left the Jews with a third of their harvests. His father reasoned that his grandfather had been too soft. His point was proven when the Jews still managed to survive with less in their granaries. The Governor, when he took over from his father, had done as his father had and left the Jews with a third. Once his father died, however, he reduced the amount even further, leaving the Jews with a quarter. The Jews still survived, so he surmised that his father had also been too soft on the Jews as well.

It had been a perfect setup, until the bloody peasants had gone and destroyed the village and killed all the Jews.

He was about to leave his office for the day when he heard a commotion outside his office door. He could hear his secretary's voice raised as he argued with someone. He was about to go to the door and yell at his secretary and whoever was making the fuss, when he heard the word 'Jew'. That got his attention. He listened to the exchange. Whoever his secretary was arguing with kept claiming that they needed to see him urgently because a Jew had been found hiding in the German colony of Norka. His secretary kept telling the man that the Governor was a busy man, and that he must make an appointment to see him. The man, however, was not going to be sent away so easily.

The Governor flung open the door.

"What the hell is going on?" he thundered at his secretary Yuri.

"I'm sorry, sir." Yuri looked worried because he had obviously failed to do his job and send the man on his way. "This man insists on seeing you, sir. It is about a Jew hidden near the village of Norka."

The Governor looked at the man who was demanding to see him. He was nervously playing with the cap in his hand as the Governor stared coldly at him. He could see that the man was extremely nervous, which was good, because it was likely that the man would tell him the news quickly and make a hasty retreat. The Governor motioned to his office.

"You have five minutes."

It took the peasant less than three to relay his story. The Governor listened to him stone-faced. He did not want the peasant to know that the news he brought was good. As the peasant told his tale, a plan was starting to form in the Governor's mind. He asked a couple of questions to clarify a few details, and then he dismissed the man. Of course, he warned the man that he must not say anything to anyone about their meeting. He made it very clear that if the man talked, his life, as well as those of his family, were forfeit.

When the peasant was gone, he called his secretary into his office. He instructed him to arrange for a carriage, six wagons, and a small militia of bodyguards. Everything was to be ready at first light the next day.

As his secretary hurried off to do his bidding, the Governor smiled. Maybe things would turn out better than they'd been before. Maybe he had found something his grandfather and father had missed. A bigger fortune than either of them had was within his grasp, and the one surviving Jew was the key to him having the family's coffers overflowing. The Germans had harboured a Jew, and to save themselves from punishment, they would pay just as the Jews had. He would make them pay in grain and anything else he could sell to the Tsar to make himself richer and richer. Tomorrow could not come soon enough.

—◦◦◦—

At first light, the Governor climbed into his carriage. Only a dozen militia accompanied his carriage and the wagons. All had been handpicked by his secretary because each man there knew how to keep their mouth shut. They would all be paid handsomely for their discretion. The Governor would have liked to have more men as a show of force, but he could not. A dozen militiamen could still be considered personal bodyguards, whereas a larger force would mean that he was on official government business, and that would have meant a report to his superiors. His visit was strictly unofficial. He had to make sure that the Jews' village remained a secret. It was gone now – but one Jew remained.

As the carriage bounced along the rutted road to Norka, the Governor went over his plan in his head again. He marvelled at how fortune was smiling down on him. Just a few days before, he had despaired over the fact that the Jews were gone, but now he could see that their deaths were a form of salvation for him.

When they reached Norka, he directed his driver to head to the farm just to the east of the settlement. This is where the peasant had told him he would find the Jew. He hoped that the Jew had not fled, because he needed them at the farm for his plan.

Jacob, Chaya, and Liesel heard the arrival of the Governor and his entourage from the barn where they waited. They had been waiting anxiously for hours.

It was time to see if Liesel's plan would work.

After she had arrived at the Henkel's barn and endured Jacob's icy reception, Liesel had presented her plan to those in the barn. She told them over and over that it was the only way.

As Chaya listened to Liesel's solution to her predicament, she kept wondering whether Liesel was being genuine. She had already reported her presence to the Russians – why should she trust her now? As she talked, Chaya observed everything about her. She seemed truly and utterly devastated with what she had done. She might have just been acting, but Chaya sensed a real and genuine sadness. But there was something else within Liesel: disgust. She could tell that Liesel was disgusted with herself for the harm that she had caused.

When Liesel was done outlining her plan, both Jacob and his father looked at Chaya. Neither would consent to Liesel's plan. As it was Chaya's life in danger, they both said it was her decision alone, and that only she could accept or reject Liesel's plan.

Chaya mulled everything over. The plan was audacious, but if it worked it would mean one big thing – that she would not have to go away. She would not have to abandon sitting shiva, and she wouldn't have to be parted from Jacob. In her mind, there was no other real choice, so she agreed.

Once the decision was made, the trio prepared in anticipation of the Governor's arrival. They knew that he would not appear until sometime the next day, which would give them enough time to prepare.

Jacob hauled buckets of water from the well, which Chaya used to wash her hair several times. She also washed her body. The water was cold and bracing, but she needed to be as clean as possible. Liesel did the opposite. She rubbed dirt on her face and arms and rubbed handfuls of hay vigorously into her hair.

Chaya swapped clothing with Liesel. Luckily, they were roughly the same size.

When they exchanged clothes, Liesel made sure that Chaya was looking away when she slipped her knife out of her pocket. When she had Chaya's dress on, she slipped the knife into its pocket.

While Chaya and Liesel were busy getting clean and dirty, Jacob went to one of the stalls and pried two boards loose, making a small opening in the barn. The three then sat on some straw and went over the plan one more time.

It was getting late when they all agreed that they should try to get some rest. As the three climbed up into the hayloft to sleep, all were tense and no words were spoken. Jacob and Chaya curled up together at one end. Liesel lay down by herself at the other end.

Each spent the next hours of darkness agonizing over what the next day would bring.

For Jacob, he spent those hours staring at the outline of Chaya's face in the dark. He studied every beautiful piece of her face, committing each to his memory. He wanted to remember all that he loved – just in case.

For Chaya, she did not sleep either. Rather, she prayed. She prayed that the decision that she had made was the right one. She prayed for guidance from her family to help her through the difficult day yet to come. She prayed for Jacob. And she prayed for Liesel.

For Liesel, sleep eluded her as well. She could smell Chaya's sour sweat on the dress she now wore. She so envied Chaya lying with Jacob on their side of the hayloft. She pushed the thought away – jealousy was what had gotten her to this moment in her life. She should have prayed like Chaya did, but she did not. Instead, she talked to her mother in her head. She finally felt for the first time since her mother had died, that she was somewhat at peace. She knew that if her plan worked, she would finally be free. She just hoped that she had the courage not to falter, for if she did, all would be lost. *Give me strength, Mutti*, she begged.

—⁂—

In the morning, the three awoke with the cows. Chaya and Liesel stayed in the loft while Jacob completed the milking.

After the cows were turned out, the three of them ate, although none really felt like eating. They all picked at some of the food that was originally brought to the barn as provisions for Chaya's escape. Since it was no longer needed, it would have to be returned to the farmhouse.

Jacob poured out one of the pails of milk and put the remaining food in the bucket. He hated wasting the milk, but pretences still had to be maintained. He carried the pails to the farmhouse.

Back in the barn, he helped Chaya and Liesel get everything ready. They went into the loft and erased all traces suggesting that three people had slept there. They did not, however, touch where Liesel had slept.

They checked everywhere in the barn and in the loft for anything that they might have missed and that might contradict their story. Satisfied, they completed their final task, then settled down to await the arrival of the Governor.

Maybe, Jacob thought hopefully, *maybe no one will come.* But a few hours later, they did come.

—⁕—

Arriving at the farmyard, the Governor had his men dismount and fan out around the barn just in case the Jew tried to make a run for it.

He approached the barn door with two soldiers and wrenched it open. It let out a loud creak in protest. He quickly scanned the barn, thinking he might see a scurrying figure. Instead, all he saw were a young man and two young women. One of the women was tied securely to a post.

"What is going on here?" he demanded.

"Thank goodness you are here," the young man began. "We were worried that you might not come."

"Who are you, boy?"

"My name is Jacob Henkel, and I was the one – sorry, I mean we –" Jacob corrected, gesturing towards Chaya. "We were the ones who discovered the Jew."

"And how did you discover this Jew?" The Governor acknowledged the tied-up Liesel.

"I was doing the morning milking when my betrothed arrived to get some milk for her father. We heard a noise and discovered the Jew hiding in the loft. I tied her up and sent my betrothed to the Russian village to summon you to deal with her."

"And you have been holding her here ever since?" the Governor inquired. "Why not just take her to the Administration Office in Norka and have her dealt with there?"

"She begged us not to. I know we should have, and that is my fault entirely, but I couldn't deny her request. My father says you reap what you sow. I couldn't in good conscious let her bear further humiliation."

"Further humiliation?"

"Isn't it bad enough, just being a Jew? Why make it a public spectacle. We reported her presence here as we were supposed to. My conscience is therefore clear," Jacob concluded.

Something here is just not right. The Governor was not convinced with the story that this Jacob Henkel was telling him.

"Who are you?" He shot the question at Chaya.

"Liesel Hauser." Chaya's voice quivered a bit when she answered.

"Is what your betrothed is telling me the truth?" he pressed.

"Yes."

"Are you sure you weren't here for something more than milk?"

"No."

"Maybe, a roll in the hay with your betrothed? Not very honourable for someone who is not married. But more common for a hussy." He could see that her resolve was wavering. Now he could get the truth. "So, you lied to me, the both of you," he accused.

"Yes, yes, yes," Chaya confessed. "I'm sorry, Jacob," she said sadly. "I cannot do this."

Triumphant, the Governor declared, "I knew it. Tell me the truth. I am quickly losing my patience with the two of you."

"You are correct, sir," Chaya began. "I came here for more than milk." Tears were now streaming down her face. "I came to be with my betrothed. We discovered her when we went up into the hayloft." Chaya started sobbing uncontrollably. "I'm so ashamed."

"So, the plot thickens," the Governor declared, a huge smirk on his face. "The bride-to-be is no virgin." He snickered. "Maybe you should have had that one too." He pointed at Liesel. "She looks more virginal, I'd say." He snickered again. "Or maybe you did when you sent your hussy to the Russian village." He snickered yet again.

The Governor could see that Jacob was seething, for he kept clenching and unclenching his fists. No matter. He could not care less who was bedding who. He was playing with them as a cat would with a mouse. It had nothing to do with why he was here – just a little sport before he got down to the real matter at hand.

For the first time since arriving, the Governor really looked at the tied-up Jew. She was a pretty little thing. Almost as pretty as the little hussy. She just did not have those green eyes like the other one. They might have even passed as sisters, except one was tainted, being a Jew and all.

The Jew wore a filthy dress with a tear on one of the shoulders. She did not avert her eyes when he looked her over. She kept her gaze locked on him with a look of defiance. *Good, a feisty one*, he thought to himself. *That would make it even more enjoyable.*

"Who are you?" he asked in a very conciliatory tone.

No answer.

"I said who are you?" he asked again, with a slightly sterner voice this time.

Still no answer.

Her grabbed her arm forcefully and started to squeeze. She did not cry out, but he could see that he was causing her discomfort.

"Who are you?"

Liesel answered. "Chaya . . . Chaya Blumenthal."

The Governor released his grip. "There, that wasn't so hard now, was it?"

Liesel did not respond.

"Now, I'm having a hard time with their story." He indicated Jacob and Chaya. "They've lied to me and I'm not sure I believe what they are telling me. Maybe it is time for some truth telling. Don't you think? Let me just say your life depends on it. Do you understand?"

Liesel, visibly shaken, answered. "Yes."

"Good we finally understand one another. Now tell me, how did you come to be in the hayloft of this barn?"

"When the Russians attacked my village, I was in the forest. I saw smoke and ran to my village. I saw Russians looting our homes. Many of the buildings of my village were on fire. I ran for my life. I hid in the forest for a couple of days. I got hungry. I snuck into this barn under the cover of darkness. I milked a cow and that helped my hunger. I was exhausted and wanted an hour's rest before I went on my way. I climbed into the hayloft and unfortunately, I fell into a deep sleep. They discovered me there. They tied me up and had someone send for you."

"Liar!" the Governor roared as he slapped Liesel across the face. "Another liar." *How dare these people lie to him.*

"Search the barn," he ordered the two soldiers. "Be careful you don't stumble on a nest of vipers. How can you sneak into this barn without alerting anyone when that door makes such a racket?"

"I didn't use the door."

"She's right, sir," reported one of the soldiers searching the barn. "There are two loose boards in that stall over there. It is just large enough for her to squeeze through."

The other soldier returned from the loft.

"What did you find?" the Governor inquired.

"Nothing at all, sir. Just some hay that's been packed down like someone slept on it."

Damn, the Governor thought. He was hoping for some hard evidence that would implicate the Germans. He needed their guilt for his plan to work. He had to get what he needed – a confession – so that he could lord it over the Germans and start his new extortion scheme.

"You did all of this on your own? You did not have people like them helping you? Giving you shelter? Bringing you food?"

"No," Liesel replied. "No one helped me. I acted alone."

"LIAR!" he screamed at her as he smashed his fist into her mouth.

—⚭—

When the Governor had slapped her, Liesel had been completely taken by surprise by the violence.

When he struck her the next time, she was more prepared. But still, the ferocity of the attack left her head spinning.

Liesel could sense that the Governor was not accepting the story that they had concocted. She feared it would only be a matter of time before it all fell apart. She worried that Chaya might break first from the guilt of seeing Liesel tortured on her behalf. *This cannot happen*, Liesel thought. *My salvation and redemption hang in the balance.*

She could taste blood in her mouth from the Governor's blow. She had to act fast before she lost her nerve. She had to convince the Governor that she was Chaya.

"Had enough yet, bitch?" the Governor asked sadistically. "Now tell me what I want to hear. You did not do this alone, did you? You had help."

Liesel mumbled an almost inaudible response to his inquiry.

"What did you say bitch? Speak up." He moved closer to Liesel to hear her response.

Liesel looked at him, defiance in her eyes.

"Go to hell." She spat the contents of her mouth – blood and bits of teeth – straight into the Governor's face.

"You let them kill my family, you bastard. You did nothing to save them or my people. Their blood is on your hands. If I could I would tear you apart with my bare hands. You are the devil incarnate. I curse you and all . . ."

Liesel was not able to finish her tirade, for the Governor's fist smashed into her stomach, leaving her gasping for air.

"Take this bitch and throw her into the wagon," he ordered the two soldiers.

As the soldiers cut her loose from the post, Liesel collapsed onto the ground. Her insides were on fire and she could not catch her breath. The soldiers had to drag her between them as she was unable to walk on her own. They dumped her unceremoniously in the wagon. She curled up into the fetal position and continued to gasp for air.

Liesel wasn't worried that the Governor might still torture her more. She already knew what she was going to do. It was part of her plan that she had not divulged to Jacob, his father, or Chaya. The only way to set things right was if she took her own life. It wasn't a sacrifice; her life was over anyway.

Liesel watched the guard who had been left to supervise her. When he looked away, she made two deep cuts on her wrists. As she felt her life ebbing away, her last thought was of her mother.

"See you soon," were the last words that she spoke.

—ʍ—

The Governor wiped his face with a rag that he found in the barn. The Jew had confessed to acting alone, but he didn't care. He needed the Germans to confess to helping her. Real or contrived, all he wanted was a confession. He assessed the two young people clinging to each other. *Which one should he torture next? Which one would break the easiest from seeing the other tortured?*

The two soldiers had returned to the barn.

"Tie up that whore," he commanded them.

Neither soldier moved to follow his orders.

"Didn't you hear me, you idiots? I said tie her up."

Still neither soldier moved.

"Have you lost your stomach for what is necessary?" he sneered.

"It's not that," the older of the two said. "It's just that . . . that the Jew is dead."

"What!" he roared. "What did you idiots do?"

"She had a knife, sir. She slit her wrists."

"Where did she get the knife?"

"She must have had it hidden on her," he declared.

"Didn't it occur to either of you idiots to search her?"

"No sir. Sorry sir."

The Governor was not happy that he had just lost his main bargaining chip, but a confession from either of these two might still serve his purpose.

"No matter," he said. "Tie the bitch up."

Still, neither soldier moved to follow his order.

"Are you dense? I said tie her up."

"You better come outside, sir," the older one instructed him.

When he emerged from the barn, he saw a mass of people in the farmyard. He could also see that many people had gathered on the road leading to the farm. A man in the yard stepped forward.

"What is going on here?" he demanded to the Governor.

"And who are you?" the Governor challenged.

"I am Johann Henkel. This is my farm."

"Are you aware that a Jew was found hiding in your barn?" the Governor asked.

"I was not," Johann confirmed. "Is my family, okay?"

This was not the question that the Governor was expecting. *Shouldn't he be proclaiming innocence in the whole matter?* he thought.

"Who reported the Jew to you?" Johann inquired.

"Actually, it was your son Jacob and his—" *He wanted to say whore, but knew that wouldn't be prudent.* "Betrothed."

"Good," Johann declared. "He did the right thing. I am so glad that he informed you. I thought the good people of Rysincek had rid us of those Jews – I guess they missed a few."

Was this all an act? The Governor pondered in his head. Everything was falling apart.

He knew that torturing a Jew was one thing, but a German with all these witnesses was quite another. If the crowd turned ugly, he and his small contingent of soldiers would be overwhelmed. Every scenario he played out in his head did not bode well for his extortion plan. He knew a hasty retreat was his only option, as much as he hated to be bested at something. But there was no other solution.

Still, a threat would go a long way. He glared at the crowd.

"People of Norka, it is clear that this Jew acted alone and hid here without your knowledge. But know this: if a Jew ever sets foot in this town again, I will burn it to the ground, innocent or not." He let the threat hang in the air and clambered into his carriage. He ordered his driver to get moving.

No one tried to stop him or his men as they left the farm.

It was only after they left Norka and were on the road to Saratov that the Governor realized that the wagon was still carrying the body of the Jew. He called a halt to the procession and ordered his men to dump the body on the side of the road.

Let the wolves feast on the bitch, he thought as his carriage drove away.

CHAPTER 40

After the Governor departed, the crowd slowly dispersed. Many left in small groups, talking about what had transpired and discussing the Governor's threat.

Eventually the farmyard emptied, and the only people left were the Henkel family.

Jacob's mother ushered a distraught Chaya into the house where she ministered to her as best as she could. She was able to convince a tearful Chaya to lie down and rest, noting that she looked totally spent.

She shooed all the young ones outdoors, even sending the youngest one away with his sisters.

"The girl needs peace and quiet," she declared. "Outside, all of you, and watch out for your little brother."

After Chaya was ushered inside, Jacob walked out to the pasture with his father.

"What made her do it, Vati? Liesel, I mean. She said she wanted to make things right. But taking her life. If I had known she was going to do that, I wouldn't have encouraged Chaya to consider her plan. It was just supposed to be Liesel taking Chaya's place. But her life. . . Vati."

"I think that Liesel was a very troubled soul. When we tried to talk her out of her plan to switch places with Chaya, she was almost hysterical. She kept telling us that her name was the only thing left of her life that was worth anything. I don't think we could have said or done anything different. Her mind was made up."

"Do you think she intended to take her life the whole time?"

"I feel like there were many things that were also troubling her, but we will never know. I don't know if we will ever know why she did it."

"Do you think Chaya is safe now?" Jacob asked his father.

"I think so, Son," he replied. "Everyone in the town is now part of the secret. They know the consequences. If they tell anyone and it gets back to the Governor, many lives will be forfeit. Plus, they will respect the sacrifice that Liesel made on their behalf."

"I am glad that Chaya is now safe, Vati. But it came at a very high price."

"It will now be up to you to convince Chaya that Liesel's sacrifice for her was not her fault. It was Liesel's choice and God's will. You must not fail in this, Jacob."

"I will, Vati, I will," he assured his father. It was not going to be easy, but if Chaya could accept that it was God's will, then they could finally build their lives together.

"I have to go, Vati. I promised Liesel I would do something for her."

"Is it anything that I can help you with?" his father asked.

"No, thank you, Vati. I must do this for her and myself."

"I'm proud of the man you've become, Jacob."

"Thank you, Vati. I best go."

Jacob left the pasture and headed towards Norka. The previous evening, Liesel had handed him a letter addressed to her father. She told him that she knew the Governor would be taking her away from Norka. She made Jacob promise to deliver the letter after she was gone. Jacob had agreed because

Liesel had looked so desperate when she had made the request. *Had she known then that she was going to take her own life?* he wondered. He also wondered what was in the letter. But it was not for him to know. It was sealed in an envelope. Whatever Liesel had written was intended solely for her father.

As Jacob approached the Hauser's store, he was surprised to see that it had the open sign displayed in the window. *Herr Hauser would have been informed of his daughter's death, so why was the store open?* Jacob did not understand that at all.

He opened the door to the familiar jangle of the bell. Herr Hauser was behind the counter, as was Widow Fromm. Herr Hauser looked totally lost. *Hadn't the man endured enough already?* he thought. *Maybe what Liesel has written will give him some peace.*

He approached the counter.

"I'm sorry, Herr Hauser, for your loss," he began. "Liesel asked me to give this to you." He produced the letter from his pocket. "She made me promise to deliver it to you."

"What happened? All we have heard is that she took her own life because of the Governor. What was she doing at your farm, Jacob?" While Widow Fromm was grilling him with questions. Liesel's father was not saying anything. He was just running his fingers over the envelope.

Jacob had fulfilled his promise to Liesel. He ignored the Widow and her questions. Finally, Liesel's father looked up.

"Thank you, Jacob."

Jacob saw such pain in the man's eyes.

"I'm sorry, Herr Hauser, for your loss," he repeated himself, not knowing what to say. He wanted to tell the man that Liesel's death served a purpose, but he could not bring himself to say the words. He hoped that Liesel's words in her letter would bring the man some kind of comfort.

Jacob beat a hasty retreat from the store, saying he was sorry again as he hurried out.

—⚹—

For a long time, Liesel's father just stared at the envelope. He could not decide whether to read the letter or tear it up in anger. So, he just stared and stared at it, not knowing which he should do.

Finally, the spell was broken when Widow Fromm declared, "Georg, aren't you going to read it?"

He tore open the letter, recognizing Liesel's familiar script. "Vati", it began.

Vati,

I have stared at these blank pieces of paper for hours now, agonizing over just what I wanted to say to you. I have decided there is no easy way to tell you of the things that I have done, and those that I am about to do, without hurting you. For this I am truly sorry – but you deserve to know the truth.

First, let me say that I am totally ashamed for what I have done. I have brought shame on myself and my family by my actions. It was not my intention to do this, but actions I took, however misguided, put everyone in Norka in danger. You and my dearly departed mother raised me to be a better human being than I have become. I must make things right.

I tried hard to help you with the grief of losing Mutti, but you pushed me away. I know that you grieved for her, as did I, but instead of sharing this and seeking support from each other, we withdrew to ourselves. I only wished I had tried harder to break down your protective walls.

Things might have turned out a lot differently if I had. Sorry that I failed you in your time of need.

Then, before Mutti was hardly cold in her grave, Widow Fromm swooped in. I know you wanted me to call her by her given name, but I cannot – even now. Maybe she provided you with the comfort of having someone fuss over you, maybe it was because you had both lost spouses recently, I don't know what attracted you to her. Maybe you thought I needed a replacement for my mother – I didn't. Whatever your reasons, they were yours, not mine.

As the Widow was appearing in our store and ultimately our home more and more often, I began to suspect that maybe she was pursuing more than friendship.

She saw me as a threat to her plans of marriage, hoping to secure her future and the future of her snot-nosed brats. So, she threatened me. This came after I tried to tell you of her plans. You didn't believe me, but you believed her. That really hurt, Vati, but she was already poisoning your mind against me.

What I didn't know, Vati, was the lengths the Widow would go to get rid of me.

One day she made me take a delivery to Gunther. I cannot and will not call him Onkel Gunther – not after what he did. The Widow sent me to Gunther's knowing full well that THE PIG would rape me – which he did. I did not know at the time that the Widow had engineered this with Gunther, but she let something slip one day and then it all made sense. To make matters worse, Gunther impregnated me. It was more fuel for the fire. The Widow used the fact that I was carrying Gunther's bastard against me further. I don't know if she told you that I was carrying a child or not, and it doesn't really matter. Her plans were to convince you to marry me off to Gunther – where I would be raped and abused until I died.

She was sentencing me to death.

I was desperate, Vati. I had no where to turn and I knew with all of my heart and soul that she would do exactly as she said.

So, I decided to scheme and manipulate to try to save myself. I used the kindness of Jacob Henkel and his parents to help me to achieve my goal. My goal, Vati, was to endear myself to them so that they would ask you for permission for me to wed Jacob. I am not proud that I used these people to get what I wanted. They deserved better – my actions were despicable.

I even had a plan to trick Jacob into sleeping with me so that I could pass off the bastard growing inside of me as his. I knew Jacob would do the honourable thing and marry me. But what I was doing was beyond despicable. There are no words to describe how much I loathe myself and my actions.

I got desperate when I felt time was running out on me. I hadn't secured a betrothal from the Henkels, and your period of mourning was almost over. The plans which the Widow had laid the groundwork for would come to fruition.

I also believed foolishly that Jacob had feelings for me – he didn't. I misconstrued his feelings of concern and chivalry for affection.

I accidently discovered that Jacob was hiding a Jew in his barn. And to make matters worse, he was in love with her. I was angry. I was hurt. I was out of my head with grief that my plan had failed. Without even thinking it through, I went to the Russian village to report the hidden Jew. If I couldn't have Jacob to marry, neither could she.

It was petty. I was so full of jealousy and malice. I did not think through what I was doing, or the danger I was putting Jacob and his family in. I also put all of the people of Norka in harm's way – which Jacob pointed out to me. But the damage was done. And now when it is too late, I have realized the errors of my ways.

I have sinned so much, Vati. Sinned so much that I feel that I have lost my soul.

I am sorry that I have done what I have done. I can beg your forgiveness, which I don't deserve, but it is forgiveness from God and from Mutti that I seek the most.

I cried for hours over Mutti's grave as I emptied my heart and soul to her. I wish it could have been to you, but I just couldn't face you. The shame was just too great.

The only thing I can do, Vati, is to set things right. I am hoping and praying that my sacrifice will be accepted by God and absolve me of my sins so that I can join Mutti in Heaven.

Please don't mourn for me Vati – I don't deserve it. Try to remember me as I was before all of this happened: the beautiful Liesel Hauser, the loving daughter of Katarina and Georg.

Vati, I need to make things right with Jacob and his family, and for this I need your help.

I want to give the Jew in their barn my name. That way she will be safe from the authorities and then she and Jacob can wed. Please help make my last wish happen.

I love you, Vati.
Liesel

As Liesel's father read her letter, tears flowed freely down his face.

I have failed you Liesel, he lamented. *Oh, my darling girl – I'm so sorry.*

"Georg, what is it?" Widow Fromm asked, feigning concern. *Even dead the brat was still stirring up her father,* she thought. "Georg, are you okay?"

"Did you send Liesel to Gunther's farm?"

"Georg, why do you want to know that?"

"I will ask you again. Did you or did you not send Liesel to Gunther's farm?"

"Georg, I'm not sure what lies she is telling you in that letter."

"DAMMIT WOMAN! Did you send her?"

"Yes, Georg, I did. But let me explain . . ."

"There is nothing to explain. You sent her there knowing full well what Gunther had planned for her. To rape her. Maybe you even suggested it, or planned it yourself."

"Georg, why are you accusing me of such things? I did nothing wrong. You are making accusations towards me that are unfounded because of something that Liesel wrote. She was of not of sound mind Georg . . . her committing suicide confirms this."

"GET OUT!"

"You are upset, Georg, and rightly so. I will leave you and come back once you have calmed down."

"GET OUT ENID! Get out of my store! Get out of my life! Get out before, so help me God, I kill you with my bare hands. GET OUT!"

The Widow was about to protest her innocence, but she saw Georg's eyes; they were full of hatred. She feared he might do as he'd said and try to kill her, so she beat a hasty retreat.

After Widow Fromm left the store, Liesel's father collapsed behind the counter and sobbed and sobbed for the daughter whom he had failed in life, and for the wife whom he'd failed after her death.

—៳—

The next day, a number of wagons left Norka for Saratov to get supplies. Liesel's body was discovered on the side of the road by the waggoneers. It was decided that the wagon driven by Leo Baeker would return Liesel's body back to Norka, since his was the last wagon in the group. They carefully loaded Liesel's body into Leo's wagon, and he returned to Norka with his sad cargo.

Leo took Liesel's body to the undertaker. A messenger was sent to her father. Leo did not stay to see what occurred next because he wanted to rejoin the wagon train. If he pushed his team hard, he would catch them long before they got near the Kosakenwald.

The pastor of Georg Hauser's church made all the necessary arrangements for Liesel's funeral and burial. Her father was stoic throughout both.

The funeral was a small affair. Many wanted to attend but did not. The pastor had warned that a large funeral might come to the attention of the Governor. He pointed out that it would be suspicious if the funeral of a Jew was attended by many. She wasn't part of their society, so pretences had to be kept up.

It was not that the people of Norka did not appreciate Liesel's sacrifice. Her grave soon became covered with flowers of all sorts. A marker was also being made for her final resting place. The problem was that her real name could not be used. Someone suggested that her marker should say 'Daughter of Norka'. So that's what they put on it.

Liesel's father showed his pastor the letter Liesel had written. He requested that the pastor read the letter to the congregation at Sunday Services the next day. He also requested that her letter be read in the other churches of Norka as well. The pastor had tried to convince him that it was unwise because Liesel's letter told of very personal matters between herself and her father. Her father was adamant, saying "I failed her in life, I will not fail her in death. I want everyone to know what happened and why she did what she did – the good and the bad."

As per his request, the letter was read. All in Norka knew what it said.

When Jacob heard Liesel's letter, all the ill thoughts he'd still been harbouring towards her were forgiven. He now knew why she had done the things that she had. He hoped that she had been given her absolution and was reunited with her mother in Heaven.

The Widow Fromm's relatives immediately threw her and her children out of their house when they heard the letter. The Widow sought help from people who she'd come to know in the community, but all turned her away. She found she had no choice but to leave Norka. She decided to go to Saratov until she figured out what to do next. She headed towards Schilling, where she hoped to get a boat heading upstream to Saratov. Many wagons passed her and her children as they walked to Schilling, but none offered her a ride. She begged people to stop and help her and the children, but those who drove by ignored her pleas. She tried to clamber onto one wagon, but the farmer held her off with his horsewhip.

When they finally reached Schilling, the Widow tried to talk her way onto a boat. News of her treachery had already reached Schilling, and not one boatman would allow her and her family to board.

For two days, the Widow and her children hung around Schilling, stealing food to survive and sleeping on the steppe at the village's edge. Since no one would help them, she decided that they'd have to walk to Saratov.

Luck finally smiled on her. A Russian peasant took pity on her and gave her and her children a ride. Nothing more was heard from the Widow until the following year.

A group of hunters chasing game came across what remained of her in the Kosakenwald. Not that there was much left of her. The wolves had feasted on her body. A scrap of what remained of her dress, and a pin that many people had seen her wear, was all that the wolves had left. How she met her end, and the fate of her children, was never known.

Gunther died shortly after the contents of Liesel's letter became known. A fire at his farmhouse claimed his life. Some said he committed suicide. Others said he'd been assisted over to the other side – Hell being his destination.

Liesel's father left Norka a week after her death. He quickly sold the store and joined a group that was preparing to leave Russia. He did not care where the group was going – Canada, the United States or South America. The destination did not matter to him. He just wanted to leave Russia and to never think of all that he'd lost. He was a broken man. His greatest wish was that the boat carrying him across the Atlantic would sink.

CHAPTER 41

For Chaya, Liesel's gift meant that she no longer had to hide, but that she still had to fulfill her duties to her family and to the rest of the residents of Novaskaya. She continued to sit shiva for their departed souls.

When her shiva was completed, she asked Jacob to accompany her to her shtetl.

As she walked through her burnt out village, she couldn't stop crying. Jacob held her hand and she appreciated the love that he conveyed to her through his constant squeezes. She looked at where her house had once stood. All that remained were a few burnt timbers. Everything else was gone. She closed her eyes and tried to picture her home in happier times, but the pleasant memories did not assuage what had befallen her home, her family, and her shtetl.

The rest of the shtetl was like her home – destroyed. Some of the timbers still gave off their burnt smell, even though it had been over a week since the fire.

She walked to the place in the shtetl where she dreaded going, but knew she had to. The synagogue was gone, just like the rest of the buildings. A few charred timbers also remained, but unlike the other buildings, these were in a huge depression in the earth. Chaya realized that the depression was where the secret granary had been. She could smell it too. There was the smell of burnt timbers in the air, the smell of burnt grain, and another smell.

Chaya let out a long, tortured wail, and fell onto her knees. Here was where her family had died. Here was where all of the members of her shtetl were murdered. She cried for the cruel way that they had been killed. She cried for their lost lives. She cried for their souls. She cried for herself and for her loss.

As she cried, she felt Jacob's arms enveloping her. He did not say anything. He just held her and let her cry her heart out. When she couldn't cry anymore, she looked into his eyes. She saw what she needed to see – his undying love and devotion to her.

She stood up.

"Thank you, Jacob, for being here with me."

"I will do anything for you, my love. I just wish I could take your pain away."

"That is something you cannot do. I must bear it alone."

"You are not alone, Chaya. I am here. I will help you to bear the pain. I love you."

Chaya loved Jacob even more than she already did in that moment. He was such a good man. What she was going through would have been unbearable if not for his strength and love. She was so fortunate to have found him.

"Jacob, I need to say Kaddish for the dead, to tell them that they are remembered and not forgotten. It is usual for a quorum of ten men to perform it, but now I am the only one who can do it. Do you think God will accept a lone woman doing it?"

"I am sure that God will accept what you are doing. You are following your faith and are doing what you must for the souls of your family, as well as for the others. He understands, Chaya."

Jacob's words brought her great comfort. She took out a stone out of her pocket and placed it by the synagogue's hole.

"We bring a stone every time that we visit a loved one's grave, to tell them that we came and that they are not forgotten," she explained to Jacob. She closed her eyes and sang the Kaddish at the top of her lungs.

She was crying once again when Jacob led her gently away from the shtetl.

They stopped and sat on the grass in the meadow where they first met. Chaya stretched out and put her head on Jacob's lap. They talked of all the happy times they'd had in this particular spot. Jacob caressed her hair and she felt a bit better.

When they finally decided to head back to the Henkel's farm, Chaya's heart still felt sad for her family, but it also felt the love of the man who walked proudly beside her.

Chaya was glad to be returning to the Henkel farm. It had been her refuge after the attack on her shtetl, but now it had become the place where she felt the safest.

She had been given a bed in the girls' room. She shared the room with Jacob's sister Heidi, who was a year younger than herself, as well as his sisters, Lina and Anna. At first, sharing a room had been strange for Chaya, because at home she'd had her own room, but she grew accustomed to it quite quickly. All of the girls made sure that she felt that it was her room as well. She got on especially well with Heidi. She was so patient with Chaya, giving her space when she was being emotional, and talking with her when Chaya was feeling lost. If Chaya had ever had a real sister, she would have wanted her to be just like Heidi.

Jacob's parents also went out of their way to make her feel welcome within their home. In fact, all members of the Henkel household did their best to make sure that she felt loved and protected. Chaya was overwhelmed by this outpouring of love and compassion on many occasions.

Chaya did her best to help out around the farm. No one asked her to do this, but she'd been raised to work if one was able. She cleaned the chicken coop, weeded the garden, helped Jacob's mother with her canning and cheese making, hauled water, picked berries, and foraged in the forest. Over time, she began to feel more and more like she was part of the family. But a part of her still felt that she wasn't.

The people in Norka also accepted her. They greeted her as Liesel and were kind and solicitous to her. Chaya was really touched by their gestures, but like the Henkel family, she was being treated as if she was one of them, when she wasn't. She was still Chaya – the Jew. She wondered if in time if she would feel that she belonged. She had to remind herself that it had only been a few weeks. She wasn't sure what the future would bring.

Chaya loved when she went berry picking or foraging in the forest, because then she could spend some time alone with Jacob. He'd stop his work of gathering wood and accompany her to the shtetl if she wanted to go. Each time she visited, she'd bring another stone and she'd recite the Kaddish. Sometimes she went alone.

Sometimes she'd help Jacob with cutting wood like they'd done before, and he would help her to pick berries or gather mushrooms. Sometimes they'd walk hand in hand to the meadow in the forest and make love on the soft grass. Being in the forest with Jacob again brought back some of her former happiness.

Everything was going okay until she fell sick.

She contracted a mild case of the flu. Even though she was having trouble keeping food down, she felt that she couldn't just lie in her sickbed. The Henkels had done so much for her already, and she couldn't have them tending to her sickness. So, she forced herself to get up and carry on as best as she could.

Her sickness, however, had not gone unnoticed. One day when they were making cheese together, Chaya felt unwell. She didn't want Jacob's mother to know, so she pretended she was well when she clearly wasn't. Jacob's mother wasn't fooled.

"Are you unwell, Chaya?" Chaya could hear genuine concern in Jacob's mother's voice.

"I'm fine, Frau Henkel."

"You are not fine, Chaya. You are as white as a ghost."

"It's just a bit of stomach flu, that's all. I will be fine."

"How long have you been feeling unwell?"

"A week or two. I'm sure I'm over the worst of it."

Chaya was not prepared for what happened next. Jacob's mother came over to her and gave her a warm embrace.

"You are not ill. You are with child."

Frau Henkel's words shocked her. *With child . . . how could that be? Yes, she and Jacob had made love, but her monthly courses had come. Or had they?* She thought hard. *They hadn't come since before the attack.* In the pain and confusion and grief of losing everyone, she'd lost track of her cycle. *What Jacob's mother was saying now made sense . . . she was pregnant.*

She looked into Jacob's mother's eyes expecting to see disappointment, but all she saw was pure joy.

"Every child is a blessing. This child, especially, is telling you that it is time to do something that should have been done already . . . and that is to marry my son. He loves you with all of his heart. That is obvious to anyone who sees the two of you together, but he has hesitated asking you because you are grieving. God has smiled down on you two, giving you this blessing, and I for one am glad that he has. Oh, Chaya, you will make a wonderful wife and mother."

A wife and a mother. It was almost too much for her to take in. It was what she'd hoped for when she'd realized that she'd fallen in love with Jacob, but she'd thought that it could never be. *But now it was possible. Or was it?*

"How can I marry Jacob? We are of different faiths?"

"God will find a way. You just have to accept that this is part of His divine plan. Chaya, your news has made me so happy."

Chaya wished that she could share Jacob's mother's optimism, but she couldn't. *How was God going pave the way for a Jew to marry a gentile?*

Jacob and the rest of the family were also overjoyed at the news of her pregnancy. Jacob's father hustled Jacob out of the farmhouse shortly after he received the news. Jacob returned a short time later, got down on one knee, and asked for her hand in marriage. Chaya realized that Jacob's father had taken him outside to tell him that he must propose to her. Even though she still had reservations, Chaya accepted his proposal. Only when they were alone later did she voice her concern.

"I want to marry you, Jacob, I truly do, but how will it be possible? I am still a Jew and you are a Christian. How can we marry? I cannot turn my back on my faith and convert, not now after everything that has happened. I have to respect my family."

"I never asked you to convert, Chaya, nor shall I ever ask you to make that choice. My father told me that we should talk to our pastor. He believes that he might be able to find a solution."

"Your mother believes that God will make it happen."

"Well, with God's help and the good pastor's, we shall be married then." He twirled her around and then kissed her passionately. "I can't wait to be your husband, Chaya."

"I can't wait to be your wife, Jacob, but . . ."

Jacob placed a finger on Chaya's lips. "No buts, Chaya. Tomorrow we will go and see Pastor Weitz."

When they met with Pastor Weitz the next day, Chaya instantly liked the man. He smiled at the couple and he nodded his head encouragingly as they told him of their plans to marry. They even told him of the baby. Chaya had expected condemnation from this man due to them having premarital sex, but he did not judge nor condemn either of them.

"You two have so much love between you. I am sure that the blessed baby will also receive much love from the both of you."

Chaya couldn't keep her anxiety at bay any longer.

"Pastor, we truly love each other, but how can we be married? I cannot give up my faith."

"God has provided, my child. You can get married to Jacob without giving up your faith. In fact, it will be my pleasure to marry the two of you."

"How is that possible, pastor?"

"You are now Liesel Hauser. Liesel was baptised in this very church, as was Jacob. Both can marry here."

"But wouldn't it be committing a lie in the House of God?"

"Liesel bequeathed her name to you so that you could be free. Free to live a life without fear of being persecuted for being a Jew. Free to marry the man you love. She sacrificed her life so that you could have a life with Jacob. She believed that she had sinned and that this was a way to receive forgiveness and to atone for her sins. I am not, nor am I asking you, to lie in a House of God, I am only fulfilling a request of a congregant and being God's instrument in what He has already preordained. God knows that you have suffered so much, my dear Chaya. He is offering to give you some peace, and more importantly, some happiness."

Listening to the pastor, Chaya felt a lump in her throat. Liesel's huge sacrifice came back to her once again.

"If you are sure, pastor . . . then yes."

"However, there is one thing. Your children must be baptised as Christians." The pastor's last words were like a blow to her chest.

"Why?"

"It would be suspicious if the children of Jacob and Liesel were not baptised when both of them had been. It might raise the suspicions of the Russian authorities. For the safety of yourself and for the children, this is how it must be done."

Chaya pondered the pastor's words. He was right. It was to protect her, but more importantly, it was to protect their children.

"You are right, pastor, the children must be protected. I will consent to them being baptised."

"You have made a wise decision, Chaya."

—⁂—

Two days before the wedding, Chaya journeyed alone to her burnt out shtetl. She went alone because she wanted to tell her parents and her brother her news.

She approached the spot where the synagogue had stood, and placed another stone on the small pile that was there.

"Hello Abba. Hello Ima. Hello Herschel." She spoke to the depression in the earth. "I have news to tell you all. I'm . . . I'm . . ." This was more difficult than she had thought. She steeled herself. "I'm with child. I'm sorry if I have disappointed you by having relations with a man out of wedlock, but he is a good man – he truly is. He loves me and I love him. I know that if you knew him like I do, you would love him too. He is a good man." She realized she was repeating herself. Telling them of the baby was hard, but her other news was even harder.

"We are to be married the day after tomorrow. We can be a family. His family has been so loving towards me, they have given me shelter and protected me. I owe them all so much. They have all been there to help me through my grief. You all would love them." She paused. *Why was it so hard to tell them?*

"The man I love, Jacob, he is my bashert. But I'm . . . I'm . . . sorry . . . I'm sorry, but he's not Jewish. Oh Abba! Oh Ima! Oh Herschel, I'm sorry. It just . . . it just happened. I love him with all of my heart . . . Please understand. I am not turning my back on my faith. I am not turning my back on you . . . it's just . . . it's just complicated. I am still your daughter, your sister, your Chayaleh. I have to do this. No, I want to do this. I want my child to have a happy family, I want my child to be safe. I want you to understand that what I do is for our child. I make this pledge to you that I will protect them with every fiber of my being. I will make you proud. I love you."

Chaya wiped the tears from her eyes and then sang the Kaddish.

On her way back to Norka, she stopped at the meadow. She sat on the grass and made another pledge. She placed her hand on her stomach.

"I will protect you, little one. You are the baby of Jacob and Chaya. Your uncle was Herschel, and your grandparents were Mordecai and Sara. My blood and the blood of my ancestors flow through your veins. I love you."

—⁓—

Jacob and Chaya's wedding was a small affair. The early harvest was in full swing, so only Jacob's family attended the wedding. Pastor Weitz said that was for the best since a large wedding at harvest time might arouse suspicions. Throughout the ceremony, Chaya kept one of her hands on her stomach. She wanted the baby to know that she was thinking of them. Her other hand held Jacob's.

As the pastor finished, she said a silent prayer in her head. She hoped that God wouldn't mind a Jewish prayer in a Christian church.

ABOUT THE AUTHOR

Danny was an elementary school teacher for 30 years. After retiring from teaching, Danny decided to pursue writing. Danny's ancestors lived in Norka, Russia, for a number of generations. His great-grandfather, along with his family, immigrated to Canada prior to the First World War. Danny researched Norka extensively. As he got to know more about his link to Norka and of the Volga Germans, he felt there was a story to tell. His family was able to get out of Russia when many Volga Germans were unable to do so. This is the story of one family who never left Norka.

ACKNOWLEDGEMENTS

A big thank you to my friends April, Diane, and Marlee for reading my manuscript and for giving me so much positive feedback and encouragement. To my family who are always there for me, I am eternally grateful. To my ancestors who called Norka home, I thank you for giving me the inspiration for this story. To my project manager Redjell and the awesome team at Tellwell Publishing, thank you for helping me to fulfill my dream of becoming a published author. And to my incredible editor Chloe, thank you for all your insight and positive comments about my book.

If you are interested in learning more about Norka, Russia, the website norkarussia.info is an invaluable source of information.

Manufactured by Amazon.ca
Acheson, AB